"You've thus far received more out of this tryst than I. Would you not agree, Donally?"

"Is this your idea of a tryst?" He came to his feet, his cloak swirling around his boots and dislodging a cloud of leaves. "I can certainly make our reunion more interesting."

Looking at her now, David remembered her as he had first seen her long ago—tall, proud, regal—Meg Faraday. She wore no finery, but she had not changed. "What does one say on an occasion such as this?" he asked, closing the distance between them. "'Hello, Meg. How are you after all of these years? I'm so glad to see that you did not drown.' Hmm? Or .... gracious, David, I .... alcutta.'"

.... e ever would have .... emptress of a trai- .... l but magnificent

.... Nothing to say before I take you to jail, sweet wife?"

"How did you find me?"

He considered not telling her. He considered slapping her in irons and handing her over to Kinley.

He considered all of these things, yet did none of them.

Other **AVON ROMANCES**

Melody Thomas

Angel In My Bed

AVON BOOKS
An Imprint of HarperCollinsPublishers

This is a work of fiction. Names, characters, places, and incidents are products of the author's imagination or are used fictitiously and are not to be construed as real. Any resemblance to actual events, locales, organizations, or persons, living or dead, is entirely coincidental.

AVON BOOKS
An Imprint of HarperCollins*Publishers*
10 East 53rd Street
New York, New York 10022-5299

Copyright © 2006 by Laura Renken
ISBN-13: 978-0-06-074233-1
ISBN-10: 0-06-074233-X
www.avonromance.com

First Avon Books paperback printing: April 2006

Avon Trademark Reg. U.S. Pat. Off. and in Other Countries, Marca Registrada, Hecho en U.S.A.
HarperCollins® is a registered trademark of HarperCollins Publishers Inc.

Printed in the U.S.A.

10 9 8 7 6 5 4 3 2 1

For my wonderful mother, Faye Joann.
I love you.

Chapter 1

England
Autumn 1873

On a gust of biting wind, David Donally walked into the Wild Boar Tavern, his cloak swirling about his calves, a whisper of dead leaves trailing in his wake. The frigid weather was as volatile as his mood as he remained like a shadow in the arched doorway of the common room. His towering height gave him the advantage, and he surveyed the length of the room filled with smoke from a roasting pig sizzling over the open stone hearth. He felt the eyes of the patrons this night and let them look their fill, knowing most contemplated what wealth he carried on his person.

His sweeping cloak concealed his black trousers, shirt, and riding boots. A full cowl covered his head and face, his beard all that the eye could distinguish of his features. A cynical smile shifted the line of his mouth as his gaze moved over a room rumored to cater to murderers, smugglers, and thieves. A stiletto braced his calf inside one boot, a cutlass at his side, his weaponry no more than an extension of his own dangerous temper.

Tonight, he was the hunter.

And hunt he would.

"What be yer pleasure, guv'nor." A pale-haired whore slid one fingernail across his beard before he wrapped his black-gloved hand around her delicate-boned wrist. Her once pretty mouth slipping into a pout, she sidled against him. "I'll be whatever pleases ye tonight."

"Point me to Stillings," he spoke, making his disregard of her obvious as he returned his attention to the crowd. "I believe he is here."

"You've come to trade, 'ave ye?" She tossed her thick hair, for his dark eyes had fallen on her again. This time he let them linger. Caution seemed to replace some of the fire in her eyes. Nodding toward the man sitting in the corner watching David, she shrugged. "'As soon throw ye in the river as trade anything ye got to offer."

David smiled crookedly from the shadow of his cowl and, pressing a half crown in her palm, leaned nearer to her ear. "I'll take that as a much-appreciated warning," he said with a hint of Irish in his voice.

She gazed up at him with the bluest of eyes. "In case ye be needin' a quick exit there's a door down that corridor."

Surveying the darkened hallway, he nodded. She squealed as someone behind her wrapped an arm around her hips and pulled her to a nearby table. David watched as two men fought over her. He began pressing through the unwashed bodies toward the back wall. The smell permeated every breath that filled his lungs. Disgust made him grimace. He had come to this tidewater town on the shores of the Cuckmere River for one purpose, and he was as unimpressed by the bloated show of force among the locals as he was by the depravity of their nocturnal habits.

Sipping froth from his ale, Stillings watched his approach like a military man who sensed a new enemy at his gates. Stillings wore a sleeveless leather vest over a blue woolen shirt unbuttoned at the throat. But for the narrowed eyes that took his measure, any naïve fool might have considered the man's face friendly enough.

David came to a stop next to the table, blocking the light behind him, his height forcing the man's chin up. "Stillings, I presume?" He didn't extend his hand.

Shoving the toe of an expensive boot against the man sitting at the table with him, Stillings snapped, "Off with you, Franks. Can't you see we have a distinguished guest in our midst?"

David accepted the proffered chair and sat with his back against the planked wall.

"I'm the sheriff," Stillings said, leaning forward on his elbows. "Appointed by the most noble Nellis Munro himself, magistrate and protector of these humble shores. He owns most of the land in these parts. Or is about to." With a flick of his hand, Stillings brought a harried barmaid to the table. "Your pleasure, guv'nor."

It would please him to bathe the stench of this place from his clothes. David softened his next statement with a smile. "I believe we have business to attend. The sooner we finish, the sooner I can attend to my own pleasures."

"Naturally," Stillings complied, sending off the girl. "But a man like you wouldn't last five minutes in this town."

His slow grin affable, David took note of Stillings's men moving around the room. Though David kept his face void of expression, he had the distinct impression that the sheriff expected him to be afraid. "Why is that?"

"Because it's a dangerous place for outsiders," the man challenged with an air of amusement.

Only one thing had brought David out of retirement, out of seclusion, and back to England.

He slid a red velvet pouch from within his cloak. Drawing open the string, he dumped the trinket onto the table. A bloodred ruby and diamond earring rolled into the sphere of golden candlelight. Light glinted from the brilliant stones, an open invitation for every greedy eye in the room to stare.

"I've traced this earring back to here," David said. "I'm willing to pay a handsome sum for the necklace that matches this bauble."

"Forgive me." Stillings scratched at his chin. "Where did you say you were from?"

"The pawnbroker who had this earring directed me here." David leaned away from the candlelight, the hilt of a stiletto in his glove. "Claimed to do business from around Alfriston. Said if anyone would know about the bauble's previous owner, that man would be you."

"Did he now?" The sheriff folded his massive arms over his chest. "Why would I know such information?"

"You are the sheriff. He must have presumed that you knew everyone in this area. This particular earring came from an unsolved theft in India some years ago."

"India?" Stillings regarded David with a hint of new interest in his brown eyes. "I'm not saying I know there is a necklace that belongs to this bauble," he clarified, lest David construe his obvious greed for anything except what it was. "But I am wondering how you would know of such a necklace's existence, if ye don't mind me asking?"

"Truly, Sheriff." He used the title loosely. "What difference can it make how I know? I'm willing to pay for the object in question. A thousand pounds to be exact," he said, knowing many a man would sell his own family for that kind of wealth. "The people I work for are willing to offer a cut of the profit to any man who will help locate the necklace."

Stillings's eyes sharpened. "A thousand pounds, ye say?"

In truth, the necklace was considered priceless—part of a decade-old theft of artifacts stolen from the Calcutta royal treasury. A theft that had cost him the life of a friend and his very soul. No one knew why a single earring had turned up after all these years. Nine years ago, the stolen cache was believed to have been on board a steamer that went down off the coast of Bombay, along with everyone on board.

"A theft ye say?" The big man rubbed a finger across his clean shaven chin. "Maybe it's not the necklace you're after. Maybe you are a thief after a thief who has something more that you want," he said, before finally surrendering his full attention to the ruby and diamond earring glittering on the table. "If that earring is any clue to the value of the necklace, methinks it is worth more than you say." Stillings reached out a gloved hand to claim the earring.

David slammed the stiletto into the trestle table just in front of his grasp, startling the man's hand back. "This earring belongs to me, Sheriff."

Stillings's eyes narrowed as if he had made a mistake in dismissing David as no threat. "Do you question my authority to pursue this as a legal matter?"

"Come, Stillings." His tone and smile belied the odds of his capture. "You do not mean to take what belongs to me. I've offered to pay well for the information I seek."

A confident smirk lifted one corner of Stillings's mouth as he stood. "I can see we have a problem."

"Then we have something in common."

"Seize him!" the sheriff shouted.

David reached beneath the table and, with both hands, heaved it over. Mugs, plates, and silverware spilled over the planked floor, splattering food and ale over unsuspecting patrons. In the same motion, he sprang to his feet and leaped atop a second table. Tossing out a handful of coins, he threw back his cloak and swung around, revealing the sword at his side.

"Another day, Sheriff."

Men and barmaids dove for the shillings in a clash of screams, teeth, and flailing limbs. A call rang out. "Don't let him escape, you fools!"

David leaped to another tabletop and strode its length, his boots scattering trenchers and mugs. Shouts ensued as more men joined in the fray. Glass shattered, a bench overturned. David stepped onto another table, turning to check the sheriff's progress, and saw him fighting through the tangle of limbs, barely missing a collision with a punch as he scrambled to recover the earring David had left him on the table.

His cowl billowing around his shoulders, David dropped onto a bench before touching his boots to the floor and striding out the door into the black chill of a bright moonlit night.

Chapter 2

"It is freezing out here."

Setting a crate of jelly jars into the cart, Victoria Munro turned at the sound of her stepdaughter's voice. Seventeen-year-old Bethany stood in a shaft of moonlight, her arms folded tightly over her torso. With only an eleven-year age difference between them, they had always been more like sisters than stepmother and stepdaughter.

A lone lantern sitting in the barn's doorway cast light over Bethany's white wrapper. "Whatever are you doing at this hour? And on a night like this?" the girl scolded.

"We are helping your grandfather deliver these to his patients tomorrow." Glass rattled as Victoria set a second crate in the cart. "Since his illness, he can no longer—"

"Cousin Nellis was here again tonight. I saw you arguing with him in the garden," Bethany said, running to Victoria and wrapping her arms around her. "That awful man will see us driven from our land won't he? And Peepaw can do nothing."

As Sir Henry's closest male relative, Nellis wanted Bethany's grandfather declared incompetent, a fact that was bound to occur if Sir Henry's illness weakened him further. Victoria would fight Sir Henry's sneak thief of a nephew every inch of the way before she sat back and watched Nellis become the family's benefactor and take over their holdings.

Victoria covered the cart with a canvas tarp and bent to secure the fastenings. She was confident they would make it through winter and still have a roof over their heads come spring, despite Nellis's illegal machinations, but she was not so sure of next year.

"'Tis a dangerous duel you play with Nellis, Victoria. He's getting more persistent with you about his desires. How can you not be afraid?"

"Bethany . . ." At seventeen, her stepdaughter was too naïve to understand real evil. But Victoria was neither young nor naïve—and she understood evil too well. She could handle Nellis, she told herself. "Would you rather we concede?"

Bethany tucked a wisp of her hair behind her ear and looked away. A velvet canopy of stars lay over the countryside. Behind her, the tree swing creaked in the steady autumn breeze. "It's just . . . you make me afraid when you fight Nellis the way you do. He won't care now if you marry him or not. He wants this estate."

"Your cousin isn't a nice man, Bethany. Both your grandfather and I will fight him before either of us surrenders anything to him, and that includes this estate. Besides, even if I wanted to do such a thing as wed, I could not."

"Because you don't love him?"

Victoria absently fastened the iron rings that rimmed the cart, her cloak doing little to shield her from the chill.

Moving to this cottage down the hill from Rose Briar

should have proven to Nellis that she would not relent in her decision. Could not relent. But he had become even more obnoxiously persistent in the last few months, and she did not understand why. She had managed to save the plot of land on which this cottage sat with the income she and Sir Henry earned from their medical practice, but they were not going to be able to save the ancestral home on the bluff or the three thousand acres of nearby farmland. Nellis had already put everything on the block for unpaid taxes. No one would dare purchase the estate for fear of reprisal, and Nellis would get it for nothing. In a few weeks, everything but this cottage would be in Nellis's hands. After that, he would be going after guardianship of her son.

"Come," Victoria beckoned. "You can help me finish tying down the tarp. With Nathanial still with your cousins in Salehurst, you and I will be too busy to worry about anything else for the next few weeks."

"Oh, look." The younger girl pointed a slim finger at the sky. "A shooting star. Did you see? Make a wish. Hurry."

Victoria's gaze moved across the trees and over the land that had been her home for the last nine years. Closing her eyes, she made a wish before the tail of the star fizzled in the sky. The people most important to her lived here. She wished for a miracle that would help her fight Nellis, and discovered she would bargain with the devil himself.

A black cat leaped on the cart, and Victoria lifted the purring feline into her arms. "Where have you been, Zeus?" She nuzzled the cat. "Don't you know it's dangerous for you out here at night? An owl lives in our barn. Nathanial would never forgive me if I allowed you to get eaten."

She missed her son. He'd been gone since the hops harvest began in September. This was the first year she'd allowed him to go, and had done so because one of his best friends had moved to Salehurst last year. Nathanial was almost ten years old, after all—the age at which many of his friends were already being sent to boarding schools.

"Victoria?" Bethany's small voice came from behind her. "Riders are approaching."

"Get inside," she said as a group of darkly clad riders crowned the hill above the cottage fifty yards away.

"But why would they be coming here?" Bethany whispered. "We have a full moon tonight. Smugglers don't—"

"I said go inside, Bethany." She continued to hold the cat. Sheriff Stillings should not be calling tonight, and she wondered what foul luck brought him her way. "See that Sir Henry doesn't awaken."

Her stepdaughter turned away and, in a billowy cloud of white, ran across the yard and into the cottage. Oaks pillared the drive, and Victoria's gaze touched the canopies made more eerie by the silver light filtering through their limbs. She would not have expected this particular crowd to be out roaming the woods on a cold night when they could easily have found warmth and entertainment in town.

A rider separated from the group. Sheriff Stillings rode directly toward her and pulled up his beast of a horse just before he ran her down. Gravel sprayed her and sent the cat in her arms into a frenzy.

"If it isn't the lady doctor come to welcome me." Stillings chuckled. "You aren't going to padlock your stables again, are ye?"

Infuriated that he bullied her so, she let go of the frightened cat, and he shot off between the legs of the horse. Startled, the gelding sidestepped and reared, as the rider attempted to subdue it. The cat streaked like a trail of smoke up the nearest tree, leaving the maddened horse nervously prancing and the rider nearly unseated.

"Bloody, bloomin' hell."

Shoving the hat off his eyes, he looked into the derringer Victoria pointed at his heart. "Be careful, Tommy Stillings." She was taller than most men, and her aim was crack. "I would not wish to think you an intruder and accidentally shoot you." She lowered the gun to the much prized point between his legs.

She had known Stillings for all the nine years she'd lived in England. She knew the men who rode with him, knew what they were capable of doing. Six months ago, they had started using her horses to haul their illegal caches from the river to heaven only knew where. Bethany's spotted mare had been injured on the trail; it might have to be put down. "As for you ever using the horses out of my stable again, I assure you, you will not."

"Bloody hell, my lady." Slapping his hat against his thigh, he glanced around the drive as if to find an army hidden among the bushes, then glared at the men behind him as someone snickered.

"I am alone," Victoria mocked. "Unlike some, I don't need others to fight my battles."

Stillings's teeth showed white in the darkness. "That's what I like about you, Lady Munro. You're no sniveling coward. Must be because you spent so much of your life among the natives in Calcutta. Being an innocent orphan and all." He tossed something to the ground at her feet. "Pick it up," he demanded. "You can put the gun away, too. If I wanted to attack you, I would have run ye down already."

Her gaze reluctantly dropped to the object at her feet. And the world froze around her.

"Do you recognize that little trinket?"

Pulse racing, she knelt. Her hair fell loose around her shoulders and touched the ground at her feet, shielding her face as she lifted the earring. Her gaze chased her panic to the hill where the sheriff and his cronies had appeared.

"I'm told there is a necklace that goes with that bauble," Stillings said, dragging her eyes back to his face. "Is there such a necklace?"

"Who brought this to you?"

The sheriff leaned forward on his saddle, his muddy boots creaking with the movement. "We had a visitor tonight at the Wild Boar. My guess is he's interested in getting his hands on more than some costly necklace."

"Go." She threw the earring at him. "And take that with you. Don't you think if I had such a necklace, I would have used it to pay the taxes on Sir Henry's estate?"

Stillings's cynical smile did little to bolster the hope that he might believe her. He looked at the cottage, his expression growing thoughtful. "Seeing as how you saved my life once, I could take care of the outsider for you. I'm a man who likes to see his debts paid."

"You have a strange sense of honor for a cutthroat smuggler, Tommy Stillings."

"I take insult to your words." He laughed softly. "Especially since I've decided to offer ye my services."

"No doubt this enterprising partnership would include murder."

"Maybe. But think on this, Doc. Tonight's visitor left me this trinket on purpose. If I were the owner of this earring, I'd be askin' who in these parts can protect me from *him*."

Stillings spurred his mount and galloped back to the other riders. Together they thundered up the long drive, leaving a layer of dust hanging in their wake. Victoria remained braced against the cold and the terror that turned her blood to ice. She closed her fist over the derringer.

Zeus mewed, jolting her from her paralysis. Kneeling, she called for the feline, relieved when he loped across the drive into her arms. An owl launched from the high branches of an oak and, wings widespread, drifted into the barn. "Shh," she murmured into the cat's neck, backing out of the drive into the shadows. "It's all right."

But watching the owl's flight across the yard, she held the cat against her, knowing the words of reassurance were a lie. What she'd dreaded for too long had finally come to pass.

Someone had found her.

Chapter 3

Leading the steeldust mare up the hill, Victoria took a deep breath and looked back at the cottage. She'd managed to sneak out of the house and saddle the horse in relative silence. She swung into the saddle, worried that the creak of leather would bring one of the servants. Fighting back her fear, she reined the mare around and rode out into the night. Five minutes up the road, she switched to a back trail and changed directions as she found the narrow, wooded shortcut that led to the main house on the bluff.

She'd tucked her long, dark hair beneath a battered hat and pulled the rim lower to protect her eyes from the frigid temperature. Branches clipped her sleeves. Bending over the mount's neck, she maneuvered through the woods. Woolen trousers and heavy stockings beneath her boots protected her legs and feet, but nothing shielded her face from the stinging autumn chill. She pulled her coat collar tighter around her neck.

Panic had driven her into the house to change her clothing. Panic spurred her forward now. Fifteen minutes later, she glimpsed the silhouette of the sixteenth-century stone tower that belonged to what remained of the timber-framed church. It overlooked the cemetery where Sir Henry had buried his only son, Bethany's father, nine years ago after his body had been shipped home from India. The aged burial ground had once served the families who lived and worked Munro land. A fire had ravaged the church five years ago. Now, with the exception of nay doers and one lone groundskeeper, few ventured here.

Reining in beneath the iron arch that opened into the graveyard, she let the silence fill her and attempted to quell her panic. After Stillings had left, she'd waited in the cottage, looking at the yard and the road from her bedroom window, watching the shadows in the night, watching to make sure no one was outside. She'd waited for everyone inside the cottage to go to sleep before she came here.

She wanted to believe that the earring turning up had been an awful fluke, but someone knew about the stolen necklace. Someone knew to come to this town in search of her. Upon seeing the bauble tonight, her first terror-filled instinct had been to go after her son and flee England.

But she could leave neither Sir Henry nor Bethany alone, or the life she had built for herself and her son over the years—the only life and family Nathanial had ever known.

A fog clung to the ground, hovering like a ghostly breath over the aged and mossy stones, hiding their eternal secrets. She nudged the horse around the graveyard's perimeter, but could not see the soil to know if anyone had been here recently.

She rose on her legs to swing out of the saddle, when her mare's ears pricked forward and she froze. She whipped her head around to look down the road she'd just traveled and scanned the darkness. Her heartbeat pounded in her ears, but no other sound fell around her. Still, she eased Sir Henry's old revolver from her bag.

How long had it been since she'd gone out into the night with the intent to kill a man? Shaking with cold and apprehension, she backed her mount away from the iron fence into the trees. Tension vibrated the night air and moved over the yard like a slow-growing mist, engulfing her.

Held frozen, Victoria was consumed by something she could not explain. Someone had followed her. Someone she could not see, but felt with every instinct in her being.

"Who are you?" she called.

Looking to her right at the path that led away from the grounds, she started to edge the horse deeper into the copse when a rider separated from the darkness—a silhouette forged by the light of a full moon hanging in the sky behind him.

"I should be asking you that question, Meg." The haunting voice came back to her from across the graveyard. From across ten years of her past and a world she had escaped four thousand miles away. Recognition seized her lungs along with a fear even greater than the one she held when Stillings had left her tonight.

"Or should I call you Lady Munro now?" he asked, the tenor of his words seizing her completely. "But then what is adulterer when added to con artist, thief, and murderer?"

"Go away, David!" Her heart beating double-time, she edged the horse deeper into the woods. "I mean it. Go away."

A gust of wind whipped his hooded cloak around him like a hawk's wings and the black horse he rode pranced sideways, giving her a view of mount and rider. For a terrifying moment, she expected his apparition to take flight. "I cannot do that, Meg," he answered from the heavy shadows. "You know it as well as I."

Victoria whipped the reins and kicked her horse with her heels. The horse came out of the wooded copse and leaped the smaller picket fence that bordered the overgrown church-yard. She ducked beneath a low-hanging branch as David shot out of the woods at the bottom of the rise and blocked the path.

Without hesitation, Victoria swung the mare around and headed for another path. She didn't want to ride toward the bluff, but she would go anyplace to evade capture.

The horse hit the field separating the churchyard from the bluff's steep embankment and lunged into a run. She leaned low over the mare's neck and urged the horse flat out across the field, pulling on the reins to slow the mare as she flew over the steep embankment. The pace was too fast. Caught off-stride, the horse stumbled down the loamy hill, but like the Irish stock the horse was, it recovered its balance. Filtered moonlight laid a path through the treetops. She followed the old drover's trail serpentining down the hill. Branches tore her hat and coat off her body. Over her own thundering heart, she heard David's horse gaining. Then like the owl that would devour Zeus, he was riding beside her on the path, a huge winged shadow in the night.

Both horses collided. A scream died in her chest as David plucked her off the saddle. Pressed on one side by brush and open to the slow-moving river on the other, the path narrowed next to a hill that plunged fifty feet down to the water's edge.

David had misjudged her strength. Or her desperation.

He reined in his black and it skidded in the leaves. An elbow dug into his ribs as she kicked and screamed. Her head banged him in the mouth. He caught her wrist.

Before he realized what was in her fist, a gun discharged near his cheek, deafening him. Both horses reared in terror, throwing him backward off the saddle, his arms still locked around her.

With an oath, he hit the slope and they tumbled downward, rolling and scattering dead leaves, until they finally landed in a heap of tangled limbs and dusty clothes.

Somehow, she ended on top, straddling his hips. "Bastard! Why couldn't you just let me stay dead?"

Her sable hair spilled around him in a fragrant mesh of vanilla. For a moment, he was too stunned by his emotions to repel her attack and did not see her swing her fist. Barely evading contact, he rolled her, fighting and squirming, the evocative fullness of her body soft beneath him as they slid another few feet together. The scuffle shoved up her shirt and caught her hair beneath her bottom.

She coughed and choked. "Get off me!"

David found himself lying between her legs. He captured her wrists and braced them on either side of her thrashing head. His chest crushed her breasts, and he could feel her heart thundering against him. The shock of her wriggling jolted him. His gaze fell first on the curve of her lips, then rose to her flushed face, and he suddenly welcomed the doubt growing in her eyes. "Now, Meg." He tasted blood from a cut on the inside of his lip and spat to the side. "Why would I be wanting to do that?"

He burned to touch her, to wrap his hands around her throat and choke the life from her. A beautiful enemy was the deadliest of enemies, as she had proven long ago. For nine years, he'd thought her dead. Nine bloody years she'd disappeared.

She had managed to elude the most powerful country in the world, and he found his interest in her little tempered by his grip on his will. He'd been hunting the owner of that earring—and now reeled from finding her alive.

"How fitting that we met again across a graveyard." He let his hands slide over her waist and her legs as he checked for more weapons. "Indeed, what does one say on an occasion such as this? 'Hello, Meg. How are you after all of these years? I'm so glad to see that you did not drown.' Hmm, or, perhaps, 'Goodness gracious, David. I thought I left you for dead in Calcutta.'"

She glared back, eyes glistening with fury—and confusion. She was beautiful bathed in moonlight, the brilliance surrounding them emphasizing the hint of wet violet in her eyes.

"What?" he rasped with barely restrained fury. "Nothing to say before I take you to jail where you so aptly deserve to hang?"

"You are a madman, David Donally. Get off me!" she screamed.

"Quite the contrary." He covered her mouth with one gloved hand and forced her to look at him. "I am saner than I've ever been when around you. But you *will* understand, with the current residents of these woods, I suggest you quit making so much bloody noise."

Her eyes flashed hot. "You are the only one in danger here."

He smiled, appreciating the threat. "From you? Or that band of ruffians with whom you are so familiar? Are they the company you've been keeping for nine fooking years, Meg? Why am I not shocked?"

The Irishness in his voice seemed to alert her to the deadliness of its tone. "Therefore you throw me off a cliff?" She renewed her struggle, bucking futilely. "Get off me, you bastard."

"What were you doing in that cemetery?"

"I wasn't in the cemetery." Her words came out in gasps. "I was on my way to the bluff house when I heard you . . . and took shelter."

"Then you were out for a predawn ride? Before the roads became busy. Is that it?"

"I don't need to explain my actions to you. If I'm not mistaken, this is private land. My husband's family lives here."

"If I'm not mistaken," he said against the curve of her mouth, "Faraday is not the family that owns this land on which we are currently lying so lovingly entwined. And the only husband you still legally have is square on top of you. Unless you are trying to count that death certificate I have as a divorce."

She stopped her struggling. Her shirt sleeve had torn and spilled off her pale shoulder. She didn't weep, not that she ever would have in his presence. Not his proud, temptress of a traitorous wife, torn and disheveled but magnificent still.

"Will you let me up?" she said through clenched teeth. "You are . . . squashing me."

David hesitated, then rolled off her. His ears still ringing from the pistol shot, he set his elbow on one raised knee, looking at once for the revolver. Meg rolled to her feet as if that made her situation less precarious. Or made her any safer.

Testing the cut on his bottom lip with his knuckle, he let his eyes move over the length of her. She was still breathing hard and the mounds of her breasts were visible behind her shirt laces. Following his gaze to her gaping garment, she snatched her shirt together and presented him her back.

"I wouldn't want to think you unduly bruised." Having never remembered her modesty, he found himself amused to see it now. "Are you?"

She whirled and eyed his swollen lip. "For the sake of argument, I'd contend that you've thus far received more out of this tryst than I. Would you not agree, Donally?"

"Is this your idea of a tryst?" He came to his feet, his cloak swirling around his boots and dislodging a cloud of leaves. "I can certainly make our reunion more interesting."

She jumped backward, poised to run. Looking at her, David remembered her as he had first seen her long ago, tall, proud, regal Meg Faraday. She wore no finery, but she had not changed. At the same time, she assessed his dark hair and cropped beard. He wore no gentleman's riding jacket beneath his cloak, but black shirt, breeches, and boots. He knew he looked like a highwayman—a man who lived in the shadows—as he had always lived when he'd known her.

"How did you find me?" she asked, not so proud in bearing as she had been seconds before.

He considered not telling her. He considered slapping her in irons and handing her over to his superior. He considered all these things, yet did none of them.

Staring down at her, fists clenching and unclenching, he forced the emotions to subside. "After the earring turned up at a pawnshop in London, the Calcutta files were reopened." He didn't recount the weeks it had taken to get to this point. "We located the passenger manifest list from the steamer that went down off Bombay. There were seventeen survivors. Six were women, two of whom had already passed away. Two other women were in their fifties, and one was a forty-year-old companion. That left one Lady Scott Munro, wife to Sir Scott. Do you know how many Munros live from Brighton to Rye?"

"Please, can't you just go away? Pretend you never saw me? I'm not doing anything illegal, I swear."

"With your history for respecting the law, it hadn't crossed my mind, Meg."

Shoving a hand through her tangled hair, she shook her head as if dazed. "I think you gave me a concussion," she murmured, her gaze hesitating on the revolver lying in the leaves at her feet.

David saw the gun at the same time and read her intent. "Don't think about it, Meg. I will break your wrist if you try."

"What are you going to do?"

He bent and picked up the revolver. "Exactly what I came here to do. Smugglers, murderers, and my wife not withstanding."

"Listen to me, David." She caught the soft fabric of his shirt, just above his heart. The shock of her contact against his chest seemed to jolt them both. "I mean . . ." She dropped her hand as she fumbled for composure. "Isn't there anything I can do—"

"It won't work, Meg." He smiled at her uncertainty. "But if you want to spread your legs for me, for old time's sake, I'll certainly accommodate your desire."

Tears welling in her eyes, her arm lashed out, but he easily caught her wrist.

"You're a cold-blooded bastard, Donally."

"Temper, temper, sweet, docile Margaret." He held her easily. "You always did like disparaging my paternity."

"And you haven't changed." Shoving away from him, she swiped the back of a fist across her cheeks.

"Something you will do well to heed."

Aye, she should be afraid, he pondered as she turned and took flight up the hill, sending leaves and dirt skittering in her wake. "Where do you think you can run, Meg?"

He took the time to empty the gun chamber, letting the bullets plop to the ground, before he flung the gun into the woods. He was upon her in three steps and flipped her onto her back. He knew he was close to physically hurting her and forced his temper back, reining it in as he did the passion she'd so aptly roused in him.

She lost the ground she'd gained. Something like pain groaned out of her. "To think that I ever loved you!" She scrabbled harder to escape him, but her fight had weakened. "I hate you. I truly do."

"No doubt. That explains why you tried to kill me. Twice."

"I didn't try to kill you earlier." Breathing hard from the exertion, she flung a handful of dirt and leaves at his legs. "The gun discharged when you pulled me off my horse."

"You're a liar, Meg." He gripped the tree limb above her for balance. "You lied to me in India. You're living a bloody lie now, taking on someone else's life like the con artist you are. How many people around here believe you are some kind of saint?"

"I've built a real home, David." Her eyes glistened with entreaty. "Margaret Faraday is dead. She died nine years ago off the coast of India. Can't you please let her go?"

"Did you murder the woman whose identity you stole?"

Her eyes snapped wide. "No!" She scooted another two feet up the slippery incline. "Lady Munro . . . I met her on the way to Bombay. Her husband had died after only a few weeks of marriage. She was returning to England to her husband's family. She had no one else. We became traveling companions. When the boiler room blew, when the steamer sank, she was not among the survivors. I was given a chance to change my life. I took it."

"Along with a hundred thousand pounds worth of stolen artifacts and treasure? Where is that? At the bottom of the Arabian Sea? Or somewhere closer?"

"You have no idea what you've done by coming here." She kicked at him. Then the tears began to squeeze out from beneath her lids. "No idea at all. I hate you for doing this to me. I truly do."

David stared at the top of her bowed head, the desperation in her eyes no longer shielded by the tangled cape of her hair, and it seemed as if something inside him softened. She'd fought him, plied him, spat names at him, now she would call upon his sympathies. She had to know that her fight was as futile as it was over. "Oh, I have a fairly good idea I'm not the only one you've been hiding from for all these years. No telling the termites that will come out of the woodwork now to hunt you down."

"Then if you ever felt anything for me at all, let me go."

The words grabbed at his chest like a fist closing around his heart and roused his fury, along with memories he had no business revisiting. Unable and unwilling to go down that path ever again, David surveyed the trail far above them for a way out of here. "Let's hope the horses are still up there." Wrapping the length of his cloak around his forearm, he pulled her to her feet. "Walk."

"I can't." She stumbled to her knees. "You really did hurt me."

"Aye," he said with bittersweet humor, lending his shoulder for her to walk. "Wasn't that always the problem between us, Meg?"

Once they reached the road, she was trembling. He gave his cloak a thorough shaking before applying it to her shoulders. "Unfortunately for you, I need you alive."

"I don't want anything from you." She struggled to throw off the bulky cloak. "I would rather freeze to death."

Despite her height, the cloak swallowed her, making her look frail, and a protective, possessive part of him reared its head. "Just take the damn cloak," he said, brushing aside her hand as he worked the clasps at her neck, attempting to discard the sudden surge of his emotions. "It's too cold. You need it more than I do."

Her eyes locked on his, and his hands stilled.

His gaze slid up from her wind-reddened mouth to swim in her eyes, and he fought the pull to touch his lips to hers, the travesty of his position mocking him.

He could not have foreseen her effect on him, could not have realized how much he wanted to touch her. To hold her. Still.

He could never allow himself to forget what she had done to his life, or that she was wanted for treason and murder. He could not forget why he was here. Indeed, their past marked them both, and it would never allow him to make the same mistake twice in one lifetime.

"Thank you," she murmured, "for the wrap." Her chin lifted as if in a show of strength. But she was not all of a piece and faltered.

He hated that he cared. One arm under her knees, the other beneath her shoulders, he lifted her against him.

He hated that even after everything that had gone before them, he still mourned her. For in his heart, Meg Faraday had died on that steamer nine years ago. She had been correct about that. And he had never stopped thinking about her. Or forgotten how much he had loved her. "Don't thank me for anything," he said, his eyes steady on the path as he felt her head loll against his shoulder.

For Meg Faraday would never be free again.

Victoria awakened groggy and sore in a warm bed. Turning her head, she peered at a fire crackling from the hearth. The rococo-style bedstead where she lay was half-hidden beneath gold velvet hangings that dominated the room. Her gaze moved over the well-appointed chamber, then followed where her senses led to the pillow beneath her head, last night's memory cascading over her. No matter the years past, she would recognize David's scent beneath the spicy soap he used. She was in his room.

His bed.

Confused and struggling to her elbows, she tried to separate the calm logic from the cloud that had settled in her throbbing head. She wore nothing beneath the sheets except a bandage that wrapped her ribs.

No wonder she could barely breathe. She must have cracked her ribs when she tumbled from the horse. And he'd drugged her, she realized as her fingers tested a bruise on her temple. She could taste laudanum and feel its liquefying effects on her muscles.

Daylight slivered through a crack in the drawn drapes. Moving to the edge of the mattress, she sat up, but didn't wait for the room to quit spinning before dragging a blanket off the bed. The room gliding through her senses, she staggered for balance, determined only to reach the door. And run.

"I wouldn't go out there if I were you."

She whipped around at the sound of the familiar masculine voice. David stood framed in the dressing room archway, shrugging into a shirt, acting as if she were a paramour he'd left in his bed. Her heavy-lidded gaze roamed up his arms, encompassing the pull of white fabric against his shoulders as he tended to his buttons, his movements no longer casual as she met his gaze and, for a moment, neither moved.

He had shaved—she could smell his soap permeating the air. She blinked to clear her head, for what she had seen in the darkness behind his beard last night could not compare to his clean-shaven countenance now.

David Donally was undeniably the most attractive man she had ever known. And still was. The stark white cloth of his shirt contrasted with his coffee brown hair, cut short at the nape. Shorter than he used to wear it. Black trousers shaped his long legs and tucked into high riding boots adding another inch to his imposing stature.

He was her husband.

And she hated him.

Yet, even after all these years, she was aware of him in a way she remembered. The physical kind of awareness that made her conscious of her femininity. In that regard, time had erased nothing and only seemed to ignite the embers inside to flame. She had married him ten years ago because she had been in love with him to the point of blindness. He had used her then. Her instinct for survival warned her to run from him now. Her hand tightened around the glass doorknob at her back, and she opened the door.

"Let me give you some advice, Meg," he said, tucking the shirt into his trousers. Wary of his approach, she lifted her chin rather than retreat. "You're a beautiful woman. I wouldn't leave here wearing only my blanket. You'll never make it to the end of the street."

Her mind seemed to float around his presence. Caution and fear. These things no longer asserted themselves. "Leave it to you to find humor in my distress, Donally."

He stopped in front of her. "I have to admit, I always did like you best wearing nothing more than a sheet. Or nothing at all. I remember when you were the most beautiful woman in all of Calcutta and knew it, too."

"Don't blame me for your lust. It's not my fault you couldn't keep your hands off me."

"Ah, Meg." He tilted her chin. "You still have a wee bite with that lovely mouth."

"And what of *your* mouth, David? Do you still possess that legendary . . . vigor?"

He reached over her shoulder and shut the door none too gently. "You were right about the cracked rib and the concussion." He turned her face from side to side and looked at her eyes. "I believe you've also suffered brain damage."

Suddenly so hot in his presence, she stared up at him, vaguely wondering if maybe she was dreaming after all. "Is that your expert diagnosis?"

"I know enough of medicine," he said neutrally.

"So do I." She traced a finger along the faint pattern of delineated muscle beneath his shirt, finding renewed fascination with his body. "I once sewed up a man's scalp that had been lacerated from temple to neck. A terrible mess."

The look in his eyes told her he didn't believe a word she was saying, but she didn't care. "Where have you been living these past years?"

He didn't answer at first, then, "Ireland."

"Alone?"

It was all she dared ask him, all she wanted to know, though she used to look at the stars and wonder if he also looked up at that same sky and thought of her. Or wondered what they might have had with each other if she had been different.

His palm remained on the door, trapping her against the heat and scent of his body. "What are you doing, Meg?"

"Did I ever tell you opiates make me do and say insane things?"

His eyes pinned her where she stood, clasping the blanket to her breast. She was annoyed that she couldn't read his thoughts.

But then, she had never been able to read his thoughts, and in her laudanum-induced reality she found herself resenting that strange sense of bliss she'd always felt in his presence. "Where have you brought me?"

"A safe place for now."

"Safe?" She laughed, a contradiction if she'd ever heard one when she stood in front of him aware of her own nakedness and a strange burning inside. Leaning her head back against the door, she closed her eyes. "So this is God's great jest on me. Only the angel hails from Ireland." Her eyes flashed. "Be content that you have ruined my life. Be content that I will never laugh again. That you have won at last."

"Are you finished?"

His quiet voice, his complete and utter control ravaged hers.

"No." Seized with a fortuitous recklessness to take control, abetted by the laudanum swimming hot through her veins, Victoria raised her arms to his neck. "Are you?"

His reflexes more honed and practiced than hers, he caught her wrists. But not before the blanket tumbled to the ground at her feet. She trembled as the fire in his eyes burned her to the quick. "Not even for old time's sake, David? You and me?"

Lowering her hands to her side, he bent and picked up the blanket, returning it to her shoulders. "You insult yourself, Meg."

She hated that he pitied her. "I don't want your mercy, David." Bewildered by the tightness within her, she turned her face away from his. "But when they hang me," she whispered, "I want you there." Despite her instant and instinctive desire to dig her fists into his shirt and pummel him with all the fear and frustration knotted inside her, she could say nothing else as the dormant memories she'd buried so long ago began to awaken.

"Is there anyone you wish to contact?" he quietly asked. "Your family, perhaps?"

"My family?"

His family. The son he'd never met.

She no longer felt protected by the numbness in which she'd encased her life for so long. A place she had retreated where she could love her son and know peace, where she had tried to make up for what she had done in her past, pay her debts to society and, in her own way, deal justice to those who had deserved to pay.

Her secrets would go with her to the grave.

Sir Henry had shown her too much kindness to suffer because of her. He loved Nathanial and her.

Except he loved Victoria Munro, not Meg Faraday. No one had ever loved Meg Faraday.

David least of all.

She had already lost any chance to keep her son. But neither could she bear to see Nathanial ripped from the arms of his family and put into the care of a heartless stranger.

A heartless stranger who now managed to hold her despite her struggles and let her weep into his shirt.

A heartless stranger who, with his strength, managed all over again to pull the foundation from under her life. She had not wept like this since she buried Zeus's mother two years ago, she thought irrationally, remembering the cat she had fished out of shark-infested waters off Bombay. She'd brought that rangy black feline with her to England, the only companion to a pregnant nineteen-year-old with no where else in the world to go. They had been such a pathetic pair.

"It's the laudanum," she sniffled when David took her back to bed and covered her with blankets that smelled like him.

"I know."

"I hate you," she lied, closing her eyes as he tucked the corners around her.

"I know."

She had tried to hate him. For years, she had tried, but in her confusion, she now tried to remember why.

"Sleep, Meg."

And somehow, she did.

Chapter 4

$\sim\!\sim\!\bigcirc\!\bigcirc\!\sim\!\sim$

David danced through the master's wheel with the same precision he attacked his life, with finesse and resolve to finish what he started. Sword in hand, he lunged and retreated, crossed his back leg over and began the advance again. Sweat trailed into his eyes. He'd been working the wheel for an hour, his saber a driving force in the hushed silence, broken by the sound of his breath. He paused in momentary riposte.

Pamela Rockwell watched from the doorway, her arms crossed beneath her bosom. She had been his partner since he had rejoined Kinley's team three months ago. Blond as sin, she was skilled at hunting down information. If he gave her half the chance, she would know his every secret. She was also married to his other partner on this case.

Her verdant gown and petticoats rustled as she swept into the studio. "Don't let the point fly, darling. Movement is about balance and speed. You're off your game today."

"Thank you for the remark, Pamela. I wasn't aware that you fenced."

"You won't use a gun." She glided to a stop in front of him. "But you keep your thrusting skills honed? Isn't there a double standard in that?"

"Only if I stab someone through the heart with the tip of this sword."

He yanked a towel from a peg on the wall and blotted his face and hair dampened from the workout. He wore a long-sleeved shirt and black trousers that disappeared into calf-hugging boots. Casual working attire, but too hot, even as cold as it was outside.

"Do you wish to go another round before you face Kinley then?"

He peered at her over the edge of the towel. "If you feel the need to worry about my sense of duty, I'll spare you the trouble. My duty is intact."

"Then you won't have a problem surrendering your prisoner to him? Kinley has wanted this trophy on his wall for years."

"Indeed." David tossed the rag on the floor next to a pitcher of water. "How is that, since we've only known she might be alive for a few months?"

"You walked off the case nine years ago. Willingly, I might interject. Maybe I need to remind you of your job, David. Lest you become a risk to this mission."

"This mission, Pamela? How long has Kinley known Meg was alive?"

Pamela brushed lint from her sleeve, blindly unaware that Kinley's obtuseness had always been a black spot in David's relationship with his former mentor. "I'm not your enemy, David. I'm on your side. Remember?"

"And I'd certainly never assume that the foreign office dealt in anything less than the truth. Or that you would ever lie to me."

Pamela sighed in her usual melodramatic fashion and pulled away. "Do you know how hard it is to salvage a wreck in turbulent seas?"

He assumed she was talking about the sunken steamer. "Depending on the depth, I imagine it's not impossible. People do it all the time."

Pamela stood against the sunlight pouring through the mullioned window. "When Kinley couldn't find any trace of what was stolen from the treasury on that ship, they assumed Miss Faraday was never a passenger. He has had agents in and out of every British port from here to Calcutta for the past five years. You should be proud that you found her in less than three months."

"Kinley has bloody known for five years that Meg might still be alive?"

"What do you care? Obviously, she still has a connection to her father. Who else could she have been going to meet when you intercepted her last night?"

"You do realize she is my wife."

"Kinley told me the circumstances of the investigation ten years ago made it difficult to get into Colonel Faraday's circle any other way." She peered at him from beneath her lashes. "Clearly most men see no problem that you chose to mix pleasure with business. Who wouldn't have done the same in your place? Even you have vices, it seems."

"Surprise, surprise, Pamela." He returned the sword to its place on the wall. "I'm not the saint everyone bloody thinks I am. And maybe Meg isn't the devil, either."

"Oh, please, David. You didn't get that scar you carry skeet shooting," Pamela reminded him. "Meg Faraday is guilty of everything of which she's been accused, and I do not believe you've forgotten the mission already."

"I've forgotten nothing."

He had returned to Kinley to finish this job—for his heart, for justice, for answers to questions he had buried in the last decade—at least that was what he fed his conscience every morning when he looked at himself in the mirror.

He didn't know why he should not deliver Meg over to Kinley and be done with her. Maybe he wanted the truth to what had happened years ago when she fled him and disappeared. He could deduce from her behavior that she was guilty. But of which sin, he was no longer sure.

Then again, maybe her fear was part of her superb acting skill, and she'd been waiting for her father's return before making a move. It wouldn't be the first time she'd fooled him or lied.

But then soul to sin and all sanctimonious accusations aside, ten years ago, were her lies any different from his?

Still, he knew his duty. Had always known his duty. He folded his arms and leaned against the wall. "Don't worry, Pamela. I have no intention of shirking my job."

She stopped in the doorway and planted her palms on her hips. "Then give good behavior a crack, won't you?" Her teeth were white against her coral lips as she smiled. "Because Kinley is upstairs in the green salon waiting for you to deliver his prisoner."

Victoria sat on the mattress, her head buried in her hands, the memory of her earlier behavior uppermost in her mind as she battled a throbbing headache. Someone had thrown open the draperies, and she groaned through splayed fingers at the late-afternoon sunshine that dappled the floor.

Finally, dragging the sheet off the bed, she padded to the window on stiff legs. She could see the familiar banks of the river over the village rooftops. She had to get word to Sir Henry that she was alive. He and Bethany would be worried by now that she had not returned home.

She found the dressing room and thumbed through shirts and other articles of clothing folded there. The armoire held more clothing, but no weapons, as if David would be so careless. She gave up searching for her clothes and eased her arms into a black and silver brocade robe she found thrown over a chair beside the bed. The fabric was soft and lay against the ache in her shoulder muscles. She found a mirror and leaned into the glass to inspect her temple. A lump filled out the bruise, coloring her skin a lovely shade of lavender. She grimaced. Doing nothing for her sleep-mussed hair, she walked to the bedroom door and edged it open, surprised there were no guards to keep her inside.

Did David worry so little about her escaping?

A worn Turkish carpet muffled her steps as she followed the hallway, until she heard the low rumble of David's voice and slowed. Clutching the robe tighter against her chest, she moved to the archway of the salon. Fading sunlight cast the room in a warm yet somber brilliance that seemed to match the mood of those present.

David stood near the fireplace, one hand on his hip, an elbow propped on the mantel, clearly agitated as he spoke to the paunchy white-haired man on the chair. Another younger man and woman were present on the red-and-white-striped settee. Victoria hadn't expected anyone other than servants to be present in the house. She should have anticipated that David did not work alone.

She must have made some sound, for he turned his head, his glass arrested halfway to lips, and she fell into his gaze. She remained frozen beneath the archway, wearing his black and silver brocade robe, appearing as if she belonged to him. The robe's hem touched her ankles and made her conscious of her bare feet.

She tucked a long length of her hair behind her ear, the halting movement betraying her lack of calm. Now, as they all stared, she fought the urge to turn and run. "I wish to go home," she said to David, since he was the one who had offered to bring word to her family. Would he allow her to see them one last time? "My family will be worried about me."

The bewhiskered man in the high-backed chair laughed. He stood, his intimidating mien unsettling her composure. "You have a lot of cheek, Miss Faraday. You haven't the right to see anyone again. The only place I'm taking you is back to London."

"I'm a midwife." Her eyes lifted to David, who found interest in his glass in seeming abandonment to her plight. A muscle in his jaw twitched. Despite her crumbling defenses, she drew her spine erect and returned her gaze to Kinley. "No matter what you think, there are those who need me. You have to allow me to make arrangements."

"Is that your latest deception, Miss Faraday?" The white-haired man again inserted himself in her line of sight.

"Sir Henry Munro is a well-respected physician. I've worked with him for nine years. This is what I do."

"Not anymore it isn't."

Behind his spectacles, his hazel eyes watched her, and a vague memory grabbed at the undercurrent of her thoughts, making her ill at ease. Like an overly hot room on a full stomach. He wore his white sideburns thick and bushy on a round face that had suffered the consequences of too much drink. His presence only amplified the misfortune of her current position.

"How did you get the earring?" she asked, hating that her voice trembled. But she had to ask. The earring David had given to Stillings had once belonged to her father. "Tell me my father is still in prison . . . or dead."

Silence followed the query. As Victoria looked among them all with dawning horror, a sick feeling grabbed hold of her stomach. She looked to David. "Before I fled Calcutta, the last thing my father gave me was an earring that matched the one you brought to Sheriff Stillings last night. It was to be a signal between us. How did you get it?"

"A pawnbroker brought it to the attention of our office," the man sitting on the settee spoke when David did not, his voice hinting of a faint upper-crust accent. "He knew the piece from a description of those jewels stolen in the Calcutta theft."

"Did anyone question how a pawnbroker knew so much? Was he some historical scholar with a decade-old memory?"

"He's dead," David answered, setting his brandy on the mantel. "His shop was burglarized three days after he handed the earring to this office."

"And my father? Tell me he is still in prison!"

"Kinley?" David directed the question to the man standing nearest to her.

"Your father escaped," Kinley said.

Appalled at the ramifications, Victoria drew in a breath and met Kinley's stare with accusation. "Why wasn't this mentioned in any of the newspapers?"

"For all intents and purposes, Faraday has been dead for nine years," Kinley said.

"You kept him alive because of what he knows. Now you led him directly to me. To my entire family. You did this on *purpose.*"

"We can save your family," Kinley said, the menace in his voice amplifying the threat, "if you tell us where the jewels are."

David set the glass on the mantel. "That's enough, Kinley."

"Even if I did know where that treasure was, I would never tell you. The gems are cursed." Victoria shifted her gaze helplessly to David's. "How many people have already died because of them? How many lives ruined? Let them stay buried."

David pierced her with dark eyes, the quiet intensity of his gaze seeking to understand that which she had not meant to surrender. "Why are you afraid of your father, Meg?"

His voice was gentle, and Victoria was conscious of an irrational surge of panic. Her father had a reason for hunting her, and Victoria realized David no longer believed with even the slightest possibility that the treasure had gone down off the coast of Bombay.

"My name isn't Meg," she snapped. "It's Victoria Munro. Margaret Faraday died the night that ship went down, along with everything she thought she loved. She will never be back. Do you understand that?"

The younger man sitting on the sofa spoke into the sudden silence. "Would you help us bring in your father? Obviously you are concerned that he will show up here."

Shaking her head, she yanked her gaze from David to the man and woman, with their perfect blond looks. "You don't know him." Breathing hard, she felt crushing pain in her chest. She'd sooner be dead than show her fear to the likes of anyone in this room, but she was already turning to run from the room.

David grabbed her before she reached the door. Somehow, he had made it past two chairs, a curio table, and a delicate crystal lamp to reach her before she'd taken five steps. "Meg—"

"Let go of me!"

Spinning her into the solid restraint of his body, David turned with her in his arms and faced Kinley. "You've known she was Colonel Faraday's target from the beginning. How?"

"We were never even sure she was alive," Kinley mumbled, yanking his black waistcoat over his belly. "We had to find her first, and you did that."

Clearly, Kinley had an inflated opinion of his own consequence, Victoria thought, certain she could escape if she could get away from David. No lock had been made that she couldn't pick. She would be free before the overstuffed fool knew what happened. Better to run than bring her father down on Sir Henry or face a public trial in London and forever leave a mark of shame on her son. Hadn't her father always accused her of bringing ruin to everyone she'd ever loved? She wouldn't do it!

"I voluntarily surrender myself to interrogation," she said.

"Is that right?" David demanded.

She whirled to face him. The very air crackled as they faced each other, two opponents in an unfinished duel, awareness arcing between them like live sparks. "Kinley can take me to London and learn for himself that I do not know where any treasure is."

David took a seat on the arm of a chair and surveyed her in that lazy, perilous way of his, as good at hiding his feelings as she was. "We won't catch Faraday without her." David shifted the brunt of his gaze to Kinley. "Or have you forgotten the primary objective of this mission?"

"He's right, Kinley," the blond Adonis agreed. "If Faraday wants her, it makes sense to keep her here."

Panic infused every limb in her body, but she froze as David returned his attention to her. "Rockwell, send a note to Lady Munro's family and tell them she left last night to deliver a baby. Then tell them she had a riding accident on the road."

"They won't believe you," Victoria whispered. "I've never fallen off my horse."

"Maybe Meg Faraday isn't as skilled a rider as Victoria Munro thinks she is." His unfathomable eyes seemed to challenge her. He was handsome, devastatingly so, and if she was not convinced that he was taunting her on purpose, she would have flown at him. "What is there not to believe?" he asked. "I've seen the bruises myself."

"Naturally. Do include my concussion with the accounting of your brutal behavior toward my person as well as drugging me senseless."

His eyes were on her. "As well as your attempt to shoot me?"

She answered with equal focus. "If I had ever wanted you dead you would not be standing here now. There is nothing you can do to entice me to help you."

"Nothing?" he asked. "It is common knowledge that Sir Henry's estate went up on the block for overdue taxes."

"Overdue?" she scoffed, wondering how he would know such a thing. "The chief magistrate would steal from his own uncle."

"What if we could get Sir Henry's estate back, Meg? Would you help us then?"

"Bloody hell with that," Kinley protested, the epitome of skepticism. "An hour ago you were ready to roast her on a spit. This is insane."

David folded one arm loosely over the other. As he awaited her reply, she was aware of his eyes on her face, and looked away. His hands were dark against the white of his sleeves, and he wore a gold wedding ring on his right hand. Her fingers went to the loose band on her own hand. She had not noticed the band on his finger before, and clearly he had not been thinking enough to remove it, for he lowered his hand. "I need a place to live and work," he said when she again raised her gaze. "Lady Munro can use a long-lost relative at her back. It would behoove her to cooperate."

"You won't be able to fight Nellis Munro. He wants Rose Briar."

"Let me worry about your local politics, Meg. I'm not without my own resources."

"Sir Henry knows I haven't any relatives."

"And you never keep secrets?"

He said nothing else, the charge coursing between them now electric, knowing she was trapped by the consequences of her own sins and mindful that he was also the only person standing between Kinley's brand of interrogation and maybe the end of a rope. Any observer would have thought them longtime lovers, trusted friends, not mortal enemies.

Yet she sensed the strangest tension had seized his limbs.

"Are you so anxious to be hanged then?" he quietly asked.

Victoria clutched the robe's fabric against her chest, her desolation growing. Of course she did not wish to be hanged. But David was as dangerous to her as her father.

"She's in my custody," he told Kinley. "I'll bring her in when it's time."

Kinley moved in front of her. "Everyone eventually talks, Miss Faraday. Everyone."

"Kinley." The quiet warning came from David. "I suggest you move away from her before she gives you a black eye."

"And I'll trust you not to turn your back on her. Next time she may not miss when she tries to kill you."

"I'll keep that in mind."

"Do. Find Faraday." Kinley snagged up his coat on his way out of the room.

In the silence that followed his departure, the beautiful blond woman brushed her palms. "Well," she said with flair. "That went well for us all." Looking at Rockwell, she plopped her fists on her hips. "What were you thinking, Ian?"

The man rose to his feet. A head taller than the woman, he glared down at her. "I was thinking we have a job to do, Pamela."

He strode from the room, the same path Kinley had taken. Victoria had not moved. As if her silence could enfold her in a mantle of invisibility, she was not even aware that she had fallen back into an old habit until she saw David watching her, and straightened.

"This is the Countess Cherbinko's town house," he said, introducing Pamela. "Our own faux Russian royalty, trained at the consulate in St. Petersburg. She took you in last night to help you recuperate from your injuries. She is our eyes and ears in this town. Nothing will get by her." He fixed his gaze on Pamela. "Will it, countess?"

In a rustle of emerald silk, Pamela slid her arms around his neck and pressed her mouth to his ear. "Tell me not to worry about you up on that hill by your wee lonesome, David."

But Victoria had had enough of their cozy little love scene. Tears burning in her eyes, she returned to the bedroom and slammed the door. She did not understand her reaction, only that she would never again look at the stars and wonder what David had done with his life since leaving India, or whom he'd been with for business—or for pleasure. She would never wonder whom he might have loved.

She didn't care.

For all his upright principles, everything about him still screamed of duplicity. He was a clever, manipulative, and experienced spy who played life like a game of chess. And she was just another move on the chessboard, as he maneuvered his way toward the conclusion of a game that should have ended nine years ago.

None of them knew what they were asking her to do.

She thought of her father roaming free, and attempted to harness the pace of her heart. Outside, gray clouds darkened the sky over the bluff as an early winter storm hovered over the channel. Catching herself on the window casement, she looked down into the empty courtyard below, then leaned nearer to the glass, searching for a way to escape. Her gaze ran up the length of heavy draperies across the thick wooden dowel and down the other side. She tested their strength before turning her attention to the armoire for suitable clothing. She would have been better off taking her chances with Kinley.

She had to escape now. Her father was out there.

He frightened her. Her father finding Nathanial terrified her.

She had known people who had no sense of moral right and wrong. She had known people who drank because their bodies craved the libation or opium-addicted sufferers who could not live out a day without the drug. As a little girl, she met many of them in her father's circle of acquaintances. But her father suffered no such moral ambiguity. He knew the difference between right and wrong. He just didn't care. Playing the game had been his opium. Name the hunt and it became his sport. He'd always loved the chase, the game of fox and hound, cat and mouse.

He and David were alike in that respect.

"Damn you, Donally!" Frustrated beyond belief, she crossed her arms over her midriff, turned back into the room, and froze.

David stood with his back against the door, looking much as he had that morning when she'd thrown herself naked at him. "You would not have escaped Kinley, Meg."

"Why is that?"

"Because I would have been with him."

She gritted her teeth, truly aware of how much she disliked him. The firelight burned in the dark depths of his eyes as he continued to watch her. "Who is Nellis Munro to you?"

"He is Sir Henry's nephew. He wants control of all Munro holdings."

David pushed off the door. "All?"

She was unable to meet his eyes. "Does everyone know that you and I . . . ?"

"Share the sanctity of wedlock? My circumstance is no secret."

"Then they must appreciate the terrible sacrifice you made for God and queen."

He stopped in front of her. "Not all of it was a sacrifice, Meg."

She tried to push past him. "I don't want Sir Henry involved. You can't protect him. My father is a master of disguise. He could walk into a room and his own mother wouldn't know him unless he wanted her to know—"

"What happened between you and your father?" He touched the bruise on her temple.

The contact was hardly threatening; yet she recoiled. "Why are you doing this?"

"Look at me." He slid his palm around her jaw and tilted her face. She could have sworn she heard his heartbeat pounding almost as loud as her own. "Give me your word you won't run," he said. "Or I will take you to Kinley tomorrow and do this myself."

He would, too, she realized, knowing she would promise him nothing. Margaret Faraday still had it in her to fight him, even if Victoria Munro did not. For Meg, being the more streetwise of her two selves, trusted David no farther than she could throw him. But if he was anything at all, he was a man who carried through with his threats.

"What are the odds," she asked, "that some jeweler would recognize that earring, then bring it to Kinley, the very person who would know what to do with that piece?"

"I only know that Kinley received the original before he came to me."

"The original?" It had been so dark that night Stillings had come to the cottage. She hadn't noticed that the earring was fake. "Of course, you wouldn't hand a priceless antiquity belonging to the treasury of India over to someone like Stillings."

"The forgery was very well done. Don't berate yourself over the fact you didn't recognize the earring was a fake and got yourself captured. Nor does it take away the value of the matching one still somewhere in your possession."

With a sigh that pressured her ribs, she sank to the floor, and sat with her back to the armoire, painfully aware that she would not win this battle as they squared off again like two enemy combatants. She should hate him more. "Wouldn't you rather tie me to the bed and torture me? Do I have to make promises to you?"

He crouched in front of her, the lean hard muscles of his thighs smoothing out his trousers. "I would rather tie you to the bed. But I doubt you will let me have my way with you now that you are in a more rational state of mind."

She looked into his eyes—eyes like the twilight, so dark blue they were nearly black. He had stolen her anger and her thunder, and Victoria stared in awe at his transformation.

She narrowed her eyes. "How could you be so arrogant to come into this room and remind me of my boorish behavior this morning?"

"Maybe I thought it was endearing. So much like old times."

"I don't want to like you, David. So don't even try to be charming. It won't work."

"Do I have your word you won't run?"

What did her word mean to him, anyway? Faraday blood ran in her veins. "I won't run," she yielded, knowing she had him on a semantic loophole.

"Nor walk," he clarified, "nor ride a horse or a cart, nor row a boat, nor skip out of this town with the sole purpose of escaping. I'm dead serious. If you run, I will hunt you down."

"All right," she snapped. "I give you my word, for what it has ever been worth to you. But you had better protect my family."

"Your family won't be left unprotected. Ian Rockwell will join your household staff," he said. "And I will see that Sir Henry does not lose the estate. I give you my word."

That thought and the hope it inspired served to halt her protests. She thought of Sir Henry. A man who was more of a father than hers had ever been. He had taken her in when she'd had no other place in the world to go, and given her life focus and purpose. Maybe when this was over, she *could* give something back to him after all. And Rose Briar was the only home her son had ever known. The land was his future.

"Mr. Rockwell looks barely out of nappies," she relented.

One corner of David's mouth lifted. "He's not so young. And he knows his job."

"Like you?"

"There are worse men out there than me, Meg."

"Not to me," she whispered, aware of a strange ache in her chest where her heart used to be, and she suddenly found herself staring up into the breathless beauty of that gaze, wanting desperately to believe in someone, wanting to believe that David wasn't worse than her own father was.

"Are you really a midwife?" he asked.

"Are you and that child who was hanging all over you lovers?"

"That child, as you call her, is a very skilled operative."

"You didn't answer my question."

His eyes captured hers and smiled. "Nor do I intend to."

He brought her to her feet, but she pushed his hands away. "Please don't . . . touch me."

He caught one wrist and easily captured the other, bringing both to the flimsy armoire door at her back. The heat thickened between them. He was tall, but so was she, and even at four inches over six feet, he did not tower over her. "Just don't tempt me to put my hands around your throat, Meg. We have an agreement."

"Are you sure my throat is where you want your hands, David?"

The other corner of his mouth lifted, but whatever he'd been about to say was cut short when a knock sounded.

"My lord?"

An older woman wearing a mobcap and white apron over a black dress peered around the corner of the door. "I didn't mean to be disturbin'—"

"It is of no concern, Agatha." David shifted his gaze to the nervous servant, and his eyes lost their stoic command. "You weren't disturbing us."

"You told me to bring Her Ladyship victuals and a bath."

"Go ahead and send in everything."

After the woman left, Victoria raised a slim brow. "You are no lord."

"You are no lady. I imagine that gives us some common ground." He swept into a cocky bow, ever the debonair gentleman, before his long stride took him to the door. "What is mine is yours, Lady Munro." He made a flamboyant gesture of his hand. "Enjoy your meal as if it were your last. Rockwell will return you to your humble cottage in a few days when everything is in place."

If she'd held anything in her hand, she would have hurled it against the door. He was worse than a wicked snake, entwining himself in her thoughts and bending her will. Yet, strangely, with his departure, the last tremulous ray of warmth vanished, and the room grew cold. Maybe it was because her life as she knew it had just come to an end.

Chapter 5

$\sim\!\!\circ\!\!\bigcirc\!\!\bigcirc\!\!\circ\!\!\sim$

Victoria stood in David's dressing room, grateful for the hearty meal Agatha had brought up after she'd awakened from a nap. After three days in this room, she would maim anyone who tried to stop her from going home. At least her head no longer ached, and the egg-sized lump near her temple had receded to a tender swell.

Unable to wrestle with her thoughts any longer, Victoria drew on her drawers over her stockings and tied them at her waist. Given the debacle that was now her life, she considered wallowing in another good cry. One that she could appreciate without a layer of laudanum in her blood. But what she really needed was to see her family.

She stood in front of the long mirror in David's dressing room, examining the bruises on her ribs. She looked as if she'd been in a brawl. Maybe she had when she considered her unorthodox departure from her horse at David's hands.

She had not seen her husband since the morning of her interrogation with Kinley. From Agatha she'd learned that David left every morning after breakfast, only to return late. She didn't know where he slept. Last night, she thought he'd been standing beside the bed, but when she rose on her elbow and looked around, the room had been empty.

Victoria touched the bruises against her ribs, and, unbidden, memories returned. She knew, without having realized, why her thoughts kept returning to David. After all, no other man had ever lain with her or touched her in all the ways that he had. The bruises on the outside didn't nearly match those on the inside. She closed her eyes, for there was pain and anger that even the years could no longer keep buried.

Nine years ago, she almost killed him. She had discovered who he was, whom he worked for the day she had come from the consulate physician, preparing to surprise him with the news that she was carrying their child—only to find her father's bungalow in chaos. Hurrying to her bedroom, she'd found a man bleeding profusely from a wound in his chest, but still strong enough to hold a gun on her, demanding her silence while her father's men looked for him. He'd told her who David was and that a raid was about to take place on the house. Orders signed by her husband that included her arrest.

Victoria only remembered confronting David with the gun the agent had held on her before he'd died. She warned him not to touch her, to let her go. She'd pleaded. It was the closest she had ever come to killing another human being: the closest she'd ever come to pressing the barrel of a gun against her own temple. Only the fact that she had carried another life inside her body kept her from ending her life. But instead, she had run from all that she knew and loved, and never looked back . . . until now.

Her mind spun even further back to the first time she'd met

David, and knew the exact moment when her life had truly changed, the catalyst that had set her fate in stone. She first glimpsed him on the polo field, riding a low pony and leading his team to victory. He'd been a new arrival in India, working in the diplomatic corps. No man had ever made her breath catch as hers did when he walked his horse off the field, turned his head, and looked directly at her on the sidelines. He'd tipped his riding hat, and she'd watched as he led the horse back to the stables, aware of the whispers around her.

She remembered feeling young and silly that he singled her out and that she had blushed, her reaction so completely girlish that she evaded him for a week afterward—until a dinner at the governor general's house brought them face to face.

To her discomfort, she'd watched him through the entire meal, barely aware of her own thoughts. In truth, she had never been like other girls her age. She found the cosseted female gender childish and shallow. She disliked the superficial layers of their society, but she played the social game well because it served her purpose. That night she shone.

After all, she was the infamous Meg Faraday, who had spurned the attentions of a wealthy duke two months before. She was the girl all the other girls whispered about behind her back because her mother had run off with a captain from the Bengali army.

Meg was ten years old at the time, and had neither seen nor heard from her mother from that day forward. One never discussed the topic in the Faraday household. A little girl in need of love, she had become her father's perfect daughter. She learned the lessons well. There was nothing more terrible than when he withdrew his love for some perceived wrong she committed, nothing more frightening than when he left her standing alone in a room wondering if this would be the moment he'd leave her like her mother did.

At first, Colonel Faraday had encouraged her friendships with the daughters of diplomats. She learned where valuables and important papers were kept. In the beginning, she bought into his lies that these people were somehow a threat to England. He worked for the security of the consulate, after all. What fourteen-year-old would not believe her parent? She became a valuable asset to him. She could climb into third-story windows and unlock doors as deftly as she could scale rooftops.

By the time she was seventeen, she suffered no more illusions about her father or her own crimes against those she had befriended. She never suspected that the governor general had launched an internal investigation into her father's activities or that she was the key target, the weakest link; she only knew that she wanted out of a life that had descended her into a nightmare.

A week before her eighteenth birthday, she had met David on that polo field and had fallen in love, never once suspecting the truth behind his appearance in her life or the motives behind his whirlwind seduction. For the first time, another man became a bigger presence than her father. Here was a man who could have had any woman at his calling, and he had chosen her. David Donally had been the first man to love her for only herself, not for what she could give him in return; at least that was what she'd believed. She let him into her bed and her heart like the novice virgin she was. Then she'd brought him into her father's circle, never knowing how cleverly David had manipulated her every move to get there.

What were a young girl's dreams worth, after all? she remembered wondering as she'd watched her future die beneath her father's indoctrination of her husband.

Victoria closed her eyes and drew in a deep breath to clear her mind. She wiped the dampness off her face with the back of her hand and turned away from the mirror. Outside the dressing room, someone was removing the tea tray. Victoria slipped into her shift and eased the stays around her ribs. She had been in the changing area for an hour. Agatha brought her the clothes Mr. Rockwell had retrieved from Bethany a few days ago when he went to tell Sir Henry her whereabouts.

Another voice intruded, and Victoria knew David's countess and partner had entered the bedroom. Her flowery perfume wafted into the dressing room.

"Where is she, Agatha?"

"She be in the dressing room, mum."

Victoria slipped the dress over her head, and slid her arms into the long sleeves as a knock sounded. "Miss Faraday?"

She hated that everyone insisted on using that wretched name. "I suggest that if you wish to carry off this ruse, you call me by my correct name," she said, walking out into the main room to retrieve her shoes.

Pamela was wearing a lemon yellow satin gown trimmed in Chantilly lace as bright as sunlight. A glittering pair of emeralds in her upswept blond hair gave her an elegance to match her faux title. Indeed, she looked like a spoiled countess as if born to the role.

Agatha stood in the doorway and spoke to Pamela. "Mum, Mr. Rockwell is here to return her back to her family."

"David has sent a message with arrangements to see you delivered to your family," Pamela said. "He told me to tell you that everything is in order."

Victoria hesitated. "Does that mean he paid the taxes on Rose Briar?"

"I believe that it does."

She was struck silent as she instantly forgot that she disliked him immensely. Of course, it would be dangerous for her to forget this was only business, his side of a bargain. Nothing more. Nellis would be furious, she thought.

"David is very persistent when it comes to the job," Pamela reminded her, the woman's use of his first name not going unnoticed. "If he says he will do something, I guarantee he will. It is one of those qualities a woman can count on."

Victoria slipped her feet into a pair of old slippers. "Do you know Mr. Donally well?" she asked after a moment, turning to face the other woman.

"Since he rejoined the team three months ago, we have gotten to know one another. One does under such circumstances." Pamela nodded to Victoria's bodice where it sagged off her shoulders. "Do you need help?"

Victoria could not fasten the buttons at her back. Hesitantly, she turned and lifted her hair. "Thank you."

Pamela's fingers deftly finished the buttons. "He was somewhat of a legend in his day, and most people were as surprised by his departure as they were by his return," she continued. "It even surprised Kinley that he came back. After all, they had barely corresponded in the nine years he was away."

"David left London? When?"

"Three months after your ship went down. It took him that long to recover from the wound you gave him."

"Three months?" Victoria laid her hand atop the back of the chair. "I didn't know."

"I suppose you didn't. From what I understand, despite his

injury, David tore up Calcutta looking for you after you disappeared. Kinley had sent every available man to bring you in dead or alive. David was the one who finally found your father. He and Kinley had a falling out shortly after that," Pamela said. "No one ever knew why."

Victoria looked at the gold band on her finger. David's robe lay draped over the chair beneath her hand. "How did they finally catch him? My father, I mean?"

"Someone tipped off the authorities. David captured him boarding a ship to Alexandria."

"I see."

"He's an adept agent." Pamela drew the robe through Victoria's fingers and, dropping it on the bed, turned with a lift of her brow. "And he never belonged to you, Miss Faraday."

David turned up the collar of his woolen greatcoat and came to a stop at the top of the hill. The sleepy stillness surrounding him did not fit the uncertain mood of the pewter sky. His tall boots hugging the barrel of his horse, he withdrew his field glasses and looked down at the cemetery spread around the burned-out shell of an old church. He quartered the thinning forests and distant fields.

One corner of his mouth lifting in a meager smile, he returned the field glasses to their leather casing and tucked them inside the haversack behind his saddle. A stiff chill found its way beneath the lapel of his coat. He kicked his horse into motion and cleared the ditch in a graceful arc as he continued down the back road into the cemetery. After a few days of rest—or as Meg accused him in his absence, her captivity—Ian Rockwell would be returning her to her cottage this evening. David had stayed away from her—as far away as he could while he sifted through the facts of this case. He'd already risked compromising this investigation by demanding that she remain in his custody, but he knew Kinley had been manipulating him from the moment he'd shown up in Ireland and asked David to rejoin the case.

One gloved hand resting near his thigh, David kept his gaze on the ground, alert to his thoughts as he lifted his head and looked out across the rows of stones. Meg had come straight to this place after Sheriff Stillings confronted her with the earring. David suspected the reason was more complicated than anyone thought.

She'd said the earring had been a prearranged signal with her father. But her fear of Colonel Faraday had been as genuine as her love for Sir Henry and his family. If Meg had betrayed Colonel Faraday in some way, when she was faced with the realities of what happened to those who betrayed the colonel, her terror of her father would be justified.

So why did she come here?

Leaning over the stallion's neck, he found the tracks he'd been seeking and urged his mount around the wrought-iron fence surrounding the churchyard. He established the point where Meg had stopped that night—before he'd alerted her to his presence and she'd pulled the mare back into the woods. He looked across the row of stones nearest him and considered the possibility that she had been telling the truth when she'd said she'd hidden here upon hearing someone following her. But he doubted it.

David slid to the ground and looped the reins around the fence. In one easy movement, he placed both hands on the iron railing and vaulted to the other side. He dropped to his haunches in front of the headstone nearest to the fence and cleared away the dead leaves that had blown against the marble. It belonged to a woman who had passed away in 1856. One arm resting across his knee, he scooped up a handful of duff from the ground and let it filter through his fingers.

For years, the whereabouts of stolen priceless artifacts and relics had remained unknown. Kinley believed Meg had absconded with the treasure. Then why would she be living a life in genteel poverty, struggling to take care of an old man and his family if she was in possession of such wealth? Would she not have purchased Rose Briar herself? How would she have gotten something like that out of India?

Too many unanswered questions lay at the threshold of his thoughts. His eyes came to focus on a distant trail of gray smoke rising from the treetops, bringing him back to the present. Colonel Faraday was still his biggest threat. Maybe even hers.

His horse snorted, warning of someone's approach. David stood and saw a young girl standing at the arch entrance. She carried a straw-plaited basket. With her hair hidden behind the hood of her cloak, he could not tell her age.

Dusting off his hands, David shoved them in his pockets, and remained at a standstill. She did likewise as she seemed to debate the wisdom of approaching a lone man in the cemetery.

"She's my mother," the girl finally said, clutching her cloak.

"My apologies." He stepped off the mound. "It is not my intent to frighten you. I saw the church steeple from the bluff."

"Who are you?"

"A new resident." He shrugged a shoulder. "I just paid the taxes on Rose Briar before it went on the block. I was told the owner lived around here."

"Grandfather?"

"Is your grandfather Sir Henry Munro?"

The girl walked beneath the arch and approached. "You must be the Most Noble Baron Donally of Chadwick?" The breathy title came from her lips in a foggy mist. "Victoria told us about you in her missive. You are her cousin."

Her hood had fallen around her shoulders. She was pretty, with long blond hair that framed a heart-shaped face. "You must be Miss Bethany Munro," he said as if he and Meg were remotely close and that he hadn't wrenched what little knowledge of her family from her as he could.

She smiled. "I am Miss Munro. We had no idea that Victoria had a family, much less a baron in the family."

"I've only just returned to England after some time away."

"Her note said you've been on an adventure across the world. That until your surprising return, she thought you had met an untimely and tragic end."

"Did she?"

"How very exciting to go on an adventure. But not one that would find me eaten by cannibals, mind you. One day I wish to cross the channel and visit France."

Smiling to himself, David refrained from replying.

"When Victoria wrote that you might be able to help against Cousin Nellis . . ." She paused. "You have to understand. We were so worried until we received the note. Peepaw hurt his foot three weeks ago in a fall. I fear I am no use to him, not like Victoria. My mother passed away when I was very young," she said, then nodded to the grave where he stood. "Victoria brings me up here weekly. We help the groundskeeper keep the site clean and bring him victuals. Mr. Doyle lives in the woods behind the rectory."

David looked around the grounds, curious that someone lived here.

"Not exactly in the woods. He lives in a cottage that is in the woods. Though I don't know where he is. I was supposed to leave this basket." She looked around the cemetery as if expecting him to appear out of the ground. "Victoria has taken over Peepaw's responsibilities with the tenants. I've been trying to do everything she would want me to do. But I don't like this place."

"Cemeteries make me nervous, too."

"They do?" She beamed. "Peepaw used to come here to visit Father. But not much anymore, since he has difficulty moving."

The girl knelt and cleared away the dead leaves that had blown against the second headstone. "I never knew my father. He was a brave soldier in India. Victoria married him a few weeks before he passed away. She practically adopted me when she came here."

"Your father's remains were returned from India?" David dropped his gaze to the headstone, every sense on alert as he read the name carved in the stone.

Sir Scott Davis Munro
September 24, 1828–November 28, 1863
Cherished Son of Sir Henry
and Lady Matilda Munro

Meg had left India December of 1863.

"My father is Sir Henry's only son," Bethany continued. "Father must have been wonderful for someone like Victoria never to marry again. One day I'll find a man to love as much."

David frowned at her romantic nonsense. "That's my cousin, the poetic troubadour of romantic causes."

Bethany lifted her gaze and he quickly asked, "Do you live alone with your stepmother and grandfather?"

"Oh no, I have a brother as well. He is visiting family in Salehurst. My mother's side of the family grows hops. We used to, but our last crop failed three years ago."

His gaze still on Sir Scott's headstone, David wasn't listening as she spoke of bad weather cycles and lack of tenants to help with the land. He wanted to ask her questions about her father's military unit. Mostly, he wanted to know why Munro's casket hadn't been on the same steamer that left Bombay as Meg.

"If you drink ale in these parts, I guarantee it is my family's brand," she was saying. "Victoria wants Nathanial to learn to manage these lands. Unfortunately, as you can see, he may not have land to manage by the time he comes of age." Her blue gaze lifted to the church, and she sighed. "Not much remains anymore. Most everyone has left. Including many of the servants. Except for Mr. Doyle. He works these grounds."

David looked past her, through the thicket of trees. Higher on the bluff, the yellow stone manor peered out over the countryside from a throne of brambling roses and crowning oaks.

"I'm afraid it will be difficult for you to move in tonight," she said. "Will you come to the cottage and meet Grandfather?" she asked, the top of her blond head barely reaching his chest as he stood. "Besides, it is getting late and you must be famished. Sir Henry will be pleased to meet you, especially since you've paid the taxes on the land. We can wait for Victoria together."

Turning away to release the reins of his horse, David wondered what Meg would think walking into the cottage and finding him present. He was suddenly quite famished.

"Are you always this friendly to strangers?"

"You're no stranger to Victoria." The brisk chill brought apples to her cheeks. "And I do see a family resemblance. You have dark hair and you're tall."

A rainstorm was pummeling the ground by the time Victoria arrived at the cottage after dark. The back door flew open and Bethany appeared like a silhouette against the light. Mr. Rockwell sat on the front seat of the buggy, his face hidden beneath a wide floppy hat. A black slicker swallowed him.

"Someone is here," he yelled over the rain.

Victoria tightened the hood around her face and looked toward the barn where she saw a beautiful black horse pulled out of the rain. A stiff wind whipped up her skirt and cloak, and she captured its length with her hand. "Mr. Shelby is in the barn. He'll see that you get dry clothes. When you're finished, Mrs. Shelby will feed you and give you a bed for the night. Tomorrow we will see to your permanent lodgings."

She directed him to the barn, then to the smaller cottage behind. A steady rain had softened the ground into mud. Victoria lifted her skirts as she ran across the yard and over the cobblestones that marked the path to the back door. The former hunter's cottage was an unassuming two-story, gray stone thatched cottage. A century's growth of ivy twined through the crevices in the stone. She could smell smoke from the chimney.

"Victoria!" Bethany launched into her arms as she entered the mudroom. "I was in the kitchen and heard the buggy. Look at you. I was beginning to get worried. Are you all right? You said little in your note. You must be freezing."

Water dripped into a puddle at her feet. Bethany helped her remove the sodden cloak she had stolen from David's closet. "I'm sorry I couldn't get back sooner. How is your grandfather? Has he been soaking his foot?"

"He's playing cards."

Victoria remembered the horse in the stable. "Who is here?"

"I've got the most wonderful surprise for you."

Bethany took her hand and led her down the long corridor to the back of the cottage. Men's voices sounded from Sir Henry's bedroom.

David was sitting beside the bed, his sleeves rolled up to his elbows, cards in hand, as he finished the shuffle. A fire crackling in the hearth radiated warmth in the room. Beside him, lying on the bed, his left foot bandaged, sat Sir Henry, his craggy face split into a wide grin. Victoria had not seen the elder so animated in weeks.

David turned his head and saw her standing in the doorway. The light from the lamp cast a shine over his dark hair and accentuated his classic features. She couldn't ignore the strange flutter she felt inside her chest. "What are you doing here?"

"I met His Lordship today near the church," Bethany said.

Victoria had momentarily forgotten David was a baron, or that he was supposed to be her long-lost relative returning from the jungles of some continent. "The church?"

"He cheats at cards, I'm sure of it." The man she loved liked a father chuckled with glee. "Victoria? You've finally introduced me to someone worthy of my time."

She looked at David, confused by the camaraderie between the two. He gave her a wink. "Sir Henry drives a hard bargain."

"Well, I say if His Lordship can swindle the swindler at rummy, then he deserves to win, Peepaw," Bethany said, lifting that evening's dinner tray from the nightstand. "You should not have behaved so ornery in the first place. He is our guest."

"Pish posh," Sir Henry snorted. "I'll not be signing over Rose Briar to any man lest he can prove himself up to a challenge. Nellis never could play cards worth an owl's hoot."

"What did you say?" Victoria moved into the room. And David dared call *her* a thief? "What papers have been signed?"

"The agreement I've made is with Chadwick. Men's business, if you will. Now, help me out of bed and let me look at you. Bethany, make Victoria a hot toddy."

"Yes, Grandfather," Bethany murmured obediently, and with the tray departed.

"Where have you been?" Sir Henry demanded after Bethany left. "We've missed our appointments for three days. What madness possessed you to fall off your horse?"

"Tommy Stillings's wife is with child," Victoria said, telling Sir Henry the truth at least on that account. "He was worried about Annie."

"Worried, my bum." Sir Henry raised his gaze to David. "Watch out for Stillings," he warned David. "He's my nephew's puppet. Run most of the decent folk away from these parts. He came here the other night and scared my granddaughter senseless. We thought he'd dragged Victoria away. He and Nellis—"

"Really, Sir Henry." Pulling her skirt aside so as not to touch any part of David, Victoria inserted herself between her husband and the bed. "I'm sure my *cousin* isn't interested in our problems. Your foot is not healed," she warned the older man when he moved to the edge of the bed. "Have you been soaking it in hot water and salts?"

"Yes, yes." He waved an impatient hand. "Now let me look at your head. Bethany said you had a concussion. Though why you should suddenly grow clumsy—"

"I'm fine, Sir Henry."

"I'll decide that for myself, young lady. A concussion isn't to be taken lightly."

Victoria obediently bent her head for his examination, wincing as he tenderly probed her skull. "Nellis has decided he wants Victoria," Sir Henry said.

"I'm sure Lord Chadwick isn't interested . . . ouch."

"Nonsense. You can't allow a man to walk blind into the middle of a family feud." He held up two fingers. "How many?"

Frustrated, she glared. "Four."

"You'll live." He patted her cheek. "Now help me out of bed."

"May I look at your foot first?"

"See what I have to deal with?" Sir Henry said to David as he eased off the bed. "The girl insists on hovering over me."

Victoria followed Sir Henry's hobble across the room. "I don't hover."

"I wish I was still sailing those balmy West Indian waters. At least I never had a case of aches as I do in this chill." He fumbled through the vials and bottles on the shelf. "Ah, here 'tis," Sir Henry murmured. "My medicine."

"What is it?" Victoria stepped forward with every intention off sniffing the contents.

"It's mine, that's what it is," he said, taking a swig. "The finest Irish whiskey ever made. Now off with ye, girl. Go fetch your toddy and change your clothes. Your dress is damp, and I'm to bed. That young man over there has exhausted me."

She stood in front of Sir Henry, suddenly wishing David was out of earshot. The past few days had made her emotional, and, as she pressed an affectionate kiss against his whiskers, she wanted to throw her arms around him. "Thank you, Sir Henry."

"For what," he murmured.

How would she ever explain the truth to him? "For worrying about me."

He huffed a great show, but she knew he'd missed her, and in his roundabout way was trying not to show that he'd been worried. "Off with ye, Victoria." He patted her arm, and she watched him limp back to his bed before she realized David was watching her.

Feeling exposed, she straightened. "I'll see you in the morning, Sir Henry."

Chapter 6

David stood aside, allowing Meg to pass into the corridor first. "Truly, I cannot believe what you did," she whispered, sweeping past him and affording him a glimpse of her uptilted breasts impressed against the damp fabric of her bodice.

At once, he became interested in the rest of her attire and stepped back to look just as she swung around to face him, hand outstretched, dragging his gaze to her face.

"May I see the paper Sir Henry signed and gave to you?"

He withdrew the folded document from inside his waistcoat pocket. "As you wish."

"Maybe you should have tried harder to lose at cards, David."

"Me?" He laughed, astounded by the conclusion she'd drawn. "Sir Henry is a shark."

He had not come here today to take an old man's property from him, and as Victoria read the contract of sale Sir Henry had signed, David found he easily traded the direction of his thoughts for another. His glance dipped from her full lower lip to the damp blue gown Meg wore, settling on the sensual flair of her hips.

While in captivity these past days, she had washed in his soap, and he could smell himself all over her. When he again contemplated those violet eyes that could say so much to a man, he found them narrowed on him.

"What can I say?" He shrugged off the carnal intrusion with the same lack of self-reproach as he did any other vice someone caught him committing. "You look nice all wet."

"You're a cad, David." She refolded the document and tossed it at him. "I've not only allowed you to steal back into my life, but now I've abetted you into taking Sir Henry's ancestral home. You were only supposed to pay the taxes. Now you own Rose Briar and all three thousand acres that surround it?"

"Meg—"

"How dare you charm yourself into the bosom of my family."

David lowered his voice. "Do you think this is the proper place for this conversation? We're supposed to like one another."

"Oh dear. Have I been remiss in welcoming you into this family, Cousin David, Baron Donally of Chadwick just back from the jungles of central Africa?" She planted a dutiful kiss on his cheek and whispered against the shell of his ear. "Admittedly I was disappointed to learn that you had not been devoured by cannibals. My loss, dear cousin."

He wrapped an arm around her back. "And yet I was saved the fate of countless others in my hunting party. Your loss is my gain."

Her palms caught against his chest. "Let go of me, David."

He smiled, reading her reaction to him in the rapid beat of her pulse at her neck. He liked that he could make her uncomfortable and agitated after she'd so effortlessly sucked his libido through every pore in his flesh. "I should show you my scars, colleen."

"You're still a tyrant," she managed between clenched teeth. "You and your fake title go well together."

"So does yours, Lady Munro," he said against her hair.

Except that she did wear her title well, he realized. He loosened his hold on her. She fell away from him, her eyes wide, and he was aware of the confusion his words caused her. She retreated a step, then turned in a slide of damp fabric. Adjusting his trousers, his eyes narrowing on the swing of her skirts, he waited a moment before following her down the corridor.

In the kitchen, Bethany had made two hot toddies and handed one to Meg. "I made them strong," she said with a smile.

"Where is Lord Chadwick's cloak?" his wife demanded with the clear intent of throwing him out into the storm.

Bethany handed David the second toddy. "Oh, but you mustn't think about leaving us tonight, my lord. We have room here."

"Oh, for goodness sakes, Bethany—"

"He could ride off a cliff, Victoria."

Content to allow Bethany to fight his battle, David fixed his eyes on Meg from over the rim of his glass. She stood in front of the fire blazing in the hearth. "I'm sure His Lordship knows the way quite well. The storm isn't that bad."

Thunder rattled the eaves. She took a swallow of her

toddy, and switched her gaze to him as if to blame him for the weather. His eyes continued to hold hers above the pewter. "I think my cousin still hasn't forgiven me for tying her pigtails in knots when she was younger," David said to Bethany, but he spoke to Meg.

"He did that?" The girl laughed.

His eyes smiling into Meg's, he reminded her that he had done far more than loop her hair around the bedstead. He had stripped her naked and put his mouth on places the memory of which even now brought a heated blush on her cheeks.

His mouth edged up. "She never could beat me on a horse, either. Methinks she holds a grudge," he said behind his hand in a mock whisper.

Rain began to pound the cottage. Bethany turned to Meg. "No one should be out on a night like this. We have room here." She smiled at David. "As long as you don't mind Zeus, Lord Chadwick."

"Zeus?"

"My brother's cat. It sleeps on the bed in Nathanial's room."

David looked at Meg, who, clearly flustered, had found solace in her toddy. He felt a twinge of guilt to see her so outnumbered and outmaneuvered, first by him, then by Sir Henry, and now by Bethany. "Only if it's acceptable to Lady Munro." He set his toddy aside. The last thing he wanted to be inside was warm and cozy.

"Of course it's acceptable." Bethany turned her eyes on Meg. "Isn't it?"

"I've not changed the bedding."

"I don't mind," he said.

"He doesn't mind," Bethany echoed.

Meg's mouth went flat. "You haven't any clothes."

He opened his arms, willing himself to be humble in the wake of her defeat. "I'm wearing them."

"Wonderful!" Bethany clapped her hands together as if that decided the matter. "I'll show him to his room."

"You'll do no such thing, Bethany Munro," Meg snapped. "I believe it is time for you to retire." She added on a softer note. "His Lordship and I have some catching up to do. Family matters, as it were."

Bethany turned to David. "Will I see you tomorrow?"

He shoved his hands in his pockets. "Count on it, Miss Munro."

"I think it's wonderful that you're here."

"Good night, Bethany," Meg said, hurrying her on.

Bethany dipped into a curtsy. "Good night, my lord."

Recognizing a crush when he saw one, David watched Bethany flounce from the room. Clearing his throat, he turned and glimpsed the cloudy expression on Meg's face as she also watched her stepdaughter, probably pondering the same thing.

David wondered if Meg had ever been as young as Bethany or as vulnerable. He had met her when she was only a little older than Bethany was now. His eyes moved over Meg. Firelight from the hearth rippled through her long ebony hair damp from rain.

It was madness to be so absorbed, yet he could not force himself to look away. And as if his thoughts somehow transcended the distance separating them, she turned her head and he suddenly found himself staring at the most beguiling enigma of all.

His wife.

"That was interesting," he said.

"Don't be too flattered. Bethany falls in love with someone new every month. Clearly she's picked you for October."

Duly cut down to size, he quirked his mouth. "I'll not let it go to my head."

Looking away, she seemed to grapple for thought. A flash illuminated the window behind her, and he saw that she was not as indifferent to him as she appeared.

"Be sure that you don't. It's just that she's enthusiastic . . . and young. She hasn't had to face true hardship, yet." Meg set the empty toddy mug in the wash tub behind her. "I have no desire to pretend that anything is somehow different than what it is with you, David."

He stopped her from sidestepping around him. "You and I made a bargain about the house. I won't go back on my word."

She snatched up the lamp sitting on the trestle table. "I fear we haven't any servants to help with your toilette." Ignoring him, she stepped around the table. "There is a cistern pump in the sink if you want water. Linens for a bath are in the closet off this kitchen."

"Paying the taxes on Rose Briar isn't enough to secure the property."

"Esma serves breakfast early."

Again, he stopped her. "I know what you think of me . . ."

"You cannot possibly understand what I think!" She shook her head, and then looked at him directly, pain in her eyes. "This family isn't yours. These people aren't yours. I don't want them hurt. The only thing you are here to do is catch Colonel Faraday."

"I may not be particular about the fate of a known traitor and murderer, but I do keep my word, Meg." Why was he even defending himself? In frustration he looked at the ceiling, then outside at the storm. "Where is Rockwell sleeping tonight?"

"In the gardener's cottage." Her voice hesitated, and he saw that she had marked his mood. "After tonight, I will see that he is moved to one of the linen closets off the kitchen."

"No doubt he will appreciate the accommodations."

"It's a big closet." In the dim light, her eyes shone softly. "If he is here to protect this family, he'll need to be inside."

David agreed. They stood for a moment longer, suddenly awkward in the warm silence of the kitchen.

"I should show you to your room."

She walked him past a well-appointed drawing room and up the wooden stairs, a creak marking their every step. "The Shelby family lives in the bigger cottage out back. Mr. Shelby and his son tend to the stables. Esma and her daughter cook and help with the chores. But if you want anything to eat tonight, you are on your own."

"I already dined with your family. Have you eaten?"

"Mr. Rockwell and I stopped at an inn on the way."

He followed her to a room tucked at the end of the hallway. The ceiling slanted low enough that David could not walk three feet into the room and stand straight. Stopping just inside the doorway, he looked around the walls filled with charcoal drawings of trains before glimpsing the simple iron bedstead big enough to fit two people. Meg set the lantern on the maple dresser and struck a match to another lamp. The room was free of dust, and he guessed that someone spent a lot of time in here.

"Is Nathanial very much like Bethany?" he asked as more light filled the dark interior, curious about the two children she had inherited upon her arrival from India all those years ago. She would have been nineteen, he realized.

Meg blew out the match. The scent of sulphur drifted in the air. She replaced the glass bulb on the lamp. "They are very close." With her dark hair spilling over her shoulders, she folded her arms and turned. "Sir Henry is dying, David. He thinks he's found a way to protect this family from Nellis when he is gone."

"What are you talking about?"

"He has a cancer inside him. He doesn't want me to know but from what I can tell, he has been drinking more to hide the pain."

"Hence, Nellis has decided to move in on all of you."

"Nellis is the son of Sir Henry's oldest brother and the chief magistrate for this entire region. He is a middle-aged widower married some years before I returned to England. He fancies himself this family's guardian. Six months ago, for whatever reason, he became interested in Sir Henry's land."

"You mean he became interested in you."

She plowed her fingers through her dampened hair. "Sir Henry thinks by giving you the estate, he has somehow secured our future, and for some reason because of your alleged relationship to me, he trusts you to protect all of us." She laughed. "The irony is brilliant, don't you think?"

"Except if Sir Henry should die before Nathanial and Bethany come of age, as the closest male relative, Nellis would still become their guardian regardless of Rose Briar. My owning the estate means nothing in that regard."

Her attention returned to the dresser. "That won't happen," she said, her voice a whisper. She opened a drawer and replaced the box of matches. "Sir Henry won't die."

Aware that he was feeling proprietary in his intentions toward her, David knew he couldn't allow her to suck him into her life. He'd already done enough by seeing that Nellis did not receive the estate—at great cost to him. Outside rain sheeted against the glass. All around him the scent of myrrh and quince drifting from her made her smell like an exotic houri girl who should be in some sheik's harem.

"Your feet are going to hang over the bed," she said.

David peered at the bed. A flash of lightning brightened the red squares in the quilted comforter. "Is that quilt one of yours?"

She gave him a brief glimpse of a rare smile, and he found himself lost between the logic and lust that began to war inside him. "My first and only quilt," she answered cheerfully. "Patience is its own reward, so I was promised. It's a lie."

He touched a length of her hair and looked into her eyes. "Is it?" The contact was an error in judgment, and he knew it the instant he touched her.

She reclaimed the captured curl. "This isn't part of our arrangement. I agreed to help you catch my father, not to sleep beneath the same roof with you."

Hell, he wanted to sleep in the same bed with her, do more than sleep, and he had the nerve to laugh at his own weakness. "Don't make the arrangement sound so intimate. I'm not asking you to share my sheets."

"It doesn't matter." She tucked the strand of hair behind her ear. "I mean it doesn't matter in the sense that it will never happen."

He followed her retreat. "What will never happen?"

"It . . . intimacy between us will never happen."

"Because you don't want intimacy?" he asked, annoyed that she was doing everything in her power to avoid touching him. "Or because you forgot how to be intimate?"

"Spare me your boorishness, David. Surely you have other woman to torment." She swept past him.

He caught her arm and pulled her around. "None to whom I'm married."

Color tinged her cheeks. He noticed that about her. For all of her courage when facing down brigands in the night, she behaved like a virgin with him. Or maybe he was the one behaving like a virgin. How long had it been since he'd been with a woman?

He lifted her hand into the light. The band on her finger flashed gold. "You're still wearing my ring. Why?"

She tried and failed to snatch her hand away. "You should know the answer to that."

He didn't give a damn if she was pretending to be a widow; he wanted to know why she still wore *his* ring. "No, I don't."

His fingers went to her chin and traced her mouth. He felt the softness of her lips against the pads of his fingertips. She still felt perfect to him.

He moved closer, sank his other hand into her hair and tilted her face, but whatever he'd been about to say died when he heard her whisper his name. It fell against his lips in an intoxicating blur, and his ice-cold world cracked with the promise of warmth. He'd never had any control around her. No restraint.

He should have kept his hands off her, but he knew from experience the feat was impossible. He closed his mouth over hers, parted her lips, and, sinking all ten fingers into her dampened hair, lost himself completely in the kiss.

He savored. He tasted.

His hands gently framed her face. With a half sob, she stepped into his arms.

Groaning deep in his chest, he felt the kiss deepen; then felt nothing else but the blood rushing through his veins. Heat flooded his body, filled his loins, and he backed her up until she hit the dresser. His breathing coming more rapidly, his grip tightened. Logic whipped at his lust. This was a bad idea on so many bloody levels, he didn't know where to start, or how to stop. Or if he wanted to stop ever.

Hunger spiraled to edge out his control. Outside the storm cocooned them. Inside it raged silently. It raged past barriers and memories. Past emotions that crumbled into tiny shards and fell to his feet—until he realized that he had pulled away slightly, but not so far he couldn't taste her on his lips or breathe the air that she pulled into her lungs. He could feel her full breasts against his chest, feel the hard bite of her nails against his shoulders.

"When was the last time you had a lover?" he asked.

When she didn't reply, he looked into the violet of her eyes. The light that bathed her was golden and warm, beckoning and promising. "When?"

"You." Her eyes searched his. "You were the last, David."

He stared at her hard. Her lips were still wet from his kiss. "I don't understand . . ."

She was more passionate than any woman he'd ever known. Once, long ago, men of every country had fallen all over themselves for her attentions, and he was sure she had used that to her advantage when robbing them blind. "You can steal a fortune and kill a man?" he asked, "but adultery is out of your realm of sins?"

With renewed anger, she shoved hard against him. "I did not kill your partner. He was in our bedroom waiting for you that day when I walked in and found him hiding," she added on a whisper. "He had already been shot. I only know that the papers he had on him were arrest warrants with your signature, David. So do not preach your ethic to me."

His expression set, he remembered that morning as if it were yesterday. He had walked into the room to find his partner dead, and a gun in Meg's hand pointed directly at his heart. Even now, he couldn't believe that she'd actually pulled the trigger. Or maybe he could. "You are not innocent of everything, Meg."

"Don't you think I know that?" She pushed past him.

David turned just as the door slammed in his face and brought him up short. Next to this chamber, another door shut hard.

Rubbing one palm across his bristly jaw, he looked around the cozy little room and mentally groaned at the erection pressing hard against his trousers. A wooden train sat on the floor next to a stuffed purple cow and a rocking horse, the innocence of his surroundings suddenly making him feel all too depraved.

"You're an idiot, David," he muttered, softly addressing the rafters, the demons, and all the ugly ghosts in his soul. "A complete and bloody idiot."

Victoria didn't awaken until noon.

In disbelief, she threw off the covers and, unmindful of the cold floor, washed and cleaned her teeth. She dragged a brush through her hair and pinned it in a chignon, then dressed and checked Nathanial's room. The bed was perfectly made as if no one had violated the sanctity of her son's chambers. As if David had never been there at all. As if he had never kissed her, and she had dreamed up the entire past week.

If only Providence were so kind, she thought, feeling restless and edgy, the cause of her frustration clearly defined in her mind as she realized how hopelessly banal she had already become. Her room next to this one, she'd listened all night to David's movements, as she imagined him attempting to find comfort on a mattress too short for him.

What had she been thinking to allow him to kiss her?

She shut the door and hurried downstairs in time to hear the tall clock on the stairway bong twelve times. Checking on Sir Henry, she found him asleep, before wading through the familiar smells of baking bread and mulled cider coming from the kitchen.

"Good afternoon, mum." Esma Shelby turned from the stove as Victoria walked to the cupboard and removed a ceramic mug. Wisps of damp mustard-colored hair curled around Esma's face. "Sleep has brought the apples back to your cheeks."

Victoria grabbed a mitt and lifted the tin coffeepot from the stove. Steam emerged from the spout as she poured. "You shouldn't have allowed me to sleep so long, Mrs. Shelby."

"What is one to do in weather like this? You need rest. His Lordship said so."

Annoyed that David thought he had any authority here, Victoria wrapped her hands around the cup and held it to her nose. "How long ago did . . . my cousin leave?"

"His Lordship was up at the crack of dawn." Esma stirred a wooden spoon in a pot of pumpkin soup. "Spoke to that young man you hired, mounted that black of his and left. Don't rightly know where he went but he said he'd be back for supper."

"Did he?" Victoria leveled a look at the housekeeper. "Just like that? He invited himself?"

Esma's brows lifted. "Seeing that he is your family, he probably assumed he was welcomed here."

Victoria buried a reply in her cup. David could charm the fangs from a viper. She was disappointed how easily her entire family had fallen for him. "Just be cautious. He is a stranger regardless of his relationship to me. You should not just naturally give him your trust. After all, I haven't seen him in years."

"He came to your aid, didn't he?" her housekeeper challenged.

Victoria refused to comment, and Esma took her silence as agreement. "He be a fine-looking man, mum," she said on a sigh that belied her sweet, grandmotherly façade. "A gentleman he is, too. Helped carry in the coal for the stove and thanked me proper for the porridge he ate. Bethany has taken after him, smitten child that she is." Esma chuckled. "Seems like something about him is familiar though . . ."

A log burning in the hearth collapsed in a shower of tiny sparks and Victoria startled.

"Good heavens, child." Esma set down the spoon and propped both hands on her ample hips. "You're as jumpy as Zeus. That tom has been hiding beneath Sir Henry's bed all morning. Probably heard the hounds baying earlier."

"You heard hounds?"

"Near dawn." Esma checked the fire beneath the blackened pot. "Pity the poor animal that caught their scent."

Victoria leaned toward the window and looked up at the churning sky with a frown. "Where is Bethany?"

Esma told her Bethany was in the stables tending to the mare that Stillings's men had injured last month. They had not padlocked the stalls last night because Victoria had not felt it necessary to do so during the storm, but she was never sure when the stables might be visited at some point in the night. The hounds usually came out when the smugglers were about.

"Forty years ago, the Munro name carried weight." Esma dropped a dollop of bacon fat in an iron skillet. "No one would have dared steal a horse for such nefarious purposes," her housekeeper said as if there was ever a good excuse for stealing. She cracked two eggs in the sizzling fat. "It's come to a point where decent folk aren't safe. We need someone who will care for these lands and its tenants as much as you do, mum, and that man isn't Nellis Munro." She sniffed, delivering a plate of eggs to Victoria.

Unfortunately, it wasn't David, either.

Yet, despite the chaos and upset he caused in her life, his presence made her feel safer. Shaking her head, as she finished her breakfast and set the plate in the wash basin, she only knew that the contradiction of her emotions made a mockery of logic.

Outside, the wind continued to blow. Victoria moved to the window. The drive had turned into a muddy stream that would require hours of refilling the ruts with dirt. "I should go to the churchyard and check on Mr. Doyle. He has those chickens he coddles like pets."

"Bethany was up there yesterday, mum. Ye shouldn't worry so."

Victoria did worry. The weather looked none the better and the temperature had dropped below freezing since yesterday. "Are you positive Bethany brought him victuals while I was gone?"

"I packed the basket myself," Esma replied. "Gave him our boysenberry jam we still need to deliver to our other tenants."

Victoria had not forgotten the crates of jam she'd packed

the night Sheriff Stillings had come here. Turning away from the window and folding her arms, she leaned against the countertop. Her gaze fell on the wicker case sitting beside the breakfront.

"That basket?" Victoria pointed.

Esma turned and her hand flew to her mouth. "I don't understand . . ."

Victoria remembered that Bethany had found David at the cemetery yesterday.

"Where ye be goin', mum?" Esma asked when Victoria walked into the mudroom to retrieve David's cloak drying on the wall. In lieu of her own coat that she had lost, she'd borrowed it from his quarters yesterday before returning here.

"Someone needs to check on Mr. Doyle," she said and settled a bonnet on her head. "I'll speak to Bethany when I return."

"She does her best, mum."

"She's going to have to do better." Victoria flung David's heavy cloak over her shoulders.

She wore woolen stockings beneath her warm gown and should remain protected from the cold for at least the walk up to Mr. Doyle's cottage. "I'll cut through the woods and be back before Sir Henry awakens from his nap."

Besides, she wanted to look at the cemetery while she was up there. As Victoria tightened the strings on her half boots, Esma stood in the doorway between the mudroom and the kitchen. Her ruddy face held a hint of worry. The same worry she'd held when Victoria had gone to her last night and requested that her son go into town when the weather cleared and drop off a post to Nathanial. Nathan would be safest with Bethany's cousins for now. She would deal with her emotions when it came to her son later.

"Don't worry, Esma." Victoria fastened the cloak. "If Sir Henry awakens, make sure you heat water on the stove for him to soak his foot. Don't feed him until he does."

Outside, the wind nearly snatched the cloak from her person. She dipped beneath the trellis, hoping Mr. Rockwell wouldn't see her leaving, preferring him to stay with her family. Victoria never went anywhere without the derringer, and today was no different. She could take care of herself. Her family could not.

The shortcut through the woods took less than fifteen minutes. Mr. Doyle was a lonely man who liked boysenberry jam, had chickens for pets, and fed the pigeons that roosted in the bell tower of the burned-out church. He had been the groundskeeper for the old church for decades. He'd been old to her when she first arrived at Rose Briar. He was still old. Last year his wife of forty years had passed away, and Victoria had been making regular visits to him ever since. He had no other family.

With winter setting in earlier this year, she needed to see that Mr. Doyle had fuel enough to heat his cottage. As with the other tenants remaining on Munro land for whom she was responsible, Mr. Doyle had fallen under her jurisdiction since Sir Henry's illness.

Sleet or snow was not far off, she realized, pulling the cloak's hood over her bonnet to shield her from the wind. Carrying the basket, she felt like Little Red Riding Hood as she came out of the woods onto the field near a dilapidated farm shed, a remnant from the farming glory days where hay was stored after harvesting. A fluffy red squirrel poked its head out of a mound of wet leaves. It saw her and skittered up a tree.

The cottage lay fifty yards behind the rectory. She saw no smoke coming from the chimney. Uneasy, Victoria approached the cottage. She knocked on the door, before edging it open and sticking her head inside the gloomy interior.

"Mr. Doyle?"

No answer came. Fearing what she might find, she entered the small cluttered front room. She checked the bedroom where an unmade bed lay among disorder. She walked out the back door. The chicken coop had been destroyed. Feathers lay everywhere. Those damnable hounds had been here this morning.

Forcing herself to remain calm, Victoria scanned the church and called Mr. Doyle's name twice. A bolt of lightning flashed over the treetops followed by a roll of thunder. Tenting her hand over her eyes, she wished now that she'd not come up here alone.

Chapter 7

David reined in his horse at the top of the hill overlooking the cottage just as sleet started to pelt his shoulders. A stately black carriage sat at the bottom of the drive, and two footmen huddled behind the boot, attempting to stay out of the brisk wintry wind.

Scanning the yard, David didn't see Rockwell and, with a quiet oath, nudged his horse down the drive. He rode into the warmer interior of the barn, slowing as Mr. Shelby hurried down the row of stalls to greet him.

Shelby took the bridle. "You've returned just in time. Nellis Munro arrived ten minutes ago."

David swung to the ground. "Cool the horse off." He patted the horse's rump. "We've been riding hard, hoping to beat the weather."

"Is that a valise behind the saddle?" Shelby asked.

"Leave it," David said, raising his coat collar against the

chill as he walked to the entrance. "I won't be staying to-night. I'm moving up to the manor house."

He sprinted across the yard, nodded to the two uniformed footmen, then strolled up the stairs into the mudroom. Inside, as he stomped his boots, he could hear raised voices coming from the kitchen. Without removing his greatcoat, he dipped through the doorway and stopped.

A low fire burned in the hearth. The smell of fresh-baked bread floated in the air. Sir Henry sat at the table, Bethany beside him. Mrs. Shelby stood to one side of Sir Henry with a pot in her hand, pouring tea. The table was set for dinner, but the man lording over the pair didn't seem interested in join-ing the family. David looked at everyone present, but he didn't see Meg.

". . . I have been patient, Uncle." Nellis paused in his per-oration to nail Sir Henry with a glare. "As patient as a man can be under the circumstances. The least she owes me is a little of her time for all the worry she has put me through. Bloody hell"—he slapped his gloves over his palm—"I was unaware that someone of the countess's distinction had even let the Sprague House until my servant informed me this morning."

"We have not conspired to keep you in the dark about any-thing," Sir Henry said.

"You will forgive me my insistence to see Victoria then, will you not? You are all my responsibility. If she needs med-ical assistance, my own physician will look after her."

Removing his gloves, David stepped from the doorway. "She is not your responsibility."

Nellis whipped around, saw David, and whatever dressing-down he'd been prepared to administer died in a cough. "Excuse me?"

"There"—Sir Henry waggled a spoon in David's

direction—"you want to talk to someone about your unfortunate circumstances? There's the man with whom to speak."

David unbuttoned his coat and approached. "Have I missed something of import?"

Nellis perused David with a mixture of fury and disbelief. "You are the one who purchased Rose Briar over a game of cards?"

Looking over Nellis's shoulder at Sir Henry, he said, "I believe that would be me."

"And, who pray tell, do you think you are?"

"Baron Donally of Chadwick," Bethany volunteered as David stopped at the end of the table, inserting himself between Nellis and Meg's family. "Victoria's cousin."

"Cousin?" Nellis scoffed. "She doesn't have any bloody family but us."

"I assure you, I am her closest family."

Wearing a dark suit and cloak, Nellis was a tall man with graying temples and brown hair to match the mutton chop whiskers that framed his jaw. He still carried his hat and gloves in one hand. Nellis's eyes narrowed perceptively. "Have we met?"

"Not unless you've traveled in Africa," Bethany said.

"Africa?" Nellis swung on the pair sitting at the table. "This is bloody mad. How could you sell to a stranger, Uncle? For hardly more than the taxes, no less."

"I don't recall your offering to purchase Rose Briar, Nellis," Sir Henry dipped his bread in a bowl of pumpkin soup. "As a matter of fact, the only thing I do rightly recall is Victoria having to defend herself from you every time you decide to grace us with your esteemed presence. If you want to blame anyone for my decision, blame yourself."

"Victoria should be grateful I offered for her at all. Next

time, I won't bother behaving like a gentleman." His gaze landed on David with practiced intimidation, but something in his eyes must have warned Nellis to shut his mouth while he still had his tongue. "Your purchase isn't legal, my lord," Nellis said, his voice modulated several degrees.

"Everything is legal, Mr. Munro." No longer worried about the dark tenor of his own voice, David withdrew an ivory packet from his pocket. "The deed was recorded this morning. If you continue to fight me, it might look as if you're using the powers of the bench for illegal acquisition of private property. Rose Briar is now mine and, unlike your uncle, I have the means to fight you."

"Are you accusing me of an indiscretion with my own family?"

"If I did, I might force you to call me out." David recognized Nellis's type. He'd seen men like him enough in Ireland. Men who used their powers to gain title to land. "Aye," he said quietly. "I know the justice system well enough."

With exaggerated casualness, Nellis reapplied his gloves. "Give Lady Munro my regards, Sir Henry. You may also tell her I am a patient man. For you won't live forever. From the looks of your health, I doubt you will even last out the year."

"How could you say that?" Bethany cried.

"Get out!" Sir Henry toppled the bowl of soup, spewing hot liquid down his trousers.

David took a protective step toward Sir Henry. "You've been told to leave, Nellis."

"And you, Chadwick." Nellis settled his hat on his head. "You'll have to have more than will and money to work that land around Rose Briar. Your tenants have left in droves. They won't return to work your fields. Fear does that to a soul."

Nellis slammed out the back door. Bethany sniffled. A moment later, he heard the rattle of Nellis's carriage wheels up the drive.

"Do either of you want to tell me what that was about?" David asked.

Sir Henry leaned on his palms against the tabletop. His hands shook, and he had difficulty wiping the soup from his lap. "Maybe I should have warned you," he admitted.

Sir Henry could hardly stand, and David walked around the table and braced his shoulder beneath his arm. "Aye," he muttered. "I can see why you forgot," he agreed none too kindly. "I'm taking you back to your room." He looked at Esma kneeling on the floor wiping up the spilled soup. "Bring more soup and tea, Mrs. Shelby."

"Lady Munro told me to have him soak his foot in salts." Esma sat back on her heels and wrung her hands. "But he's not at all cooperative, my lord."

Once in Sir Henry's room David settled him into a chair and, after helping the elder remove his trousers, eased a woolen sock from his swollen left foot. The start of an ulcer tortured his large toe. "How long has this foot been like this?" He braced his arm across his thigh and regarded Sir Henry with a frown.

"Long enough to know what unhealed ulcers can do to feet." He rubbed his temple. "I've tried to do what I can so she won't worry. She has worries enough with the children and trying to keep a roof over our heads. I couldn't let her see this."

"Lady Munro is correct. You should be soaking in salts. I've seen injuries like this heal and sometimes I haven't. But you have to take care of the infection."

Sir Henry's eyes grew speculative. "You're a doctor?"

David knew enough about practical medicine from his former job in Ireland to qualify as a physician in most parts of the world. He also knew that what plagued Sir Henry would pass the point of a cure in a matter of weeks if he did not work diligently to fix the problem. "I've worked around enough people for the last decade to learn how to set a splint and birth a baby," he told Sir Henry.

Esma and Bethany arrived with a pot of hot water and salts. "Will he be all right?" Bethany sidled beside her grandfather.

David's gaze moved from the old man fussing at Esma about the water temperature to the low ceiling above him, wondering if Meg was ill in her room not to have heard the commotion. He didn't want to feel responsible for these people in any way.

David stood. "Mrs. Shelby? See that he soaks the foot."

He returned to the kitchen to wash his hands. Leaning both palms on the countertop, he stared out the window.

"Thank you." Bethany had followed him. She wore yellow, the same color as the bright curtains that draped the windows. "For what you did for us—"

"I didn't do anything, Miss Munro."

"But you did. Not just for Sir Henry, but for standing against Nellis. I fear it will not go well for you. You don't want to make him an enemy. But I guess it's too late for that."

He plucked a towel hanging from a wooden peg and dried his hands, looking down at the younger girl. "What happened to the tenants on this land?" he asked.

"Most have left to find work," she said, studying the toe of her slipper. "With the river and the channel a short distance away, this area has become a haven for smugglers. If Tommy Stillings hasn't put the fear of death in our souls, then the hounds running loose over the countryside have. The tenants remaining do so at their own peril."

Forcing down a spark of anger, David reminded himself that these people were strangers. When he left, he would see none of them again. "Yet you're still here," he said.

"For the most part, Sheriff Stillings leaves us alone," Bethany said. "Victoria saved his life once, and, out of some sense of honor, he has not treated us the same as he has others. But she'll stand up to him one too many times, I fear."

David remembered the night he'd first come to this village, and the fact that Sheriff Stillings had come here with the earring. "The excise officers know nothing about this?"

"Oh, sometimes soldiers and the excise officers come. The smuggling stops. Nellis does nothing at all." Bethany looked away. "I fear it is very possible that you made a poor investment with your purchase of Rose Briar."

"Do you think?"

He walked to the window and edged aside the yellow curtain. Even as he watched, the last of the light fell away from the sky, leaving sleet sheeting against the glass. "I heard the hounds this morning," he said.

Esma snorted in disgust. Carrying a pan of water, she walked past him and dumped it in the sink. "Yes, they were running about. That's why Lady Munro left this afternoon to check on Mr. Doyle." She wiped her hands on her apron. "He's the groundskeeper at the church. She should have been back hours ago. We did not tell Nellis—"

"Lady Munro is gone?" Moving away from the window, he looked between Mrs. Shelby and Bethany. "Why didn't someone tell me this sooner?"

"Mr. Rockwell left to find her just before Nellis arrived."

David forced himself not to run as he pulled his gloves out of his pocket, but he was already walking out of the kitchen; then sprinting across the backyard toward the stable.

With Colonel Faraday loose, he cursed Meg's foolishness. Then there was also part of him that feared she had fled.

The old part of him that knew the old part of her as he knew his own soul. Victoria Munro might be close to sainthood in Sir Henry's eyes, but Meg Faraday could look down the sight of a gun and kill a man. It was only a matter of time before she ran again. He just didn't want to believe it could be this soon.

"I've a mind to marry ye, mistress," Mr. Doyle's voice rasped over Victoria's cheek.

Easing him onto the bed, Victoria smiled, if only to acknowledge she'd heard him. He still suffered from hypothermia. She had found him in the burned-out rectory hiding beneath the desk, clutching a chicken for dear life and shivering beneath a heavy woolen blanket. "In a few years I may consider your offer." She adjusted the pillows behind his back. "Mr. Rockwell has started a fire in the front room. I'll fix tea. But I want you to stay warm beneath those blankets. You've suffered exposure."

Thin hands grasped hers. "She's been gone a year, my lady."

"I know." Victoria tucked his hands inside hers.

Spidery purplish veins marred his cheeks and nose, and he squinted up at her, his left eye coated with an opaque film. He had been blind in that eye for five years. "I remember when she had hair the color of yours," he said, half asleep.

"You miss your wife. Is that why you were at the church?"

Victoria knew he spent a lot of time in the burned-out

structure. Sometimes she would find him sitting on the floor in front of the crumbling pulpit.

"Ye tell Sir Henry that Doyle says he best be findin' ye a husband soon. 'Tis a shame to see sturdy stock go to waste."

Victoria sat back on the bed and gave Mr. Doyle a stern look. "Since you're so spry, maybe I should send you to Widow Gibson's place to spend the winter."

"You wouldn't send me away, would ye, my lady?"

Victoria had to send him somewhere for his own safety. Mrs. Gibson was the former Rose Briar cook. Last year she'd moved in with her son, who still managed to farm a spot of land on the estate. "She can cook a good meal, and it's safer for you. She could use help around the farm. You'll have a place to keep your chickens."

"Then ye be knowing the truth of it." Thoughtfully rubbing his chin, he peered at her through his one good eye. "It isn't safe these days." He lowered his voice. "Ol' Doyle can tell ye a thing or two about what I seen some nights that would stiffen the hairs on your neck, mum. There be ghosts in the belfry. Not even the hounds went in there last night."

Victoria bent over the nightstand and dimmed the lamp. She would have to go over to the church and find out what had frightened Mr. Doyle. Looking out the window, toward the church, she suspected the ghostly specters were lantern-carrying humans and part of Stillings's group of smugglers.

Closing the curtain to curtail the icy draft, Victoria looked over her shoulder at the man in the bed. He might have died had she not found him this afternoon. "Don't leave me, mistress," his voice carried to her as she blew out the lamp on the dresser.

"I'm only going in the other room." She stood at the end of

the bed. "But tomorrow I am going to take you to Widow Gibson's place. All right?"

Mr. Doyle's one eye focused on her in the dark. His voice came to her softly. "Will ye tell Bess? She'll expect to see me and won't know where I'm off to."

Victoria moved to the end of the bed. "I'll tell your wife, Mr. Doyle."

"Promise?"

"I promise."

"We were happy together, my lady," he murmured.

Her heart pounding for some illogical reason she couldn't explain, Victoria stepped out of the room and, closing the door, leaned her head against the jamb. She never wanted to know that kind of love. The kind that made a person do foolish things like stand on a grave and talk to a headstone.

Or conceive a child.

Drawing her shoulders back, Victoria turned into the room and nearly leaped from her socks.

David was half leaning on the back of the settee, his coat draped beside him. Instinctively, her hand went to her pocket, where she now hesitated, waiting for her pulse to return to normal. "Mary and Joseph! Where's Mr. Rockwell?" she asked, alarmed as he unfurled his long body and came to his feet.

David had seen the movement and, by the hard look on his face, guessed that she carried a weapon. "I sent him back to your family. I told you never to leave without him."

Despite the fact that she refused on principle to retreat before any man, she found her feet had taken a step backward. She bumped the wall, but he kept coming. Beads of water glistened on his hair, and she could feel the chill on his clothes as if he hadn't been long out of the storm. "What are you doing?"

Without a word, he retrieved her derringer from her pocket before she had a chance to stop him. "Not that I don't trust you with a loaded gun." His eyes on hers, he checked the load—as if she'd carry an unloaded gun. "But I don't."

Folding her arms, she didn't argue his wisdom. She wouldn't trust Meg Faraday either when it was so tempting to shoot him and be done with it. Her eyes traveled down the length of him. The light caught the silver threads in his waistcoat and made him look expensive. "Why are you so angry?" she asked.

"Do you have a death wish?" His rasp came out sounding proprietary as if he had some claim on her or right to be worried. "You're not supposed to leave the cottage alone."

"I can take care of myself. Rockwell stays with my family at all times, not with me."

"That wasn't our agreement. Unless you are expecting a pleasant father-daughter reunion." One finely arched brow shot up as he considered that possibility. "Come to think of it, you still haven't told me why you don't want him to find you."

"What is *wrong* with you?" She pushed against his chest, knowing the instant she yanked her hand back, it was a mistake to touch him. Especially when he was standing so close, and the chill on his clothes had turned to heat.

They stood, neither moving, except to breathe. Barely. He was close enough to kiss her. Close enough to dig his hands in her hair and open his mouth over hers as he had last night. She wanted her anger back. Not this stark terror that she might do something stupid and step into his arms.

His jaw clamped tight. Then he shifted his gaze to the bedroom door and stuffed the derringer in his vest pocket. "Is Mr. Doyle all right?"

"He's suffering from hypothermia. I can't leave him tonight. I was on my way to make tea."

Stepping a wide arc around her husband, she walked past the small maple dining table with its two spindle-back chairs and into the tiny kitchen.

She'd lit the stove earlier and set a kettle of water atop the fire to boil. She dragged three cups from the cupboard and set them on the counter next to the wicker basket that she'd brought earlier. She pulled out a wooden tray.

From her peripheral vision, she could see David settling a shoulder against the wall. Hovering with eyes that burned, watching her pour steaming water into a china pot. Somehow, she kept her attention on the tea in an attempt to quell the flutter of her pulse. The cottage was too small and cluttered for them both to spend a peaceful night beneath this roof. An uncomfortable silence settled between them as she rummaged through her thoughts for something relevant to say.

"Who owns the hounds that came through here last night?" he asked.

"Most of them are wild dogs. I can't prove it, but I believe Nellis is responsible for their presence. When I find out . . ."

David just looked at her, and some of her righteous anger faded. She was surprised that he'd even asked. Or maybe she was tired of fighting alone and appreciated that he seemed concerned. "The sleet will change over to snow tonight. If they come again, they'll be easy to track," she said.

"I don't need snow to track them."

She blinked away the urge to tell him tracking those hounds was not his responsibility. "They're dangerous, David."

"As is your father. I prefer only one canine at my back." He moved into the kitchen and leaned his backside against the counter. "How many tenants do you have left?"

"Seven families." She arranged the sugar bowl on a tray but her movements slowed. Her knuckles still bore the scabs from her flight off the horse. "A few years ago, there were thirty families. Mr. Doyle takes care of the church grounds. We used to have four groundskeepers who cared for the parkland surrounding the bluff house."

"Is there only one road leading up here?"

"No," she said, knowing he asked purely for professional reasons, not because he was interested in Rose Briar. And a sadness came over her. For up on this bluff was everything that she loved. "One road comes up from the valley to the manor house. There is a more traveled road north over the ravine that comes in from Halisham and Salehurst and goes on to the coast. Then, of course, there are all the secret trails in and out of the woods." She glanced his way. "I know them all."

"In case you've thought about it," he said, looking at her with absolute promise in his eyes, "there isn't anywhere you can go that I won't find you, Meg."

She placed the lid on the teapot. "Because you hate me so much?"

"Hate was never the problem between us." He turned his hip against the countertop. "Now I've somehow found myself owning land, a house, and a family that you love. Can you explain that?"

Her hand fell away from the pot to linger on the tray as she remembered the shooting star that first night he had returned to her, and the wish she had made for a miracle that would help her save Rose Briar. The adage that God worked in mysterious ways had never hit her so hard. "Perhaps something once so alive doesn't deserve to die," she said, looking up at David when he didn't reply. "Rose Briar really is worth saving."

"Is that all worth saving, Meg?"

"There are the fields and orchards as well. The tenants have spent their lives up here. They consider this land their home." The thought turned her away from the topic, and she studied a hairline crack on the sugar bowl. "Have you eaten supper yet?"

"Are you offering to cook for me?"

"There is a jar of boysenberry jam in the basket." This time she spared him a coy glance. "I was planning to share my spoon with you."

The corner of his mouth tilted. In the dim firelight, the smile caught Victoria.

"Maybe I should cook for us then," he said.

"Can you?"

"Give me a potato. I'll make you a pie. Do I look underfed?"

Her gaze encompassed his shoulders and briefly touched the rest of him. For all of his shortcomings, David still had the kind of hard body that forced women to carry smelling salts. Again, her mind flashed memories of that kiss he'd given her last night—the same kiss that had kept her up all night.

As the silence stretched between them like a taut violin string, she suddenly had an urge to pluck out an entire symphony.

He'd awakened that wicked part of her she'd thought lay dormant beneath the prim Victoria. He was the only man she'd ever known who Meg Faraday could not control with her sexuality. That had always been part of the attraction. The challenge.

But only part.

"You should do that more often," she said, placing one hand on the lid of the teapot and pouring.

"What exactly should I do more often?"

"Smile as if you mean it." She slanted him a saucy glance. "You have nice teeth." Like a wolf, she didn't add.

He shifted his body, and one hand went into his pocket. "I told Rockwell you wouldn't return to the cottage tonight. I was worried about the weather."

"Then why didn't *he* stay and you return to the cottage?"

It was an impulsive schoolgirl question to ask. "On second thought," she said, "maybe neither of us should evaluate that answer too much."

His eyes told her he was thinking about that kiss, too.

And she realized this wasn't a battle she'd prepared herself to wage. Not ever again. But she couldn't breathe the same air David breathed without remembering what it had once felt like to know the heat of him against her naked flesh—to know all of him—as if she'd forgotten he was a first-rate charlatan.

As if she'd forgotten he was exactly like her.

"I need to stable my horse." He shoved off the counter. "I'll make a round over the grounds before I lock up for the night. Shut the curtain behind you and lock the door."

Of course, he would not let down his guard. He still had her derringer tucked away in his pocket. She looked over her shoulder out the window at the layer of ice caked on the glass, only to startle as he tipped a finger beneath her chin and turned her face into the light. He was standing so close, she could feel his warmth all over. It was suddenly obvious to her—as it must have been to him—that she was going to sleep with him again.

"Patience, love." He rubbed the rough pad of his thumb across her bottom lip, before he cloaked the hot, possessive glitter in those eyes behind a wall of stone. Blunt. Predatory. "When I kiss you again, it won't be while you're playing Florence Nightingale in an old man's cottage."

Victoria refused to respond. It was not concern about what he might do to her but worry about what she would allow if she followed the promise in his eyes. When he left the kitchen, she placed her palms on the smooth wooden counter and listened to the whisper of cloth as he slid his arms into the sleeves of his coat. She didn't breathe again until he shut the front door behind him.

Chapter 8

ఠఠ

"**H**e's been out there most of the evening, mistress," Doyle murmured from the bed behind Victoria.

Not realizing he'd awakened, she turned from the window. Doyle clutched the blankets to his chin. The only light in the room came from the woodstove in the corner. "His Lordship fixed a mighty fine soup," he added, his one good eye brilliant in the faded orange light. "He ain't like other no-account lordships, mum."

"No, he isn't," she agreed. Because he was no true lord.

But he was an excellent cook. David had managed to make a delicious meal out of old potatoes, carrots, and the ham remaining in the smoke shed in back. But it was when he'd helped Doyle out of bed to perform his evening ablutions that something inside her shifted. He'd managed the task with the elderly man's dignity intact, as if he'd performed such tasks a hundred times before, his compassion contrary to everything she remembered about him. She had looked away from him when he'd come out of the room, afraid of her confusion.

"I feel he'll be the one to bring back Rose Briar, mistress." Mr. Doyle's eyes drifted shut as Victoria pulled the covers to his chin. "I feel it in my gut."

"Why?" she asked, struggling to delve through her own conflicting emotions about David's character.

"He's out there chopping wood so we don't freeze tonight." Mr. Doyle chuckled. "And I've seen the way he watches you when you're not looking. That young man has feelings for you."

"Lord Chadwick?" she laughed at the notion.

David didn't watch her any differently than he would any other criminal who'd been handed over to his keeping.

Doyle peered at her from beneath bushy brows. "I'm not as blind as I look, my lady."

No, he only sees spirits in an old burned-out church. Victoria stood next to the bed. "Are you warm enough?"

"Aye, mistress. I've not been so warm in a long time."

After a moment, Victoria left the room. She walked to the hearth and put another log onto the fire before returning to the kitchen.

David had told her to keep the curtains closed, but she lifted aside one edge and looked toward the stable. The wind had slowed to an occasional gust, and earlier the sleet had turned to snow. Huge flakes fell and coated the ground in a layer of white. Light from the stable seeped out of the crevices between the slats, making the ground glisten gold. She could hear the muffled but steady *thwack* of an axe chopping wood. David had been outside almost two hours.

Grabbing a ragged mitten, she lifted the kettle from the

fire. She poured coffee into a chipped mug. At the back door, she wrapped David's heavy cloak around her shoulders and headed for the stable. Her boots squeaked in the snow. Once there, she gripped the wooden latch and edged open the wide door. The movement lifted David's head, and, despite her will and all the lies she told herself, her heart skipped a beat. Even without benefit of the shadows playing around his face, he was tall, handsome, and looked extremely capable with his hands wrapped around the long axe handle. Her estranged husband had enormous presence and the ability to become a part of his surroundings, even in a dilapidated old barn and wearing attire suited to a lord. She had to force her attention back to the coffee in her hand as she turned and shut the door.

"It's freezing out here." Holding out the hot steaming cup, she offered a tentative smile. "No weapons. Promise."

"Scalding liquid against this axe?" He smiled, but his wasn't nearly as tentative as hers. "I'd rather be holding the axe."

"What a fine domestic couple we make," she said. "Talking murder as easily as we talk about the weather."

Straw littered the ground. Mr. Doyle's chicken had found a place to nest near the stall where the stallion mulled over a trough of hay. David wrapped his palms around the mug she offered and captured her hand. He wore his woolen coat unbuttoned, and it opened as he bent to inhale the steam. "Then you are reassuring me that I needn't have you take the first drink?"

Victoria edged the mug to her lips, aware that his eyes were on her mouth. She drank, not because he'd bullied her into doing so, but because the coffee was the only warm thing in the stable. "I make great coffee, if I say so myself." She stepped away, confident that she had at last made him uncomfortable. "I'll be taking Mr. Doyle to Widow Gibson's in the morning. They are good folk."

David drank the coffee. Peering at her over the ceramic rim, he looked at the cloak she wore, but did not ask why she should be wearing something belonging to him. She could have told him because the cloak was warmer than anything she had.

"Is this weather common for this time of year?" he asked.

She studied a wood chip. "We get a storm like this every three or four years. Once, we had a hurricane come through. Brighton received most of the damage."

"I remember. The Dublin rags carried news of that."

She looked up and found his eyes on her. He had read about something that had happened to her, she realized, wondering if that was the same as looking into a sky filled with stars knowing those same celestial entities filled David's sky as well. Glancing away, she moved out of the lantern light nearer to the horse.

"You were very capable with Mr. Doyle tonight," she said.

He put aside the axe, saying something inane to the chicken that brought a smile to her mouth. "You don't talk about yourself much, do you?" she asked as he moved beside her, stirring straw with his steps.

Don't panic, she told herself, holding her hand out to the stallion behind the door. David's coat brushed her cloak. He set down the cup and turned to the horse as it leaned its neck over the stall in greeting. "I've worked in many a hospital. Not as a physician, but close enough to people sometimes to be one."

"A far road from the one you traveled in Calcutta."

"Roads have many forks," he said.

"That's the beauty of roads," she agreed. "They fork."

One corner of his mouth tilted. "The more forks the better."

He was skilled at keeping a conversation moving when he wanted to as he talked about everything except the topic at hand. She imagined that making love to him again would be about as breathtaking as burning up on a beach of hot sand. India had been like that. Sultry and tempestuous. Jasmine and sunlight.

Death.

"I don't want to bed you," she said without looking at him.

His hands stroked the horse's ears and neck. "It's cold in here, isn't it, Old Boy?"

His presence achingly intimate, she felt pinned by the gentle movement of his hands, captured by the mockery of their circumstances and conflicting desire. "I mean it, David. Don't ask me. Especially when we both know why you are here."

"Why did you venture out here?" he asked, rubbing his hand down the horse's neck.

She glanced up at his shadowed profile, knowing she couldn't answer that question, without admitting how easily he seduced her. The sensation left her dizzy.

"What's his name?" She nodded to the horse, and this time David grinned, the kind of smile that could light up a dark night, or in this case the inside of a frosty stable.

He looked directly into her eyes. "Old Boy."

Her mouth crooked into a smile before she caught herself and frowned. Stepping around him, she walked toward the barn door, the cloak flowing around her like wings. "I wish I hated you." She opened the door and turned. "But I don't."

David remained where she left him standing, stroking the horse, aware that the blood rushed faster in his veins. He could still smell his soap on her. The scent of her hair. He'd come out to the barn tonight to get away from her, and now found that he did not want to escape at all.

"Not good, Old Boy," he murmured, distracted, the words as much a warning to himself as they were an admonition that the line he walked was thin indeed. "Not good at all."

"She said ye like peppermint, my lord."

David threw off the covers someone had laid over him in the night. He sat on a chair in front of the hearth. Mr. Doyle stood beside him, a cup of hot tea extended. The weathered, blue-veined hands shook with age. A glance around told him Meg was gone.

Furious, he slid his feet into his boots. "Did she also tell you to remain quiet until she'd left?" He walked to the kitchen window and looked outside at the stable.

Tracks led from the stable in the snow. She'd taken the horse. He dragged up his coat from the sofa and, walking outside, looked toward the church.

It was there he stopped. One set of fresh tracks left the churchyard from the old rectory. Yet there were no tracks leading inside, which meant they did not belong to Meg.

Someone had been inside that church since the snow had begun to fall after midnight. Shoving his arms into his coat sleeves, he looked across the field into a network of distant ravines and hillocks that eventually turned into woods. Old Boy's tracks joined the footprints a hundred yards out and disappeared over a hill.

"You were sleepin' like a babe when she left this morning," Doyle said, standing inside the doorway wrapped in a blue-checkered blanket. "I told her last night I seen the spirits in the church. Sometimes they glow in the rectory. Some-times in the belfry. I told her. She believes me now."

Muttering an oath beneath his breath, David stepped off the porch.

"Y-you won't be leaving me, will you?"

He pulled his gloves out of the pocket and turned to see the old man following him. "Pack what you will be taking to Widow Gibson's. I won't be gone long."

"Bless you, m'lord."

David decided it was a good idea Meg was taking Doyle to another place for winter—if he didn't wring her neck first, he thought as he trudged through snow toward the churchyard.

"Who are you today?" He paused to study the tracks. "Lady Victoria, good Samaritan? Or Colonel Faraday's protégée?"

Meg, Maggie, Victoria, Lady Munro. He'd never known a more talented chameleon than Margaret Faraday, beautiful daughter of a Bengali garrison whore and a convicted mur-derer. Except maybe her father.

Squatting, David splayed his hands over the footprints, studying the depth of the snow. A big man wearing large boots and a cloak had made the tracks. He could see the fab-ric striations atop the icy surface. A man's cloak usually touched his calves, which made this particular ghost of Doyle's at least six feet tall. Colonel Faraday was six feet tall.

David looked north and continued following the tracks, plowing through the snow, a lone figure in black wool and clothing too nice, certainly inappropriate for a winter stroll. Yet the farther he walked, the more time seemed to stand still all around him, the air breathtakingly silent, the landscape strangely beautiful encased in snow and ice.

Like Meg, he thought, an ice queen atop the lifeblood and

heartbeat of her soul. Fate and deception had made her his wife. The force of his own passion had brought her back to him. He had forgotten the true depth of that passion. The danger she posed.

This was the second time in as many days he'd allowed himself to worry about Meg. David laughed—a knife-blade edge of anger—a dead giveaway that he would bloody throttle her this time. It wasn't a reassuring sound.

Not when he wanted her as he wanted the warmth of sunlight at this moment.

"Too long in Ireland," he murmured in disgust a half hour later, his breath clinging like a cloud to the air. He had difficulty catching his breath in the cold. He stopped to assess the tracks and to breathe. Bracing his hands on his thighs, he glanced over his shoulder, back at the cottage, surprised that he'd traveled so far. In front of him, in a wooded copse, long clump grass peeked through places bared of snow by the wind. Pushing off, he moved on, but slowed when he glimpsed another pair of smaller tracks.

A woman had met the man here. He found where a horse had been corralled behind a windbreak. Moving on, he followed the horse's tracks another hundred yards to the top of a hill that looked down over a sweeping valley.

In the taut silence of his thoughts, David saw the band of riders crest the knoll in front of him. They had seen him at the same time he stopped on the rise.

Bloody hell.

Out in the open as he was, he had no place to go. If he ran, the horses would be upon him in less than a minute. As the riders neared, he identified Stillings in the lead. Even in a heavy cloak, hat, and beard growth, the man was unmistakable. Only eight to one, he mused aloud. Two men broke away, and the riders widened into an arch. David recognized a flank attack when he saw one, backed a step, and prepared to fight.

One horse bore down on him, the rider wielding a cudgel.

David ducked, rolled, then came up on his feet. Two men dropped from their horses and tackled him from behind. His body slammed against the ground. He felt a kick to the ribs, but evaded the second boot to his chest. David rolled to his feet, his coat swirling around his ankles as he turned and met the third rider holding the club.

"Bloody grab him, Franks," Stillings shouted.

A man's bulky arms wrapped around his torso, his heavy breathing measuring a physical exhaustion that won David precious few seconds. He raised both feet off the ground and kicked the man holding the club, sending him sprawling on his backside. Lowering his chin against his chest, he touched both feet to the ground, gripped Franks's forearm, and flipped him flat onto his back into the snow. In one swift movement, David dropped to one knee, his arm a vise around the man's neck.

Breathing hard, he lifted his eyes to Sheriff Stillings. "Pull your men off me." The words came out in a puff of steam. "Fooking now!"

The four men surrounding him stopped in their tracks, all of them looking to Stillings for direction. No one moved.

"Two of my men were killed last night," the sheriff said. "Not a mile from here. Their necks were broken."

David let loose of the man whose throat he gripped in the crook of his elbow. Gasping, Franks crawled away. "What are you talking about?"

"You're a stranger in these parts."

"He is with me," a decidedly furious feminine voice said from behind him.

David's head jerked toward the voice. Meg sat atop his high-stepping stallion. "I lost my derringer," she said, "and this shotgun will hurt, Tommy Stillings."

The barrel in her hands did little to persuade David that he was any safer from her than he was from Stillings. As if reading his mind, she said, "Mr. Doyle keeps a shotgun in the barn."

David wiped his mouth and spit blood into the snow. Not that he'd ever trust her anymore than he appreciated being in her direct line of fire. "I'll try to remember that next time you and I are sleeping beneath the same roof for a night. I will be the first to know if you decide to shoot that thing, won't I?"

"I told you it was dangerous for you alone out here."

"But not for you," he said deadpan, coming to his feet and managing not to flinch from the pain in his ribs. "Have I interrupted a secret assignation?" David looked between his wife and the sheriff, who seemed bemused by the exchange. "Why am I not surprised?"

"Do you two know each other?" Stillings asked.

Meg pulled her gaze from his and raised her chin. "You have just tried to kill Lord Chadwick, my cousin and the new owner of the land where you and your men are trespassing. He purchased Rose Briar two days ago."

"Did he now?" Leather creaked as Stillings propped his elbow across the saddle and gave David the full import of his gaze. "The new owner. Dressed all nice-like for church. Inspecting your land?"

The men around him chuckled. Stillings nudged his horse

forward, eyeing David's clothes. "No gentleman I know fights the way you do."

"He didn't kill your men," Meg said, the shotgun leveled at Stillings's chest.

Stillings frowned. "You shouldn't be aiming that at me, Doc. I might get the impression you're trying to shoot me."

"Oh, please, Tommy. I would think that after the other night, that fact would be abundantly clear." Her gaze touched David's. "The sheriff thinks I'm a thief. He's under the impression that I'm in possession of a necklace that will make him a wealthy man."

"Interesting." David cocked a brow. "Are you?"

"Naturally." She glared at him. "That's why I live like a pauper in a hunter's cottage."

"Does our magistrate know you own Rose Briar?" Stillings asked David.

"I had the pleasure of informing the honorable Nellis Munro yesterday."

Stillings's horse stamped in a circle. The barrel of Meg's shotgun followed his chest. "Why are you on this property, Tommy? Aren't you a little off the main roads?"

The sheriff's smile was white against the black stubble on his face, but his eyes had grown hard. "What have I told you about talking that way to me in front of my—"

"How is your wife, Tommy?"

Something flickered in Stillings's gaze.

"I saw her three weeks ago in town," Meg said. "I'll need to check on her progress next month. Unless, of course, you prefer that she birth that babe alone. I want you off this land. Even I have my limits when you threaten my loved ones."

Stillings straightened in the saddle. "You know what I

think, Doc? You'd not let Annie birth that babe alone no matter what I did." He laughed as he waved his men away.

His men mounted in a rattle of bridle chains and creaking leather made stiff by the cold. The horses galloped down the ravine toward the wooded copse, and finally reappeared on the opposite knoll before vanishing into the woods.

"Your loved ones?" David spit out blood over a laugh. "Wasn't that overdoing it?"

"When did you talk to Nellis?"

He tested his bottom lip with the back of one gloved hand. She was wearing his cloak. The one she'd worn last night in the stable. "Ask your bloody family."

"Did you kill Stillings's men?"

David squinted against the bright glare of the sun, tempted to yank the shotgun out of her hands and pull her off the saddle, if his head didn't feel like he'd dropped it out off a second-floor balcony. Clearly, she wanted a reason to distrust him as much as he distrusted her. He began to relax, as much as he could around her.

"I was in town yesterday. Where were you before Rockwell found you?"

"Oh, please. I'm not strong enough to snap a man's neck. Isn't that your forte?"

"Whoever was in that church last night, I can assume didn't belong to Stillings's group?" he asked.

Unless she already knew. But she wasn't looking at him, and he couldn't see her eyes. "I followed the tracks into the woods about a half mile down the hill." She pointed to the ravine. "I saw signs that a horse had been left in a lean-to on the other side of where an old hay barn sits. I was there when I saw Stillings's men."

David wanted to look away but found he could not. She'd been nowhere near that lean-to or surely he'd have seen her. "Why did you go alone this morning, Meg?"

"Shouldn't you be thanking me for saving your life?"

He fixed his eyes on the shotgun. "Is my life safe in your hands?"

More than a warning, his voice held a question. Her gaze dropped to his stance, to his hands before lifting to touch his eyes. Awareness of her—of danger—coursed like a current through his veins. Even at her mercy, he would have time to kill her before she swung around the shotgun and pulled the trigger.

Maybe.

If he didn't hesitate.

As he had years before. Jeopardizing the mission and the lives of the men who depended on him. Nearly costing him his life. Certainly his soul.

"Shooting you is underrated," she said quietly.

"Or maybe you'll be hunted until you die. This time without benefit of a fake death to cover your trail. These people aren't your family, Meg. They aren't your people. Why are you even here standing up to a man like Stillings?"

"I don't expect you to understand." She shoved the shotgun in the sling hanging from the saddle and, leaning into the stirrup, lowered herself to the ground. Snow crunched beneath her boots as she approached him. "You're hurt." She pulled aside his coat.

He stopped her from touching him. "Why would you save me from Stillings's men?"

"Maybe I like your personality. I don't know. You tell me."

He couldn't.

And thrice his heart thumped in response to her standing

before him. A breeze whipped at her voluminous cloak. The curves of her body looked supple and inviting. He lowered her hands to her sides. In no way did he want her to touch him.

"I should look at your ribs."

"No." He walked past her. "You should not. If I wasn't chasing you, this wouldn't have happened."

She followed him to the horse. "Don't be such an infant—"

He bent and snapped up the reins, trailing in the snow. "I don't want your help, Meg. I don't need your help."

"No, you only want me as bait to catch my father."

"Bait?" he scoffed.

"Wasn't that all I ever was to you, anyway? Bait?"

Victoria watched as he stepped into the stirrup and swung his leg over the saddle with a grimace of pain. The sun was behind his shoulders. "You obviously know how to shoot that shotgun," he said, "so keep it and go back to Doyle. I want him packed to move." He swung the horse around. "Today."

"I've already followed those tracks." Victoria glared at his rigid back. He was going to leave her to walk, the bastard. "Obviously you've kept your fighting skills as well-honed as they always were," she called, resenting the tears that welled, the sense of abandonment, the way he had always made her feel. "But still not well enough to keep you from running away. I would have left India with you had you just asked, David! Why couldn't you have asked?"

The horse stopped on the incline, but Victoria was too deep into the throes of her temper to take heed of her tongue. "I know you must have felt something!"

The beast reared and pranced irritably in a circle as David turned back up the hill. A shadow passed over her at his approach. Her gaze traversed the length of a shiny boot, past a thigh snugly attired in dark trousers. His gloved hand gripped the reins. "What the hell did you expect to happen between us, Meg? You and me?

"Didn't you think I knew you danced only when your father pulled the strings? Why do you think he let me marry you?" Her horrified gaze held his probing colder one. "You never knew. Did you? He learned who I was before you did. There was never anything but the game and the chase. Bait? Your father dangled you in shark-infested waters ready to feed you to the treasure gods, Meg. You never once asked for my help. Not one bloody time in the three months we were married did you ask."

Tears welled. Hot, terrible tears that threatened to rise up and choke her. "You knew what my father was like. You *knew*. But it seemed I let the shark into my own bed. What a laugh that must have been for you, David."

"Oh, yes. I've been laughing for nine fooking years."

"And what did you do for those nine *fooking* years tucked in Ireland? Spend your days in hospitals? Slay evildoers at night? Practicing for the day you could resume your fight against me? Cheers for the winning team. They brought you out of retirement so you can finish your precious job."

His eyes nearly blue in the sunlight, he looked down at her standing in the snow, wrapped in his cloak, waiting for him to respond. "God only knows . . . whether you like it or not, I am your only hope of survival, Meg."

"There's a name for people like you, David." She backed a step and tripped on her cloak in the snow. "Hypocrite."

"Priest," he said, his eyes shuttered.

"Pardon?"

"County Wicklow, Ireland." He held Old Boy's reins as the

stallion danced a circle, turning his head to look at her over his shoulder. "That's where I went after I left the Foreign Service nine years ago."

Stunned, Victoria watched him ride away and would have followed if her feet weren't already beginning to feel like frozen stumps.

"Impossible." Her voice caught up to her thoughts, but David had already reached the wooded ravine. "You never even believed in God!"

Chapter 9

"**P**eepaw says I should wear spectacles in places of poor light," Bethany said idly. "Or I shall be blind by the time I am your age."

A single glass lantern swayed from a hook attached to a heavy wooden rafter above the workbench where Bethany was helping Victoria label glass jars of newly dried medicinal herbs.

"My age?" Victoria arched a brow. "Please don't put me in my grave, yet."

Bethany perched herself on a three-legged stool behind the bench where she and Victoria had been working for most of the morning. "Tory Birmingham gave me these spectacles when we were in town yesterday. She said that spectacles are all the rage in Mrs. Winston's reading circle. I think they make me look older."

A red kerchief restrained Bethany's hair. The spectacles

magnified her eyes and made her look like an owl. Victoria tried not to smile. "You look quite old enough."

"Maybe Lord Chadwick will attend Tory Birmingham's Yule soirée this year." A hint of eagerness tinged the girl's tone. "Have you thought any more about a new gown for me?" Bethany set aside the jar she was filling with dried herbs and grabbed another. "All I would need is fabric and I could make my own gown."

With an exasperated sigh, Victoria returned her attention to the jar of peppermint in her hand. "Please, can we not have this discussion again?"

Bethany's eyes, more gray than blue beneath the light, regarded Victoria with concern. "You didn't used to be such a recluse," the girl said. "Or cry out in your sleep at night and jump at shadows everywhere."

Startled that Bethany would notice that and a little ashamed, Victoria averted her gaze to the jar at her elbow. "I haven't been feeling well of late."

"Are you afraid to go anywhere we might see Nellis? Is that why you haven't wanted Nathanial home?" Bethany asked. "Because of Nellis?"

Victoria wiped her hands on her apron. "It's complicated, Bethany. If I could send you to Nathanial, I would. But your grandfather needs you when I can't be here."

"Peepaw doesn't need me. He only needs you. And sometimes Mr. Shelby with whom he plays rummy."

"That's not true, Bethany."

Bethany retrieved an empty jar from the stack and moved down the bench to the chamomile. "He has a mistress," she said quietly.

Victoria's eyes widened. "Who has a mistress?"

"Lord Chadwick. Melinda told me yesterday when you

and Peepaw were at the apothecary. Her father owns the general mercantile on Main—"

"I know who Mr. Carter is. We see him every Sabbath."

"Countess Cherbinko's servants shop at his mercantile. He carries rare spices that the countess likes. Servants talk. I saw her leaving Goodchilds Boutique. She is beautiful. Doesn't it bother you that Lord Chadwick *keeps* her at a town house?"

Victoria set down the jar. She'd listened to the same gossip at church the past two Sundays. She didn't want to think about David's nocturnal activities. What he might or might not be doing behind closed doors with Pamela. In another woman's bed. Yet, thoughts of him, his past—and hers—had filled her every waking moment these past weeks since he had ridden off and left her in a field to walk back in the snow.

"Lord Chadwick's private life is not our concern."

"But you're his family. And he paid the taxes on Rose Briar. I thought he was different from Nellis."

"He *is* different from Nellis. Now can we please change the topic?"

As she watched Bethany move down the bench, Victoria found the pencil she'd set aside to begin labeling the next set of jars on the shelf, but her mind no longer focused on the task.

In the days that followed Stillings's attack on the bluff, she had been careful to keep her distance from David, though she shouldn't have bothered. He had stayed away from her. She had not seen him since he'd helped her take Mr. Doyle to Widow Gibson's. He'd brought her home afterward and not returned until yesterday, when he'd stopped by the cottage and spoken briefly to Mr. Rockwell. He didn't even see her as she walked around the cottage and watched him ride out of the yard, or scarcely seemed to care where she went as long as Mr. Rockwell was with her. Clearly, not only did he want nothing to do with her; he didn't trust her to be alone for a single moment. Or maybe it was more.

David had been correct when he'd said her father relished the chase. He was a man who enjoyed the game more than he enjoyed winning the prize. Yet she'd not once considered that the footprints she'd followed after the storm had been Colonel Faraday's. She had gone after the culprit, thinking those prints belonged to one of Tommy Stillings's men, only to betray herself in David's eyes.

Why it mattered to her, she didn't know.

Except he had promised to deliver Rose Briar out of Nellis's hands, and had done so. He had already begun the process to put the estate in a trust for Nathanial. She had seen the papers in Sir Henry's surgery office that morning, picked them up and nearly wept in relief, realizing she was in danger of admiring her husband, realizing she was traversing the very same emotional path she'd traveled when he'd entered her life before.

David was a man who acted on his promises and never promised what he couldn't deliver. She'd learned from Esma what he'd said to Nellis in the family's defense and what he'd done for Sir Henry afterward. He'd been kind to Mr. Doyle as well.

And she was beginning to realize what had drawn her to him all those years ago, what was drawing her to him now despite the apocalyptic threat of doom he brought to her life. Beneath the mask he oft wore hid a man of deep principle and courage. There was goodness inside him whether he realized it or not. A sense of duty to law and truth. To people. Whereas Meg Faraday was a thief.

Her life was and always had been filled with duplicity and deception. One huge lie from the beginning to now.

Yet, ten years ago, she had somehow touched David's life in the same way he had touched hers. And a strange sort of miracle had happened amid the chaos and tragedy surrounding them. They had fallen in love with each other. She was sure of that now.

Then they had done the only thing they could.

They had run.

Now, needing to talk to David had suddenly become a reason to see him. A reason to ask a hundred questions on her mind. She wanted to touch him again, and might have remained content with her years in a celibate state had he not kissed her, then boldly underscored that act with the promise of giving her more.

Was he still a priest?

". . . someone is living in Mr. Doyle's cottage." Bethany concentrated on a tiny leaf in her hand and, as Victoria looked up, she realized Bethany had been talking for some time. "Mr. Rockwell said he works for Lord Chadwick. A big Irishman with red hair. I saw him yesterday when I went past the cottage on the way to Rose Briar."

The statement put the skids on her thoughts. "You went to Rose Briar? Alone?"

Bethany lowered her chin guiltily. "Esma made apple pies. I thought it would be nice to take one to Lord Chadwick." She drew tiny hearts in the loam at her elbow. "He thanked me. Then brought me home like an errant schoolgirl and told me never to go back to the house alone. I saw him talking, rather testily, I might add, to Mr. Rockwell before he rode out of the yard—without even saying good-bye, mind you."

So that was why David was here yesterday. Victoria wiped her hands on her apron and stripped it over her head. He'd hired men to watch the bluff. No wonder he wasn't worried about where she went. He probably had other men following her everywhere.

"He was right to bring you back," Victoria said.

"We haven't had any trouble in weeks," Bethany said. "I didn't think it would be dangerous in the light of day and, since you don't seem interested in courting his friendship, even after everything he's done for us, I thought I would."

"The fact that it has been quiet of late doesn't mean the woods are safer or that it's proper for young unmarried girls to go flitting about bachelor's houses alone." Victoria gathered up the labels and pencils and set them in a wooden tray. "Family or not."

"You just told me I was grown up. I'm almost eighteen."

"In ten months, Bethany. He's old enough to be your father."

"But we could be his family." Bethany set her chin. "I want to own a dress that hasn't had the seams let out of the bust for the past two consecutive years. I'm tired of going to sleep at night wondering if someone is going to steal my beautiful horse again and use her for illicit purposes and their ill-gotten gains. All thieves should be hanged! I hate them!"

Disturbed by the girl's outburst, Victoria dropped the soiled apron in a basket beside the shelves. "I wish I held the power to fill yours and Nathanial's world with eternal sunshine, Bethany." She wished she had the power to keep them out of danger and safe forever. And shield them from the horrors of the world. "But sometimes life isn't fair and you get what you get. One cannot choose one's parents."

A stricken look passed across the younger girl's porcelain features. "This isn't your fault, Victoria. I know you loved my father, but would it be so wrong to invite someone else into our lives? Maybe Lord Chadwick hasn't any other family to love him."

Victoria dipped her hands into a bucket of icy water and washed the soil from her palms, her hair falling over her shoulders and shielding her face. She didn't know if David had any family. In truth, she knew little about his life, except that he had gone to Ireland after leaving the Foreign Service.

And he had a son.

Every day these past weeks, she'd awakened with the thought that today would be the day that she would tell him. Then she thought of the life she and her son had built here with Bethany and Sir Henry. She was not so much afraid of telling David the truth about Nathanial as she was afraid of what that truth would do to her son's life and to Sir Henry.

She didn't know where to turn when intuition kept warning her to run, and the deeper she rooted her heart into the ground, the more she began to question if she possessed the strength to withstand the upcoming storm, wondering when David would decide to suspend the investigation and take her to London for the tribunal.

Or worse, wondering when her father would find her—and in finding her, learn about Nathanial. David had been correct when he'd said that he was her only hope at survival.

Yet her reasons for needing to see him today were ingrained in more than survival. They were personal, for there were certain truths he had inadvertently revealed to her. Why would someone leave the Foreign Service and become a priest? She knew only that the fire spiraled wildly around her and she lay undefended in its path.

Perhaps so did he.

"Do you think Mr. Rockwell will want some apple pie?" Victoria absently blotted her hands on a rag.

"I wouldn't know." Bethany snapped the lid closed on another jar.

"Why don't you ask him on your way back to the kitchen? I'll wager he's doing some chore outside the cellar door as we speak."

"I don't like him, Victoria. He's . . . he treats me like a child."

"Please, Bethany."

"But I'm not finished here."

Victoria lifted the lantern from its hook. "I have other work to do today. I can't be here to supervise this."

Another lie, she realized as she watched Bethany climb the stairs out of the root cellar a few minutes later. Victoria looked down at her work clothes; a pair of form-fitting boy's riding trousers and woolen shirt that she'd taken to wearing when she worked in the dirt. She'd learned long ago, it was easier to wash trousers than a skirt and petticoats.

Dragging a chair to the sliver of window, she peered outside toward the stable, then glanced at the cottage, before she wrapped David's cloak around her shoulders and snuffed out the lantern.

She eased the door open and stepped outside, ready to jaunt across the yard to the stable, only to stop in her tracks. Ian stood next to the woodshed, muscular arms crossed, leaning a wide shoulder casually against a tree.

"Mrs. Donally," he said, as if he hadn't just caught her in subterfuge. His breath hung suspended in the chill air, yet he wore nothing heavier than a woolen shirt, tucked into work trousers.

"Don't ever startle me like that again." Victoria didn't even pretend she wasn't attempting escape and shut the root cellar door. "Why aren't you inside eating pie?" Like any normal younger man, she wanted to add, defiant in her un-willingness to accept a man younger than she was as her jailer. Even if he did have broad shoulders and a dimple where he smiled. "And don't call me Mrs. Donally."

His green eyes twinkled. "Donally told me if I ever let you out of my sight again, he would have my ball—head. And he usually does exactly what he says he'll do, my lady."

"Is he at the manor house?"

"I believe today he is."

"I really need you to remain with my family."

He nudged his chin in the direction of the barn. "I'm not the only one watching over your family. Donally brought in his own people. They've been here for a week."

Stepping from beneath the trellis into the bright afternoon sunlight, she tented her hand over her eyes. She didn't see anyone and looked at Mr. Rockwell doubtfully. "Who are they?"

"Honestly?" He lowered his voice and leaned nearer, giving her a whiff of his soap. "I suspect they're Donally's Fenian bodyguards from Ireland. Criminals," he whispered with his usual boyish charm that had its way of softening Victoria's dislike for him. "An Irishman's answer to British toll collectors and certain local smugglers, so I'm told. Clearly, our Lord Chadwick has an affinity for criminals."

She set out for the stable. It was just as well that David treated her like a criminal, someone he could never trust. And she told herself she didn't care.

Yet another lie so easily spoken.

Even to herself.

Chapter 10

"I 'll fetch His Lordship at once, mum." David's stoic butler eyed Victoria's attire, clearly not trusting her alone in the foyer. "If you will await him here."

"Rest assured I won't steal anything," she promised facetiously beneath her breath as he walked up the staircase to the second floor.

Even as she wondered where David had found someone so perfectly persnickety in such a brief time, the balding man disappeared. She glanced nervously at the tall clock in the entryway, the *tick-tick* counting seconds in the silence.

After a moment of restless pacing, she walked into the drawing room and set her cloak on a chair, surprised and a little saddened to see the furniture still draped in ghostly canvas. Dust layered everything. Throwing open the golden damask draperies, she let in the sunlight. Beyond the low stone wall, the white valley below stretched into the old orchard. Victoria traced a finger over the painted red rose stained glass at the top of the door, before wrapping her arms around her torso and turning back into the room.

Rose Briar once contained a beautiful collection of Flemish Mortlake tapestries and paintings. Walking to the middle of the room, she stopped beneath the Venetian chandelier and, making a slow turn, raised her gaze. The ceiling motifs still shone gold, made even brighter in the afternoon sunlight. This wasn't her home, yet it was. For it had become the keystone on which she had built the last nine years of her life.

With a sigh, she looked toward the sound of approaching footsteps.

David walked through the archway, saw her, and stopped. His hands gripped the ends of a towel draped around his neck. His hair, almost black against the white of his linen shirt, was tousled and damp with sweat. He didn't look pleased to see her.

"No apple pie from Esma this time?" he asked.

Victoria pushed her chin up a notch and managed to smile. "Thank you for bringing Bethany back home yesterday."

A dark brow rose slightly. "For some reason, I don't believe that is why you are here. Should I be worried that you're armed?" he asked, looking her up and down.

Her boyish attire revealed more than it hid. He could have been born an aristocrat, she thought then, letting him look. It was in the way he held his head, his uncompromising bearing, and the dark fire in his eyes. Never mind that those eyes had the ability to strip her bare. Easily they could. For they knew what lay beneath her clothing.

She tightened her arms over her chest. "Are you still a priest?"

He gave her an indecipherable look, then something in his eyes softened. "No," he said after a moment.

"Why would you do that, David? Become a priest? When you were so well-trained in the art of seduction, death, and bedlam?"

He cocked a brow in barely veiled amusement. "Why don't you tell me?"

"Guilt?" she queried. "Atonement for your sins? Why not become a faceless champion for the hapless souls who need you?"

"We all have sins to atone for. Do we not?"

"Anyone who goes to so much trouble to find me after nine years must still feel something."

He did not move, but neither did he dispute her conclusions. Just what he felt, she was no longer sure. "Does your job also include hiring your own men? Men who have no connection to the Foreign Office. Isn't that above and beyond the call of your duty to me?"

"I am a man of my word, Meg."

It had suddenly become difficult to look at him. She ran her hand along the back of the settee. The gold wedding ring on her finger captured the daylight surrounding her. "Nellis will attempt to find some way to disclaim your purchase of Rose Briar."

"Have you considered he might have a right to Rose Briar?"

"Sir Henry inherited Rose Briar from his mother, who was Nellis's father's *stepmother*. Nellis holds no blood tie to Rose Briar, hence no claim to the land."

"But then neither do you, love."

The irony did not escape her that she was more mistress of this place now as his wife than she ever was as Lady Munro. "Why haven't you removed any of the coverings on this furniture?" She stripped the canvas sheet away, revealing a worn yellow damask sofa. "How do you expect to make yourself at home in a place filled with ghosts?"

He didn't reply, so she stripped the canvas from both of the high-backed Queen Anne chairs, then others from the chairs beside the glass door. Today she would not allow his barriers anymore than he allowed hers. "You must learn that touching everything is essential to owning a new identity. Once you have staked your claim, it will be harder for someone to recognize the mask for what it is."

For one brief moment, she believed that her words had connected to something inside him. He gripped each end of the towel. "What do you want, Meg?"

Looking at him standing in the doorway, she suddenly knew exactly what she wanted to do and how many times. He was her damnation. Her secret salvation. And everything he made her feel combined to create one more question mark in her future.

"I've just figured out something about you today."

"Only just?" He stepped into the room and shut the double doors behind him. "That is slow for you."

"I want to know why you involved yourself with a case you left years ago. Pamela said you retired shortly after I—"

"Kinley brought me in."

"That's it?"

"That's it, Meg." He drew closer. "No secret motive. No clandestine need to make right the wrongs of the world. I came in to finish something I began over ten years ago."

"Because you thought I was alive."

It was a statement. One he didn't answer.

"Tit for tat, David Donally," she challenged.

He stopped in front of her. Theirs was a familiar dance. One that he knew how to lead with the skill of a master. She couldn't let him. Not this time.

He spoke without touching her. "You mean you'll answer my questions if I answer yours?"

She didn't reply. Instead, she closed the small distance separating them. "Were you in love with me?"

Something dark seemed to veil his eyes. "Is this the part where you try to seduce me in earnest?"

"Do you ever regret not having a family, David?"

"As a matter of fact, I have a very large family."

The thought startled her. "I don't believe you."

"Because I never talked to you about them? Why would I do that? If it appeases your curiosity, I never told them about you, either."

She had never considered that he had another family. Never thought that she might be completely wrong about him. "I can see that I shouldn't have come here today."

"No, you shouldn't have." Lifting a strand of her hair, he tilted his face. "But since we're tit for tat and you're so interested in me personally, don't you want to know more about them?"

More appalled by the memory of the deep marks he'd left on her soul, she wanted only to leave. She tried to move around him, but he stepped in front of her, suddenly seeming dangerous. "My oldest brother is married to an earl's daughter," he said. "My sister is a duchess. My youngest brother holds two seats on the London stock exchange. I have two other brothers and thirteen nieces and nephews. So I ask you"—he'd followed her retreat as if they were dancing a waltz—"what do you have to offer me in return for your future, madam, that I don't yet have? I've already taken your virtue."

"Bastard!" She raised her fist to shove him away, but he caught her wrist. "Why do you insist on ruining everything that I try to do?" The glass door was suddenly behind her.

He clasped both her wrists in one hand above her head and frisked her. "Tit for tat, Meg, remember?" He shoved his knee between her legs and pinned her to the thick glass, immobilizing every inch of her body with his. "A heart-to-heart between a husband and his wife. Isn't that what you want? Unfortunately, I don't want to find myself maimed."

"I didn't bring a gun this time."

She ceased struggling when he found the shiv inside her boot and removed it. "That's what I like about you, Meg. Your dishonesty is predictable."

"You can't keep taking my weapons, David." She followed his hand with her eyes as he stabbed the knife in the paneling high above her head.

She tried to hit him with her other hand, but he caught that one in his grasp as well. "Tit for tat, Meg. Questions first. Before we get on to other things." She met his angry gaze, felt his breath on her lips. "For your sake, I'll begin easy."

"Oh, please." She pushed against the grip on her hands, furious that he had so easily outmaneuvered her. "Why play easy now? When rough is so nice."

To her surprise, he was in no mood to play at all. He just held her, waiting until she stopped fighting. He watched her for a moment, not even breathing hard. "Have you ever killed a man with a knife, Meg? Looked into his eyes as you feel his lifeblood seep away into your hands?" He finished patting her down. "Because that is what you do. It isn't clean and it isn't pretty, and you wear the smell of blood for a long time."

"I know the smell of blood," she said, horrified to feel his knee beneath the vulnerable apex of her thighs, even more horrified by the tenor of his words and what the revelation meant. Had he killed men in his past?

"That morning after the storm, when you decided to follow those tracks from the church, did you get off your horse?" he asked. "Did you meet anyone?"

"I thought the tracks belonged to someone in Stillings's group. I didn't see anyone."

"Why would you go after anyone in Stillings's group?"

She hated the tears that welled in her eyes. "You would never understand."

"Try me, Meg."

She could not move her gaze from his face, from the seductive promise offered in his eyes, the promise of peace and security she longed for. At least a war with Stillings gave her the illusion that she was not powerless. If she could vanquish just one evil, maybe she could vanquish them all. "Not everyone is bad. Sometimes . . . people have a reason for what they do."

"Aye, Meg. Give me a wee violin." He laughed, and it was an honest sound. "I've witnessed firsthand Stillings and his merry men. Or were you referring to yourself?"

"Spoken like a self-righteous puritan," she said between her teeth, mad to think he had an ounce of compassion. Mad to have come here at all.

"I don't need to understand a man's reason for committing a crime to know it is still wrong."

"And here I'd thought you'd gone all soft in the heart, David. Or maybe you care about everything more than you want to admit."

He lowered his voice. "*Soft* isn't exactly how I would describe my state of mind . . . or anything else at the moment."

Leaning his palms against hers on the door, he imprisoned her between his arms. "You're a sham, Meg," he said against her lips. "A bloody born liar. But God help me, at the moment, I don't care."

The smallest sound escaped her as his lips slanted across hers.

She had meant to turn her head—or maybe she didn't—but as soon as his mouth touched hers, she kissed him back, a tempestuous reminder that passion thrived between them. It heated and burned like the hottest fire. Sheer perfection and mind-melding electricity. He slid his fingers into her hair, cradling her nape—and deepening the kiss with a primal sweep of his tongue. She felt like laughing and crying, embarrassingly close to finding release astraddle his knee.

Surely there were worse things than losing this battle.

Then he broke the kiss.

Her mouth wet and swollen, she lifted her gaze and, touching his, saw the darkness within their indigo depths. She could see he was fighting his own losing battle. And in that brief connection, she recognized they were both in the same unholy place.

"Victoria." He said her name as if testing the fit of it on his tongue, his arousal hot against her softness. "Who are you right now?"

She no longer knew and, closing her eyes, no longer cared. She used her freed hands to cup his face and pull his mouth back down to hers, attempting to take him as completely as he'd abandoned himself to her.

Whatever was happening was not what he'd planned, or it was proceeding too fast, she sensed, as she heard him swear under his breath. Then he was kissing her again, hard and deep, one of his hands against her jaw, the other on her breast. He jerked her shirt out of her waistband. This was insane.

"David . . . we . . . should talk—"

Shouldn't they?

"Not bloody likely."

His reply sent a sense of satisfaction coursing through her veins—that familiar and seductive sense of the power Meg Faraday could still wield.

Meg Faraday, that sleepy dark shadow that still clung to her life and refused to go away. Meg taunted and flirted with danger as she'd always flirted with death, and David had so aptly let her out of her cage to play. David, who could also rein her in with merely his presence. She reached up and touched his hair, traced his ears with her thumbs. He didn't pull away when she followed his tongue into his mouth, refusing to grant him room to retreat.

He slid his free hand up the small of her back, over the ribbed stays she wore, and bunched her shirt in his fist. "God rot the bloody thing, Meg." He stripped the thing over her head.

Her bottom hit the small curio table between the glass doors, then he was pressing her hard against the pillow of heavy draperies at her back, and she was pushing against him, seeking more of the growing sensation building inside. This was not what she'd expected to feel. She must have made some sort of noise, because he lifted her and she wrapped her legs around his hips. He was fully aroused and hard against her and she rode him for sheer physical pleasure. Her body wanted him.

Closing her eyes, she gasped, for his mouth was moving from the erotic arch of her throat to the valley between her breasts. Winded, she gripped his shoulders and the corded tendons straining beneath the cloth of his shirt. Then her bare shoulders were pressing into the draperies and he was suckling her nipples through the thin cloth of her camisole, cupping her intimately.

And she began to tremble.

Warmth and musk and a hint of something exotic clung to the fabric of his shirt. She whispered his name, little realizing her feet were touching the ground. And then he was tilting her face with his palms before his mouth again laid claim to her lips. Somewhere in the tempest of her mind that separated her pleasure from his, reason and logic tried to rear their conjoined heads, only to be crushed by the intimacy of David's hands moving inside her pants and sliding them down her hips. Far enough down her legs that he could lift her and with his other hand wrapped around his erection, guided himself between her thighs.

Sin created desire in many forms. The glitter of a diamond in lamplight, the taste of chocolate on strawberries, a gold sovereign. Then there was David, she thought, opening her eyes.

Wrapped within golden damask of the curtains, she felt her voice catch in her chest. He was large. He hurt her, and seemed to know that he did. With what little control he seemed to have left, his dark hair disheveled, his shirt hanging open, he was looking at her with smoldering eyes all but scorching in their intensity.

"Myrrh." She clung to him, adjusting to his size, her senses flooded by the weight of his memory. "I've finally figured out the other scent in your soap. Quince and myrrh."

"My one vice in Ireland that I could not rid myself."

Only one vice? She wanted to laugh. Her breath broke for

a moment, and she closed her eyes as he pushed deeper. "I wish—"

One hand braced against the wall, his thrust filled her completely. "What do you wish?" he whispered in a velvety hush.

Her heart scurried to answer. That she could go back and change the past? That she was anyone but who she was. "The curtains," she rasped, and felt his hand grip the cloth behind her, sending the draperies another few feet to dim the light in the room.

Her eyes held his for a raw moment. His gaze flicked down to her wet mouth. "I confess . . . I have not done this in a long time."

"A long time?" she echoed on a watery laugh, her body adjusting to the hot brand of his, her smile tremulous. But it was a smile, and she'd not felt so alive in so long. She traced her palms across the uncompromising contours of his chest. "It's unfortunate we don't have a bottle of wine to celebrate this moment," she said against his throat.

"I don't need wine."

She felt the defined muscles of his back strain, then his mouth was again upon hers, crushing her lips. His hands splayed wide over her hips and lifted her higher before he leaned into her, his breathing rasping into her ear. "Not when I have you."

David was drowning in the scent of her. Her body consumed him. He could feel the thud of her heart, her breath against his ear. "That's it, Meg." The words were hot against her mouth. "Take me deeper."

She opened her mouth and he caught her cry in a slow, deep kiss. He braced his legs, thrusting unrestrained in his need to possess her. He tried to remember to breathe, but lost in the hot friction from moving inside her, a gasp ground from his throat instead. Even as he held her crushed against him, she held him tighter, panting in his arms, taking his thrusts deeply into her body. He drove into her, all conscious thought lost in his shuddering climax. When he could no longer stand, he sank to his knees with her to the floor, and she was suddenly beneath him tangled in her hair and clothes. He hovered over her braced on his forearms, his hands in her hair, his lips opening against her temple, a sensual shudder going through him.

Meg lay beneath him, her chest rising and falling with every breath. He had taken her still wearing his boots and his trousers. It was a long time before he opened his eyes. Before a sliver of sanity returned to malign his conscience and kick him in the arse. More than years of celibacy had ended here tonight.

Suddenly her mouth drew down at the corners, and he realized she was watching him with steady eyes. "Nothing ever goes the way it should between us, David. Does it?"

Her hair spread around her, lush in the daylight. Hunger undeniable and fierce still burned within him. "Did I hurt you?" The words sounded harsh, even to his own ears.

"Don't feel guilty," she said softly. "I wanted it as well."

"It?" David pushed against his palms.

"A roll, a toss, copulation? Whatever you wish to call what just happened."

"Thank you for putting it in perspective, Mrs. Donally. But I wasn't feeling guilty."

Her beautiful eyes collided with his. "What were you thinking then?"

His gaze eased over her breasts and to the shadow of hair at the damp apex of her thighs where his body joined hers. "I was wondering what one says to an estranged wife—who is no longer quite so estranged."

"Don't think too hard on the matter." She pressed her palms against his chest. "I might want to come back tomorrow and do this again. Longer next time."

Narrowing his eyes, David eased himself almost painfully from her body. He moved onto his back, where he adjusted his trousers, giving his hands and his mind something to do. He was the one still in torment, and he wondered how any woman could have so much power over him, filling his thoughts so completely at every hour day and night, taking such a place in his life that he would champion her to the exclusion of all else. There had never been anyone like her, but she had always been a complication. That fact hadn't changed.

He got to his feet, then pulled her up and helped her dress, because she was making no move to repair herself. "Look at me, Meg."

"I don't want to be Meg." She raised her gaze, and his eyes stared into hers. "But when I'm around you, I can't seem to help it. You bring out the worst in me."

Stuffing his shirt into his trousers, he laughed, almost pulling her into his arms before he realized what a mistake that would be. "You've changed. But not that much. I think you've proved that adequately enough."

She looked up, her eyes liquid bright and filled with hurt. "I really did think those footprints belonged to one of Stillings's men. I want you to believe *me* for once."

Hell, Meg could frustrate him faster than any single person could. He had never bloody intended to get involved with her again. Not in this way. Not when he recognized the dangers, and knew they had no future. When he didn't even trust her not to poison his tea. Certainly not with Colonel Faraday somewhere at his back.

And still, he wanted to touch her, because being with Meg

did something to him inside—as if selling his soul to her once was not enough.

He waited until he had her full attention. "If I put a Bible in your hand, would you swear that you didn't rendezvous with your father?"

She hesitated several seconds, as the question began to sink through the muddle of her thoughts. "You actually think I went out that morning because you believe those tracks belonged to my father and you thought . . . ? After everything you know about him—"

"I don't know. You tell me. There is a Bible in the other room."

It was just like David to trust what anyone would swear on a Bible to be true, no matter the crimes and sins in a person's soul. She started to tell him she would put her hand anywhere he wanted. Before the thought stopped her heart.

The family Bible held the births and deaths of everyone who had ever lived in this house. Nathanial's birth would be recorded there. Was she ready to tell him her deepest secret?

Suddenly, she was terrified for her son all over again, afraid of telling anyone the truth, when there was so much danger around her. For a moment that afternoon in the cellar, she had forgotten that David was part of that danger. She had forgotten who he was and what he wanted. His only purpose to find her father and finish what he had begun years ago.

"Is this where tit for tat ends?" He put his finger to her jaw, and she sensed a strange unsteadiness in his hand. "No more spousal heart-to-heart?"

"Is that what happened between us just now?" Victoria adjusted her boots and swept past David to retrieve her cloak. "I have to go."

He pulled her around, and she faced him with eyes flashing. "The problem with you, Meg, is that you have always known the difference between right and wrong. Yet you choose wrong. Who are you trying to protect with your silence? Your father?"

Her fingers trembled as she tried to disengage his hand. "I don't need insight into my character, or any rousing stiff-upper-lip, God-save-the-queen speech. Obviously some of us don't have your moral clarity. Let me go."

"How hard can it be to choose?"

She yanked her arm from his grasp. "Some people make choices that no one will ever know about."

"Tell me why you are so afraid of your father?"

She walked to the chair where she'd laid her cloak and stopped, hating the wretched memories that came with the helplessness. But she composed herself and spoke of something she had never told another soul.

"When I was a little girl, my father told me my mother hated me and ran away with an artillery officer in the army. Years later, I tried to find her." Her voice faltered.

"What happened to your mother?"

Scraping the hair from her eyes, she looked at David. "I found out that the artillery officer in question had vanished one day shortly after he and my mother had gone away. Months later, his shriveled head had been discovered in his bed, but no body and no blood was ever found in the bungalow." She straightened her shoulders. "I have no doubt my mother committed adultery or that my father believed his act of vengeance was justice. All while he used me to rob people blind. My sire, if God wishes to call him that, is a monster. Don't ever accuse me of siding with him again."

He paused there, looking at her. "Yours was the anonymous tip that led the authorities to him all those years ago. Wasn't it?"

Her heart skipped then thundered. She could not say the word, so deeply buried was her betrayal. She'd spent nine years protecting Nathanial from the threat that one day her father would find them. Except it had been David who found her, and now she was just as afraid, no longer at peace in a life that had given her nine years of happiness.

"I'm not asking for your approval." She folded her arms to keep from touching him.

"You did the right thing with your father." His voice held her gaze, his eyes her heart, and she did not know how to tell him everything else. Only that she should. "I cannot imagine what it must have been like for you growing up as you did," he said.

"You were in Calcutta. You knew what my father had been like. Will you insert yourself into my mind now? Soften me up?" She flicked at the V of his shirt, easily rallying around her anger when he was wont to let her vent now. "Or is this the part where you'll offer a few more minutes of ecstasy in exchange for all the secrets in my soul?"

His eyes lost their expression and grew still. "I am glad that your pleasure and mine still coincide so completely, Meg. Fooking you is the best thing I've done in years."

She gasped. "And that out of the mouth of a former man of God. Maybe you didn't retire." She pointed a finger at him. "Maybe you were run out of Ireland with a stake at your back, your halo shattered when people began to see through your mask."

"Have I touched a nerve?"

Ignoring him, Victoria arranged her hair to one side and

flung the cloak over her shoulders, nearly sweeping a crystal lamp from the table between two winged chairs.

"Someone needs to touch something inside of you. Hell, I don't know." He scraped his fingers through his hair, leaving the ends standing all over the place, then peering at her as if his state of frustration were her fault. "Maybe all we both need is another round at each other. Upstairs in bed. Nothing so miserly as a few minutes between us next time."

"Truly, David. You can be such a bore." She flipped up the hood on the cloak and waltzed past him into the foyer.

This place needed dusting, she realized in some distant portion of her mind as she yanked on her gloves. Retreating in silence, she didn't want to think about this house, any more than she wanted to dwell on David or his hateful accusations. Or wonder how she would ever reconcile her life now to her past.

Her hand pausing at the door, she shut her eyes. "I swear, I have not seen my father in nine years," she said after a moment, her voice muffled by the cloak.

When he didn't reply, she looked over her shoulder and found him leaning negligently against the newel post, his eyes burning with something other than anger. "Beware of dead men and the secrets they hold, Meg," he quietly said, folding his arms. "If you want to live, then I suggest you stay away from cemeteries."

A hot flush stained her cheeks. But if David thought he knew her reasons for going to the cemetery that night, he was wrong. "There are some things in which I am innocent, whether you believe me or not, David." She flung open the door to the late-afternoon chill, the cloak flowing out around her as she hurried down the steps.

Stepping outside onto the porch, David watched her flee,

her head and face hidden by the cloak's hood. Rockwell waited with the cart on the drive, but Meg swept past him.

His mood remained mired in uncertainty, because she was his wife—and he wanted her, despite everything. With her height and her hood shielding her face, no one would have recognized her finer feminine side, hidden beneath the heavy layer of the cloak.

Unfortunately, he knew all too well that ivory perfect flesh, and ached to touch her again. Let her think she was fleeing him.

"Go after her," David said, as Rockwell looked in his direction and shrugged with that now-what look of exasperation that seemed to plague everyone when dealing with Meg. "It's a long walk back to the cottage."

Still standing in the doorway, he was ready to turn, when a flock of blackbirds startled and rose from the fields, swirling like a black funnel cloud against the stark blue sky. His sixth sense kicked into alert just as a rifle report sounded from a distance, like a hunter's shot. An innocent enough sound, but not on his property. He looked toward the church steeple visible above the other buildings.

Rockwell's shout drew David's focus back around. Ian had leaped from the cart and was moving at a dead run to where Meg should have been standing.

Chapter 11

~~GO~~

Victoria struggled to push herself up on her hands, raising her head as Ian knelt beside her. "Jaysus, my lady."

"I'm all right." Her heart thumping wildly, she wiped the back of her hand across her mouth, tasting blood. "I . . . bit my tongue."

"Meg—" David was suddenly kneeling beside her, his breath misting the air. He put his hand on her waist to support her effort to stand, then pulled it back. Blood covered his palm. She felt a stream of warmth soaking her clothes.

She smiled weakly. "You wouldn't by chance have a lump of alum on you to stem the bleeding?"

Two servants came running toward them on the drive. David yelled for them to go back for the cart. "Bring the horses around," he told Rockwell, easing his shoulder beneath hers and helping her to her feet, lifting her. "And get my coat. Now!" he said when the younger man hesitated a heartbeat too long.

"I can walk, David. Find the man who shot that rifle."

"Whoever fired that shot is gone." David carried her to a spot beneath the cover of a tree and lowered her feet. "Or he'd have taken another shot."

"This makes no sense," she said, too angry to feel anything but numbing shock, and shook off his help. "My father wouldn't shoot me . . ."

David opened her shirt at the waist. "The bastard would cut your heart out if you let him, Meg." He gripped the fabric, rending it easily with his bare hands. "I bloody should have killed him years ago."

She watched his hands work to stem the tide of blood. "Vengeance, David?"

Another length of fabric gave way in his hands. "Whoever did this just made the biggest mistake of his life."

Closing her eyes, she schooled her pain into a calm façade.

"You're hit just below the rib." He tied the cloth at her waist, then rose to his feet when he'd finished. "The stays will help with the pain. The bullet didn't pass through the cloak. The wound isn't deep."

She listened to the rhythmic rattle of approaching hooves. "Is the blood dark?"

The ice had thawed from his eyes. "No," he said quietly.

That was good news at least. She started shivering and looked away. The pain helped bludgeon her emotions into an impression of calm. "This must be an accident," she said in a weakened voice. "Someone poaching." *But what if it wasn't?* another part of her questioned. "Someone needs to get to the cottage."

David's arms came around her. "Come here," he whispered, fitting her cheek easily against his shoulder, and just when she thought she would not be affected by his actions, he sundered all her carefully tended illusions in half.

"The cart is almost here," he breathed against her temple.

"I've ruined your warm cloak," she said, shivering. "It's the only wrap I've ever worn that fit my height perfectly."

"I'll buy you a fur-lined one," he said against her hair.

She smiled into his collar. As she spoke the words against his shoulder, she could hear the crunch of gravel as the cart came to a stop. "I thought priests were supposed to give up all their worldly possessions?"

"They are. And I did. But it seems my family kept some of my worldly shares of certain family enterprises locked away in a trust."

"Are you wealthy?"

"Not by any means." His voice rasped in amusement. "But I like expensive soap."

She inhaled the scent of his hair. He was warmth and security, and a hundred memories all wrapped into one. She'd felt this way long ago when he'd taken her into his arms and danced her across the breadth of a glittering ballroom floor. "Do you believe in fate? Everything happens for a reason and all that?"

"Meg . . ."

"I'm glad we had our little . . . discussion today."

David heaved an exaggerated sigh of surrender. "There was nothing little about it."

The comment made her laugh. She flinched against the pain that the movement caused. A few minutes later, David had her loaded into the back of the cart with orders to take her to the house. Ian galloped up on a fine bay mare, holding the reins of David's horse and a greatcoat in his other hand.

"I'll be back as soon as I can." Shoving his hands into his coat sleeves, David spoke to another man standing with the driver, one of his people that he'd brought from Ireland.

"Make a perimeter check. Keep everyone inside for now."

"David?"

He looked down over the side of the cart at Meg. "Shh." He placed a finger against her lips and walked beside the cart as it started to move. "We'll discuss anything you want when I get back."

"I need you to make sure Nathanial is safe."

"I'm sure he's safe, Meg."

"You cannot know that for sure."

"Sir—" Rockwell said from behind him, "someone needs to fetch Sir Henry."

"We'll get her inside the house, sir," the driver said.

Standing in the drive, David watched the cart move away.

He had promised he could protect her and her family. But he didn't have men to send to watch over Sir Henry's grandson, nor did he believe the boy was in any danger.

Stepping into the stirrup, David mounted his horse. He held the high-prancing stallion in check as he looked over his shoulder at Rockwell. "Go to the churchyard. That shot was fired from there."

"Deer overrun these bluffs. Maybe it was an accident."

"Think about it." David's gaze went to the remote church steeple. "To hit anything at all from the distance that shot was fired, the shooter would have had to have been high off the ground. A tree? A belfry maybe?" The horse pranced sideways. "Blakely is staying at Doyle's cottage. Get over there and find out what he might have seen."

Back at Sir Henry's cottage, David dismounted and, glancing around the empty yard, jogged up the back steps. He opened the door into the kitchen. Esma Shelby and Bethany were standing inside, and he saw them as he ducked out of the mudroom.

"My lord, 'tis you." Esma's hands crushed the skirt of her apron. "Sir Henry heard a gunshot. He went to the fields with my husband. Sometimes there be poachers about. He was angry that someone would be shooting so near to people in their homes." She dabbed her eyes with the corner of her apron. "But what if it be Tommy Stillings, my lord. That blackguard doesn't hold the same favor toward Sir Henry as he does Her Ladyship."

"I'll find Sir Henry and send your husband back," David assured her, knowing he had no time to smooth away her fears. He looked at Bethany. "But right now, I need you to go upstairs and pack a change of clothing for Lady Munro."

The girl's eyes widened. "But why?"

"Just do it, Bethany," he said. "I don't have time to explain." As he returned his attention to Mrs. Shelby, his tone became softer. "Show me where Sir Henry keeps his medical bag."

She led him to Sir Henry's chambers in the back of the cottage. A few minutes later, David uncovered the physician's bag beneath a quilt someone had thrown atop a chair.

"Everything else be back in the surgery, my lord." She pushed aside the folding panels connecting to yet another room, then set a sulphur match to the lamp. "He sees his patients here. Since his illness, he has not traveled so much anymore."

Medical books filled one entire cabinet, some penned by Sir Henry Munro himself, David realized as he looked in the case next to him. Bound by a thick ornate frame, Sir Henry's royal commission in the navy hung on the wall next to a medical degree. He'd taught at a medical university in London.

"Check on Bethany," David said over his shoulder.

Vials and jars lined glass shelves stretching across one

wall; boxes, canisters, and bandages filled yet another. He walked to the cabinet and shoved accoutrements into the bag. Nearly three dozen miniature photographs and daguerreotypes lined the top of the cabinets and followed the shelves along the back wall to the heavy mantel over the fireplace. Too many faces to be family.

The rattle of a cart sounded from outside. David peered out the window. Esma's husband had ridden into the drive. He was alone. When David turned from the window, he knocked a pair of photographs from the desk. One shattered on the planked floor.

Caught by the image of Meg, he picked up the frame, shaking away the shards of broken glass and dropping them into the refuse can. He held the image in the sunlight. He recognized Bethany wearing a ruffled frock, no older than twelve, and Sir Henry standing beside her. A dark-haired boy dressed in black velveteen short trousers and black-buckle shoes sat on Meg's lap. He tilted the photograph, caught by something he could not explain.

"My lord." Esma bustled into the room, flushed and breathless. "My husband has just returned. Sir Henry is at Rose Briar. He sent my husband back for his medical bag—"

"How long ago was this likeness taken?"

Mrs. Shelby glanced down at the image in David's hand, too shaken to enlighten David about dates. "I don't know, my lord." She twisted her hands in her apron. "Some years ago. Please, my lord. Sir Henry is waiting for his bag."

David shoved the photograph into his coat pocket.

"Swallow the medicine, Victoria."

Warm licorice passed between her lips. She drank.

She didn't remember much after Sir Henry cauterized the

wound. Only the voices. She drifted away again and became lost in a fog of pain and frightful dreams. Dreams that involved Nathanial. She searched for her son and, with a mother's instinct, knew he was in danger. She called David's name.

Someone came to her side, but it wasn't David.

Later, she remembered a young girl helping her with her private ablutions and eating soup. She awoke again at daybreak with streamers of sunlight squeezing through the cracks in the curtains. Sir Henry was sitting beside the bed, an unlit pipe between his lips, his blue eyes bereft of his usual good humor. Confused by his presence, she faced him with a thudding ache in her head.

"He's been up here twice asking about you," Sir Henry said.

In the firelight, her sight touched the familiar bed frame, the tiered yellow and lavender fabric draping in swathes from the canopy. She was wearing a clean nightgown. Her entire body felt as if she'd been shoved through a meat grinder. She found the simplest movement brought pain and with it a renewed sense of urgency as she realized she had not been having some awful nightmare.

Someone had shot her. Why?

"How long have I been asleep?" Her words came out sluggish as she tried to coordinate her mind and her tongue.

"Most of two days." The crinkles around his eyes deepened.

He had kept her sedated; that was why she felt so sluggish and incapable of thought. She tried to prop herself on her elbow. Sir Henry was suddenly beside her, his black jacket rumpled, and his expression determined in the light. He held a syringe in his hand. Liquid spurted from the tip of the needle.

"Don't you dare give me that stuff again, Sir Henry—"

He showed not the least inclination to obey her. "I've cauterized that wound and I'll not have you tear the flesh. Let the poultice work or you'll be facing sepsis."

"You're a bully," she whispered, knowing he was right.

"And you're a poor patient," he countered, equally resolved to see her bedridden, and gave her the shot.

"No worse than you," she argued. In a test of wills, Sir Henry would win. She lay back on her pillow. "Where is David?"

"Lord Chadwick went to pay a visit to Mr. Doyle yesterday." He set the syringe on the night table next to a vial of carbolic powder and picked up his pipe. "He hasn't returned." He folded his lanky form onto a chair beside the bed. "Do you want to tell me how you really know Chadwick? You asked for him in your sleep, Victoria."

She tugged the down comforter to her neck. Unable to look Sir Henry in the eyes, she turned her head. "I knew him in Calcutta."

"I thought so. If I were a gambling man, I'd wager you two know one another well."

Sir Henry's voice became distant as she began to drift away again. *Of course I did,* a whispery voice answered in her head.

I was in love with him.

That revelation engendered nothing new to her battered heart. Indeed, she had always loved him. They had made a child, the one good thing they had done together. David could protect Nathanial. Even as she recognized David could never be hers, she needed him. He was capable of giving her son a future when she was not. She recognized that now.

In her drugged and veiled state, she felt Sir Henry gazing down at her, perplexed for reasons he could not name, and worried for reasons he could probably name well enough if he set his mind to it. But someone had shot her, and she needed answers that only she could get. She had to get to the cemetery. She had to know the truth.

David returned to the churchyard well past the time he should have heeded the chill and found shelter. He had ridden the last few hours over a frozen landscape. Now, stomping the cold from his feet, he tied Old Boy's reins to the fence and followed the glow of lantern light. No moon rousted the shadows tonight, but lay well-hidden behind heavy clouds. Snow fluttered in the air as if the weather had suddenly grown timid.

Watching the disembodied glow of lamps move through the decaying skeletal structure, David could understand why Mr. Doyle believed in ghosts. He pulled himself up through an opening and stood transfixed by the destruction surrounding him.

Fire had gutted the church one long ago day. Wooden benches sat askew against the opposite wall. The room stank of rotten timbers and animal offal, a strange juxtaposition to the downy white snowflakes floating around him.

". . . people don't bloody sprout wings and fly." David heard the voices, and maneuvered through the debris toward the rectory.

"I'm not sayin' the shot didn't come from the church, Mr. Rockwell. I'm sayin' if someone was in that belfry, he did not leave by way of any door or window."

"We're not dealing with ghosts," David said from the doorway, despite Mr. Doyle's claim that spirits haunted the church. "There is another way inside this structure."

Eight men stood in the rubble. David looked at each of them before turning his focus on the mountain of a man standing amidst the group. Ralph Blakely, a longtime Glenealy,

Ireland resident, was David's sometime bodyguard, hailing from the days David first went to work in the shantytowns near Dublin's ports seven years ago. Blakely was one of the few men he'd ever met who was as tall as he was.

David moved away from the stone wall and shifted his focus. This church looked to have been built around Cromwell's era—a time of great political upheaval. Any priest knew a room such as this held a passage that would take him to safety in case of incursions, and he should have considered that possibility weeks ago when he'd realized the extent of the lucrative smuggling commerce that fed too many of the people around here.

He looked at Blakely. "Find the vicar who used to work and live on these grounds."

"Did Doyle have anything to say?" Rockwell asked.

"Whoever he's been watching in this church has been here for weeks."

"Weeks?"

"Two of Sheriff Stillings's men were found dead two weeks ago near the old drover's trail. Go down there and look around."

David stayed another hour before mounting Old Boy and taking the back trail to Rose Briar. After his initial visit to Meg yesterday, he'd remained at Doyle's cottage. Now with another night upon him, he had not found a single piece of evidence that could point to a particular shooter. That, and the fact that someone would intentionally shoot Meg, who might or might not be the key to locating a stolen treasure, made no sense. The only thing that bothered him more was the fact that she had been wearing *his* cloak.

In addition, everything about his current state of emotions vexed him as he continued to refine his feelings toward his

wife. No longer abstract, they had formed a permanent con-
crete seal in his thoughts, preventing reason from finding its
way back into his head. He was no longer coming at the case
as an investigator but as a husband—an impossible circumstance, he realized, especially when he was detailed with the
job of turning her over to Kinley.

Snowflakes floated through the amber light cast by the
lantern behind him as he rode into the stable and paddock.
He did not intend to keep this property, but he had ensured
the sanctity of his agreement with Meg by purchasing Rose
Briar himself and putting everything in his name. But as
David handed Old Boy's reins to the groom, he turned up the
collar on his coat and looked toward the house, a proprietary
sense of ownership touching him. Meg's bedroom faced the
orangery. He could not see her window, but he felt her presence and recognized that he was thinking about more than
just the land and this house. Everything from here to Alfriston belonged to him—including Meg.

How did a man throw something like that away?

Twice.

A young chambermaid had just shut the door to Meg's
room when he appeared. David recognized her as one of the
girls Blakely brought with him from Ireland. She held a
wicker tray topped with blood-soaked rags. "My lord. I
didn't see you."

His gaze on the door, David removed his gloves and
stuffed them in his coat pocket. "Is she conscious?"

"Oh, yes. Sir Henry asked me to bring her tea." The chambermaid hurried away.

Sir Henry stepped out of the bedchamber, closing the door
behind him as he saw David. "You're back," he said and,
without preamble or temperance, handed David the spot of

lead in his hand. "I forgot to give this to you yesterday. Whoever shot her was not hunting game, unless one uses an Enfield rifle," Sir Henry said. "Old issue."

His heart turning over in his chest, David closed his fist over the mini ball and considered the implication that a military-trained sharpshooter or assassin had fired the shot that took Meg down.

"Do you know anything about caves in this bluff?" he asked.

"They've been sealed for fifty years. Before I came to Rose Briar. I couldn't begin to tell you what manner of fool would go inside the caverns as dangerous as they are."

"Someone must know something. Someone familiar with this area."

"Then maybe you know more than I do and can explain who would shoot Victoria," Sir Henry said as David stepped around him to enter the room.

Remembering her brazen confrontation with Stillings, David used all his self-control to keep from naming off the first dozen names that popped to mind. "This place isn't exactly a haven of morality, Sir Henry."

"I'm not obtuse. I know the manner of men who ride these roads." Sir Henry set his leather physician's bag on the curiosity table beside the door and clipped shut the lock. "They are a useless lot. But Victoria has gone in the middle of the night to sew up their wounds. She has helped birth babies those men have fathered. Nursed their sick wives and sisters. No man-jack in this area would shoot her down as if she were an animal. Now she's worried that whoever did this will go after her son."

David let his hand slide from the door latch. "What are you talking about?"

"You tell me, Chadwick. At first, I thought you were here

because you were related to her and genuinely wanted to help. But there is more to you than meets the eye. More to the both of you. A blind man would see it, it's that glaring."

"You need to speak about this to her—"

"I *have* been speaking to her. For two nights, young man. Morphine is an unwelcome bedfellow for those with secrets. She knew you in Calcutta, which explains a lot. She was in trouble there."

Sir Henry pulled out a handkerchief and dabbed his upper lip. "Victoria has worked hard to teach Nathanial values and to respect the land he was supposed to have one day inherited. She sent him to Bethany's cousins so he can take part in the hops harvesting. But this year she kept him from returning home. I thought at first it was because of Nellis. I am now prone to believe that it is for an entirely different reason. Why is she so afraid of you? Why has she been waking up to nightmares for weeks? Now this."

"Hell, I don't know," David said, wary of Sir Henry's observations. "Why don't you tell me?"

"Because you are connected to the same people she fears will go after her son."

Before David could respond, a noise in the corridor dragged his gaze toward the stairway. Rockwell appeared on the landing, his cloak sweeping around him as he stopped, his presence snapping the tension like a tautly wound string.

No longer chafing beneath the older man's verbal flagellation, David shoved his hand into his coat pocket and felt the photograph he had put there when at the cottage.

"I take it that man is no ordinary servant, either?" Sir Henry said, coughing into his handkerchief.

"He works for me," David said.

"I see." Glancing between David and Ian, Sir Henry took a step backward, almost self-consciously as he stuffed the handkerchief back into his pocket. "Then if you'll excuse me, I will leave the two of you alone with your business."

"Sir Henry?" David stopped the older man. "How old is Nathanial?"

Sir Henry stopped in his tracks. And turned. "Why don't you ask her?"

A momentous silence rocked David.

Mumbling something about having tea brought up, Sir Henry whirled on his heel. Rockwell stood aside as the man hurried past him in the corridor. When David still had not moved, Rockwell gave him his full attention.

"What just happened?"

David swept past him. "I'm not sure."

Descending the stairs, he led Rockwell to the bookroom, as far away as he could go from Meg's chambers. He didn't light any lamps.

"How is Lady Munro?" Rockwell asked.

"Alive."

Without removing his coat, David walked to the window. He had not shaved in two days, and his reflection bore the hint of a man who had not slept.

Rockwell's voice hesitated. "How alive?"

David met the younger man's gaze in the glass. "Thank you for that bit of confidence. I haven't murdered her if that is what concerns you, though I don't know why it should. Did you find anything on the drover's trail?"

"No one has been on that trail for days."

"Then why aren't you at the cottage?"

"Pamela wasn't at the town house last night. I'm concerned. I should try to find her."

David shook his head. "Her absence isn't abnormal."

"Perhaps not, but that doesn't mean—"

"Dammit, Rockwell." David said flatly, then cut off the rest of the sentence. "You knew what your job would be like before you married her. She would not appreciate your interference in whatever she is currently doing. Would she?"

Rockwell's jaw tightened, but he said no more. The very mercenary trait that had once made David faultless at his job made Pamela a valuable commodity in the realm of British espionage. He recognized the attribute and, as he looked out onto an ice-encrusted, picture-perfect world, he knew a part of that man still thrived inside him—he felt it now—its dark presence lurking like a shadow just beneath the surface.

After a moment, he looked away from the window, knowing he had no right to lose his temper with Rockwell. "I'll find Pamela tonight myself and have her send a message to Kinley. I'll check on her," he said.

"Is there anything else before I go, sir?"

If there had been, David had forgotten and, for a long time after Rockwell left, he stood at the window. The snow had stopped and moonlight fell in a crisscross pattern over the polished floor.

Finally, he withdrew the photograph.

Moving the image into the narrow beam of light, he studied the impression, peering at the child's face.

His jaw clenched, and it was a labor to remember to breathe as he moved the image back and forth in the light. If Scott Munro had died in India, the child was too young to be Meg's stepson.

The chambermaid he'd met upstairs appeared in the doorway. "My lord, I can light a fire. This room is chilled."

David looked dispassionately at the fireplace, the rich paneled walls and ornate bookcases, and felt only the heat of a fast-growing anger. "No thank you," he replied after a moment. "If I want a fire, I'll build one myself."

"Yes, my lord."

His gaze paused on a rostrum. David had seen the Bible on that stand the first day upon his arrival. The Munro family Bible.

The one Meg didn't want to place her hand upon and swear an oath of honesty to him.

He found a tinderbox in the desk drawer and lit the oil lamp beside the globe. David brought the book to the desk. He flipped the ornate cover open and peeled back page after page until he found the birth listings. He ran his finger down the long list of names and stopped when he recognized Meg's handwriting.

Nathanial's date of birth was the last entry. Born May 14, 1864, five months after Meg disappeared from Calcutta.

David's body went icy cold.

Five months.

Bracing both palms on the desk, he closed his eyes.

Five bloody months. While he'd mourned her.

And returned to Ireland to take up the cloth, she'd given birth to his son.

He'd been a father for nine years.

"A man would have to be blind not to see the resemblance between you and my grandson," Sir Henry said from the darkness behind him. "I thought you knew."

His palms still braced on the stand, David glared at the ceiling and mentally cursed Meg's lying, treacherous heart. Anger began to roll off him in a crescendo of comprehension. She would have let him leave here never knowing the truth.

"Victoria was just a lass, not even twenty when she showed up on my doorstep heavy with child and nothing but a gangly cat to her name," Sir Henry said.

In no mood for benevolence, he faced Sir Henry. "As much as I'm sure this story—"

"That woman upstairs is a daughter to me. If my son married her for whatever reason . . . then he must have loved her very much."

"Don't count on that."

"Victoria is the only mother Bethany has ever known," Sir Henry said from the shadows behind the settee. "I love her as if she were my own blood. I love that boy. If they are in trouble—"

"Trouble?" David spoke, furious.

Sir Henry moved nearer, an old man hunched with age and, for just a moment, David felt sorry for him. "Whatever she's done in the past, she's made a good life for herself and her son."

"She has no bloody life," David said, his growing wrath unchecked, even when he saw the man flinch. "And she's in trouble. Buried in it up to her neck."

Unable to stomach his own emotions, David stepped around the settee, his long stride carrying him toward the door.

"I don't know who you are, Chadwick," Sir Henry said from the darkness behind him, "if that is really your name. But whatever happened to her . . . whatever she was running from all those years ago, Nathanial was born a Munro. He legally belongs to my family."

"You're mistaken, Sir Henry. He belongs to me."

Chapter 12

When David stepped into Meg's room, he knew immediately that she had fled. He stood in the doorway, staring at the bed frame and the rumpled feather tick. He strode to the dressing room. Her nightgown lay crumpled on the floor. The clothes he'd brought for her and his heavy cloak were gone.

"Little fool!" he mumbled.

He left the room and collided with the chambermaid carrying an armful of linens. "When was the last time someone checked on Lady Munro?" he asked her.

"An hour ago, my lord." She dipped her head. "I brought her tea and biscuits at Sir Henry's request."

"Was she in bed?"

"Yes, my lord. She told me she wanted to sleep."

David descended the stairs three at a time. How far could she go in her condition? The chilly night air was as brisk as a slap to his face and stopped him on the stone steps outside.

161

Retrieving his gloves from his pocket, he looked toward the drive. The snow had stopped, and the moon was a bright orb in the sky, clinging to the naked treetops and reflecting across the landscape like fine crystal. At first, he saw no tracks in the snow small enough to belong to Meg. Then some sixth sense made him walk up the drive. His boots squeaked in the hushed silence. Finally, he stopped, tamped down a grip of fear, and let his anger rule him instead. Switching directions, he returned to the stable and his horse.

Once mounted, David picked up her trail in the woods just off the drive. Her prints continued north toward the church. Twisting around in the saddle to look at the house, he frowned over his shoulder. She must have gone through the servants' passageways and left from the back of the house to have escaped unnoticed.

David nudged the horse off the drive and followed the lone set of tracks, bending low as he weaved through the trees. Something kept niggling at his thoughts.

Remembering the other female prints he'd seen a few weeks back, he finally slid from the horse and squatted beside the path. Meg's footprints had not been those in the clearing he'd seen after the storm—that much was patent by the length of these prints and width of her stride. Meg was taller.

Bracing an elbow on one knee, David looked down the path at her footprints in the snow. A frown touching his brow, he realized she was heading to the cemetery.

Her cloak spilling around her, Victoria scraped the snow from beneath the tall granite stone belonging to Sir Scott Munro, Sir Henry's beloved son. She clawed at the frozen earth until, frustrated, she sat back on her ankles, and waited for the wound in her side to quit burning. Being here felt sacrilegious. Wrong. She had never been afraid of this place, but as she looked upon the lifeless burned-out church, she felt fear.

Victoria picked up a rock and began chipping away at the space of hardened earth where she knelt. Tears filled her eyes. Her father would never have tried to shoot her. Not when there was something valuable he wanted—that he knew she had. Not when vengeance could be exacted in so many other ways.

Somewhere, a horse whickered. Heart racing, she froze and listened to the night. She wiped the back of her hand across her cheek and startled.

A fierce figure in black stood a few feet from where she sat. David. His horse was tied to the iron rail that caged the cemetery. In a night so quiet she could hear the hush of snow falling from trees, she didn't know how had he had entered the cemetery and come upon her.

"Go ahead, Meg. Dig."

She stared at him with something of her old defiance. "I had hoped to be back before you found me. This isn't what you think."

"Tell me what I should bloody think. When everything between us has always been a lie."

Movement behind him grabbed her attention. A bear of a man ambled beneath the iron archway leading into the cemetery. She looked back at David who didn't seem concerned. He peered into her face. "Tell me, Meg."

He might be an adherent of moral right, but in this, they were on the same side. Forcing away her dizziness and her uncertainty, she returned her attention to the headstone. She leaned forward and wiped the last of the wet leaves and snow from the base of the stone. The effort was stealing her strength. The morphine Sir Henry had given her might have dulled the pain, but it did not shield her from exhaustion or the frigid cold. Worse, it did not protect her from David's furious presence.

She slid aside the marble piece that usually held flowers. Beneath the stone lay a rusted tin she'd placed there almost a decade ago. The one that held her half of the pair of earrings that had been recovered from a London pawnbroker.

"It's still here," she whispered, so sure it would be gone. She removed the tin. For a moment, all she could do was stare in disbelief. "I thought . . ."

David took the metal box and withdrew the velvet pouch.

"I buried it years ago." She drew in a breath and winced at the pain. "I needed to know if the earring in your possession had really come from my father, and that someone hadn't found this one. I needed to know for sure if my father was dead or alive."

"This proves nothing in that regard," he said.

With effort, Victoria looked up at him. David's eyes held an icy chill she had not recognized before. "This is what you were after that night I found you?" He stood beside the mound tall and angry, his eyes challenging. Something else was wrong with him, she realized. Something terrible.

He hunkered down beside her as she returned the marble to its proper place in front of the headstone. His heavy coat spilled around his boots and his eyes even with hers seemed capable of piercing her innermost secrets. "This is valuable enough to have paid more than the taxes on Rose Briar for years. Why didn't you use it?"

She bowed her head, realizing he thought she was saving it for a night like tonight, for a time when she needed to run. He would never understand that in her mind as long as that earring remained hidden, she remained free.

"You were wearing my cloak," he said. "Have you considered that whoever fired that rifle may not have been shooting at you? That maybe I was the intended target?"

She raised her fist to her chest. "You?"

"Why wasn't Sir Scott's body on the same steamer out of Bombay as you were?"

"I stayed behind another week because his wife became ill. The captain would not allow her to board."

"You took a chance on capture."

Pressing her palms on her thighs, she started to shiver. The hood shielded her face. "We'd ridden the train together from Calcutta. She knew I was . . . not well, and had been kind. I couldn't abandon her when she later became sick."

"But then playing lady's maid was just another convenient role for you."

Knowing he was right, for that was exactly what she'd done, she met his gaze with determination. "There *is* no treasure hidden here. That treasure left India long before I did."

His heavily lashed lids narrowed slightly. "You're bleeding, Meg," he said abruptly, but not harshly.

She was not frozen by his tone, but by his lack of emotion. She looked down at her side and saw blood had seeped through the bandage and stained her bodice. She could barely walk before. She knew she would not be able to stand without help now.

David was suddenly pulling her to her feet before she felt herself lifted into his arms. If it meant she had abandoned all pride, she didn't care. Too weak to argue, she laid her head against his shoulder and listened as he spoke to the man waiting for him at the gate.

"Your guard?" she asked when David put her on his horse.

He stepped into the stirrup and settled behind her. His horse breathed a cloud of steam. Reaching around her, David gathered the reins with one gloved hand and wrapped his other arm protectively around her, careful to avoid her waist. Heat from his body wrapped her in warmth. "His name is Ralph Blakely," he said, turning the horse toward the path. "He doesn't answer to anyone but me."

Clenching her jaw against Old Boy's jerky movements, she didn't understand David's quiet fury. David slowed the horse to a more bearable pace. "This ride isn't going to be comfortable no matter what," he said.

"I'm all right, David."

"Of course you are. The blood on your bodice is a prime example of your sterling health. And the brain in your head your wit. You could have waited until tomorrow to come here."

"Do you really think that you may have been the target?" she asked, leaning her head against his shoulder.

"At this point, I believe anything is possible. You yourself have proven that."

They rode in silence to the cottage.

"Why are you bringing me back here?"

Without answering, David slid to the ground and helped her down. One lamp burned in the kitchen, which meant Rockwell was making his perimeter check around the property before retiring to the cot in the pantry. She stumbled and, without breaking pace, David lifted her into his arms, conveying her up the stairs with a sure and steady grace that spoke of his strength. She raised her arms to loop around his neck.

David shouldered open the door to her room. With three long strides, he set her on her feet beside her bed and unfastened her cloak. Bright moonlight spilled through the parted curtains and washed his face in shadows.

"Where will you be staying tonight?" she asked.

He removed her cloak and tucked it beneath his arm. "I assure you it won't be here."

Her mind in confusion, her reserve fled. "David—?"

"Keep the earring." Something plopped against the comforter. He'd thrown the velvet pouch on her bed. "You've earned it for being the preeminent liar of my lifetime."

Still carrying the cloak, he strode across the room, his footsteps soundless on the red rope carpet. He'd reached the doorway before Victoria finally regained her voice.

"What is wrong with you? I've done nothing wrong here."

He turned and found her shivering where he'd left her standing. "Sir Henry knows, Meg."

"He knows what?" she asked, her voice quiet in the hushed silence of the house.

"That Nathanial is my son."

Her hand went to the polished iron bedstead. "Wait."

But he had already stepped out of her room. She stumbled to the hallway and saw David open Nathanial's door. Her heart raced, and she suddenly felt sick.

David knew.

Somehow, he'd learned the truth.

"I would have told you," she whispered.

His head came around. He walked back to her and, despite her desire to stand tall in the face of his accusing eyes, she could not. "You kept him from me. I will never forgive you for that. Ever. You want to chafe against caring for your own health or run away so badly, go ahead. Ye can go to hell, Meg, and I won't lift another bloody finger to stop you."

"You don't understand." She braced a hand against the

wall. "How could you after everything you did?"

"Everything I did?" He raised his voice. "What part of your life in Calcutta do you not remember? You were a thief stealing gold and jewels as easily as you stole state secrets. A member of the Circle of Nine—"

"We were married for three months. What did you think could happen? Yet, in your mind, I was still expendable." Tears burned her eyes. "How dare you think you have any rights at all."

"How dare I?" He advanced on her, a dark menacing figure in black. "I have a son, Meg."

"What are you going to do?" She lifted her chin, and the seedling of rage inside took root as he walked past her.

"I'm going after my son."

"You can't . . . He doesn't know who you are."

David turned on his heel and backtracked three furious steps until he stood toe to toe with her. "Of course he doesn't know me. You made sure of that, didn't you? But he has a right to know that he has a father. A real living, breathing father, not some fooking lie that you invented to save your own bloody skin—"

"You hypocrite!" She shoved him with more strength than she thought possible and, caught by the force, he stumbled backward. Nine years ago, she had learned why he had married her. All those nights she'd spent in his arms laughing and dreaming of a future that would never be hers, believing he'd loved her. She had been nothing but a job to him.

"Whose lie was worse? Mine because I chose to fight for my life and that of the child I carried, or yours because you surrendered your soul to queen and country, like some scheming Lothario knowing that everything you did with me was a sham. Do not preach to me about lies, when you committed the worst lie of all." She slammed her fists against his chest, but he caught and held her hands immobile. "If there's any forgiveness to be had between us, you should be on your knees seeking mine. You have no heart!"

She felt the hard muscles of his body tense against hers. "Do not believe you ever knew my heart."

But she was finished with civility. Finished blaming herself for all the mistakes in her past. For falling in love with a bastard using some higher agenda as an excuse to bed her. "Your precious superiors condemned me to the gallows ere there was a tribunal. My father set his cronies on my trail for betraying him. I did the only thing I could. I ran. I survived. I made a life for my son and myself."

"You're tearing your wound."

He let her go and she stumbled backward, gasping for breath. "I could have killed you that day. But I didn't!"

His eyes blazing, he suddenly turned his head. Victoria faltered. He was looking at Bethany standing in the hallway, her hand clutched to her wrapper, tears shining in her eyes. "Victoria?" the girl whispered, her pale hair visible in the darkness.

"Go back to bed, Bethany." David bent and retrieved the cloak he'd dropped. "It's all right."

Tears in her eyes, Victoria turned the force of her attention back to her husband. Of course, it wasn't all right. But Bethany obeyed, and Victoria heard the door click shut. "Don't presume that your high-handed orders carry any authority in this house, David."

"I bloody *own* this house, Meg."

Rooted to the floor, Victoria watched in shock as he turned away. "Nathanial knows Mr. Shelby," he said over his shoulder. "I will take him with me to Salehurst. So you needn't worry that I will have to kidnap my son."

"Then what?" she asked in a shaky voice.

He stopped on the stairway landing, his gloved hand resting on the banister, her pride and soul bared by his gaze. "I haven't decided."

Then he was gone, and somewhere a door slammed downstairs. A deathly quiet descended over the cottage. She'd never felt more alone. Or lost. Or frightened. Her breath caught. She turned into her room and, heedless of the cold and her blood-stained clothes, dropped to her bed, anger returning to her some measure of calm. She listened to the sound of horse's hooves riding away.

"Victoria?" A slim arm came around her shoulders, and suddenly Bethany was holding her tightly. "It will be all right."

The gentleness was too much. It was as if her lungs ceased to breathe, and when she finally gasped, she could not hold back the tide of tears. They flooded down her cheeks, then became a deluge. "I'm so sorry."

And as Victoria turned her face into her pillow, she knew nothing would ever be all right again.

David raised a pitcher of water over his head and poured. The icy shock jolted his whole body, but still he poured, raising his face as he rinsed the last of the soap from his hair. He stood in a hip tub, caring little that he had not ordered the water heated before he'd bathed.

He set the pitcher on the commode and leaned his palms against the countertop. His muddy boots stood beside the tub. Buttons lay scattered over the floor where he'd torn his blood-imprinted shirt off his back and stripped away his trousers. He had not wanted to return to Rose Briar and instead came to the town house. Hell, he'd have ridden through the night straight to Salehurst if he'd thought he wouldn't kill his horse.

Movement in the doorway turned his head. Pamela stood next to the silk screen watching him. Her gown was a deep crimson with a full sweeping skirt and low décolletage trimmed with creamy lace. Tendrils of her blond hair curled around her shoulders.

He felt the glide of her eyes, and if his reaction was anything less than any other male's, she didn't appear shocked. "Your dressing room door was open," she said.

David stepped out of the hip tub, sloshing water to the floor. "The door wasn't open."

"It was unlocked." Her gaze shot back to his as he walked toward her. "I had a key?" She dangled a metal object in her hand.

"Convenient." David snatched the key from her hand.

"For your information I knocked," she said, as he reached over her shoulder and yanked the robe he'd draped across the screen. "You weren't answering the door. I was worried. Especially after everything that has happened. I wasn't expecting you to be here."

David slid on his robe. "Where have you been since yesterday?"

"Is there a rule that requires me to spend the night here?"

"Don't even ask me to begin to understand that answer. Ian was worried about you. I told him I would check in on you."

"The local magistrate is here," she said, folding her arms. "He's asking questions about you. I believe he is on his way to London with the intent to find evidence that will declare you a fraud. Especially after he was refused admittance to Rose Briar an hour ago. Something about your orders?"

He belted the tie around his waist. "Is that all?"

"Do you want more?" Flashing him a smile that was part coquette and part street doxy, she nodded to the tiny bite mark on his neck. "Though I see someone has already been inside your clothes."

His eyes hard, he trapped her gaze. Despite everything she projected, he knew some of it was an act. He just never knew for sure which part. "Do you fancy yourself the whore, Pamela? Or are you so used to the part you play that you no longer know the difference?"

David stepped past her into his room. She leaned a shoulder against the doorway as he passed. "Even after all of your reassurances to Ian and me, you're still in love with her, aren't you?"

His hand shaking slightly, he withdrew a crystal decanter of whiskey from the sideboard, as if alcohol could burn away his thoughts. "Love has nothing to do with what is between Meg and me."

"Then you're in lust. For most men, I'd say there is no difference. But not you." She approached in a whisper of crimson silk. "Have you considered she's not the same woman she used to be?"

"People don't change that much."

"You did." She flicked a long scarlet nail at his robe. "You once had no qualms about killing a man in cold blood. From what I understand, yours was the shot that took out the treacherous grandson of the Prussian archduke in Munich. How many years ago? Thirteen? Fourteen? What a scandal you caused in the international community," she prodded sweetly. "The identity of that assassin still remains a secret."

David didn't question how she would know that manner of confidential information. "Obviously not."

"If there was any job dark and dirty to be done, they called you. How old would you have been when you fired that shot?"

He'd been twenty-two when he'd pulled that trigger and ended the conspiracy to assassinate the queen. Twenty-four by the time his reputation made him one the most sought after agents in the service. Twenty-six when he met Margaret Faraday.

He'd seen her the first time on a polo field at the British consulate in Calcutta. The beginning of the end to his way of life.

His sin and his salvation.

His curse.

"I'll be away for a week or so." He sloshed whiskey into a glass. "Maybe longer."

"Now? You're leaving now?"

"I have personal business to attend." Without offering her a glass, David peered at her over the rim as he drank. "You're our liaison with Kinley. While I'm gone, I want you to find out where Faraday has been living for the past nine years, who was paying the cost and how many of his former cronies are still alive."

"Why?"

"Oh, I don't know, Pamela," he said facetiously, aware of his sarcasm and the mood driving at him. He was impatient to be on the road. "Maybe it has something to do with the fact that someone may have tried to kill me and shot Faraday's daughter instead."

"What makes you think you might have been the target?"

"She was wearing my cloak." David studied the bottom of

the glass. "Why would someone shoot the one person suspected of knowing where a fortune in jewels and gold is hidden?" He set down the glass. "Even if shooting someone at six hundred yards was Faraday's modus operandi, after nine years in prison he would be fortunate if he could hit the broadside of a barn at twenty feet."

"There are only a handful of men in England who could make that shot." She smiled temperately. "Since your whereabouts could be accounted for, maybe less than a handful."

David shut the cabinet door none too gently. It was never easy to keep his patience with Pamela, and he sometimes wondered why she provoked him so, as if she always had something to prove, especially when he was sharing the same assignment with her husband. He walked to the bedroom door and swung it wide. "I don't intend to be gone long," he drawled.

She stopped in the doorway. "You still haven't explained why you are you leaving."

"I have a son, Pamela. Now"—ignoring the knot in his stomach, he offered her an indulgent smile, inviting her to leave—"for my safety, go."

"A son? I see," she said after a moment. "I'm sorry, David."

"For what? It isn't your fault that no one knew."

"What shall I tell Mr. Munro about you? He isn't happy that you have seen fit to steal Rose Briar out from beneath him, and now you have barred him from seeing Lady Munro. I warned you when you came here that you needed to be careful of him."

"Usher Nellis out the door." He started to turn then hesitated. "Then after you have finished contacting Kinley, do a little background investigation on the magistrate while he is in London. I want the history on Rose Briar and why he wants that property so badly."

Chapter 13

❦❧

"**G**ood gracious, child." Esma met Victoria as she entered the kitchen and put a hand to her cheek. "You're still feverish. It's only been a week. What are you doing out of bed?"

"Determined to remain on my feet." Victoria set Zeus on a chair and watched the cat dart straight for the bowl of cream on the floor. "Sir Henry isn't in his room."

"He is in the herbal, mum."

Victoria accepted a cup of hot tea. She disposed herself as comfortably as possible on a stool and watched Esma begin cutting carrots for supper. "Has Sir Henry spoken to you since last night?"

Esma shook her head. "He has kept to himself since Lord Chadwick left to fetch Nathanial."

Victoria hurt, and the ache had nothing to do with her injury. David had sent no messages. Despite her want to push him out of her head, his absence as much as her concern for her son's welfare kept her awake when she'd needed to rest.

Sir Henry had continued to care for her wound, though he had shut himself away from the deeper one in her heart.

She loved Sir Henry like the father she'd never had. He was the only grandfather Nathanial would ever know. She had no right to ask for his forgiveness, but he'd had a right to know the truth no matter the cost to herself.

When he had come to change her dressing yesterday, she could no longer bear the lie. She told him about her marriage to David in Calcutta ten years ago, from whom she had been running when she'd left India and met Scott Munro's widow.

She could find no words to express her sorrow for the hurt she had caused.

Yesterday had been the first time since her mother had left her that she opened herself so completely to another human being. How much of that honesty Sir Henry would choose to share with the world was up to him. It was enough that people would learn that Nathanial was David's son.

This morning she had risen to change her own bandages.

Laughter outside diverted Victoria's attention to the window. Mr. Rockwell and Bethany were in the yard with the mare Bethany had been nursing back to health, just as she had been caring for Victoria.

Frowning, she set her teacup onto the saucer. Other than a dimple on his cheek, Ian Rockwell, Foreign Service agent, had nothing to recommend to a sunny seventeen-year-old.

"He has done nothing untoward, mum," Esma said, reading her mind as if she had spoken her doubts aloud. "My William told me Mr. Rockwell knows about horses, and that girl loves that horse."

"Bethany should be with other young people her age."

She should have a new dress every once in a while and attend teas and other social functions that allowed her to meet nice boys.

"And when might that be, mum?" Esma scraped the carrots into a pan of water. "She hasn't said another word about the Yule soirée this year. She knows we cannot afford fabric for a new gown. But it's a shame you'd not ask Lord Chadwick to sponsor her."

"I can't do that, Esma."

"It's not my place to ask what has happened between you and Sir Henry and His Lordship. Maybe Lord Chadwick's coming here has not been such a good thing. It is a shame to be sure. I like that young man." Her housekeeper changed the topic. "But since he did open up the manor house, you should speak to Lydia Gibson about returning to Rose Briar. The household doesn't have anyone cooking for them."

"They did, until you insulted the cook yesterday."

Esma waggled the knife in her hands. "If you count boiled chicken a meal. Those men up there need nourishment and I can't be leaving here to feed them."

"Mrs. Gibson is caring for Mr. Doyle—"

"Mr. Doyle will be over the moon if you asked him to ready the bulbs in the orangery for spring planting. There's many of us what would be mighty beholdin' to His Lordship to see Rose Briar come alive again like it used to be around here in spring. It would do all of us good, including you, mum."

Except David's purchase of Rose Briar meant nothing to him. Looking down at the cup in her hand, she absently touched a chip on the once-flawless ivory porcelain. How could she explain to Esma who David really was and his purpose here? She could not even tell Esma if David planned to return Nathanial or that she would not even be here come spring. People should not ask impossible things of her.

Esma quit chopping and set both hands on the wooden block. "None of us ever asked what ye were runnin' from all those years ago, because some things don't need to be talked about. But you've been here a long time, and we are family now. If ye wish to talk, not a word of it will ever leave my lips."

"You and William have always been so good to me, Esma. But I fear this is something I must figure out how to fix myself. I should go see Sir Henry," she murmured.

Victoria pulled her cloak from its place on the wall and slipped it around her shoulders. David had taken his warmer one away.

Once outside, sunlight hit her face. Snow was still on the ground where it had drifted against the cottage. Avoiding the wet spots on the drive, she made her way across the yard to the herbal and let herself into the cellar. The single sound of a spade cutting into the dirt broke the silence.

Chop. Scrape. Chop. Scrape. The cinder walls amplified the noise from the back of the cellar. She compressed her lips. A cold, tight feeling formed in her stomach as she approached the noise. If there were worse things than being a pariah to one's own family, then it was having no family at all.

"What are you doing out of bed, Victoria." Sir Henry's voice carried to her from the dank shadows.

Aware that he continued to use the name by which he knew her, she remained next to a lamp on the workbench, unsure whether to go forward or retreat. "I want to talk to you, Sir Henry."

"If you're well enough to walk and talk, then hand me a jar."

Victoria pulled a jar from the shelf. She turned up the lamp on the workbench. Sir Henry had dug holes everywhere in her garden. She dropped to her knees beside him in the loam and helped place the delicate tuber in the jar. Later, she would lay it out to dry. It couldn't remain in a jar like this—surely he knew that.

Watching his hands work over the soil, she realized he was doing the same task repeatedly with no real purpose. She looked at his profile and felt a rush of tears before turning her attention to the jar. "I've put much of last month's herbs in jars. The others—"

"Will he bring my grandson back?" Sir Henry continued to chop at the mound of dirt.

Victoria's hands paused on the lid, but she nodded, even if it might be a lie. "David holds no ill will toward you, Sir Henry."

"I want you out of the cottage, Victoria. You can take what you want to Rose Briar. There is nothing here to which I'm attached, except for my books. When I am dead, you may have my books. If you decide that you will carry on here."

She blinked at his profile in confusion. "I don't want your things, Sir Henry."

"Your place is with your husband." He sat back on his heels. "You belong to Chadwick whether you recognize that fact or not."

"I do not recognize that fact."

"How much do you love your son?"

"How can you ask me that?"

"Will Nathanial be safe with his father?"

Wiping the back of her hand across her cheek, she nodded. "David will never allow anything to happen to him."

"Then so will you be safe in his keeping as well."

"You are mistaken," she said, looking at Sir Henry as if he had lost his mind. "He despises me."

"Pish posh, Victoria." Using his favorite phrase, Sir Henry wiped his hands on his trousers. "That man is in love with you."

A shocked denial formed, yet she could not voice the thought to Sir Henry, who already knew her to the core of her soul. But loving someone was not the same as trusting that person with your life. On as many levels, David was as big a fraud as she was.

A pale shaft of light from the cellar window behind her speared the garden. "There are few gifts in this life." Sir Henry returned to the spade. "Family is one. Love is another. I had both with Scott's mother, only to learn that life is too short. I don't care who you both were ten years ago. You will take responsibility for who you are now."

Victoria eyed Sir Henry through the gloom. "It isn't that simple."

"I'm an old soldier and a doctor, Victoria," he said, forcing her to meet his ardent gaze. "My son and I were estranged long before he joined the ranks of the East India Company and went to find his fortune. He left me with Bethany and the responsibility to see her properly raised. My son didn't have the courage or steadfastness to manage his life or that of his daughter's."

Victoria had once heard rumors that Scott Munro and Sir Henry had quarreled and were estranged up until his son's death. But she'd never felt it her place to know more than what Sir Henry told her. "What happened between you and your son?"

"After Bethany was born, I wanted him to take his place at the head of the family. Rose Briar needed him. His daughter needed him. This town needed him. But he forever rebelled against the constraints of his station." Sir Henry dug the spade beneath the root. "We argued one night, and he left angry. I found him the next morning on my way to see a patient. He'd had a carriage accident. One should never allow a loved one to go away angry. I should have fought harder for both of us. Six months later, Scott had regained most of his health. But he and I remained estranged until his death."

"Why are you telling me this?"

He shook his grizzled head regretfully. "After the accident, Scott was physically incapable of fathering any more children."

Victoria startled. "Then you've always known . . ."

"For whatever reason, I thought Scott loved you enough to marry you and give your babe a name. That was sufficient for me." He sat back on his heels, looking older than he had yesterday. "I will never come to terms that it was all a lie no matter my deep affection for you. But I could not let you leave here angry."

Wearily Victoria nodded, wondering vaguely why no tears came.

"A person only has two roads to follow in life, Victoria. You can do what's right, or you can do wrong. Everything else forks from those two arteries."

He pulled a fat tuber from the loam and set it in another jar, closing the lid. "When next I see you, we will speak of this conversation no more. Do you understand?"

Without looking at her, he struggled to climb to his feet. Victoria's hands curled into fists and she resisted reaching out to steady him as she followed him to his feet. He would not appreciate her help. "That young whippersnapper . . . Ian Rockwell"—he pointed the spade at the narrow window—"take him with you to Rose Briar. I don't want you at the house alone."

*   *   *

Victoria tossed and turned in bed, her hand finally going to the small clock on her dressing table to check the time. Having administered to herself a dose of hartshorn last night, she had fallen asleep before eating dinner. She set the clock down and let her eyes go over the bedroom. The house was utterly silent in the hours before dawn.

It had taken her only one day to move into Rose Briar. She had nothing that belonged solely to her. What she did have, Ian moved from the cottage for her.

"Mum?" a girl said from the doorway. Victoria recognized Moira, one of the girls who had come with Blakely from Ireland. "I heard ye cry out."

Victoria turned her head. "I did not mean to awaken anyone."

Certainly, it was not her intent to cause worry among the sparse household staff.

"Shall I add more coals on the hearth, mum?"

"No, I am fine. You may go back to sleep."

After the girl left, Victoria dragged herself out of bed and washed with the pitcher of water Moira left out last night. Looking into the mirror, she examined the discoloration at her waist. The silvered glass was not kind. The skin surrounding the wound was a mottled red and still proved tender to the touch. The wound was healing, but not quickly enough for her satisfaction.

She dressed, took the lamp, and left her bedroom. The two chambermaids and the butler David had hired slept somewhere on the other side of the house. Moira did not.

Victoria quietly walked the corridor and up the back staircase that led to the attic. Her shadow wobbled eerily over the walls as she stood in the center of the room and raised the lamp. Her surroundings were cold and layered with dust and spiderwebs. Trunks, crates, and old furniture, looming like ghostly shapes, were piled against walls in no particular order of age. Beyond the dormer windows, the morning sky remained dark.

Kneeling next to the second dormer window, she dug through a pile of needlepoint tapestries, and sundry other relics stacked against the wall over the years. At last, she reached the bottom and dislodged a piece of pine floorboard. The box remained where she'd hidden it years ago. A monument to all that she would forget, but could not.

She withdrew the satin box and lifted the lid. A golden locket lay on a puff of aged velvet. She released the latch, and inside was a daguerreotype of her mother. She could have been looking at an image of herself. There were no dates engraved, only a Latin inscription and a scarred emptiness that revealed so much more of her heart than the terrible secret it hid.

Her father had given her the locket for her seventeenth birthday. A gift that shocked her for all that he loathed her mother, but one that she had treasured nonetheless, for it was a link to her mother. It had been a private gift given to her away from the small gathering of her father's cronies—the Circle of Nine. It would not be until much later that she began to believe the locket meant something insidious, and that it had been given to her not out of affection, but out of an obsession to tie her to him. She had not lied when she'd told David that she didn't know where the treasure was buried.

But her father knew.

In the years since running from Calcutta, Victoria had prayed he would take the treasure's whereabouts to his grave, always believing that if it was never found, it could never be connected to her.

For she had been as responsible as anyone who had taken part in that crime. She had been sixteen, and already a skilled thief. She had gotten her father into the vault. The theft had been clean and so beautifully executed that it had been six days before authorities discovered the loss. By then the treasure had been secreted out of India with plans to retrieve it later. But as the months passed, her father's bloated arrogance began to defeat them all. By the time Victoria turned eighteen; she had met David and only wanted out.

But nobody left Colonel Faraday.

When the authorities closed in on her father, she took the locket and fled Calcutta. The pragmatist inside her knew that piece of gold might make the difference between escaping or dying in some foreign country. But she had not been able to trade it. Blame that on the sentimental part of her. She could not throw away her only link to her mother.

Closing the locket, she looked away.

Next to the lamp, she recognized the trunk belonging to Nathanial. Her small cry broke the heavy silence as she rummaged through baby clothes and toys stored through the years. Pulling out his baby blanket, she held it to the light and, caught by the tears trapped in her eyes, pressed the well-loved fabric against her cheek. The yellow quilted squares, frayed from constant handling by little hands, still smelled like him.

Something brushed her hip. She startled when Zeus climbed into her lap. She had brought the old tom with her from the cottage for company. "You miss him, too, don't you?"

No matter what David thought of the choices she'd made, Nathanial had been raised in a loving home. His birth had been a blessing in so many ways. She had changed her life for him. She'd become the parent her mother might have been had she lived longer and her father could never have been if he'd lived a hundred years. Sir Henry had supplied the foundation to begin her life anew, and she had built on it one brick at a time, struggling even through failure because she was working for something greater than herself. She'd begun to read the books in Sir Henry's surgery, taking on the role as his assistant, expanding her participation in the affairs of this town, and eventually finding her place as a person people respected. Slowly she'd learned to celebrate each triumph as a new milestone. She'd dared to believe she could become something special, never truly comprehending that the past was not something she could escape, but a part of her.

Now, having lived the lie for so long, she didn't know how to fix her life or if that was even possible. Sir Henry said a person could only choose between doing what was right or wrong, but for her it was a choice between doing nothing at all—or turning around to fight.

She had reached, without fully understanding it, a crossroads that would decide not only her life, but the kind of woman she really was. She only knew that for her son's sake she could no longer do nothing. She had never had a real home, and the significance of this one to Nathanial and Bethany became all the greater in her heart, for her father threatened that which she held most dear. In many ways, she and David had always been on the same side.

Victoria shut the trunk lid. Snuggling against a purring Zeus in her arms, she walked to the dormer window and stroked the black cat as she looked out. The first pale line of light appeared above the treetops and, like golden wings spreading across the sky, the sunrise topped the distant belfry.

Her gaze held to the steeple as if she had the eyesight to

see beyond the vague shadows, and wonder if someone was even now watching this house.

Had that someone really tried to kill David and shot her instead? The idea frightened her. Under the circumstances, it would make more sense, yet neither Mr. Rockwell nor Pamela had been attacked, and they were all here for the same purpose. Her father was many things, but he was not a sharpshooter, even on his best day, which meant someone else was working with him. Someone who knew about the caves that honeycombed these bluffs, a nice place to hide and never be found.

Local legend told stories of those caves, once used by pirates, but they'd been sealed half a century ago. The excise officers didn't even know where to look anymore on their yearly inspections of the area. But there was someone she suspected who did know.

And his name was Tommy Stillings.

For a timeless interval these past weeks, Victoria had been without real purpose, suffering from more than just a physical wound on her body and in her heart. But there was more than one front to this war, and as the sky began to pinken and daylight replaced darkness, she turned out the lamp and padded downstairs in soft-soled slippers, returning to the beautiful golden drawing room where she and David had made love. If she could realize one feat in her lifetime, then let it be in finding a way to save Nathanial's future.

It seemed symbolic somehow, that she should begin her crusade in this room and, with both hands, stripped the remaining canvas shrouds from the furniture.

For Margaret Faraday Donally was finished running.

* * *

Victoria knocked on the door. When no one answered, she stood back to look up at the second-story window where green curtains were drawn against the sunlight. Carrying her physician's bag beneath her cloak, she stepped away from the house.

"Maybe no one is home," Mr. Rockwell said, his hands in his pockets as he warded off the afternoon chill.

Sheriff Stillings's cottage sat amid a quiet glade of beeches and chestnuts just at the edge of town. Victoria turned to walk around the back of the cottage when the door squeaked opened. "My lady?" Annie Stillings swung the door wide. "Whatever are you doing here?" The younger woman stood aside to allow Victoria entrance. Her white blond hair lay mussed about her face. Six months gone with child, Annie had begun to show. She looked pale and tired. "We all heard about the accident, I'm glad to see you about on your feet, my lady."

Of course she had heard. The entire town had heard and attributed it to a poaching incident gone awry. Yet she had come here to wage her own battle and traded her discomfiture for determination. "How are you feeling, Annie?"

"Not so well," she admitted. "I was abed."

Victoria told Mr. Rockwell she would not be long before closing the door behind her.

"May I fetch you a pot of tea, mum?"

Victoria set her physician's bag on the table beside the sofa. "How long have you been feeling this tired, Annie?"

She laughed. "I'm always tired, mum."

"I told your husband that I would check in on you."

A promise was a promise, Victoria had decided. Besides, she liked Annie. Only a few years older than the other woman, Victoria had worked with her often in the poor house when Sir Henry used to visit the children residing there. They spoke about the weather as Victoria examined her, side-stepping any topic that had to do with her husband.

"Your baby is active, I might say. I can leave licorice and chamomile tea for stomach upset. But you need to make sure you are eating all of your meals."

"Will you be with me when my baby comes, mum?"

Her hands stilled in the act of closing her medical bag. "Why would you ask that?"

"People are talking." Annie sat up, averting her eyes as she fluffed her skirts. "They say you have moved back to Rose Briar. Rumor also claims that Lord Chadwick is Nathanial's father."

Victoria sank beside her on the sofa. How would someone know that already? she wondered, appalled. Nor was it something she could simply deny. "Lord Chadwick and I knew each other many years ago when I lived in India. We were separated by terrible circumstances and, until recently, he thought I was dead."

"You wouldn't be the first to marry another to give your child a name, mum."

Victoria managed to breathe the words, "Is that what people believe?"

She knew tolerance only went so far and that some would ostracize her. She didn't care about what people in general thought of her, for her days as a midwife were over the day David stepped back into her life, but she did care about Nathanial and Bethany.

"How many years have you given to the people in this town, my lady?"

"Maybe not enough."

"You may be a scandal, but you're our scandal, my lady."

Annie said passionately and took Victoria's hands before she could speak or more like choke. "Lord Chadwick found you, mum. He owns Rose Briar now. He is a fine one, to be sure. Do you realize what he can accomplish when he tills the fields this spring?" Annie's round face brightened. "People are already talking about the tenants he will need to farm the land. Some people will be cruel, but most of us are looking to *you*, my lady. Nellis Munro was never any good for this town."

Hands folded in her lap, Victoria turned her head. A cradle sat next to the fireplace.

"Tommy made that," Annie said when she saw where Victoria's eyes had strayed. "With Mr. Munro still in London, he has not been so busy with . . . other matters."

Looking at the cradle, Victoria was struck by the contrast to the man who could labor so long creating something so beautiful to the man who worked for Nellis.

"My husband is not a bad man, mum. Sometimes circumstances force us to make choices to protect others and ourselves. Don't condemn him."

"I understand more than you think, Annie." She stood. "Do you know where I can find him? It's important."

"He's out back, my lady."

Wrapped in her cloak, her hood shielding her face from the cold, Victoria walked out the back door to a smaller cottage nearly hidden among the trees. As she stepped through the doorway, she saw Sheriff Stillings in the back, whittling away at a toy duck. Her glance touched two massive oak timbers stretched across a ceiling that angled into a loft as she shut the door. Intent on his work, he didn't see her until her shadow passed across him.

"Lady Munro . . ." He nearly choked as he set down the carving. He wore a clean woolen shirt, rolled up his forearms, and appeared almost urbane if one could overlook the scar on his cheek. Quickly recovering, he stood. "What brings you here?"

"I told you I would see Annie. You will be a father before spring, Tommy." Victoria looked from the toys spread across the workbench and picked up a wooden block. "You have a secret life, Sheriff."

He plucked the block from her hand. "I understand you do as well, my lady."

"Was my getting shot an accident?"

He tossed down the rag in his hand. "I had nothing to do with what happened to you." Even wearing boots, Stillings did not have the advantage of height, and this was one of the few times Victoria appreciated her stature. She could stand her ground among men.

"None of my people would have shot you," he said.

"I believe you. None of your men could have made a shot that accurate. But you work for Nellis. You might know things the rest of us don't."

Stillings walked to the window and looked out at the back of his cottage. She knew Ian would find her the moment he realized she'd left the cottage. "Is it true that you are not living with Sir Henry any longer?" he asked, dropping the edge of the curtain.

"It's true enough." She set her medical bag on the workbench. "Is there another way into the Briar Hill Church? You've lived here your entire life. Perhaps you know something the Munro family does not."

He leaned a shoulder against the window casement. "A man would be a fool to go into the caves. They were sealed decades ago."

"And maybe you unsealed one."

"You and I don't agree on much," Stillings said. "But you've been square," he added as if his words mattered to her when he'd hurt her horses and forced most of her tenants from their homes. "If you want my help, you understand that I always have a price."

"As do I, Tommy." She called him that on purpose because she had always called him that when he used to bring Nathanial wooden toys after she or Sir Henry had visited his ailing mother, never realizing he had made them himself. He used to attend church and seemed to care about local problems. Before he'd found himself in trouble and Nellis got hold of him. "In exchange for your cooperation, I won't turn you over to certain authorities along with all the names of your men and locations of your various tariff-evasive enterprises these past three years."

A malicious smile formed. "A comrade in arms, my lady. What a novel idea to learn that you and I are more alike than I thought."

From over his shoulder, she saw Mr. Rockwell step into the clearing. Stillings observed him. "I'd say it is just as well we can't continue our chat. Your turnkey has grown worried for you."

"Mr. Rockwell works for Lord Chadwick."

Stillings walked to the door. He opened it wide, inviting her departure. "Curious about Chadwick showing up the way he did after I brought ye that earring. A fine man with the countess, I hear."

Pushing back the hood on her cloak, she loosened the frogs against her neck as if the thing impeded her breathing. "Lord Chadwick isn't some naïve coxcomb," she warned. "If you were wise, you would grab on to what you have here and find a new livelihood. You should be on his side. Trust me when I say crime will only earn you the end of a rope."

He forced a laugh, a faint suggestion of comprehension in his observant gaze. "Is that the right of it, my lady?"

"That's the right of it, Tommy."

"Our fine magistrate, Munro, is confident that Lord Chadwick will be gone by the end of the year. Someone wants him out of the way."

A chill settled in her spine. "Nellis said that?" His threatening comment only brought about the inevitable to her mind. Then David was correct when he'd said that bullet had been meant for him. She wondered if Nellis wasn't working with her father. But how?

"So, you understand why my loyalty will stay where it is, my lady."

"Did Nellis say who? If you know anything—"

"I don't. You can ask him when he returns from London." Stillings folded his arms over his chest. "Nellis Munro has a fondness for French brandy and fancy baubles, my lady. Lately he's added Rose Briar to his list. You should know, you can't win against someone who is stronger than you are. Haven't you learned that by now?"

"But what if we could win, Tommy?"

"You cannot do it alone, my lady. And that is exactly where you stand. Alone."

Chapter 14

"**I**'ve never seen fabric this beautiful." Bethany pressed the blue velvet to her chest as if it were a living thing in her arms.

Victoria sat in front of her vanity watching the girl twirl about like a bright golden top. Bethany met her gaze in the mirror. "However did you afford this, Victoria?"

"Finished, mum." Moira set down the comb in front of the looking glass.

Victoria didn't answer Bethany's question. She looked at herself in the mirror and raised her brows. The gown she wore was reserved in its lines but fit her like a glove. Since discovering the old forgotten trunk of clothes in the attic, and with a little alteration to update the style, she'd added three new gowns to her wardrobe. This afternoon, dressed in a red and green muslin skirt and ivory blouse belted at the waist, with her wealth of dark hair piled atop her head, she looked the picture of sophistication.

Shouts from downstairs roused her. "A carriage is approaching, mum!"

"A carriage?" Victoria stood in a rustle of petticoats.

The distant jangle of an approaching coach pulled her through the boudoir. She ran to the window facing the orangery. A black carriage rumbled past. Even before it came to complete stop, the door flung open and a boy leaped out.

"Nathanial."

Victoria whirled in a flurry of muslin and hurried down the corridor. She stopped on the landing as the front door flew wide.

"Mama . . ." Her son hurtled himself up the stairs.

Tears in hers eyes, she met him halfway and, kneeling, took him into her arms. "Look at you." Holding him at arm's length, she examined his face and arms. "You've grown two inches since I saw you last."

"I outgrew my trousers, Mother." And he proudly displayed his arm in demonstration of his newly gained muscles from working real machinery. He filled Bethany in on the state of his many cousins' affairs and that Janie kissed Peter at the apple dunking, which was why he had not arrived earlier than today.

"Because Janie kissed Peter?" Bethany asked from behind them.

"No, you goose." Nathanial rolled his eyes and returned his attention to Victoria. "We stayed and celebrated the harvest." He added with relish how his uncle Fred allowed him to sip a mug of the family's ale.

Victoria looked over his head at David standing in the foyer, looking tall and beautiful, wearing a new suit of clothes, his hair nearly black in the sunlight of the day.

"Lord Chadwick let me stay." He leaned nearer and whispered in her ear. "He danced with Bessie and Mildred and Frannie. She wants to marry him."

"Frannie?" Bethany scoffed. "She's hardly out of swaddling. What does she know about marriage?"

Frannie was Bethany's age and her rival at family functions. "No doubt His Lordship has that effect on younger women," Victoria said.

"Where is Zeus?" Nathanial leaned over the banister.

"The last I saw that cat, he was sleeping in the bookroom." Victoria gripped the spindles on the stairway. "Be careful, Nathan. The floors have just been polished."

But her son paid her no heed. Her eyes met David's and she rose to her feet.

The color rising in her cheeks as he took in every detail of her appearance, she rested her hand on the polished banister. Despite everything, her world seemed safe and whole again, though she knew it was neither.

Bethany stepped around her. "I'll check on those tarts Mrs. Gibson pulled out of the oven. Nathanial is probably hungry."

She fled, leaving Victoria alone with David, her heart racing against her ribs.

"I half expected to find you gone," he said.

"We had an agreement," she said, electing to stand on moral high ground in lieu of remembering that until a few weeks ago she'd planned on fleeing. "How did you know I would be at this house?"

"Rockwell rode out to meet the carriage. He told me what happened between you and Sir Henry. I'm—"

"Do not think to apologize. He has a right to his opinion of me."

David moved to the bottom of the stairs, and she looked

into his upturned face, caught by the sweep of light and shadow in his eyes. "I only meant to say I'm surprised you told him the truth."

She lifted her chin. "Does Nathanial know?"

"Everyone in Salehurst thought my *family* tie to you explained our resemblance. Another lie, until we can sit down and talk to him. I won't allow my son to grow up thinking his father is dead."

She listened to Nathanial's exclamation as he found Zeus. Dare she tell David that they were already the topic of town gossip? "Are we prepared to answer his questions about us then, David?"

"You have caught me well and good on that score, madam." His quiet scoff raked over her. "By the very dynamics of our relationship, it would serve us both if I removed myself from this case and walked away forever."

She held her tongue, stricken by the fear he would do exactly that, yet knowing she had no right to ask anything from him. But she wasn't prepared yet to lose her son. David had brought him back. She was beyond trying to rationalize her relief. "Can we please agree that we want the best for our son?"

"Mother?" Nathan bounded from the bookroom, holding Zeus with both arms. "May I see Peepaw?"

"I'll take you to your grandfather," David said, pulling his gaze from her.

"Lord Chadwick said I'm going to see Big Ben." Grinning, Nathan bounced back on his heels. "We came home to see you and Zeus and Peepaw, too. And to fetch my pillow."

Thrusting down sudden panic, Victoria looked at David. "You're taking him to London?"

"A train leaves from New Haven tomorrow night. I've already made arrangements."

What he didn't say, but what was evident in his eyes, was that he had brought Nathanial here to say good-bye. So this would be the way it was between them? David had already made the decision. Even as a part of her recognized that Nathanial might be safer in London, she was not prepared for the knife-sharp pain in her stomach, and dropped to one knee in front of her son. How would she ever tell Sir Henry?

"I'll visit the menagerie when it opens in the spring, Mother," Nathan said. "And I'll get to go to a school like Ethan Birmingham. He learned fencing last year."

Victoria touched his cheek. Her son spoke with so much enthusiasm, that she could not bear to let him see her sadness. "You'll need to pack more than your pillow, Squirrel."

"I shan't be gone forever, Mother," he reassured her, suddenly sounding like the man of the house and not her baby. "All the boys go to school. And when I get back, Ethan Birmingham won't be calling me a brat anymore."

"I thought you, Ethan, and Robbie were best friends?"

"We were till Ethan went to school last year."

She smoothed a lock of dark hair from his brow. "Mrs. Gibson pulled fresh tarts from the oven less than an hour ago. Why don't you see if they are ready?"

With an exclamation, Nathan whirled on his heel. Her side hurt. She couldn't stand. David's steady hand was suddenly at her elbow. "Who is taking care of you?" he asked.

She withdrew her arm, and it was all she could do not to collapse on the stairs. "I don't need anyone's help. I can fight my own battles, David."

"Bravo, General Faraday." He stepped back, his smile hinting at amusement that did not reach his eyes. "I'm glad to know that your frail physical condition has not changed your disposition."

"I'll take my son to the cottage. There will be things—"

"I'll see that he gets everything he needs in London."

"Of course you will." There was a dull thudding in her head. "Does that include a new mother as well?"

"Hell, it might."

"If you divorce me, you'd have to actually admit in public you married Colonel Faraday's treasonous progeny. There will be a terrible scandal. Even you would not survive unscathed."

She watched in disbelief as he removed a cheroot from his pocket and stuck it between his lips. "Which is why I would seek an annulment," he said, striking a match against his boot heel. "I believe I can still work the occasional miracle."

Narrowing her eyes, she took a firm grip on herself. "When did you start smoking those awful things again?"

"It would have behooved me never to have quit," he said, shielding the flame with his hand as he observed her flushed expression. "Do you want to know why?"

He waved out the match and dropped it in a brass pot beside the banister. "Even if you didn't have high treason charges hanging over your head—not counting, say, the hundred thousand pounds' worth of stolen artifacts and jewels still missing, the death of my partner, and my own brush with mortality at your hands—you and I would never be a family." He dabbed ash off in the pot, and she followed the movement with her eyes. "But maybe if you're nice, I won't throw you out of this house upon my return. For you see, I still have tender feelings for you. Enough not to shake you where you stand."

"Feelings?"

"I've done naught but think about you since I left. I have a son and I never thought it possible. In some bloody way, I even agree with what you did." He moved toe to toe with her, the slight movement peeling away her meager temper. "I find myself admiring your courage in the face of defeat, unable to comprehend what you must have felt like all these years knowing that I betrayed you and my child. Asking you still to trust me. I don't want to take Nathanial away from you. Tell me those aren't feelings for stalwart fools to suffer?"

Entrapped as she was within his stormy gaze, she peered at him with watery eyes. "Sometimes, I find myself completely baffled by you, David."

He gave her a mocking salute. "Likewise, madam. I baffle myself," he said leaving her staring at his back as he shut the front door firmly behind him.

David leaned against the carriage boot as he finished the cheroot. His coat collar lifted against the icy chill, he wore a fur-lined hat to cover his ears and wondered irritably if he still wasn't underdressed. He brought the cheroot to his lips, knowing he didn't have an answer to the way he was feeling at that moment.

He should be downstairs in the kitchen with Meg and their son. He should be, but he wasn't, and didn't quite know what he'd say even if he were. So what did he do, but come outside to freeze his bum off?

His eyes narrowing against the smoke, he peered toward the distant church tower, then straightened as an old wagon crawled into sight. He recognized Mr. Doyle. A towheaded boy sat between him and the second man hunched at the reins.

Recognizing the Widow Gibson's son from his visit to

their homestead a few weeks ago, David dropped the cheroot to the ground and crushed it out with the heel of his boot. The wagon came to a jangling halt in front of him on the drive.

"Lord Chadwick." Mr. Gibson wiped his hands down the front of his coveralls, then introduced his son. "This is my son, Robbie," he said. "He used to spend much of his time here when I managed the estate. I'm glad to see you back. I hope you are here to stay."

David remained silent in his reluctance to pursue this tack of conversation. Beyond having purchased Rose Briar as his side of an agreement with Meg, he held no other connection to this house or the land. Nor did he want to.

The door behind him flew open and Nathanial appeared.

Robbie suddenly came alive. "Nate!"

"We didn't know the nipper was back," Mr. Gibson said, his face lighting beneath his hat.

"May I see him, Papa?"

Mr. Gibson deferred the decision to David, who could not have stopped him if he'd tried. "You're friends, are you?"

"The best, my lord," the boy said as David stood aside in time to escape being trampled.

Robbie ran to Nathanial, who was halfway down the cobbled walk. David realized he knew nothing about his son's life here, except what little he'd discerned on the trip back from Salehurst. His boy was bright, confident, and seemed popular wherever he went, a trait he'd not failed to notice.

David's gaze touched Meg standing on the pathway as she said something to Robbie that animated both boys. They rushed inside out of the cold.

Wrapped in her cloak, looking very much the lady of the manor, Meg straightened and smiled at Daniel Gibson. Watching her, David felt as if someone had hit him in the chest with a staff. Meg wasn't pretty in the traditional standard. She was extraordinary, like stepping into sunlight after years of living in a cave, and when she smiled, it took a moment for him to breathe.

She approached the two men in the wagon. "Mr. Gibson. Mr. Doyle. I see you have been taking care of yourself."

An icy gust whipped her skirts around David's legs as she leaned into the wagon to adjust the blanket on the old man's lap. "He didn't want to come, mum," Mr. Gibson said.

"Don't you want to work in the orangery?" Meg asked, worriedly noting Mr. Doyle's nervousness. "You love flowers."

David followed the man's gaze, listening for what it was no one would say. He seemed afraid of the house. "You will like that there are other people around to talk with," he heard Meg say. "I've put you in the cottage the other side of the orangery. Mr. Gibson's mother has already kindled a warm fire."

Doyle's forehead disappeared in a set of wrinkles. "There be no spirits in the orangery?"

"Not a single one. You're safe," Meg quietly said.

She stepped away from the wagon and stood next to David as it lumbered away. "I've never seen him like that," Meg said, still watching the wagon—as David couldn't help watching her—the extent of his discontent with her vastly abridged as he'd observed the ease of her affection for these folk. "I hope I've done the correct thing bringing him here."

"Has Doyle said anything more about what he might have seen in the church?"

"No, but there are caves in this bluff. Sheriff Stillings confirmed it."

"You went to see Sheriff Stillings?" He would bloody throttle Rockwell for allowing Meg anywhere near Stillings.

She looked up at him as if they'd been remotely civil to each other since his return, as if he wasn't suddenly thinking of committing some spontaneous act of self-destruction with her—and something else very much like possessiveness flared inside him. Clad in a gown he had not seen on her before today, she presented a striking figure as she met his scrutiny with growing defiance.

"You have given orders that have made me a prisoner." Her eyes locked with his. "But you did not order that I couldn't talk to people or make certain decisions regarding the welfare of those for whom I feel responsible. If you haven't noticed yet, I shall point out that I've not been idle."

As if for the first time, David glimpsed a groom walking out of the stable to help Mr. Gibson. Of a sudden, he looked at the manor house, the clean mullioned windows and gardens cleared of weeds. Two chambermaids he didn't recognize were outside beating a rug, their laughter carrying to him on a gust of wintry wind.

He returned his gaze to rest on her face. Both his eyebrows lifted in response, his state of awareness akin to the way he'd felt in the drawing room when he'd pressed her against the curtains and buried himself in her body. "You've been busy during my absence. Are you planning on staying for any length of time?"

Meg brought up the hood on her cloak to cover her hair. "Nathanial and Robbie are eating lunch. I sent Mr. Rockwell to the cottage to let Sir Henry know that I will be bringing Nathanial shortly. I need to be the one to do this. Until then, you're welcome to join us for lunch," she said from behind the bow of her perfectly shaped mouth. "Mrs. Gibson is an excellent cook."

"What did you do with my cook?" he thought to ask her.

"Esma discharged him. He's better with horses. No doubt most of your hirelings are spies, but I added some of my own. People who actually know how to cook and clean."

The corners of his mouth softened. "I shall keep that in mind lest I'm tempted to take a meal here."

"Truly David," she chided. "Don't fill my head with ideas."

Dismissed like a servant just taken to task, he raked his gaze over her backside as she breezed past, their stalemate no longer intact. He was still staring at her when she turned and caught his gaze, his actions only adding to her bewilderment—and his.

Emotion banked the embers in her eyes. "Do you mind that I take Nathanial to the cottage?" she asked in a voice oddly vulnerable to him. "It is not my want to exclude you."

He nodded to the carriage and said, "Use the coach and four. I will join you later."

"David?" Their eyes locked, and he knew in that moment of reckoning that he was surely a fool for having granted her any wish at all—but for some reason couldn't bring himself to care. "I promise I won't instruct Mrs. Gibson to poison you. I'm over wanting to kill or maim you."

David allowed a brief grin to form. He could read in her eyes that she wanted to say more. But it was one thing to loosen his grip on his son and an entirely different problem altogether to forgive her. Or forget where they stood with each other.

He might have been a priest at one time expounding eternal forgiveness upon all, but this was personal.

Yet it was precisely for that reason he had returned.

"Did you really ever want me dead, Meg?"

"No." Her eyes held his. "I just wanted you. Period."

David did not attempt to temper his reaction to her answer. Watching as the door shut behind her, he lifted one eyebrow in an incredulous arc, cognizant of how easily a single two-letter word followed by one substantial sentence could change the timbre of their discourse and touch the very fabric of their relationship.

Chapter 15

David reined in Old Boy just past the cemetery, peering up at the church tower as he rode into Doyle's enclosed yard. As he tied the reins to a post, a familiar Irish hail greeted him from the direction of the burned-out church. "If it isn't himself come ridin' over the hill." Ralph Blakely stood in the weed-infested churchyard wearing heavy leather boots and a thick woolen shirt. His gold tooth flashed upon David's approach. "Will ye be stayin' long, Mister Donally?"

David followed him into the rectory. Once out of the wind some of his body warmth returned. "Only tonight. I have business to attend in London. I'll be back in a few days."

"Ye told me not to be leavin' the church till I found the tunnel."

"Are we that fortunate?" Peering warily at the thick wooden beam overhead, he ducked to avoid a splintered shaft of wood and stopped beneath a blackened overhang that opened into the nave. A bright patch of blue sky appeared. Unlike certain members of his family, he wasn't a structural engineer, but good sense told him this place was as close to collapsing as any dilapidated tenement flat, of which he'd seen plenty of in his lifetime.

Blakely shoved his thumbs into his waistband. "No, but the boys and I, we've done everything else you've asked. We found the hounds a few days back. They're part of a pack someone let lose up here what roams these hills and kills the livestock. Seems to me someone 'as done his utmost to run off every tenant. Also found the vicar what used to work in this church."

David pulled his gaze back to Blakely. "You spoke to him?"

"Wish I could say I had. He died a few months ago and is buried in Halisham. His missus said I wasn't the only one what visited her askin' questions aboot the old tunnels. Some months back, a dark haired-woman and a heavy man with white hair nosed aboot askin' the same questions."

"A white-haired man . . ."

Kinley.

The description fit, maybe too conveniently, and it was precisely that initial assumption that put the skids on his thoughts, that and the dark-haired woman. But Kinley was six feet tall and could fill the footprints David had found leading from this church the morning after the snowstorm.

A crisp breeze disturbed the dead leaves at David's feet. His gaze touched the blackened stones, lingering on what remained of the chancel and pulpit. He felt an odd connection to this place. Meg and his son had attended services beneath this roof. Nathanial had been christened here.

David moved away from the stone wall and shifted his focus. He had never been in a church that did not hold tight to its secret vaults and chambers. Meg had confirmed there were caves beneath these bluffs. Yet chances were that most of the tunnel network had probably not been used in centuries and was unsafe, which would account for the locals not knowing much about them.

The *clip-clop* of an approaching horse drew David around. He looked out across the graveyard to see Rockwell approaching. "Do you still have someone watching Nellis's residence?" he asked Blakely.

"Aye. He's not returned from London."

"I would prefer not to involve anyone else for now in our findings past or future," David said. If he trusted anyone at all, he trusted the men he'd brought with him from Ireland. None of them worked for Kinley. "I will find a stonemason. In the meantime I want this room shored up completely before we begin taking out the walls."

His attention moved to the belfry. If there was a way in or out of this place, he wanted it found and permanently sealed.

A few minutes later, David mounted Old Boy and met Rockwell coming up the small gravel path to the churchyard. It bothered him that his suspicion of Kinley transferred to Rockwell, by his very association with Pamela. For David had also found a woman's tracks that day after the storm. Pamela had blond hair, but could have worn a wig if she had been with Kinley. Clearly, someone wanted him to believe that woman had been Meg.

Rockwell slowed at David's approach. "You appear troubled."

"What were you bloody thinking taking Meg to see Stillings?"

He looked affronted and amused at once. "You try stopping her from doing something once she sets her mind to a task."

In no mood for musings, David nudged his horse with his heels only to hear Rockwell yell. "I wouldn't go to the cottage just this moment, sir."

He reined in Old Boy. "Why not?"

"Is that boy your son?" Rockwell asked. "Is that why you went to Salehurst? It's already town gossip, Donally."

Biting back an oath, David looked away. He had told only one person his purpose for leaving. "That *boy's* name is Nathanial," David answered shortly. Rockwell could figure out the complications on his own time. "I'm taking him to London tomorrow night and handing him over to my sister until . . ." Shaking his head, he crossed one hand over the other and glared across the cemetery. "Until I close this case."

"Until you hand his mother over to Kinley, you mean?"

David's features hardened, the truth of that statement only exacerbating his temper.

"And since you are as incapable of shirking responsibility as she is of shifting it to others"—Rockwell shoved his hand into his pocket and tossed a gold locket to David—"I came here to give you that."

David caught the trinket and turned it over in his hand.

"I rescued it after your wife bartered it for a bolt of fabric." Rockwell's horse sidestepped and had to be reined in tighter. "She wanted to give Miss Munro a new gown. Or else she just wanted to get rid of the locket. I suspect both."

A sinking feeling in his gut, he snipped the latch. Someone had tried to remove the woman's image inside. The miniature daguerreotype was Meg's only remaining possession of a woman her father had viciously exorcised from her life. But Rockwell's reasons for giving it to him were hardly rooted in sentiment. "Let me guess the conundrum." He shut the lid.

"This was not among the things she packed and brought from the cottage when she moved back to Rose Briar, which meant she retrieved it from inside the house *after* she returned to the manor house. Maybe you're mistaken."

"I know exactly what she took because I helped her move."

"Why not take this straight to Kinley?"

"Kinley is impatient," Rockwell finally said, *sans* the boyish dimple that made him look less than his twenty-six years. "I suspect his concern over Colonel Faraday is not nearly so top shelf as gaining a percentage of the spoils on this case. That locket may not mean anything, or it might mean a lot. I thought I'd leave it to you to find out. Not him."

David's gaze remained on the cemetery as his mind dwelled on the riddle surrounding Meg's last few weeks in India. A part of him recognized this locket might hold significance. He knew her father had given her the trinket. Knowing what he did now of Meg's mother, David understood that the locket meant something else entirely to Faraday.

He also respected the symbolic gesture of Meg's defiance against her father when she had quit wearing the locket shortly after they were married. He suddenly realized he knew exactly at which point she had begun to take a stand against her father.

Even then, he recognized that as Colonel Faraday allowed David into the inner Circle of Nine, Meg was trying to escape.

Shoving the locket into his pocket, he looked at Rockwell. "How is it you and your wife were assigned this case?"

"Kinley contacted me shortly before he contacted you. My father was Kinley's aide-de-camp when they worked on this case in India."

"Your father worked on this case?"

A ghost of a frown flitted across Rockwell's features, as he became aware he'd revealed something that he shouldn't have. David was thinking of that damnable earring that miraculously came into Kinley's possession, and who might have had it all of these years, for Faraday couldn't have kept it with him in prison.

"My father is dead. I have as much a personal stake in this case as you do."

"How is that, exactly?"

"You and I depend on each other," Rockwell said, avoiding the question. "Trust me to do my job as I trust that you'll do yours."

"What I depend on is loyalty and the assurance that no one is going to undermine me. That this is a sanctioned operation." He no longer took pains to avoid the topic uppermost in his mind. Nor would he rely on Pamela's loyalty. "And I trust if someone wanted to kill Meg or me, it wouldn't be someone working for my own government."

"Listen to yourself." Rockwell laughed. "Have you considered that the woman you came here to apprehend has twisted your bloody breeches in a knot? Or is it always your habit to populate every country where you work?"

David smashed a fist across Rockwell's jaw. Both horses reared. Rockwell tumbled from the saddle. David gripped the reins of his own startled horse to keep from trampling his partner to bone and dust. When he brought Old Boy under control, he slid from the saddle and dropped to the ground in front of Ian, his heavy coat brushing his calves.

"You have never impressed me as being thick-witted, Rockwell."

"Maybe I lack finesse in my delivery, but I believe I have gotten my point across." Ian struggled to his elbow. "You would know that if you were not so singularly wrongheaded. Face it, you have a bloody *tendre* for your wife, Donally."

Hell yes, he did. "Meg stood up to Faraday ten years ago. Even when she had nowhere to turn and every bloody person betrayed her, she did the only right thing she could and she did it alone. It was because of her that we caught Faraday the first time."

"And are you willing to betray your oath to save her now? That is the question pressing on your soul. The one that makes you dangerous to the rest of us on this case."

Staring down at Ian, David found his temper sorely wanting of common sense. What the hell did Rockwell or anyone else know about his soul?

"If you're finished going cork-brained on me, help me up, Donally. I'll be lucky if I'm not crippled for life."

In no mood for charity, David crouched in front of Ian. "How long has this operation been ongoing?"

"Faraday disappeared shortly after he was transferred to Marshalsea six months ago. That's all I know." Ian wiped the back of his hand across his mouth and examined his glove for blood. "Kinley was the man in charge of overseeing his incarceration. He is also the one who sanctioned this operation. My father was part of Kinley's team in Calcutta. Kinley owed me."

"What did he owe Pamela?"

"Bugger off, Donally. Your only job is to keep Meg Faraday alive."

Rockwell's life and career centered on his service. David had read his exemplary files. He would be the agent the foreign secretary called in to investigate another operative. "It was your idea that Meg remain here as a lure for her father.

Kinley wasn't expecting that. In fact, he was in a royal pisser about the idea. Who is the *real* target? Kinley or Faraday? Or someone else?"

"You've just proven to me you're bloody compromised. Don't think you're getting anymore answers. And all records concerning this case are in the foreign secretary's office. So, unless you know Lord Ware, you aren't going to find out anything else."

"You're a fooking bastard, Rockwell." David surveyed Ian's sprawled form, his beaver hat askew, and somehow, he tempered his anger as he stood.

"Take your son, Donally. In fact, I suggest that you do, but Meg Faraday stays. If you compromise this case, Kinley will arrest you for treason. He's still your superior."

"Who shot Meg?"

When Rockwell didn't look to be any more cooperative than he had thirty seconds before, David fixed his boot on the man's chest. "I swear I don't know."

"Has Kinley ever been up to this bluff?"

"I know you two have a long history—"

"Kinley couldn't find his way out of a glass jar if someone dumped it upside down. If the bastard is ghosting us then someone else is pulling his strings." *And the Foreign Office is after whomever Kinley is working for.* "Tell me one thing. Is Faraday dead or alive?"

Rockwell's jaw clenched but the brief fire of defiance yielded to the threat apparent in David's own expression. "That's part of the problem. We don't know. We only know someone wants his daughter enough to kill to get what she has."

A treasure worth the meager price of an oath—certainly worth the kingdom it could buy. So why hadn't Meg taken the bloody thing and run when she'd had the chance?

But as he looked around him at the church and the dome of blue sky above, he knew the answer. He knew in his heart that even if she had the treasure, she would never touch it. For Meg had found a treasure more valuable to her than that offered by diamonds and gold. It lived in the people who loved her, the family she had never had, the trees, the land, the house on the hill. It lived in her son.

"Pamela is investigating a lead," Rockwell said, still on the ground. "So, if your oath to this crown means anything, bloody stay here and do your job and allow us to do ours."

David recognized a spoken threat when he heard one, but it was the unspoken one that troubled him because it came from Rockwell himself. It was unfortunate the younger man hadn't broken at least one bone in his body, David thought, removing his boot from Rockwell's chest and offering his hand in a gesture of goodwill and concord that extended no farther than his eyes. It was also unfortunate for the young upstart spy that David did not intend to sit quietly in the background.

"Are you going to live?" David asked.

"I confess I've been deuced inconvenienced." Rockwell brushed off his cloak. "My horse has abandoned me. You can trust me not to toss down the gauntlet a second time."

He straightened just as David smashed him in the jaw, landing him back on his arse in the slush. "On the other hand." He stood over the sprawled man. "I have no such problem, Rockwell."

David slammed shut the bureau drawer and looked around the library. Having no clear thought as to what he might be looking for, he continued to methodically search each of the rooms in the town house, seeking anything of value that would help him decipher Pamela's activities these last few weeks. Moonlight spilled through the windows behind him. Having found nothing downstairs, he made his way to the second floor.

Pamela's private desk in her boudoir was a repository for bills, receipts, and invitations. Thumbing through each one, he noted nothing beyond the pale—except a slip of paper with a single address. He held it to the moonlight, then tucked it into his coat pocket before searching her armoire and dressing room for a dark wig. He discovered that she had wigs, but none of them dark.

He made his way to the window and edged aside the drapery. As he watched, the clouds parted and moonlight painted the rooftops a chalky white. The street was nearly deserted. Wherever Pamela was, it was better that he had not confronted her tonight. His gut feeling warned him to tread with cautious step. Yet, another part of him realized that neither Ian nor Pamela trusted him any longer.

A low fire burned in the hearth behind him and, without willing it, he was suddenly thinking of Meg, wondering if she had returned to Rose Briar with Nathanial. He looked down at his hand. A slim shaft of light slanted across the locket he held in his palm. David hadn't thought it possible so many forces could collide without leaving a crater in his gut.

For the first time in his life, his duty was no longer clear, as something inside him, something that lay hard and unbending in the center of his being, snapped. His thoughts so at odds with honor and integrity, he nearly laughed aloud. Not in the manner of a man who reflected on his past but of one who pondered his future and realized he had to make a choice. For, until now, doing the right thing and doing what was honorable had always been the same in his mind. He didn't know how to separate his duty from the two.

Nor did he know, as memory presented him with a picture of Meg's future, how to save what he had so carelessly thrown away nine and a half years ago. Kinley, Ian, and Pamela—whatever their respective missions might be—worked at the center of an intricate organization spanning oceans. If David helped Meg to run again, neither of them would ever be free for as long as they lived. And they had a son to consider.

He had facilitated Meg's capture. Yet, knowing without quite understanding what had happened, David realized his mission had changed.

But for a single brass sconce, the hallway remained darkened. Keeping to the shadows, David descended the stairs and let himself out the back door where he'd entered. He needed to find the sharpshooter, sure that the man who'd held that rifle also held all the answers—and maybe the key to Meg's freedom. He wasn't so much afraid of his heart as he was afraid of making a promise to her he couldn't keep. But David understood the game better than Rockwell thought. Only the difference now was that he wasn't willing to trade his soul anymore for his country.

"I do not wish to go to London, Mother."

Victoria placed a finger on the spot in the storybook from which she was reading. Sitting on the settee with Nathanial, a glass of milk in her hand, she looked down at her son snuggled against her and, utterly flummoxed by the declaration, frowned.

After leaving Sir Henry that evening, Nathanial had been inordinately quiet—no longer the exuberant boy of that morning with fearless dreams of challenging Ethan Birmingham to a sword duel. She had done her best to keep a happy face, yet, from the mournful mood hanging over the meal that night, one would have thought the world had already ended.

"Don't you want to see the city? It's all you and Peepaw used to talk about."

He stared morosely at the strawberry tart in his lap. "Not if you aren't there."

"What has suddenly brought this on?"

"Is Lord Chadwick my father?"

Meg choked on a sip of milk. Snatching a serviette from her lap, she dabbed her lips and coughed. "Is this what you and Peepaw spoke about today?" she rasped.

"Peepaw said I looked just like him. Everyone I meet says that." Nathanial's eyes, so much like his father's, lowered as he traced a circle on the tart. "Do I, Mother?"

"Nathanial . . ."

His jaw set in sullen defiance, he thrust out his chin. "I already know the truth."

She and David were supposed to do this together, but he had not returned with Mr. Rockwell from the church today. Nathanial folded his arms, looking even more like David.

"Yes, he is your father," she answered, setting the milk aside and turning to her son. "It's true. We were going to—"

"Does Father want me?"

Protectiveness unfurling in her chest at the naked vulnerability in her son's eyes, the last thing she'd expected to do was champion David. "You listen to me, young man." She took his hands into hers. "He wants you very much, or he would not have gone all the way to Salehurst to find you or dance with Frannie just so you could stay longer and dunk for apples."

A corner of his mouth relented to a grin.

"Something happened between us before I came to live with Sir Henry"—her voice was quiet—"or he would have been here sooner to see you." No longer on solid ground, Victoria wished she could blame the sudden sting of tears on anyone other than herself.

"Frannie said I was a bastard," he said.

"Well, that is quite impossible. I assure you."

Nathanial leaned his head into the crook of her arm. "I'm not?" The news gave her a peek at the first real spark in his eyes since they'd returned from the cottage. "Truly?"

"Truly, you are not, Nathanial."

He took a bite of strawberry tart and smiled. "I'm glad, Mother. I like him."

Victoria didn't quite know what to say. Although the outcome of this conversation was never in doubt, her son's response was, until she realized that except for the rare story, Nathanial had never known Sir Scott Munro. The man in the cemetery held no connection to Nathanial's world, not like a real live, flesh-and-blood father would. And David had a way of making himself the center of anyone's universe.

"Do you like him, too, Mother?"

"I . . ." She shifted her arm beneath his head. "Your father has many . . . interesting, admirable qualities. He's"—clearing her throat, she regarded her son's interest with growing frustration—"interesting. And admirable."

"He owns a castle in Scotland."

She could not understand why David would say such a thing.

"Ethan Birmingham's father is only a merchant," Nathanial continued with rising enthusiasm. "My father is better than his father."

"Don't judge people on their rank or trade, Nathanial. You know better—"

"Father will set Cousin Nellis to rights, too, Mother. You shall see. He knows how to use a sword. He practices every morning. I saw him from my bedroom window."

Victoria sank against the cushions. With a start of surprise, she remembered the ritual kata, an ancient Far Eastern form of training. She used to watch him from their bedroom window in Calcutta. He'd performed the routine every morning before sunrise, eventually teaching it to her, until the ritual had become their own, and she'd mastered the sword.

She shut the book. "Nathanial—"

"He has a large family," her son extolled. "With thirteen nieces and nephews. And Frannie says she heard him talking to Uncle Reuben in Old German. They all like him."

"Did he say anything . . . about anything else?"

"He said my trousers were too short and I would need new clothes." Nathanial yawned and snuggled against her. "He won't leave us, will he, Mother?"

Victoria pushed the hair from his brow. "He won't leave you. I promise."

After putting Nathanial to bed, Victoria grabbed an oil lamp and padded downstairs, the skirt of her nightdress billowing out around her. The white wainscoting paneling in the corridor captured the shadows cast by the light. The house was eerily silent. David had not yet returned. She wanted to know if Mr. Rockwell had any idea why not.

Returning to the kitchen where she'd last seen him partaking of nourishment, she nearly collided with him as she entered. "My lady," he said, "I didn't see you."

Noting his limp as he stepped back, Victoria raised the light to his face. She set her thumb to his chin, narrowing her gaze on his. "Do you still have all of your teeth?"

He tested his jaw, displeasure narrowing his eyes. "Barely, my lady."

The foyer clock upstairs began to ring the midnight hour. "Do you know where Mr. Donally went tonight?"

"He was rather irritable when we parted ways. I can only hope he isn't visiting Pamela." Murmuring something else about walking the grounds, he left the kitchen and pounded up the stairs before she even realized he was gone.

A small hiss emanated from the lamp in her hand. "I see," she whispered, whatever she'd wanted to say to David now lost in her hurt. "It didn't take him long, did it?"

Absently, she picked up a piece of bread crust from the floor. And started to turn when a distinct noise coming from somewhere below in the cellar jerked her around. Her hand went to her pocket before she remembered the derringer was no longer in her possession. She no longer had her knife, either.

Holding the lamp above her head, she walked through the kitchen to another room where gleaming pots and pans were stored. Silver moonlight speared the floor through an upper stained-glass fanlight set high in the wall. "Mrs. Gibson?" she called.

She walked to the door leading into the cellar, then edged it open. Zeus shot between her legs, tail in the air as he disappeared around the corner. Biting her lip to stifle a treacherous gasp, Victoria shut the door, twisted the key in the lock, and leaned back against the jamb. A chilly draft seeped beneath the door to wrap around her ankles, and she jumped away, glaring at the door as if icy fingers had just touched her flesh. She didn't like that Zeus had scared the wits out of her.

She hurried out of the kitchen with the realization that David's absence weighed on her heart and mind heavy enough that she was beginning to fear the shadows in her own beloved house. Without pausing on the main floor, she hurried up the second set of stairs, until she stopped in front of Nathanial's room.

Her hand paused on the latch, and just when her mind caught that the door was ajar, it suddenly swung wide.

"Mother Mary and Joseph!" Her breathing labored and rapid, she confronted David. "You scared the wits out of me."

Still wearing his long coat, he stepped into the hallway, bringing with him the chill clinging to the dark wool. "Why are you shaking?"

Victoria's wide eyes swept over him. The realization that his presence eased her mind troubled her as much as it relieved her that he was safe. "I thought you were . . ." She shook her head to clear the cobwebs. "An intruder."

No sconce lit the hallway, and she could not read his eyes as he closed the door. "I wasn't expecting to find anyone stirring," he said. "I didn't mean to awaken you."

A stillness settled over them, and, as her alarm subsided, she became aware of the faint essence of expensive French perfume. "What happened between you and Mr. Rockwell?" she forced herself to ask.

"We had a divergence of opinion." He walked to his room.

She followed him. "If it is about this case, I should know."

Turning in the doorway at the end of the corridor, he looked at her, then dropped his gaze to her feet. "You aren't wearing slippers, Meg."

She glanced at her toes, as if she didn't already know that fact. She wore heavy woolen stockings beneath her night shift.

"Tell me about Mr. Gibson," he asked her before she could respond. "The boy Robbie's father?"

It was an odd question in the middle of the night, and she drew her brows into a frown. "He used to hire the laborers for the fields and oversaw carpenters when we needed repair work done on the outer dwellings."

"Does he work for Stillings?"

"Not everyone who works for Stillings is bad. Some of the men do so to put food on the table."

He laughed. "So does hard work."

"Mr. Gibson doesn't work for Stillings. He still comes here periodically to ensure the buildings are in good repair."

"Did he ever do work at the church?"

"Yes, I believe he did so frequently."

Behind David, firelight shifted the shadows. She had instructed Moira earlier to light a fire in the hearth and see that the bed was turned down. Her line of sight included a glimpse of the four-poster bed and the edge of a tester canopy.

"Dare I assume you prepared my room for me tonight?"

"You may not." She met his scrutiny. "And if you are asking whether I was worried about your welfare, the answer is also no."

His mouth crooked a fraction. "That's not what I was asking, but you answered my question anyway." He let his eyes roam her face in that worrisome way that warned her he was very adept at reading people. "You're becoming less skilled at lying." He entered his bedroom and tossed his coat across a plush armchair. "I believe that is a positive step in the right direction."

Again, that wicked grin as he seated himself on the edge of his bed to tug off his boots, and Victoria felt a familiar quickness hasten her heartbeat as he looked up. "It isn't as important that I convince you that you are wrong, as it is that you try to convince yourself that you are right. I have the advantage of knowing the truth."

"Now you're a seer?"

"I passed your maid before coming upstairs. She told me." Working his collar loose, he walked past her into his dressing room. "Honesty is a potent medicine to swallow, Meg."

Honesty indeed, she scoffed. He was enjoying needling her for some reason. "What happened between you and Mr. Rockwell?" She stood outside the dressing room.

"He convinced me that I should not give Kinley an excuse to seize you."

"What does that mean?"

"It means Kinley is a Sassenach pig. More so than I remember. I'm postponing my trip to London." David returned to the doorway, his shirt unbuttoned and hanging loose as he worked a cuff on his sleeve in a way that told her something else was bothering him. "Kinley is proficient at mopping up before the game is over," he said after a moment. "There are some things I'm not ready to relinquish."

Victoria had never seen David like this. But all she could grab on to was the realization that he wasn't taking Nathanial away. "Because you are a patient man?"

His eyes smiled into hers. "Patience caught the nimble hare." He set his silver cuff links on a shelf next to his shoulder.

"To be redheaded is better than to be without a head. I believe *that* proverb belongs to the Irish."

"You don't have red hair, Meg. Anywhere that I can remember."

Victoria gasped and followed him into the dressing room. "Since we are in a state of grace and candor here, maybe you should tell your son the truth about your title. He thinks his father owns a castle in Scotland, for heaven's sake."

David regarded her with an implacable expression. "You told him about us?"

"He asked. I told him the truth. As much as I could." She scuffed a toe against the leg of a chair. "I believe that he's happy with the development."

Reaching across her shoulder, he picked a robe off the brass peg on the wall. "Do try not to let it get your spirits down, Meg."

"Don't call me that name." She would rather die than have her son know her by that name. "Margaret Faraday is not a model of womanhood anyone would find to have attractive attributes."

For a moment, she thought David hadn't heard her, not to come back with a rejoinder. "You know nothing of the inclinations of men to be so sure of that opinion, love."

She opened her mouth to reply, only to find she was experiencing a heart flutter in her chest. Looping the belt across his waist, he padded past her. "Actually only part of the castle remains. A turret, to be exact, among a pile of stones. But to a nine-year-old who dreams of knights and sword fights, those stones were easily castle walls."

"Oh, please, David." She followed on his heels. "You're not going to tell me you are also a baron?"

For a moment, it looked like he would tell her nothing. But

David, being nothing less than courageous, turned. "Once upon a time, I was awarded a life peerage for service to my country."

Folding her arms, she tapped her foot. "Of course you were."

"It isn't something people know about me."

"I see." Silently condemning him with her eyes, she smiled. "I *see* that the more I learn about you, the more I realize you are an even *bigger* liar than I am."

"Perhaps." He leaned an arm on the bedpost. "But if you don't leave my room, I'll give you an excuse to call me worse."

"Then we seem to be at an impasse." Her heart beating a wild tattoo against her ribs, she took a step nearer. "Because you are standing in my way."

His gaze flashed over her in warning. They both knew she could have walked around him. "Are you suddenly without speech, my lord baron?" Her voice was a whisper.

"Just . . ." His mouth grinned. "Not restrained, love."

Every sense leaped as if a flame had been put to her flesh, not just from his heat, but from the look in his eyes, the brush of his robe against hers, every illicit stroke of cloth against cloth, and she burned from what lay beneath the caress of fabric.

Then he stepped to the side, his hands palms out. Chin high, she hesitated, then strode past him in a billowing cloud of ivory and shut the door firmly behind her.

David waited until he heard Meg's door shut before he allowed himself to breathe again. Guilt had towed his thoughts all these years. But it wasn't guilt he was feeling now.

"Aye." He laughed and, in a moment of perfect clarity, glared at the ceiling, knowing someone upstairs surely mocked his sanity. "There is a fool born every minute and every one of them Irish."

Chapter 16

❦❦❦

"**O**n your guard, Donally!"

David parried Rockwell's lunge, testing the other's weapon, and waiting for an opening to attack. Ian's riposte drove David back two steps, their clicking foils a driving force in the studio as both men crossed the floor a second time. A leather vest covered David's white shirt. Beneath his mask, sweat trickled from his brow, and he welcomed the damp breeze as he passed an opened window overlooking the valley below. Outside the temperatures had risen and a steady drizzle of rain wiped away the last evidence of snow.

But the weather mattered little when he intended to find his entertainment inside today. Rockwell proved to be a worthy sparring opponent, which made baiting him all the more enjoyable. "You are bloodthirsty this morning." David countered the younger man's attack, his strength extending into the blade as he defeated Rockwell's efforts to score a single point.

"And you are not?"

Ian Rockwell, for all of his self-perceived expertise, was about to get his bloody clock cleaned. "Control, Rockwell."

Then as if on cue, both men switched their foils to their left hands and began the exercise all over again. The sound of steel sliding against steel followed. What had begun as a fencing match quickly degenerated into a sword fight. Rockwell ducked beneath David's blade, his breath harsh behind his mask.

"Not bad, Donally. But you still won't win."

David laughed. "I don't have to win to beat you. I only have to stop you from gaining a point."

Foils clicking, they went around the room two more times, until Rockwell finally bent over his knees and ended the drill. "I think . . . we've tortured each other enough." He breathed the words. "I call it a draw."

David waggled the foil tip in front of his adversary's nose, giving him no such satisfaction. "In your bloody dreams, Rockwell."

"Then strike your point," Ian rasped.

Despite his want to thrust the tip of his blunted foil into Rockwell's chest, despite having overslept the sunrise by an ample two hours this rainy morning, and leaving that day's tasks undone, David was feeling relatively sanguine for all that weighed on his mind. He had decided last night he wasn't playing anyone else's games. Let Rockwell know what it felt like to be toyed with and baited.

"I know what you're bloody doing." Ian swung his foil to knock aside David's and missed, as David's reflexes were still faster. "So there is no need for you to waste your time in trying to make me lose my temper. Strike the bloody point or draw."

David reached a hand to remove his mask, and found himself staring over Rockwell's shoulder. The sight froze his movement. His pulse thumped in a quicker pace to the vision of his wife and son, standing beside the potted fig tree at the back of the room. Her hands resting on the boy's shoulders, a halting movement to her chin betrayed her calm and mirrored his racing senses. For an instant, they all seemed caught by the other's gaze. Whatever irritation he felt toward Rockwell dissipated. The sun could have been shining for all the warmth that suddenly infused him.

"I hope we aren't intruding," she said.

A lock of damp hair fell over his brow as he finished removing the mask and tucked it beneath his arm. "You're not," he said, his eyes moving to his son's.

Nathanial, who had never exhibited an ounce of shyness in front of him, turned his attention to the scuffed toe of one shoe.

"Nathanial heard the click of foils," Meg said. "He wasn't sure if it was all right to watch."

"Master Nate—" Rockwell presented them both with a debonair bow. "You have just witnessed the two most excellent swordsmen in all of England spar to a stalemate."

Inwardly, David groaned and might have commented had his son's eyes not flickered with interest. A smile tilted Meg's mouth. "Indeed," she said. "Who am I to challenge a man's opinion of himself?"

Rockwell observed her. "You've held a foil then, my lady?"

"Mother knows how to handle a blade," Nathanial interjected. "Last year, she whacked Cousin Nellis's in half."

David cocked a brow at the same time Rockwell cleared his throat and said, "That must have been interesting."

"He was a poor sport about it, too." Nathanial tugged at his mother's sleeve. "Wasn't he? He never sparred with you again."

"Cousin Nellis was wise," she said pleasantly.

Softly amused, David met Meg's gaze. *What a far less pleasant meeting I might have had with Nellis had he succeeded in touching you,* the unspoken thought touched his eyes. "Wise, indeed," he said.

On that note, Ian returned his foil to its place on the wall and excused himself, leaving David alone with Meg and Nathanial.

A flush colored her cheeks, and for the briefest flicker he saw she was afraid of him. Not of him, he realized, but of losing her son to him.

But he should have known she wouldn't flinch from any challenge or duty, including facing him. "Your father is very adept with his sword." Meg smiled at her son in that brilliant, arresting way that took his breath, but her eyes were filled with something else entirely different when she looked at David. A mother's protectiveness, yes, but also a compassion for him he didn't expect to see from her. "I have work to do," she said, bending down to touch her lips to Nathanial's hair. "Will you be all right here?"

Nathanial nodded at his feet, and David wasn't certain if that was a yes, a no, or even a maybe, but at least he wasn't running out of the room.

"I'll be in the orangery if you need me," she said, and David suspected she was speaking to him. "For anything."

"Mother?" Nathanial ran to stop her at the door. "Don't you want to stay with us?"

She rippled his dark head, and without looking at David said, "Not unless you want to help me clean the orangery later, Squirrel." Meg walked out of the room.

His son looked over his shoulder at David—still standing in the middle of the floor, holding his foil and mask beneath his arm. And for a man who had been so sure of himself five minutes ago, he was surprised to feel a flutter in his stomach. They had spent two weeks in each other's company, but this was the first time they'd ever been alone as father and son.

"I should have been here for you sooner, Nathanial."

The boy shrugged. "Mother told me it wasn't your fault. She said you weren't going to go to London without me."

"No." Looking into his boy's eyes was like looking at Meg. "So you want to duel with this Ethan Birmingham, do you?"

Again, he shrugged. "He goes to school at Winchester and takes fencing lessons from the best master in all England."

"So he says." David grinned. "Have you learned how to hold a dueling sword?"

Nathanial's eyes brightened. "Only blunted foils. Mother thinks I'll cut myself."

"She's right. There is a lot more to mastering swordplay than the desire to best Ethan Birmingham. You have to know how to wield a blade and to do so without hurting yourself."

"Are you a master?"

A slow smile touched his lips. "That I am, son."

An hour after leaving Nathanial with David, Victoria quit trying to keep herself occupied in the orangery. She cast aside her gloves and returned to the studio, for there was no accounting a mother's desire to reassure herself all was well with her only child.

She pressed her ear to the door. Listening to the rumble of male voices, she felt a skein of warmth. She heard her son laugh in response to something David said. Then all grew quiet. Edging open the door, she looked inside.

David's back was to her as he walked his son through what resembled a strange dance—she recognized the kata he had once taught her. A breeze pulled at his dark hair. He wore no shoes. He'd changed out of his clothes into something consisting of a long white-sashed robe with scarlet underneath. Mirroring his father's movements, minus the sword, Nathanial held what looked like a peg leg, his profile intent, his concentration fierce, his movements precise as David spoke each of the steps aloud.

Neither of them saw her at the door.

The desire to watch, even to take part, brought her up short, and she eased the door closed. They didn't need her in there. She held a hand to her side. Her wound was not yet healed, but the ache she felt had nothing to do with her ribs.

Victoria grabbed her cloak and asked Mr. Rockwell to take her to the cottage. Sir Henry was asleep when she knocked on his bedroom door an hour later and Esma was upstairs helping Bethany sew her new gown.

Victoria left the cottage, and for the first time in days, lost herself to her work. She didn't hear the door into the root cellar open.

"They've been up at the house for three hours," Sir Henry said.

Victoria looked up from where she was shoveling loam from the herbal garden into the row of half barrels against the wall. Sir Henry stood just outside the lantern light, his hip hitched against the workbench where she'd finished labeling the last jars of herbs.

"How do you know?" She wearily brushed soil from her knees.

"I know, because that's how long you've been in here." His

mouth crooked at one corner. "I wasn't asleep when you knocked."

Outside, a beam of sunlight broke through the overcast skies. Victoria looked up at the narrow cellar window, as the room grew brighter. She returned to the workbench and began the process of cleaning. "You have a supply of peppermint. But we need—"

"Victoria." Sir Henry touched her forearm and her hands stilled their task. "Stop."

She wrapped her palms around an empty jar and set it on the shelf before turning to face him. "I didn't know it would be this hard. My son needs his father. I understand . . ."

"Think how he must be feeling."

"Nathanial?"

"Chadwick."

Victoria opened her mouth to correct Sir Henry's use of Chadwick as David's name, but she could not. Instead, she picked up a hand broom. "Nathanial's very relationship to David excludes me."

"As Chadwick is excluded by yours to Nathanial. You're doing the right thing, Victoria."

From an angle, she could see the palsy in Sir Henry's hand as he gripped the cane, and she set down the broom, her own problems no longer important. "How are you feeling?"

"Daniel Gibson and his son Robbie were here," Sir Henry said, leaning both hands on the cane as if it pained him to stand. "He said Lord Chadwick asked to see him. I've sent Mr. Gibson to the manor house with a message to bring him here. We need to talk."

"Would you like your coffee with cream, mum?" Esma asked.

Victoria looked up from the documents in her hand. She was sitting at the kitchen table. A fire crackled in the hearth and mixed with the tangy aroma of a baking pie, all familiar smells of warmth and comfort she'd grown accustomed to in this cottage. Esma stood beside her, a small creamer in her hand.

"When did Sir Henry do this?" She set down the documents.

"His solicitor returned with the papers this morning, mum."

The sound of an approaching horse drew Victoria to the window. She pulled aside the yellow curtains. David cantered Old Boy into the yard. He wore his coat, gloves, and hat, and she almost didn't see Nathanial riding in front of him on the saddle.

Mr. Rockwell came out of the stable to take the reins. David eased Nathanial from the saddle when he saw Robbie exit from the stable. Her son ran across the yard. Even from behind the glass, she heard him talk about everything he'd done all morning, and say that when he grew up, he was going to be a knight.

As if sensing her presence at the window, David looked at the cottage—at her. She did not hear what Mr. Rockwell said as David threw his leg over the saddle and slipped to the ground. She dropped the edge of the curtain and, leaning her head against the sill, closed her eyes.

This morning he'd solved the apprehension in her heart in regard to the welfare of their son. Nathanial idolized him. Yet, somehow, she'd thought it would take longer for the two to form a bond, that she would hold more importance in her son's life.

The back door shut. David ducked through the archway into the kitchen. Pulling off his hat, his eyes touching hers, he looked around as if expecting to see that something terrible had befallen her. "Is everything all right?" he asked, handing his coat and gloves to Esma as she bustled forward.

Behind him, Mr. Rockwell and Bethany entered. Sir Henry appeared in the kitchen. "Lord Chadwick," he said, and asked David to sit at the table, while directing Bethany to another chair.

Esma brought tea. Knowing what Sir Henry was about to ask David, Victoria looked at her hands as she took her place across from him.

Sir Henry was ill. No one knew better than Victoria did from the first time she'd recognized his symptoms a year ago. Two days ago, he'd decided to put his affairs in order. He didn't want the responsibility of Rose Briar. Even if he could talk David out of the deed, which at this point she suspected he easily could, Sir Henry would never be able to raise the funds needed to make the land productive again. But today was about something closer to his heart, and she sat at the end of the table half afraid to listen.

"I'm exhausted," Sir Henry said to David and Bethany, finally turning to her. "I've finished all the treatment I'm going to take, and we both know that no herbs or miracle potions exist to cure what ails me. I could live another year or die tomorrow, I don't know. But then who understands God's plan for us all."

"Peepaw—"

"Bethany, for once I need you to listen. I need both of you to understand," he said, looking between Victoria and Bethany before turning his attention to David. "I am willing everything I own to the Rose Briar Estate, and ask that you remain," he said. "That you not sell, if only because this is Nathanial's home. You have the means to put life back into this land and give something to this town I failed to do."

Victoria found she could not watch as Sir Henry pleaded his case. David might be her husband and Nathanial's father, but he worked for the British government, and in that capacity, he had made it clear he would soon be gone—and she with him.

"Under the current circumstances, Nellis will attempt to find some way to contest your claim to Rose Briar," Sir Henry continued to speak to David. "No doubt, he will make it a long and painful process. But though he may contest the legitimacy of your claim, he cannot successfully contest my will. I only ask that you think about my petition. I ask this because Bethany needs a guardian."

David looked directly at Victoria as if she clearly belonged in Bedlam for agreeing to this—a look everyone else intercepted. "She knew nothing about my decision," Sir Henry said.

Bethany was the first to react. "I don't want to be your family, *either*, Lord Chadwick." Her blue eyes glistening in the firelight, she stood. "Why are you doing this, Peepaw? You speak as if you are in the grave when you are as well as an ox. I'll not allow you to talk as if you are already dead."

"Sit down, Bethany," Sir Henry ordered.

"I will not."

Sir Henry came to his feet, the resulting uproar every bit as unpleasant as it usually was when he grew cross and accused his seventeen-year-old headstrong granddaughter of not only needing her bottom smacked but also needing a strong hand capable of finding her a husband.

"A husband?" Teary eyed, Bethany gasped. "I will pick my own husband, Peepaw."

"And this is what comes from spoiling you, Bethany Ann

Munro." He shook his grizzled head regretfully. "Is it your desire that Nellis become your guardian, then?"

"You should have asked what I wanted, Peepaw."

Victoria stood. "What is it you want, Bethany?"

"I *certainly* have no desire to go where I am *not* wanted. Nathanial belongs to Lord Chadwick, but I am not his family . . . why should he want me?" She looked from Sir Henry to Victoria. "I am nearly eighteen . . . surely if you do not stay, then neither do I—"

David scraped back the chair and, though he was the last to stand, his movement silenced the room. He started to speak, thought better of saying anything at all, and, turning on his heel, walked out of the kitchen.

David was outside, half sitting against a hitching rail when he heard gravel crunch behind him. Watching through a pale streamer of blue smoke, he inhaled from the cheroot as Meg stepped in front of him. Behind her, Nathanial, Robbie, and the Shelbys' older son were playing pirates in the stable. David had come out here to get away from the cottage—from his own thoughts. He had been angry earlier, though he didn't know why.

Or maybe he did.

"I would have warned you of Sir Henry's plan if I could have," Meg said. "But despite anything you might think about his motives, this is Nathanial and Bethany's home. I agree with his intent."

"Did you maneuver Sir Henry into making his decision?"

"I did not. Clearly Sir Henry believes you are some guardian angel," she said. "Everything happens for a reason and all that. Sir Henry is a firm believer your presence here is kismet."

"What do you believe?"

"That kismet doesn't necessarily equate to good fortune for all."

His arms folded one over the other, David tapped ash from the cheroot, acutely aware of her and wishing he was not. Clad in trousers and boots beneath her cloak, she presented an anomalous, striking figure, looking like something he wanted to strip naked and go at against some private, shady wall somewhere. The image, completely incongruous with the reality of their circumstances, turned his attention to the hills.

Indeed, Sir Henry had cleverly pried open the passageway to his innermost secret desires. Only his sense of duty remained to be questioned. The sole source of his conflict.

And he was no longer sure even of that.

Only of his doubts.

"Why is Nellis so intent on having this estate?"

"I don't know. Last year, we were at least on civil terms."

"With the exception of you whacking off his sword."

Her mouth crooked. "There was that," she quipped.

Something in the silence that followed spoke to him of warmth and shared memories. "Do you still practice your gojushiho kata or kenjutsu?" he asked.

She shook her head, and a strange sense of loss caught him. How impossibly long ago it had been when he'd taught her kendo, the way of the sword. When her laughter had filled the empty courtyard of her father's house.

Sounds of someone dying in a pirate battle drifted from the loft in the stables, and Meg looked up at the opened shutters. "I believe our son just killed Robbie," she said.

When he made no reply, she turned and, catching his bold perusal, frowned, for David did not turn away this time or bother to hide the fact that he was staring at her with less than pure thoughts. She looked at him steadily and with something akin to growing wariness. Yet, strangely, he understood her guardedness, for he now fully understood his own and the source whence it came, even if she did not yet comprehend.

Silently laughing at his own weaknesses, he remembered that one of his brothers, Ryan, once told him he'd have to set his own affairs to right before judging another's.

When had he stopped judging Meg?

"You are not the sort of woman I'd ever envisioned marrying," he said. "Yet from the first time I saw you, somehow you got in my blood. I was never quite sure what to do about it then anymore than I am now." He studied the glowing tip of the cheroot. "I've done a poor job at most everything I've ever tried to do, Meg. Certainly, I'm no angel."

"You're wrong about having done a poor job at everything."

He arched a dubious brow. "A compliment?"

"You found me."

David dropped the cheroot and ground it beneath his boot as he stood. "Maybe I was meant to find you. Meant to be here. And not in the divine sense of the word, either."

Clearly, the thought had crossed her mind as well. "You are here when you should be in London," she said. "Mr. Rockwell must have told you something new about the case, important enough for you to throw all caution aside."

Her assertion that he could be here for any other reason but for her safekeeping brought a flicker of grim amusement to his mood. Then suddenly he was looking into her incredible eyes and wanted to do so much more than touch her. He wanted her to believe in him. To trust him. "Six months ago, your father disappeared," he said. "I found out Kinley was in charge of his incarceration."

"Six months? That is about the time Nellis took an interest in Rose Briar. But . . . if someone knew where I was, why bring you in?"

"Isn't it obvious your father has revenge in mind?"

He thought she paled. "Do you think Nellis is involved? But why Rose Briar?"

"You tell me. Maybe he thinks something of great value is hidden on this massive estate." There was neither anger nor accusation in his voice, merely a question that demanded an answer as he took her left hand and pressed her locket into her palm. "Would he be correct in that assumption?"

The expression on her face didn't change, and if he hadn't been holding her hand, wasn't aware of her every breath, he would not have felt her response. But looking into her face, he realized the subtle reaction was not a response to his question, but to the locket itself. "Why did you bring this back?" she asked. "It's only an old piece of jewelry."

"You don't need to barter your possessions. I have money." He brought her fist to his lips and placed a tender kiss on the knuckles clutched over the locket. "I believe we can agree to disagree about everything else."

"Yet we both agree what will happen when this is over."

"What do *you* want to happen when this is over?" he quietly asked.

She eased away her hand. The locket had hit a nerve, or maybe only he had. He was confusing her. Probably had been confusing her since his return from town last night. He liked her confused. Vulnerability was more permeable, and he could touch more of her without wading through the mantle she wore around her like an invisible cloak. "Your mother's image is inside. Why would you trade the locket, Meg?"

She took a step backward as he straightened. "You were right. I also believe there is someone guiding our every movement. It's not safe for you here. Let Mr. Rockwell finish the job and turn me over to the authorities when it is time. But take Bethany and Nathanial with you. Start your life some-where else," she added, clearly having spent some time con-sidering that point as she rambled on about an annulment. "I'm sure any woman in England would jump at the chance to be with someone of your *impeccable* credentials."

Leaning his palms against the rough plank wall at her back, he encased her between his arms. "My impeccable cre-dentials?" There was a lightness to his eyes, self-effacing hu-mor that made him less upright and somehow more vulnerable to her tender gaze. "A moment ago you thought I should accept Sir Henry's proposal. Now you are you foisting me off on another woman?"

"It is not my desire to foist you off on anyone."

She ducked beneath his arm, but he stepped into her space and gave her no place to retreat. "Why didn't you tell me there was gossip about us in town?"

"You are the source of a lot of gossip," she said offhand-edly. "Isn't that what you set out to accomplish? To make yourself as visible a target as possible? You're a baron with a beautiful mistress, a big house on the bluff. You've started a war with Nellis. How could my father or anyone working with him not notice you and through you find me? It has worked. So go away and let Mr. Rockwell finish this job be-fore you and I end up exactly where we were nine years ago."

"What do you want to happen when this is over?" he asked her again. "You said that we both agree on what will happen when this is over. I want to know what *you* want to happen. Will we face each other as we once did before?" he forced himself to ask, forced her to look at him.

Shaking her head, she lowered her gaze. "I don't want to hate you, David."

"Then the future does not have to end the way someone else wants this to play out," he said, his eyes a little more gentle, knowing she had every right not to trust him, yet knowing she should have learned ten years ago that when he set his mind to a task, he got what he wanted. "A road of a thousand miles begins with the first step, Meg." She looked down as he closed his hand over hers. "You can take that step with me."

"Then what?" She met his steady gaze and whispered, "Do you have a miracle up your sleeve that can save me from *you*?"

"I might. But not today, love."

The last word said on an intimate breath, he leaned into her because he couldn't stop himself. When her back came up against the side of the stable, he straightened slightly, his eyes burning into hers. He saw only a wariness that he understood too well. He knew how badly he had once hurt her.

And there *was* a darkness inside her that worried him, that lay beneath the surface. A part of her that he seemed to recognize because it lived inside him as well.

He didn't kiss her. Didn't even try. Though his gaze remained a moment longer on her mouth before he stepped aside to let her pass. It was enough for now to see the desire in her eyes and know that she wanted him as much as he wanted her.

Chapter 17

A s twilight settled over the hills, David reined in Old Boy atop the knoll overlooking the cottage. He watched as Meg and Nathanial stepped into the buggy that would take them back to Rose Briar. After Meg had left him at the stable, he had not remained to sup with them, preferring instead to run Old Boy.

David withdrew his field glasses from his pack and watched the buggy's progress up the drive and onto the road until it disappeared in the woods. He could see other activity on the drive as Mr. Shelby raked hay into a trough. Bethany appeared from inside the stable, pulling the reins of a horse and, for a moment, heedless of his inner struggle, he watched her. Meg had been only a little older than Bethany when he had first met her.

What did he know of playing the role of anyone's guardian anyway, or of the responsibilities that came with owning land and people's lives? Or interpreting an old man's reasons for believing David had a right to any of it? Or thinking that he had the power to change anything for the better?

It was a familiar thought, he realized, one that he battled within every arena of his life. He had never had the power to change anything or make a difference.

The black stallion pranced in sudden apprehension. Twisting in the saddle, he turned the glasses on the countryside. He could see the distant church steeple through the trees and paused as he reflected on Sir Henry's belief in kismet or providence. David knew he would rather not attach his current fate to the workings of a capricious higher power. Yet his long association in Ireland left an indelible mark on him that he could not deny. For the very cause that brought him to Meg in India had brought him back to her now as if fate were offering him a second chance to do what he should have done the first time, and undo what he had destroyed. Fate was telling him to trust his heart.

And hers.

The buggy appeared atop the far rise, a speck against the darkening indigo sky. Even with the brisk chill in the air, cattle congregated farther away. The ridge dipped and the buggy passed out of sight again, and David was suddenly looking at Rose Briar across the vale. He was no longer seeing a house made of stone and wood. He was seeing Meg's vision and a hint of her dreams. He was seeing an opportunity for his own life, a glimpse of his future as Sir Henry saw it, if he chose to stay.

He also saw danger to everything and everyone that had come to matter to him.

The locket remained a constant in the back of his mind.

It was later, after midnight, as he stood in his bedroom at

his window, a saber weighting the sling at his side, that he re-alized he was no longer conflicted.

Dressed in black, with black boots beneath a dark cloak, he descended the narrow servants' stairs, the same way Meg had left the night she'd escaped the house. His saber scraped the walls. He lifted the lantern above his head as he walked around the outside of the house. His family was inside, and there were forces that threatened them. The foundation had been built hundreds of years before, perhaps even the same time as the church. He blew out the light.

Mounting Old Boy, he swung the stallion around and stretched out in an easy canter. As the moon continued its flight across an ebon sky, he rode the estate, high and low, from one end to the other, searching the banks of the bluff and the silent fields for the answers he sought. Colonel Fara-day could not have disappeared into thin air. Someone had to be shielding him. Or he was dead and another threat loomed. Tonight, not even Stillings's men made an appearance to temper David's quest for answers. And in the end, he knew he would find them only with Meg herself.

Victoria stood at her bedroom window, watching David complete his kata. Dawn had not yet breached the dove gray clouds. But she'd known he would be there as he had been every day for the past week on the terrace, overlooking the valley when the first rays of sunlight topped the distant trees.

Watching him, she was sure she had not wanted anyone or anything more in her entire life. Except perhaps, she wanted her son safe, and Sir Henry's illness to miraculously disap-pear. She wanted Bethany to know she was not alone, and she wanted to be free to face her own destiny.

This past week, David had switched tactics on her and, if she'd once thought her father was the target of his hunt, she knew without a doubt that it was she he held in his sights now.

He probably knew she was at her window watching him.

For watch him she did, fascinated as any artist patron would be by a masterpiece, no matter the sculptor or painter. Wearing a sleeveless, woven top and pleated skirtlike trousers, he moved with precise steps and coordination through the kata. She stared, mesmerized by his disciplined movements—her former mentor, her lover, her husband— caught by memories she had no business exploring. Closing her eyes, she felt her body stir.

"You're very good, David Donally." Her breath misted the glass, and she dropped the edge of the curtain.

Leaning against the wall, she drew in one slow breath at a time, recognizing a seduction when she saw one—David was very adept at his job. Yet, knowing that, she still wanted him. More than anything, she wanted to believe *in* him.

You can take that first step with me.

Even if it took her off a cliff?

But Victoria couldn't shake David. He'd been polite and civil, and as clairvoyant as a ghost. He managed to appear everywhere she was, as if he had the ability to read her mind and knew where she was at all times.

Two days ago, she'd thought he and Mr. Rockwell were at the church, and snuck outside to see who might be watching the stables, to see if she could sit on a horse without experiencing pain in her side.

But David had been there casually talking to the groom. Without any outward suspicion of her motives for being in the stable, he'd saddled Old Boy. He then helped her mount and swung up behind her. They'd ended up riding across the fields that had once sowed fertile crops. The horse's gait had hurt her side, but it did not affect her as much as the scent of David's presence, his warmth, his voice in her ear as he stopped to talk to Mr. Gibson and another tenant they'd met on the road as they passed the north edge of the property. Only David could think nothing of meeting others while sharing the same saddle with her in public or make her melt over such a mundane topic as the weather.

But he was busy now, Victoria thought as she washed her face and teeth, and braided her hair. She adjusted her stays over her waist. The sun had yet to rise. She eased herself into a pair of trousers, shoving her shirt into her waistband as she rushed to find her boots. Surely, David would be too occupied to notice if she'd left her bedroom.

She opened the door.

David was leaning against the wall, two bamboo staffs in his hands, clearly waiting for her to emerge. Narrowing her eyes, she realized he must have hurried upstairs after she'd pulled away from the window. A mischievous grin on his lips, he tossed her a staff, which she caught midair, surprising even herself.

"Not bad." And despite her want to ignore the backhanded compliment, she felt warmed by the look in his eyes. "Join me," he said.

"I can't, David. I'm still injured."

He continued to block her path. "All the better. I'll win."

"Oh, please, must you show me your conceit, as well?"

His open and appreciative scrutiny of her person brought a hot flush to her face. "The practice will do you good," he said. "Do you remember the steps?"

She examined the length of bamboo in her hand. "Where did you get these staffs?"

"Doesn't yours feel familiar? It's the same one we used to practice with."

"One staff feels the same as any other," she said.

A slow wolfish smile showed his teeth. "Does it now? And here I was thinkin' my staff was special in your magic hands."

She slid her fingers over the cool bamboo and peered at him from beneath her lashes. The unkempt, haphazard way his growing beard framed his jaw seemed to make his eyes bluer, like the sky at twilight or the sea at dawn. "Were ye now, David Donally?"

She never could turn down a challenge. Especially against a man encased in a whisper of scarlet and a short woven shirt that did not hide his sculpted strength. His feet were bare, and he made her remove her boots before they walked to the studio at the other end of the house.

David also made her wear the protective vest. She stood in front of him as he tied the leather strings at her waist and hips. Her braid lay over one shoulder. He moved in front of her and, taking her stance, she smiled at him over the bamboo staff. "If you feel the need to play nice because of some chivalrous sense of honor, don't."

He did play nice though, she realized, as he patiently countered each move and allowed her to relearn the necessary cadence that came with the exercise. Her muscles were stiff. The action pulled at her side, while pulling at still deeper pieces of her she had buried long ago. She struggled within the spirit of the kata, every step coming back to her in slow degrees. Their staffs clicked and they circled each other.

"You're holding back." He swayed from foot to foot, a reckless grin challenging her. "What are you afraid of?"

She slammed the staff across his. "I'm not afraid."

But she was afraid.

"Then fight me, Meg."

David met her every blow, moving with an indefinable grace and confidence that marked him as a skilled opponent. Not once did she think she had the upper hand, but neither did he overwhelm or defeat her.

They skirted a mat and circled each other. "You don't think fear controls you? Let it go, Meg. Fight me. Only then will you learn to master it."

His eyes never left her face. Her eyes never strayed from his, and before Victoria realized what had happened, she was moving with her old grace and confidence. It was as if with every blow she aimed at David, she struck at the wall of her heart and soul, only to find him always there guarding her, the teacher who set the pace and the distance, and the lover who beckoned more. She was eighteen again. He was twenty-six. She swept her staff high then low, her movements increasing in speed and dexterity, her smile intent as he countered, the hollow clicking of bamboo filling the empty sanctuary of the studio. Outside the sun topped the trees and sunlight moved into the room, across the floor in a blanket of amber as the dawn brought the warm colors of the day to life. Still David and Victoria went around the room, oblivious to the rest of the world.

"I haven't forgotten." She swung the staff at his feet, feeling more alive than she had in years.

He leaped the pole, turned, and countered, his movements restrained and carefully controlled, but not so weak that he didn't strike the staff from her hand. It flew above her head, only to be snatched out of the air as David caught it first. He did have the advantage. He was six inches taller.

She was breathing hard. Her side hurt, but she didn't care.

"One would think you practiced every day," he said, offering her the staff, which she snatched back and attacked again.

As if expecting the action, he ducked and was suddenly behind her. In a swift move, not a choreographed part of the kata, he brought the staff over her head and trapped her against his chest. "No fair, David." Breathing in the scent of him, she felt his heartbeat against her back. "You're improvising." Her mouth touched his roughened jaw.

"So are you, love."

Victoria could see nothing past the breadth of his shoulders. She possessed a desire to remain where she was. "If you were a priest, how is it that you've stayed in practice all these years?"

He let her go, and she turned to strike at him again. Her staff hit his. "There are places in Dublin that rival streets in Calcutta, Shanghai, and even Boston."

"Have you traveled to all of those places?"

"Every single one."

Again, he maneuvered himself around her back and she was beginning to feel like a mouse in the paws of a cat. Except David's body felt warm and inviting, and this time she let her bottom lean into his groin.

"Now tell me something no one knows about you," he said against her hair.

"My favorite color is lavender."

His mouth touched the shell of her ear. "I knew that."

Lord in heaven. Enticed by the bold feel of him, she cast the thought upward as if some higher power could save her from herself. "I've never told you that."

"Maybe not. But one only need look at your room."

She felt his subtle surrender as he allowed her to walk him backward. "What is *your* favorite color?" Breaking his grip with an upward thrust, she turned and pressed the length of her staff against his chest. She continued to walk him backward. "Black?" *Like sin*? her eyes challenged.

His teeth gleaned in the sunlight. "Nothing so mundane. Unless you have the ability to read my mind."

She could not read his mind, and that was the problem, but he was aroused beneath the silky scarlet of pleated pants. "I may not be able to read your thoughts, but your body is an open book, *love*."

She'd walked him toward the mat he'd left out after his practice with Nathanial last night, and his heel caught the plump edge. He wouldn't have fallen except that she took the opportunity to propel him backward by shoving him and sweeping her pole against his other foot. She thought he might have hit rather hard on his back, but without pausing, she straddled his hips and pressed the staff to his throat in the way of a Roman gladiator.

"I win, Donally." Her breath coming in uneven gasps, she smiled in triumph. "Surrender or face the consequences."

"The consequences?" David laughed unpleasantly.

"Are you hurt?" she thought to ask.

"Aye." His hands wrapped around hers on the staff, and he lifted the pressure off his neck. "My pride could use a wee bit of your kindness just now."

Straddled across him as she was, his erection pressed between her thighs, she felt a wicked stir of desire. Her chest heaved as she continued to pull air into her lungs and, in a breathtaking rush, returned her focus to the staff in her hands. "You asked me to tell you something that you didn't know. Are you willing to answer my questions in return?"

He could easily have tossed her off him with very little force. But he had been careful not to hurt her thus far. He had always been careful, she realized, protecting her in a way she'd never been able to protect herself.

He brought the staff over his head, pulling her arms straight until she was stretched taut over him, her lips nearly level to his. "Tit for tat?" He raised a dark brow.

The fact that he was allowing her to manhandle him brought a surge of confidence to her actions. "Tit for tat." Still holding the staff, she pressed his hands into the mat. "To the victor go the spoils. I get to ask the first question."

He slid his gaze across her lips down to the point where her shirt gaped opened, but she wasn't about to play modest and lose her edge. "What do you want to know?" he asked.

A hint of myrrh permeated his body heat. Victoria met his gaze, wary of her own raging desire. "What happened between you and Kinley that you distrust him so?"

"We've never been close. Fourteen years ago, Kinley blew my cover on a job in Prussia and nearly cost me my life, not counting jeopardizing the mission we had been working on for almost a year. In Calcutta, he cost me one of my team when he acted too soon to spring the trap on Colonel Faraday. And he cost me you. Had he waited . . ."

"Had he waited, nothing would be any different."

"Everything would have been different. I would have had time to get you out."

She shook her head. "And turned traitor to save me? I don't believe it is in your nature, David."

"Then my nature is a mystery even to me."

Not to her, she realized. David had always possessed an inherent integrity and honor that she had not.

Her braid fell against his shoulder. "Are you in love with me?"

"A man's heart is his greatest weakness. If I were in love with you, I would be a fool. Would I not be?"

"Were you ever unfaithful to our vows?"

"What the hell kind of question is that?"

"Tit for tat." Her grip tightened on his wrists. "Were you?"

"No."

"Not even after you thought I was dead?"

His eyes narrowed. "Then I could not be unfaithful, could I?"

She knew by the look in his eyes there had been other women in his life after her.

In one powerful move, he turned her over onto her back, stilling her fight with his body. His eyes tenderly brushed her face. "You have to take some of the blame. Your supposed demise was more than convincing. And it was two years before I became a priest."

"Get off me."

He studied her compressed lips with grim amusement. Surprisingly, he did as she asked, but there was something in his gaze that did not match the ease of his movement. As she struggled to stand and snatched up her staff, Victoria became acutely aware that he was furious.

"If you think you can fob me off with your injured airs, think again, love."

Forcing an artificial laugh, she walked to the window. "Who was she?"

"What does it matter?" His answer was barely audible above her racing heart. "I was never interested in keeping your memory alive. I was interested only in killing it."

Victoria didn't have to turn to know David had left, for the studio felt suddenly empty of his presence. Her eyes drifting shut, she leaned against the cooling glass.

For nine years, she had wondered about his life. She had lived, knowing he had never belonged to her. She was not angry that he had found sanctuary in another woman's arms, no matter how brief. She was angry that she had not fought harder for what she had.

David was lying on the bed in his bedroom when Victoria found him fifteen minutes later. His hair was damp as if he'd washed his face. He wore a black silk robe belted at the waist, his fingers linked behind his head as he stared at the heavy tapestry that bordered the high tester. She raised her hand to knock but her movement in the doorway brought his gaze around.

"Did it work?" she asked.

He sat up and slid his legs over the side of the bed. Whatever he'd been thinking when she entered the room no longer showed on his face. He came to his feet. Clearly, he had not expected to see her in his doorway.

"Were you able to kill the memory?"

"No," he said quietly.

"Why not?"

She needed to know because in seeking his answer, she hoped to find her own. But David did not reply. Instead, in the wake of his silence, the knot in her stomach tightened.

Looking around the room, she saw David as if for the first time as a permanent fixture in her life and in Nathanial's. "You're really a baron, aren't you? With your castle in Scotland. Your sister is married to a duke, and you have thirteen nieces and nephews. Is Pamela your mistress?"

"No."

Hot tears stung her eyes. Chiding herself for not being

calmer, she pulled the leather vest over her hair. Her shirt was damp and clung to her chest. "That last day in Calcutta, when my father knew the authorities had closed in on us and he gave me that earring, the last thing he told me . . . was that he loved me. No one had ever told me that before," she said. "On the same breath he then calmly told me that if you were still alive, he was going to find you and feed you your heart for breakfast for what you had done to me." She laughed, knowing now that threat had been a lie, since her father knew who David was before she did. "I remember thinking that you would be safe because you had no heart. Yet, I was also afraid that he would kill you. So I found a way to turn him in. Then I cut my hair, packed a valise, and boarded the first train out of Calcutta with a group of missionaries."

She realized, though she was still very much afraid of her father, she was more afraid that she could never rectify her past. "A part of me always knew my father couldn't love me. I was too much like my mother. I looked like her. I was impulsive and had to be forever reined in. But I never allowed myself to see how much of a monster he truly was until you came into my life, and I saw beauty. When your partner told me who you really were, I wanted to die. Maybe if you hadn't come home at the moment you did, I might have. Instead, I aimed the gun at you. If you had just walked away . . . if you hadn't moved when you did . . ."

"You were never supposed to be in the house when that raid went down. But you changed your routine that day. You were not at the consulate . . ."

Victoria shook her head, remembering the nightmare that had set her running for nine years, making no more excuses for her actions or condemnation for his. She had not been at the consulate because she had been visiting the physician about her condition. "After I left you"—she couldn't voice the word *shot*—"I realized all that I had become was all that I despised in my father. I had someone growing inside me who depended on me to survive. I didn't want my baby to suffer my own legacy. But even as I made the decision to turn in my father, a childish part of me wanted to believe he had not always been so evil."

Or that she was nothing like him. For nine years, she strove to be everything for Nathanial that her father had never been for her.

"Your father couldn't love you because he didn't know how."

She cocked her head. "You say that as if from experience."

"Does either of us really know what love is? You were eighteen when I married you. For all of your worldly experience, you were naïve about men."

"Was it all a lie?"

For a long time he said nothing, and she thought he wouldn't answer.

"None of it was a lie, Meg."

Her tears blurred his face. Somehow, he had moved nearer, and when she straightened, she was looking into his eyes. "You ask that I take my first step with you," she said. "I already did ten years ago. And you gave me Nathanial."

They remained suspended in time, neither speaking. It came upon them slowly, the way the years seemed to fall away and into bittersweet crumbs to her feet. Breathing became hard. Caught by the shifting sunlight warming the room, she was suddenly standing apart from everything she was, everything she'd become these past years.

The dam was suddenly cracking.

What was the point in trying to protect herself when she wanted to kiss him. When she wanted to feel his hands on her body and the whisper of hope against her heart. Then he put his palm on the doorjamb at her back and her uncertain eyes held his.

"Kiss me, Victoria."

He sealed her name with a tender kiss that turned all too quickly into something more. And the dam that had cracked now shattered in a flood of emotions. Why couldn't she listen to her head instead of her heart, she chastised herself, dropping the vest at her feet and looping her arms around his neck.

When they broke apart, there was no teasing glint in his eyes, nothing to drain away the building tension. They were both breathing rapidly. She felt her body's response and, leaning against him, pulled him back into the kiss. She opened his mouth to her thorough exploration, taking his groan deep into her throat. His harsh stubble abrading her flesh, he threaded his fingers into her hair, sifting them through her braid, and tipping her face to deepen the kiss.

Having lost her focus completely, she felt her head fall against her shoulders, frustrated by her own lack of self-preservation. She had not realized the depth of her need and barely registered his action as he turned the key in the lock.

"I am too soft, I think," she murmured, when he drew back to settle his mouth on the hollow of her throat.

She felt his hardness against her abdomen and the smile in his voice. "I am not soft at all," he rasped joining his mouth again to hers, his fingers scoring a path from the curvature of her shoulders to her hands.

He wrapped his fingers around her wrists and raised them

to the door. His dark blue eyes burned into hers. "And if you don't stop me, I will take you to my bed and finish what I want to do with you at this moment."

She sank against the length of him, intensely aware of the hunger they both shared. "People will miss us downstairs, David."

Their gazes met and held. "God's truth, do we care? What do *you* want?"

Victoria felt the door at her back, felt trapped by more than its barrier to freedom. The heat of his hands enfolding her wrists and the turbulent blaze of his eyes all conspired to rebuke her resolve. She didn't want to examine her needs, for she was no longer sure of anything, least of all herself.

Yet there was too much between them to deny the physical and emotional connection. They still had a thousand miles to travel before they reached the middle, but somehow the distance was not as far as it had been when she'd awakened that morning.

She belonged to him. And as that primitive reality swept through her, a bubble of giddiness threatened to overtake her senses. "I want to see you naked."

His breath was warm against her lips, and, divining her resolve, he bunched her shirt in his fist and drew it over her head. "Then I endeavor to make it so."

He swept her into his arms, conveying her to the bed, where he sat her on her feet beside the mattress. This was not the rush and desperation she'd felt before, but a wanton need to touch and feel all of him. She eased her palms across his taut shoulders, opening the robe over his arms where it fell in a caress of black silk to his feet. He wore nothing beneath. David had the kind of body a woman didn't forget, and ten years had honed his muscles. He was hard and rigid, polished perfection that sprang from the dark juncture between his thighs. As if he didn't even know he was standing in front of her naked and magnificent, he worked his hands over the ties on her trousers and slid them down her legs with her drawers. But standing beside him in her stays and camisole, she considered the ugly scar forming on her waist, and her hesitation made him raise his eyes.

There was something hot in the force of that look. Something that burned over her and made her buttery inside. Then he was easing her down onto the bed and they lay entwined, her leg over his hip. "Do you trust me not to hurt you?" he rasped, as if struggling to breathe.

She didn't want to evaluate that sentiment. She knew what he meant. He didn't want to hurt her wound. But he was also speaking about the wound in her heart that he had put there. He was asking her to believe in him as if he understood there would come a time that they would both be tested.

Rolling with her, he pulled her across his hips, speaking the words again as he opened her mouth to a plundering kiss, his hands expertly disarming her of her will but halting with her stays. Only because she recognized that he'd sensed her vulnerability, and waited for her to let him remove her camisole.

One hand splayed her back. He closed the other over one breast, then suckled the second through the frail fabric. She could feel his need in the way his hand curved down her spine, over her hip and along her thigh to claim the hot, humid center of her. Her lashes lowered. She arched, aware of his tongue on her breast and the moistness he created with his mouth. She reveled in the freedom.

Drawing his hands to her breasts, she kissed him with a torrent of pent-up need, her body ebbing with the tide of her emotions. The rasp of their breathing flowing between them, back and forth as his mouth returned to hers with her same urgency.

Dimly in the back of her mind, she had expected to feel in control. Not this wild hot rush that he let loose inside her. She had never been ashamed of her body and had always been aware of the power her beauty could hold over a man. But she had tucked that part of her away for so many years that her gradual awakening flashed like quicksilver between them.

"I trust you," she heard herself say.

When she had never breathed those words to another soul.

She was hot and restless, seeking more as she followed David's hands to the hem of her camisole and helped him remove the last vestige of clothing between them, less than a whisper of cloth to have proved so capable of a barrier.

Her hair a loosened mass around her face, she watched him look at all of her without touching, yet touching her intimately. Then he met her gaze, her uncertainty rent asunder by the possessiveness in his eyes as he wrapped his hand around her nape and brought her mouth to his.

He eased her to her back and, rising on his elbow, looked into her face. "Everything heals with time," he said, his words meaning more to her than physical healing of her body.

Victoria or Meg—she did not know herself any longer— found sanctuary within his gaze. He had his own scars, she realized, her finger tracing the ragged line across his left rib cage to the flat disk of his nipple. He spread his hand across the moist juncture between her thighs. His finger delved inside her with intimate thoroughness, touching her in a way only he had ever touched her, opening her to him. His mouth traced her jawline. Her eyes drifting shut, she felt her head sinking into the pillow. Felt her heart rise to the warmth pressed against her. She instinctively moved her hips to meet his movements.

She gave a low whimper. "Love me, David."

And he realized he had loved her always.

He'd been searching for redemption only to return to the beginning, as if he had the power to change his life and hers.

His fingers twining with hers, he rose above her and spread her thighs wide, possessing her with his eyes before entering her. He retreated, then forged deeper. Poised on his own crest, his eyes drifting shut, he could sense the drape of sunlight across his back, stripping away all restraint. She wanted all of him. She tried to catch his mouth with her lips but her head fell back. With a low astonished cry, she arched against him, her skin hot and tight to his touch.

"Don't stop."

He could not if he tried.

She followed him as he twisted with her until she was on top of him. He tested the silken strands of her hair with hands that were no longer steady. She continued to move against him. Her breasts filled his hands. Then her mouth captured his with a strength that took his breath. Taking what he gave, she sucked his tongue between her lips. His breath harsh against the back of his throat, mingled with hers. He welcomed her hunger for it fed his, and the kiss went onward, spiraling upward, propelling him higher. Her orgasm pulled the breath from his lungs, until he gripped her hips, rocking them both hard.

She pulled back, her wild hair wanton and flowing over her shoulders, her gaze capturing his with a knowing intensity. And with a violent thrust that pulled her name from his lips, he spilled himself into her.

Later, when the wild tempo of their heartbeats slowed, and

he was breathing normally again, he could feel her eyes on his face and the sunlight bright on the bed.

"Continue to stare and you will find I am not yet finished." David opened his eyes.

Meg was still sitting astride him, a cat-smile on her beautiful, wet mouth. "As I said earlier," she purred, scraping tapered nails across his chest. "To the victor go the spoils."

"Aye, colleen." He wrapped a hand around her head and pulled her to his mouth, turning her beneath him, where he enjoyed a long, luxurious kiss as he fondled her right breast. "Had I known surrendering would be so sweet, I'd have done so long before now."

Sometime later, they awakened and made love again, their drowsy state of awareness heightened as he brought them to slow completion. Reason abandoned him, but he was past redemption. For there was something impossibly selfish and futile in wanting her as much as he did. Then he was holding her tightly against him, aware that she was holding him too.

Chapter 18

Victoria awoke slowly, stretching languorously against the downy comfort of David's mattress. This morning she'd lain in the arms of an angel. For just a moment as she watched dust motes dance in a beam of sunlight stretching across the covers, she smiled, before a noise turned her head, and she found herself staring at Bethany, sitting in the chair beside the bed.

Behind her, Moira was busy cleaning the room. The girl straightened, saw that Victoria was watching her, and startled.

"My apologies, mum."

"It's all right, Moira." Her arm lay across David's pillow and she struggled to her elbow.

"Lord Chadwick ate lunch an hour ago and went to see Sir Henry," Bethany said. "Nathanial is with him. He told me that I was to let you sleep."

"Oh," Victoria breathed the word, feeling more than awkward. "What time is it?"

"It is past three o'clock in the afternoon."

Holding the blanket to her chest, Victoria struggled to sit. "Oh!" She groaned, not because she'd slept away the entire day, but because every muscle in her body screamed at the same time.

"I'll draw up a bath, mum." Moira dipped. At the door, she stopped. "Would you prefer the bath in your room or here?"

Wrapped in the blanket, Victoria slid her legs over the bed. David's scent lay all over her like a visible mark of possession. "My room, please."

Everyone and the cat probably knew she was in these chambers at three o'clock in the afternoon. It would take no scholar to guess what she had been doing in David's bed, she thought, dragging the blanket with her as she met Bethany's hostile gaze.

"I'm shocked—" Bethany flung out her arm to encompass the state of the bed. "You're a grown woman, Victoria. I thought you were above allowing a man to . . . to ravish you like you are so much chattel in his keeping. How could you even care about him?"

Watching her whirl to leave, Victoria moved away from the bed. "Don't go."

Bethany stiffened and turned. "This post arrived an hour ago," she said, holding up an envelope. "I came up here to tell you I am the only person in the entire world not invited to Tory Birmingham's Yule soirée. Scandal of your escapades has probably reached London by now. But I have decided that it matters not whether I am invited to another soirée again. Who cares about such trivial matters, anyway? Certainly not I when I am the least important person in anyone's life. I can't even get a man to like me."

"How could you believe that about yourself, Bethany?"

"What I don't understand is that it doesn't matter what *you* do, Victoria. Everyone still loves you and wants to protect you. Aren't you worried about making another baby? Or do you think another child will keep you out of prison?"

Victoria paled.

"I'm not dumb or deaf." Bethany dabbed her sleeve against her eye. "I know you're not my stepmother. And when Peepaw dies, I'll have no one. Not even Nathanial. He isn't even my half brother."

Victoria was still standing in the center of the carpet. "I'm sorry, Bethany."

"Peepaw won't tell me anything. Except that you used Father's name because someone is after you. Maybe that person isn't the only bad one here. Maybe you are, too."

The words cut straight across Victoria's heart. Not because they were a lie, but because they were the truth.

Bethany's eyes sheened with tears. Her back stiff, she strode to the door, but her hand paused on the latch. She turned, a blush climbing into her face and washing her cheeks pink. "I don't even know your real name, or what you did."

"I was a little younger than you are now when I helped my father steal part of a government's national treasure," Victoria said quietly. "When my father came under suspicion and a case began to grow against him, Lord Chadwick was the man they sent after us."

Wiping her forearm across her cheeks, Bethany gathered her composure and appeared mortified. "But they can hang you for something like that."

"I believe you are correct." Victoria drew a short, steadying breath as she approached the growingly distraught girl. "What I did was wrong, Bethany. I make no excuses for the crime. But my affection for you has never been a lie."

"Then I believe I really shall be alone, Victoria. For I will never live with Nellis. I am afraid of him."

Victoria could not get Bethany's comment about Nellis from her head. After she bathed and dressed in a serviceable blue morning gown with half boots laced to her ankles, she asked one of the footmen to take her to the cottage so she could find David and Nathanial. Sir Henry was asleep. Esma was outside in the yard feeding the chickens.

"I don't know where Lord Chadwick took young Nate, mum," Esma said. "He did send my William to talk to Mr. Gibson about hiring a stone mason."

"Then he must be working on dismantling the walls of the church." Victoria looked out across the yard. The snow had melted, but the gray clouds over the distant English Channel did not bode well for the current warmer temperatures.

Ever since David mentioned her father's disappearance six months ago, her realization that the event coincided with Nellis's interest in Rose Briar continued to nag at her. As did Sheriff Stillings's conversation weeks ago. "Has Bethany returned from the manor house?" Victoria asked.

"She is in the stables. If she had her way, I've no doubt she would live with the beasts. You have a knack for healing people. She has a knack for healing animals. It is unfortunate Sir Henry has never noted her talents before."

Victoria folded her arms beneath her cloak. "Neither have I been as clear-headed in that direction. Bethany has taken the brunt of our distractions of late."

"She is a good lass, mum." Esma pumped water into a bucket. "But while you've been distracted, you've not noticed the tender affection she's developed for the young man ye hired."

Victoria pressed her lips together, caught by an alarm that quickly escalated as her own past gave proof that young love and British spies were a dangerous combination. "Mr. Rockwell? Has he . . . ?"

"He's set someone else to take his place here. I've seen him working at the church or at the manor house but he doesn't come here anymore." Esma wiped her damp hands on her apron. "He's married, mum."

That revelation surprised her. Ian Rockwell obviously had integrity not to allow himself to become involved with a moon-eyed romantic schoolgirl. Still, as she thought of Bethany, Victoria remembered being seventeen and feeling the whole world sided against her. Mostly, she remembered feeling alone.

David had a hundred reasons not to care about the other family in her life or feel he was responsible for Bethany's future, but she hoped in time he could be swayed. Bethany needed to know that she wasn't alone and would never be handed over to Nellis.

"Did Lord Chadwick say anything to Sir Henry about the will?"

"I'm not aware if he has, mum."

"And you do not know where Lord Chadwick went after leaving here?"

"No, mum."

Victoria stopped at the church on the way back to Rose Briar. The groomsman accompanying her greeted those who were working inside the burned-out structure. Rubbing the cramp in her side, she looked at Mr. Doyle's thatched cottage. Smoke issued forth from the chimney. She was suddenly standing at his wife's grave, staring at the headstone wondering at the magic of spending forty years with another human being and the loss of having that person die. All of her life, she had never truly understood death, except it was a forever event. She'd never believed in heaven, though strangely she believed well enough in hell. A cold chill worked itself beneath her cloak and skirts, and she raised her hood, feeling as if someone was watching her, yet when she lifted her face, she saw no one.

She remained unnoticed in the cemetery. Mr. Rockwell's horse was tied to the iron gate that let out into the churchyard. She saw his tall form near the cottage, talking to the big man with the gold tooth. No one else was paying attention to her.

All week she had been trying to get out from beneath David's thumb, wanting to find a way to talk to Nellis. Now it was as if Providence had handed her a horse and a means to escape. At least a means to a goal.

Lowering her head, she said a brief prayer over Mrs. Doyle's grave as she'd promised Mr. Doyle she would. Heart pounding, she made her way to the gate, mounted, and rode out of the churchyard.

"You've a visitor, Mr. Munro."

Nellis looked up from his correspondence as Victoria stepped into his library. He sat behind a large ostentatious desk. Two griffins balanced each end of a perfectly arranged desktop. "I fear she would not wait in the foyer," the butler said.

Nellis rose and stepped around the desk. His eyes made a pass behind her before settling on her. "What a pleasant surprise." He managed to sound casual.

"I hope that I am not disturbing you."

"Shall I have tea brought in, sir?" the butler inquired.

"Why not?" Nellis waved his hand airily. "Make it our special blend. It will be an experience for her, I'm sure."

After the butler bowed out, Victoria found her stomach unsettled as she regarded Sir Henry's nephew with a calm she did not feel.

"How long has it been since I've been graced with your presence alone in my home?" As he pondered his own wit, his mouth flashed a mocking grin. "Why, never."

"It isn't necessary to be rude, Nellis."

"I am only rude when provoked. Unfortunately, I am in a provoked state of mind. Or I was until your arrival." His gaze warmed over her. He was dressed fastidiously in dark trousers, waistcoat, and jacket. "You're looking very lovely, Victoria. Won't you make yourself comfortable?"

It didn't occur to her until now that Nellis's position as chief magistrate made her current position more precarious. Deciding on prudence over hostility, Victoria removed her cloak. He did not press her to sit in any particular chair, but merely waited for her to do so. She chose the low-backed armchair nearest to the desk in deference to the view it provided not only of the room but also of the street.

"Is someone going to be pounding down my door at any moment looking for you?" Nellis inquired, leaning against the desk with certain significance as he did so—like a man at ease making life-and-death decisions over people.

"No," she replied, reminding herself to sit tall.

He chuckled. "Why do you want to see me?"

"I thought we could talk," she offered. "Bury the hatchet, so to speak, between our two families, seeing that you are Sir Henry's blood relative."

"I have been Sir Henry's blood relative for forty-one

years. You are the one who is not. And yet, there you are making a claim on Rose Briar."

"I believe Sir Henry inherited Rose Briar from his mother, who was your father's *stepmother*, hence no true relative of yours, since you didn't even know her."

His features hardened enough to tell her she had hit a nerve. They also warned her that he was not as he seemed, that challenging him outright would not work. He was toying with her, for he was not a patient man at all.

She folded her hands. "May I ask why you were so intent on taking the land?"

"Sentimental reasons, Victoria."

"But you've never lived there. I only want to do what is right and fair," she stated, realizing at once she'd overplayed her concern. Giving up all pretenses, she forced a smile. "Perhaps if you are nice, Lord Chadwick will invite you to sup with the family on holidays."

"Yes, an interesting chap. I was unaware Chadwick was so connected." Nellis reached behind him and slid a yellowed sheet of paper off the desk. "That was mistakenly delivered to my town house a few days ago. Since you are here you can take it to him."

Nellis dropped it in her lap. Victoria scanned the brief lines.

CONFIRMED. THREE O'CLOCK. WEDNESDAY.
NEW HAVEN. BE THERE. RAVENSPUR.

It was a telegram addressed to David. Wednesday was today. David had not told her where he might be going today. "Mistakenly? I doubt it."

"Lord Ravenspur works for the foreign secretary in Lord

Ware's inner office," Nellis said, ignoring the comment. "It seems your *cousin* has made quite a name for himself as an . . . emissary for our government in the various places he's served." Nellis waggled another paper in front of her nose. "I was hoping you could tell me why Chadwick would be meeting with Lord Ravenspur? It is rather curious, is it not?"

Her palms grew moist. She had no idea why David would have arranged such a secret meeting. "Why should that be your concern?"

He laughed, leaning on the desk. "Knowing him as you do, then you probably understand Chadwick is very good at what he does. Truly, Victoria," he said with sarcasm, "you have no idea the kind of man he is or you wouldn't have been so eager to invite him into your life. You don't think he's earned his accolades fanning the queen's bum, do you?"

Victoria could find no rebuttal to the crass statement. The rattle of a tray snapped her attention to the doorway. Wearing a white apron over her black dress, the servant pulled her gaze from Nellis as she set down the tray on the table beside Victoria's chair. She wondered what she'd briefly glimpsed in the woman's eyes as she accepted a cup.

"Aren't you curious about the kind of man for whom you seem to hold some fondness?" Nellis demanded after the servant departed.

Victoria gave him her full attention. "I know who he is."

"Then you know fourteen years ago, David Donally stopped a purported assassination attempt on the royal family with a single bullet to the culprit's forehead. Almost six hundred yards. He was one of a few in the world who could have made that shot. Not the first time he'd done such a job, might I add. You don't believe me?" Nellis queried, pulling out another sheaf of paper from the stack he held in his hands. "He belonged to an elite group of men called the League of the Condor. Men sent all over the world to infiltrate organizations to expose plots and bring in the worst sort of criminals."

She didn't believe Nellis. She did not know all that David had done in his service to the crown, but she did not believe him capable of assassination no matter the cause. David couldn't be a cold-blooded killer. Or maybe he was. But she had seen him fight Stillings's men. He could have killed any one of them and had not. And he'd gone into the priesthood, hadn't he?

"On top of everything else, ten years ago, his notable service in Calcutta won him a life peerage. His other honors and citations span two pages."

"His service in *Calcutta* won him his peerage?"

"Didn't you live in Calcutta before coming here?"

A mocking undercurrent chilled her. "You know I did."

"Then the question that begs to be asked is why a known assassin is here watching over someone as saintly as you. If I listen to rumor, Nathanial is his son. Is this true, Victoria? Have you allowed yourself get taken in by a notorious spy? Twice?"

Nellis came to his feet, and she involuntarily pressed back into the chair. He saw the movement, and his lips smiled, raising the fine hairs on the back of her neck as he left her with the disconcerting thought that he knew exactly who she was. That he had known for months. "I will not let you blackmail me," she whispered.

"I merely asked if the rumors about the boy were true," he said. "Though I've looked high and low for a marriage document between one David Donally and Victoria Munro, I have yet to find one. As a consequence, should something happen to Chadwick, heaven forbid, as Sir Henry's legal male heir, I would be responsible for the boy and Bethany."

Uncertainty made her light-headed. How would he know these things? Was he in collusion with her father then? Or did someone from the foreign secretary's office contact him in the course of the investigation? Or perhaps both?

She started to put down her saucer and stand when she noted the second cup of tea on the tray remained untouched. She looked down into her own half-empty cup then forced herself to meet Nellis's gaze, a chill going down her spine.

"I am surprised you came today to see me." He walked behind her and placed his hands on the back of the chair. "But then I never doubted you had courage." The tenor in his voice darkened. "Now, you are probably asking if I have done something to your tea. Do you still have the fortitude to fly at the face of danger now, Victoria?"

Nellis had been menacing to her before, but until now, she had never truly been afraid of him. "I am not afraid of you," she whispered.

Returning to his desk, Nellis folded his arms over his chest and observed her silence in triumph. "Then do I tell you the tea is poisoned and take away the suspense? Or do I let you discover the truth on your own? Either way, I fear you are doomed in the end."

Struggling not to react, Victoria set the cup on the table at her knee and rose to her feet. "Is there anything else, Nellis?"

"Ah, Sheriff Stillings," Nellis looked at the doorway, and Victoria almost fainted in relief.

"My lady." Stillings wore a heavy woolen cloak the color of his brown eyes. He grinned at her charmingly. "I was unaware that someone of your distinction was present."

"Sheriff Stillings works for me, Victoria," Nellis said, turning his best magistrate's gaze to the other man. "Don't you?"

Stillings cleared his throat. "Did you want to see me for any particular reason?"

Nellis continued to look at her. "I believe she was just leaving," Nellis said.

As if on cue, a harness and jingle heralded the arrival of Nellis's stately black carriage. It rumbled into sight of the bow window and rolled to a stop in front of the town house. "I would be remiss if I didn't see you properly escorted back to Rose Briar."

She struggled with her gloves. "I would not be seen dead in your carriage."

"Nonetheless, we'll tie the reins of your horse to the boot. You'll take the carriage." Nellis aided her with her cloak, but she snatched it away before he could touch her. "Cheer up, Victoria." He laughed, speaking in a museful vein. "I may be more valuable to you than you know before everything is over. Perhaps if you consider the idea, you may come to believe we can be allies as well as friends. Isn't that the way of it, Stillings?"

Victoria stepped next to the sheriff.

"See that she takes the carriage back to Rose Briar," Nellis spoke firmly to Sheriff Stillings. "And Victoria," he called after her and laughed, inordinately pleased with his victory. "The tea is my favorite blend with just a hint of mint."

"Stay away from Nellis Munro," Sheriff Stillings spoke as the carriage wheels rattled across a narrow bridge and climbed the drive toward Rose Briar.

Pressed as far away from Tommy Stillings as she could go within the close confines of the carriage, Victoria had buried herself in her cloak and kept her eyes on the window where twilight had darkened the sky. For the past hour, she'd sat unspeaking on the leather bench next to him, now the anxiety that had plagued her since leaving Rose Briar that afternoon returned tenfold as she came within sight of the bluff.

With his less than subtle mental warfare, Nellis had homed in on her greatest weakness, her faulty instinct at being able to read human nature and thus his intent. He wanted her to doubt David's integrity and thus herself.

Her father had been just such an expert at manipulation, subduing her will by creating self-doubt, for it was the one way he could control her. The only way he could beat her. She should have taken a shiv to Nellis's bollocks and been done with his arrogance. The urge to do so now rose and swelled on a crest of fury, building in momentum until she folded her hands into a fist, until it grabbed at her chest.

Turning her head, she found Stillings watching her with something resembling concern. "Why do you work for him?"

"Because I do." His smile came back. "My apologies if I gave you the impression that I am anything but what Nellis wants me to be."

Victoria narrowed her eyes, trying to read his in the darkness. "You're afraid of him."

Sheriff Stillings regarded the rigid set of her spine with a degree of admiration in the touch of his eyes. "Annie would not appreciate it if I broke your neck, my lady."

The carriage slowed to a stop, rocking on its springs. "Would you have killed me if Nellis so ordered?"

Sheriff Stillings opened the door and stepped down. "Get out, my lady."

Ignoring his extended hand, she departed the carriage and strode past an astonished half-dozen men gathered at the gate, leading up the path to the door. If David were anywhere on the bluff, he would have seen the carriage approach. Apprehension filled her. She didn't want to face him until she could rein in her emotions, didn't want to look into his eyes and see the truth in Nellis's accusations about his past or question her trust. She didn't want to ask him why he had taken her son away today, the same time he'd arranged a secret meeting with someone from the Foreign Office.

"What do you want me to do with the horse, Doc?" Stillings called after her, his voice no longer amused or mocking, but angry.

Victoria whirled to tell him he could go to the devil, but an icy wind gust caught at her skirts and snatched the breath from her lungs. She clutched the hood of her cloak.

"I'll take my own bloody horse." Mr. Rockwell appeared at her side, an expression of discontent evident in his eyes. "Since he does belong to me."

Her hands no longer steady, she clutched the cloak against her throat, and watched the carriage pull away. William Shelby and Mr. Gibson were standing among the men gathered around her. "Mr. Rockwell?" Victoria grabbed his arm, the movement startling him. "Is Nathanial back yet?"

"He is with his father. Someone rode out to try and find Donally and bring him back," he said, taking the reins of the horse from one of his men. "I hope you enjoyed your little outing, my lady. It cost us all a lot of time and labor."

"You would know if he wasn't coming back . . . I mean if something was wrong?" Nellis had subtly threatened David's life. And her son was with him. "You would know? Right?"

His gaze dropped to her fingers clutching his sleeve. "What happened between you and Mr. Munro?"

She pulled her hand away, curling her fingers into her palm. No longer sure of anything, she clutched the hood of her cloak, whirling on her heel toward the house. Mr. Rockwell called her name but she didn't stop. The main door opened.

Bethany appeared backlit by the foyer lamplight. "Victoria?" Tears in her eyes, she stood aside as Victoria swept past her into the foyer. "We've been worried about you."

"I can take care of myself, Bethany." She had not meant her voice to sound so harsh when she was so glad to see the girl; she had not meant her anger. "Please . . ." She cupped Bethany's tender cheek. "Just go home to Sir Henry."

Victoria strode up the stairs, her skirts billowing out around her like unfurled sails in a growing storm. By the time she reached the second-floor corridor, she was running to her room.

Chapter 19

~~~~~~⌒◯◯⌒~~~~~~

Afire burned in the hearth. Victoria lay in bed, one hand beneath her cheek as she stared listlessly into the dying flames. She'd tried to remain awake in hopes of seeing David, but it was already after midnight and he had yet to return. Her dinner tray remained untouched where Mrs. Gibson had set it on a small table earlier. Bethany had knocked on her door earlier, but Victoria could not talk to her and had turned into her pillow to sleep. A green vial of chlorodyne drops sat on her bedside table and she closed her eyes, Nellis's conversation replaying on her consciousness as she fell into a restless slumber and dreamed about a cloaked figure in the night.

She stood amid the swirling mist rising from the cemetery, wearing her mother's locket and looking across the grave markers to the church.

Should something happen to Chadwick, as Sir Henry's heir, I would be responsible for the boy and Bethany.

You can take that first step with me, Meg.

Have you allowed yourself get taken in by a notorious spy? Twice?

And still, he came into her dreams, an angel in her bed, taking her into his arms and holding her, vowing to love her in health and sickness until death.

The cloaked figure following her faded with the shadows, and she opened her eyes, swept into the swirling sensation of her dream, running through thick, black smoke. But she was not Victoria. She was Meg Faraday. She could hear the steamer chimney bellow three times. A fire had spread into the engine room and panicked passengers were flowing onto the decks. Screams. Children crying. People shoving and clawing at one another to reach the quarter boats on deck. But she was trying to get back inside the companionway. No one would let her. Someone hit her shoulder and she went into the water just before the engine room exploded. Indistinct memories formed shapes against the flames, smells of the oil-filled sea swallowing her within its depths and the sound of the dying ship sinking into the sea. She clung to debris, and somehow found a barrel floating in the sea, begging God not to pull her down and take her child with her, promising Him her soul if He would only let her live.

It had been the first prayer she'd ever remembered saying in her life. And when she'd again awakened to sunlight and the destruction around her, she was alive.

"Maaaaaggie? Where are you?"

The vivid dream shoved her straight up in bed, her heartbeat pushing blood through her veins. Only her father called her by that name. Gasping air into her lungs, she blinked away the confusion in her brain. Sanity returned in slow degrees. Her bed was empty. Tangled in her blankets, she collapsed back into the pillows. She'd only been dreaming. Lord in heaven, she'd only been dreaming.

Hands trembling, she stretched across the mattress and fumbled in the darkness for the table clock set on her night-stand. The low-burning fire cast the only light. Her room was ice-cold. Last night she'd taken only a few drops of chloro-dyne to help with the stiffness in her body. The narcotic ef-fects were worse because she'd not eaten. She was barely coherent. The little hand on the clock's face was on the four, but that was all she could read in the darkness.

She flung off the blankets and splashed cold water on her face. Remaining barefooted, she shoved her arms into the sleeves of her wrapper and, ignoring the tenderness on her side, belted it at the waist over her shift.

Nathanial was not in his room, which meant David still had not returned. Uncertainty turning to worry, she shut her son's door and, after a moment's hesitation, made her way to the studio, where she lit the fluted oil lamps that lined the walls.

Lifting one staff off its place on the wall, she turned it over in her hands, tucked it beneath one arm, and proceeded to work through the soreness in her body.

Nellis had enjoyed his little game with the tea yesterday. He had enjoyed telling her about David, and, at her most vul-nerable moment of confusion, she had let Nellis slip through the cracks in her mind and poison her with self-doubt.

And as she worked her way across the room, instead of melding mind and body to create balance, she felt only grow-ing frustration. Wasn't this what Nellis had intended? Yet, the more determined she was not to believe the worst, the more her mind gave in to doubt. The circle only fed upon itself and, by the time she worked her way across the floor, she felt only a need to impale the bloody staff through David's nub of a heart. Outside, the sky remained dark, enclosing her until she could barely breathe.

Sweeping her leg around into the next set of steps, she swung the staff over her head, turned, and came to a complete stop.

"David!"

He stood not two feet from her. Wearing his heavy coat and riding clothes, he looked as if he'd been dragged out of bed. Stubble heightened the dark look in his eyes, but it was not all anger she saw.

He lifted a dark-gloved hand and eased the staff away from his skull. "My horse threw a shoe about five miles from here," he said. "Nathanial and I were staying at the inn outside Alfriston. I didn't get Rockwell's message until two hours ago."

"He shouldn't have been so quick to summon you."

"What the bloody hell were you thinking, going to Nellis?"

Ignoring him, refusing to fall in to the volatility of her emotions, she straightened her neck and stretched out her left arm, looking over her shoulder as she bent at the knee. She stepped into the exercise, moving the staff with slow, precise movements. In nine steps, she reached the wall, pulled the second staff from its place next to the fencing foils, turned, and tossed it to David. He caught it midair.

"He knows," she said. "He knows who you and I are. He knows about Nathanial."

"Did Nellis threaten him?"

He threatened you, she wanted to shout. Calmly, she said, "He implied that if something should happen to you then as Sir Henry's legal heir, he would become Nathanial and Bethany's guardian."

"That won't happen, Meg."

She knew that she dared tell him no more. A part of her recognized the danger of telling David about the telegram he'd received from Lord Ravenspur for fear he would violently confront Nellis. Especially when she suspected that was exactly what Nellis wanted. Yet he'd succeeded in making her question David's loyalty. Even as he'd subtly threatened David's life.

"Nellis told me how you earned your title and a page full of other accolades. You neglected to tell me how well you'd been rewarded for all of your dedicated work in Calcutta. He told me you are a killer. An assassin. Are you?"

David said nothing in his defense. But a darkness descended in his eyes and he was a split second late in raising the staff against her attack. "What are you doing, Meg?"

"Fight me, David."

He evaded her next move. "I'm not dressed for this."

"Then undress. It isn't as if I haven't seen everything already." She swung her staff and cut only empty air.

"The first rule." His grin warned that she tread dangerous ground. "You don't fight angry. Angry will get you killed."

"And you are so adept at survival."

The sconces around the room provided scant light, but enough to show him that she wore barely anything at all beneath the robe. "I fear you have the advantage, dear."

"Oh!" She lunged.

Stepping to her left, he countered her every movement as if he was making love to her, with masculine precision to detail, guiding her every thrust toward ultimate surrender, and she missed her mark again, stumbling forward in a turn.

"Why did you go see Nellis?" he asked.

"It doesn't matter." She gripped the pole with both hands and pushed against his. "I found what I was looking for."

"Take it slower," he warned.

"I can't."

She wouldn't.

"Fight me, David."

"Why do you think I haven't pressed you about the treasure?"

"Fight, damm it!"

David held up his pole if only to counter the force of her attack. His eyes glittered over hers, warning her that he was perfectly capable of retaliation in kind. But he did not fight.

She swung the staff in a wide arc. He caught it with his hand, stopping her forward momentum with the same force of slamming against a wall. The contact jolted every muscle in her body. She bent over her legs, resting one hand on her side.

"You're hurting, Meg. Let me help you."

His tenderness served to disarm her. She recognized what he was trying to do for her. But he couldn't continue to carry her on his shoulders. Bethany was right in that regard. She couldn't hide behind people anymore. She had to do this for herself.

"I have nothing more to say." She yielded the staff to him, but he grabbed her arm before she could walk away. "Let go of me. I'm not like you, David. I can't dismiss the pain and make believe it doesn't exist."

He dragged her to the wall with one hand and mounted both staffs beside the foils with the other. "You *will* allow me my say, Meg."

"My name is Victoria. Why can't you just remember the name?"

"Jesu, Meg, Victoria—"

"Why can't you just let Meg Faraday die?"

He pulled her into his arms and, gripping her shoulders, placed his mouth a hairsbreadth from hers. "Because I love you, and you bloody ask the impossible of me."

In her agitated state, his words were the very last thing in the world she expected him to say. "I have loved you always." He leaned his forehead against hers and said with ferocity, "Don't you understand that, yet?"

She swiped a knuckle across her cheek. "No, I do not."

Cupping her face, David pulled her into a kiss. It was easier to kiss her than to convince her of his affection. He angled his head, opened his mouth over hers, and tasted only bliss. She made a soft sound in the back of her throat, as if awakening from a deep sleep, rose on her toes to wrap her arms around his neck, and the kiss burned into something erotic. Just like that, he caught fire. He strained to pull her closer, to climb inside her, but the groan in his chest did not rise from pleasure. Sheer frustration targeted every nerve in his body and saved him from the consequences of his lust.

"Can you please not try to kill me anymore?" he rasped, his forehead pressing against hers. God grant him self-control. There was much he had yet to say to her and, his exhaustion notwithstanding, he would have his say. "I'm not going to leave you. Not ever again. You have to believe me."

Meg pulled back, and he looked deeply into her eyes. He wanted to tell her he'd already taken steps to seek a pardon for her. But he couldn't. Not yet. He was afraid of building too much hope, then dashing it on the rocks, knowing that such a task would practically require a miracle. But no one had ever spoken up for Meg before, or defended her, or offered her a chance. "I'm not pressing you about the treasure because I need you to trust why I am here. If you tell me you don't know where it is. I'll believe you. I'm doing everything in my power to help you. Do you trust me?"

She nodded.

"Then say the words." He pushed his fingers into her hair and forced her to look at him. "Tell me you trust me to see you and Nathanial through this safely. That I know what I'm doing."

"Time is on the other side," she whispered. "Not ours. I only want to put an end to this. And I don't know how. If I could find my father . . ."

His palms tightened on her shoulders, and he moved her to arm's length. "*Then what*, for bloody sake?"

"Then I will never have any more nightmares, David. I could end this for everyone. I would be free. I only want to be free of him and my past. I don't care how anymore."

Finally, he knew. He understood. He watched her eyes become luminescent with tears that never fell. "Is that why you went to see Nellis?"

She walked to the wall and plopped down on the leather mat, but not so distracted that she didn't adjust the robe to cover her bare feet. "He's connected in some way to this case, but I'm not sure how."

He squatted on his calves in front of her, spilling his coat on the floor around his feet. "Tell me why you believe that?"

"Everything started six months ago. His interest in the land. His obsession with me. Someone must have come to him. He knows too much about us, and he didn't care that I knew that. It was as if he wanted to make sure I told you everything."

He smoothed back her tumbledown hair, knowing that he was ten seconds from walking out of this room and going after Nellis. "Did he hurt you?"

Shaking her head, she did not meet his eyes. "Sheriff Stillings brought me home. No one laid a hand on me."

"A person doesn't have to strike another person to cause pain. Something else must have happened if you're afraid I might ride over to his residence and knock in his teeth."

"Where did you go yesterday?" she asked.

David relented to the change of topic. "I found the stone mason who once worked on the church. Mr. Gibson gave me his name. The man will be here tomorrow, and I will see how many others follow his lead. I put the word out tonight that I am hiring people interested in honest employment."

"You did that?"

"I need people who are not afraid of the dark. Someone willing to hunt rats in caves. People willing to fight for themselves, and for a change."

He didn't know how he could make anything change at all, when he didn't know where to begin. But he knew this place and these people mattered to Meg. Or maybe she just mattered to him enough that he would give her anything. "Do you know what Sir Henry told me yesterday?" He tilted her face with the palm of his hand. "He believes that most of the people in this town will stand by you."

"But no one comes up here anymore."

"Do you think that may be a direct cause of my presence here more than any fault of yours?"

She laughed, striking at her tears. "Judge not lest ye be judged? You think because they are all mostly smugglers and thieves they will be more forgiving of me? Even when Nellis makes known certain facts about us? None of us will be able to show our faces again. No one within a hundred miles will trust me or you again."

"After last night, they trust I will find the caves with or without their help. They also trust me to see the caves permanently sealed when I do. And you can trust me to deal with any man who sets foot on Rose Briar without an invitation to visit. What is there not to trust? I'm an open book."

Tears clung to her eyelashes. "Do you really love me?"

Realizing he saw the mirror of his heart in her wet eyes, he held her hands in his palms and brought her fingers to his lips. He had fallen in love with her long ago from afar, he realized, knowing his heart had been in jeopardy from the first time their gazes connected from across a polo field in Calcutta. "I should have found a way to help you years ago. But I could not."

"You were honor bound to do your job, David. You still are."

Understanding honor meant that he also understood dishonor, and recognized the fine line he walked. He only knew he loved Meg, and would not allow her to die in prison.

When she spoke, her voice was nearly inaudible. "I believe I've never known anyone like you from the first time I looked at you walking off the polo field," she said. "I can even describe the attire you were wearing and the color of horse you rode. You were the only man I'd ever met who didn't lay his heart at my feet on the second encounter of our acquaintance." She withdrew her hand from his. "I have yet to meet your equal in that regard. You did your job very well."

David sat against the wall and, drawing one knee to his chest, leaned his head back. They sat shoulder to shoulder, the years between them narrowing to a thin line.

"Whatever Nellis told you is no doubt all factual on the surface. I was what I was." He braced one wrist on his knee, and pondered his life as one who studied a self-portrait that no longer resembled him. "But that is as far as it goes. I know I did things in my life . . ."

"Why did you become a priest?"

David considered the leather creases in his gloves, slowly removing them as he spoke. "I had a need to do something good in the world. To give back something I felt I had taken. Does that sound romantic or overly philosophic?"

"Did you?" she asked. "Do something good then?"

He thought about the past years and what he had accomplished. "I'd like to think I did." His mouth tilted into a grin. "I married off two of my brothers."

Meg leaned her head into his shoulder. "You did?"

"One willingly and the other not so willingly." He rubbed his jaw in memory of that latter experience with his youngest brother. It had been months since he'd thought of his family. He did so now with a need to see them, until he turned his nose into Meg's hair and inhaled the faint scent of myrrh and quince. She'd washed with his soap today.

"What are they going to say when they learn you are no longer a priest?" he heard her ask as she insinuated herself between his legs and sat back on her ankles. Her wrapper gaped open, revealing the fleshly curve of her bosom swelling against her stays.

"I wonder that any of my family ever believed it of me in the first place," he said, lifting his gaze to encompass hers, wondering how he'd managed so many years of celibacy when his mind so easily drowned in the carnal libation he drank from her eyes. "They don't even know where I am." He pulled her to her knees in front of him. "Or at least they didn't until I sent a post to my brother-in-law a few days ago."

"A post?"

"My sister is married to the undersecretary in the Foreign Office," he said as he rose on his knees to the softer leather mat beneath Meg's legs.

"I don't understand," she said in a breathy voice, dropping her head back against her shoulders as he found succor in the cleft between her breasts.

The sun had yet to rise, no one in the house stirred or was due to awaken, and he rose above her, kissing her deeply, neither gentle nor patient in his want to have her. "Where is the blessing in having a brother-in-law in high places, if I cannot call upon at least one favor in this lifetime?" he said, lowering her to her back and falling above her as he caught his hands on the floor.

"This brother-in law? He works for Lord Ware?" she asked.

David tore off his coat. "Is this a conversation we want to be having right now?" he asked, pulling his shirt over his head. He fumbled less at the buttons on his trousers.

"Wait!" she breathed between their frantic kisses.

But he'd had enough of waiting and talking. He pushed aside her robe then sat back on his heels and let his gaze traverse the hills and the valleys leading to the apex between her thighs. "Truly, David—" she struggled to sit, only to catch herself on her hair. "Maybe we shouldn't be doing this just now—"

Intimately aware of his presence between her legs, he cocked a brow. "Do you love me, Meg?"

Her hair flowered around her, framing her face and shoulders in a cloud of dark silk, and he could not pretend he was unaffected by the desire to hear her answer. Nor would he feel guilty that he asked the question. He knew on some level that she had always loved him, so the question was moot for him. But she had to hear herself say the words, as if saying the sentiment aloud made it real.

"Do we want to make another child between us, David?"

He looked at her kiss-swollen lips, then at all of her, the symbolism of that gesture not lost on her. He claimed her for his own. Her past, her present, and her future belonged to him. "Isn't that concern a little late, considering we are already well into our sybaritic inclinations? Many times over." His mouth found the pulse at her throat.

"Then consider this. What if no matter what you do, you can't prevent the inevitable? Will you be able to live with that?"

It was then David realized she was more worried about him than she was about herself. "We'll make it work, Meg." He caught her nipple between his lips and suckled, leaving her shift hot and damp above her stays. She gave a start at his encroaching intimacy, but did nothing to dissuade him from continuing. No other part of his body touched hers. He moved lower past her stomach. "Tell me, Meg," he said, awaiting an answer to his initial question.

"I love you, David."

He pushed on his palms. Her lashes framed deep pools of violet the pale light pulled from her eyes, and she could not have awakened a fiercer hunger. "You wouldn't be exaggerating, would you? Or saying that just to make me happy."

She shook her head and laughed. "I love you."

She held his gaze as he went down on her and found his way beneath her shift. He covered her thighs with his palms and pushed them farther apart. "Tell me again, love."

The hot breath of his whisper touched her intimately. "Oh, Lord," she rasped, tortured. "I love you."

And he loved her, too, with his mouth and his fingers, but

especially his mouth, claiming her possessively, claiming her as his own, making her body do things he wanted her to do. He stoked her fire, found her rhythm burning in the flames, felt her hips arch. She was where he wanted her to be, and when she cried out and clawed her hands into his hair, he felt her climax in his mouth.

He rose up on his knees and, looking into her passion-drugged eyes, fought the violent need to push inside her before he spent himself on the floor between her legs. Her gaze slid down his body, touching him like the fire burning inside her. "Do you want me to stop?"

In answer, her hands cupped his face, and she pulled him into a kiss, a moan vibrating from deep in her throat as she wrapped her legs around his hips with a predictable effect. His kissed her back. Controlled at first, then no longer controlled. He pushed inside her where she was wet and warm and welcoming.

"You make me feel helpless, David."

It was a feeling that he, too, had worked hard through the years to overcome. But as he pinioned her hands to the soft leather mat at her back, and his heartbeat quickened, some of that helplessness engulfed him.

His breath a harsh rasp against her ear, he held her with slow deep thrusts, entwining his fingers with hers, soon lost within the melody and harmony that hummed between them, until her name became the tempo of his breath. Her orgasmic cry broke in a breathless gasp. Rising on his palms, he kissed her openmouthed, taking her cries into his throat where they joined his.

And in the warming glow that filled him, the heightened tremors of her pleasure shuddering through him, he lifted his head to draw in a draught of air and thrust one last time, spilling himself deep within her. As he collapsed against her, their bodies damp and indulged, he knew the world could end around him and he would not notice.

Victoria snuggled deeper against the warm shoulder jostling her cheek. The first rosy blush of dawn had begun to stir the eastern horizon when she opened her eyes and saw that David was carrying her down the corridor to her room. She wore nothing beneath her wrapper. Her legs dangling over his arms, she smiled against his shoulder. His clothes beneath his coat remained in disrepair. "Where are you taking me?" she murmured.

"Your room or mine?"

She straightened, but he bounced her and she fell against the hard wall of his chest. "Your room or mine?"

David had done things to her body that still made her blush, but strangely, she wasn't ready to end this morning. "I don't expect we can keep this a secret any longer."

She felt the curve of his mouth against her hair. "I don't expect we ever did, love."

"My room. The bed is softer," she said.

And only when he'd set her in bed, did she remember that she'd thrown the telegram from Lord Ravenspur on her nightstand. She opened her eyes to see David standing over the lamp, reading the telegram Nellis had given her. Silently, she groaned, but it must not have been so quiet because David looked at her over the top of the paper, the dark blue in his eyes sharpening to pinpoints of black.

"Nellis gave you this?"

She released a long sigh as she took measure of his tone and nodded slowly, knowing it would be unproductive to forestall the truth. "I didn't tell you because I didn't want you flying over to his residence and give him cause to arrest you."

"That would be most unlikely."

Victoria pulled the blanket around her, not persuaded to share his confidence.

"He told you Lord Ravenspur worked for the foreign secretary." David folded the telegram in half. "He neglected to tell you that Lord Ravenspur was my brother-in-law."

"Maybe he didn't know," Victoria said. "Or he would have assumed I would have known and found no pleasure in taunting me."

"If he didn't know then that may tell me something."

"Am I supposed to understand what that means?" she asked, tucking a strand of her hair behind her ears.

"Only that Kinley would know that information," he said, his eyes focusing on something in his thoughts. David pulled out a slip of paper from the same coat pocket where he'd shoved the telegram. "Is this Nellis's address?"

"Yes. He lives on Grand." Victoria noted the writing as also belonging to Nellis. "Where did you get that?"

"From Pamela's bedroom."

She could not help the vise that squeezed her chest. "Should I be worried you found purpose to be in Pamela's bedroom?"

David sat on the edge of the bed. "Come here," his voice was less an order and more of a promise. He leaned over and dragged her across the mattress, covering her with his chest as he pressed her into the pillows. His feet remained on the ground.

"I'm very particular where I put certain parts of my anatomy. I always have been."

"I'm glad to know that."

"Nellis told you that Ravenspur worked for Lord Ware.

You thought despite everything we've talked about, I was still planning to spring some trap on you."

"My trepidation was born of my own guilt as it was our past."

He brushed a length of hair from her cheek. "Nellis neglected to tell you that Ravenspur is my sister's husband. What he didn't know is that I've petitioned the crown to see the charges against you dropped. That was my intent in contacting Lord Ravenspur. That was why I didn't tell you. I didn't know if—"

She placed a finger against his lips. "You wanted to talk to your brother-in-law first."

"No doubt when I didn't show at the depot in New Haven, Ravenspur set his sights on locating Kinley. If my brother-in-law doesn't know about us, he will soon enough."

"How will you explain to your family how you met me?"

"I met you in India," he said neutrally, unsure how to answer her question as it seemed to be one he'd been mulling over himself.

"You must have an extremely tolerant family if you think they will still want to know me once they learn the truth," she mused, and he looked at her tentative smile. "I am not innocent of that which I've been accused."

He enclosed her hand with his and gently kissed her palm, understanding her well enough to know that she was afraid to hope. "Considering your youth at the time of the crimes, and the circumstances surrounding your life with Colonel Faraday, and everything you've accomplished since, we'll get a pardon. I'm sure of it."

And as he spoke the words, so sure in the belief that he stood on the side of right and justice and that his family surely loved him as much as she did, Victoria began to be-

lieve as well. The first ray of hope was like a touch of sunlight
to her heart. He framed her cheek in his palm, and his touch
stole a little more of her breath. "It worries me that I have
brought you to tears."

"I'm not crying." She laughed and pushed at his weight.
But he was an unmovable entity, his arm cast heavily across
her chest and, suddenly, looking at the dark promise in his
eyes, she no longer seemed to care. "You make me believe in
the impossible, David. No one has ever given me that before."

"Then you'll understand if your father is here, we'll find
another way to catch him."

Her voice came quickly. "If?"

"I'm not convinced Colonel Faraday fired that rifle. Or if
he is even alive."

"Is there a possibility he isn't alive?"

"Rockwell isn't sure if he is."

"But that doesn't mean he is dead. Sir Henry won't leave
here, David. If my father is alive, he would only follow me if
I left."

Not for the first time did she feel his crushing desire to
shake sense into her. "I'm not here any longer as an agent to
the crown, Meg. I'm here as your husband."

"Does Kinley know that?"

He sifted his fingers through her hair. "He will as soon as I
speak to Ravenspur."

An unfamiliar vulnerability shone in his eyes and softened
the uncertain edges of her heart. She kissed the corner of his
mouth. "Because you hope to use your brother-in-law as an
ally? Perhaps with your own family as well?"

"It does not matter if anyone else accepts my life."

But it was the not the truth, she knew. His family's lack of
acceptance of her might not keep them apart but it would hurt

David, more so than their rejection of the choices he had made that put him in this place. "Your family has only to know you to love you," she said. "And if they love you they will love Nathanial and me, too."

He sat and pulled her across his lap, where he cradled her in his arms. "Are you saying no one can resist me?"

His shameless smile captured her. "I would dislike such an observation going to your head."

His fingers curled around her chin, and he kissed her. "I fear it has already gone there, my love."

Chapter 20

❧ ◦◦◦ ❧

An image of a buxom mermaid swung from a sign above the heavy oaken door. Thunder grumbled across a leaden sky, turning the drizzle into a downpour as David stepped through the door into the common room. Men stood around tables drinking ale and talking. Long mullioned windows opened to the main road from New Haven.

The white weather-boarded hostelry tucked away near Smuggler's Cove aptly named the Buxom Mermaid was a fitting throwback to yesteryear and owned by a warm-hearted couple David had met the first week of his stay in this part of England. Mr. Smith managed the livery while his robust wife handled the affairs of the inn. "Right this way, m'lord." Mrs. Smith held a lantern aloft as David followed her up the creaky narrow stairs to the second floor. "They're expectin' ye."

Walter Kinley looked over his gold-rimmed spectacles as the pocket doors opened and David stepped into the drawing

room, serving as Kinley's temporary quarters an hour outside town. Heat from the fireplace radiated throughout the
cluttered room, dissipating the cold. Yet, as David glimpsed
the second man standing at the hearth, a chill in the silver-
edged eyes looking back at him, the room could not have felt
more frigid.

Raindrops had gathered on the black cashmere wool of
David's coat and dripped on the floor as he surrendered the
wrap, hat, and gloves to the servant. "Ravenspur." David acknowledged his brother-in-law with a subtle nod. As tall as
David, the Duke of Ravenspur could look him in the eye.

"I see that the two of you need no introduction," Kinley
said with some industry, seemingly content that there would
be no family reunion to suffer. "Ravenspur insisted that we
talk, else you would not have been summoned. How you
leave today is up to you."

David's mouth crooked, though no hint of humor touched
his eyes. "Implying that you intend to take me out back and
shoot me?"

"Unless you prefer a rope around your neck," Ravenspur
said.

"Sit, if you will, Donally," Kinley suggested.

"Do either of you want to tell me what this meeting is
about?" David asked, giving His Grace the benefit of a second appraisal as he walked to the window though he could
see nothing in the pitch of the night. A glimpse in the adjoin-
ing room showed a servant cleaning the table of a recent dinner, but no men waiting in the wings.

After receiving Ravenspur's missive, David had ridden
through a downpour to get here by nightfall. He'd left Meg
and Nathanial at Rose Briar. He'd left a crew of workers at

the church, tearing down the burned-out infrastructure. Now, gazing at his brother-in-law dressed out in a dark jacket, burgundy waistcoat, and perfectly creased trousers, looking every bit the lord undersecretary, David felt the first sting of reality push aside the initial scope of hope that had brought him here. But if there was a man who could *not* claim to be without sin, his brother-in-law topped the list of the stubbornly defiant, a man who had more often than not in the past walked the line of sedition.

"You'll want a drink, I expect?" Kinley asked, accepting a tall-stemmed glass of claret from his servant.

For once, as David took his seat, he declined alcoholic libation. "I prefer to have my wits about me, if you do not mind, *sir*."

"I'm aware you are seeking a pardon for Miss Faraday," Kinley said.

David looked directly at his sister's husband, and felt his jaw clench. He had asked Ravenspur to intercede on his behalf for Meg. He had trusted Ravenspur with her life. Instead, he had given the London office reason to pull him off this case. "Clearly, reading my post must have been shocking to bring you racing to this corner of England, Ravenspur, when you could have relayed everything through Kinley. Have I ever called you a bloody bastard to your face?"

"Frankly? The last time I saw you, you were wearing vestments and raising holy hell in Ireland."

"You forget yourself, Donally," Kinley snapped. "Lord Ravenspur is your superior."

"And you're both forgetting that without me, there is no bloody case against her."

"We have your deposition from Calcutta," Kinley said.

"*You* forget you've already helped convict her in her absentia, Donally. Or shall I call you Chadwick or Sir David. Who are you today?"

With credible indifference, David made a steeple of his fingers and rested his chin on his thumbs. "I have been many men while working for you." He crossed his boots at the ankles. "Who is it you want me to be today? The knight errant? Assassin? Thief? Husband? I have been them all. Now you can bloody add *father* to that list."

Kinley set the claret on the table beside the chair, a movement that surprised David for the subtle emotion it entailed. "I understand your dilemma . . ."

"No, Kinley." David pushed out of the chair. "You do not."

"You don't like me, do you?" Kinley challenged David's tone. "You question my judgment. You think I am too quick in my actions. That I am pompous. That I have no regard for the instincts of those who work for me. I have every regard for yours, which is why I requested to work with you again."

"I thought it was because you were hunting my wife."

Kinley's eyes flickered, but he did not rise to the bait. "I've followed through with every promise guaranteed you," he said. "I can recommend taking everything away—"

"The deed to Rose Briar is in my name. Purchased with my coin. As for my title, I don't care what you do with it or anything else promised me. I've done all that you've demanded of me. What you choose to do, you do of your own accord."

Kinley rose. "It is clear that your feelings are engaged where they should not be. I need hardly remind you that I can revoke your status and have you returned to London if necessary until this case is closed."

"Are you threatening to arrest me for defending my family?"

"He is merely promising what will happen if you take one step out that door with any intent other than seeing this case brought to an end," Ravenspur spoke. He moved away from the fireplace. "If you are even a hairsbreadth from defecting with Faraday's daughter let me remind you that Lord Ware has the power to slap a treason charge on your head. On that score, consider your son's future if he should lose both his mother and his father."

David held up his hand staying any further comment. He was not yet at the threshold of his temper, but Ravenspur knew him too well not to recognize the weariness in the gesture. "What do you want me to say? That I won't help her run?" Hell, Ravenspur must know he would. "I won't put her through a public tribunal or let her go to some godforsaken prison for the rest of her life." Or worse.

"Sit down. Please," Ravenspur said dryly, compelled to add *please*, a surprising gesture considering the previously issued threat. "There's more you need to hear."

Rain pebbled the window behind him, growing in strength, and David shook his head, reflecting on the knot in his gut, and the ramification of Ravenspur's threat. "Would you mind if I remained standing, Your Grace?"

"Would it matter to you if we did?" Kinley drew David's attention from Ravenspur, and reminded him of another memory similar to this one. His first meeting with Kinley.

A memory that did not often plague him. His purpose for traveling here was the reason it plagued him now; he was sure.

David might have grown up poor, but he'd grown up educated. Like his brothers, he had graduated at the top of his class at Edinburgh, but unlike the rest of his family, he'd never held a desire to become an engineer or an architect—a man who built worlds. He'd wanted to *experience* the world, possessing the same romantic wanderlust he'd oft witnessed in his younger sister, Brianna. Sixteen years ago, working in the diplomatic corps, he'd been assigned to the British consulate in the Far East where Kinley eventually recruited him into the Foreign Service. And as the years aged, he did see the world, becoming many characters in his journey, and excelling as Kinley's protégé. With every job, he'd moved deeper and deeper into the darker tiers of his profession, eventually estranging himself from the very people who loved him most. He had come tonight seeking a place to begin that long journey home. Not to begin the journey all over again.

He would not go back to the beginning. He could not.

"There's more to this case than you've been told," Kinley said.

"Find Faraday another way. I won't risk my wife's life anymore."

Ravenspur dropped into the wing chair between him and the door. "Eleven years ago, you and Kinley were working operations with seven other people on this case in Calcutta." He leaned forward on the chair. "In the last year and half, every man who worked that job has died. Seven months ago, the last man, Major Rockwell, Kinley's closest friend, was killed in a hunting incident. The bullet that slew him belonged to an Enfield rifle. We believe under the circumstances, the shot fired from the church was meant for you."

David should have felt some measure of vindication for having already arrived at that conclusion but did not. "You and Kinley are the only two still alive," Ravenspur said.

"How would someone get the names of those involved in the case?"

"Kinley suspected that over the last two years, someone has manipulated or purged most of the records from the case. Important files have gone missing. Also files containing names of our agents on other cases have disappeared." Ravenspur sat back in the chair, his arms on the rest. "A week after Faraday's escape from Marshalsea, a body was recovered from the Thames. Faraday's identifying bracelet was found on the left hand of the male victim. We believed Faraday was dead. After the earring came in to Kinley, Lord Ware hired an anthropologist and we exhumed the body found in the Thames. We needed to know if the male victim matched Faraday's six-foot stature. It did. But the man was missing all of his molars. We know for a fact that Faraday had a perfect set of teeth. We have no idea who the victim was. Probably a drifter in the wrong place at the wrong time. By then, Kinley had already brought you in on the case."

Ravenspur's study remained deliberate. "Since Colonel Faraday could not have had the earring in his possession, someone else obviously had it all these years. Someone within the organization who had access to the prison. Someone who would have the ability to secure the special key to that bracelet and place it on someone else. We believe that someone approached Nellis Munro a number of months ago. That someone is the man we are after. Our mole."

David now understood Ian's passion about this case. He was after the mole who had killed his father. Splaying a hand across his nape, he met Kinley's gaze as he thought he might lose his temper completely and do something rash—like commit murder. "No one could bloody tell me this?"

Kinley snorted. "Considering your wife made a visit to

Munro's residence a few days ago, we're telling you now. Your job has been to keep her alive, waiting for Faraday to make contact. Of course, we've always given you leave to do that job any way you saw fit."

A quiet dangerousness touched David. "Meg is no bloody traitor, Kinley. She isn't working with her father."

"Does your wife have a gold locket in her possession?" Kinley asked.

Somehow, David managed to keep his expression flat. He thought about lying. "You must know that she does," he finally replied.

"Have you asked her who gave her that locket and why?"

"Her father gave her the locket. As to the second question why don't you tell me?"

"We know through past interrogations of the original Circle of Nine that it is in some way connected to the treasure. She hasn't tried to run. Therefore, if Faraday is alive, it is possible he has been in contact with her in the last few months." Kinley lifted an eyebrow. "It would be no difficult task hiding anyone in those caves beneath the bluff. People have turned traitor for a lot less than wealth enough to buy a small country in some corner of the world."

Staring at Kinley, David no longer cared that he was stepping over the line, as near to sedition as he'd ever stepped. "Did you and Pamela see the old vicar who used to live at Rose Briar church?"

Kinley startled. "Bloody hell, no."

David didn't bother launching into a dialogue about Doyle's ghosts nor did he mention the tracks he'd followed after the storm, or his suspicions about Pamela. "Someone fitting your description visited the cleric months ago asking about the caves beneath the bluff."

"You are out of order, David," Ravenspur carelessly slipped into the familiar, crossing the line from professional to family.

They faced each other across the stretch of worn carpet. "Out of order? My wife wakes up with nightmares. She has endured hell enough already. I won't let her bait your hook. I want her off this case—"

"She *is* the case." Ravenspur flung out his arm. "The centerpiece of the investigation. This is more important than your feelings. Or guilt over some perceived wrong you think you committed against her. If you can't carry out your assignment professionally, I *will* remove you from this case now."

"Hence we are back to the question of how you will leave here." Kinley studied the claret in his glass. "Or more precisely—"

"Will you leave us, Kinley?" Ravenspur clawed a hand through his hair. "I would speak to my brother-in-law in private."

Kinley set down the claret. "Is that wise, Your Grace?"

"I've handled desert brigands; I think I can handle my brother-in-law without help."

David turned to look out the window and grappled for restraint. Rain pooled in an empty flower box outside. He could not see past the Stygian darkness, and the light behind him simply reflected the room back at him.

"Do you want to tell me what that interrogation was about?" Ravenspur asked after Kinley left.

David didn't think he owed Ravenspur any explanation. Lifting his gaze, he found his brother-in-law's in the glass. There had been no quicksilver humor usually shared between them, no hint of friendship that had grown between his sister's aristocratic husband and himself. Only a sense of the inevitable.

"What will happen to her?" he asked.

"You may be willing to forgive her her crimes. But she belonged to the Circle of Nine and was tried in absentia with the others. Meg Faraday will never be granted a pardon. All I can do is make her life as comfortable as possible."

Creating a false confidence where there was none to be found had never been Ravenspur's way, but David had divined that outcome the instant he'd walked into the room tonight. "Don't try to detain me here, Ravenspur."

"I didn't tell Kinley anything of your request," Ravenspur said. "I will disabuse you of that notion now."

David looked toward the folding doors then at his brother-in-law. He didn't have to glance over his shoulder to know, Kinley was not so far away that he could not hear their conversation. "Nellis Munro has been intercepting my correspondence. No doubt, he has been reading what has been going out as well. Pamela has been investigating Munro. She probably found out and told Kinley." He elected to say nothing more. If the department didn't trust him, he certainly had less reason to trust them, including his sister's husband.

"For your information, I didn't know where you were until two months ago when Ware passed the files of this case to me," Ravenspur said. "I had no idea what you did before you went to Ireland or that you were the agent in Calcutta on that case."

"How is the family?" he asked, because he could think of nothing else to say.

Ravenspur considered his answer. "You might like to know that Ryan and Rachel are now living in Ireland. We missed you at their wedding. She is expecting their first child."

A wry smile touched David's lips. He had always known his youngest brother's heart belonged to the girl he'd loved since childhood. Yet even as well as he could read others, he had never found his own way so easily interpreted. "Ryan was right about me," David said to the window, remembering what his brother had once accused him of. "I have been running for too long."

"You have a son to consider. No one will fault you, if you take him and return home."

David laughed and, shoving his hands into his pockets, suffered Ravenspur's study. "Home?"

"Let me take this case from you. Anyone can see you're no longer made for this kind of life. What else do you have?"

David walked past him and snagged up his coat from the chair. "Five months ago, I was living on faith and thought I had everything I needed. *What else* is living on that bluff caring for a girl and an old man that aren't even her family. She hasn't left here because she won't leave them. I promised her she would be free." Retrieving his hat and gloves, he faced his brother-in-law. "Do you understand that? I am home."

David heard the carriage pull up to the town house. Smoking a cheroot, he looked out the drawing room window over an uneven landscape of stone chimneys and thatched roofs stretching down the cobbled lane to the quiet waterfront. A brief surge of moonlight stabbed the clouds and spilled into the room, a lull in the storm blowing over the channel.

His hair was still damp. He was sure he reeked of horseflesh, he reflected as he considered the failure of this entire night, the knot in his gut, and the ramifications of what Kinley had revealed to him. He ground out the cheroot in a tin tray and walked into the foyer, where he leaned a shoulder against the wall and waited.

The front door opened. Pamela wasn't alone as she stepped through the doorway unaware that she had a visitor. Her companion saw David first in the semidarkness.

"Chadwick," Nellis said. "What the bloody hell are you doing here?"

"Mr. Munro," David acknowledged, one hand in his pocket.

"It's all right." Pamela laid a palm over Munro's arm. "He tends to visit me in this manner. I will see you tomorrow."

"You are sure?" he asked.

David strode past them, opened the front door, and invited him out. "She is quite sure."

Nellis stopped in front of David and adjusted his waistcoat. "I enjoyed my visit with Victoria. I hope she wasn't too upset when she left. She does tend to get emotional over the oddest things."

"I'll save you the unpleasant consequences of going horns to horns with me, Nellis. Rose Briar belongs to me, as does the land and everyone who lives on the bluff. I am not an old man, and *will* fight to keep what is mine."

"One can only wish you luck in your endeavor, Chadwick."

"Allow me to rephrase." Leaning nearer, he lowered his voice. "My wife is under my protection. If you threaten her again, I will feed you to the fish in that river."

"Lord Chadwick!" Pamela was suddenly standing between them. "Go, Mr. Munro. I will not be a party to a row on my doorstep."

"Countess." Nellis tipped his hat before narrowing his eyes on David.

Pamela shut the door behind Nellis. Turning, she plopped her fists on her hips. "Just what do you think you are doing?"

"Keep your hands where I can see them." He spun her around. "You've been a naughty spy, playing both sides against the middle," he said against her ear, kicking her ankles apart. "Why do I get the feeling you and I are working on opposite sides?"

David removed a shiv from her thigh strap. "Lest I find it in my back." He tossed it to the table beneath the looking glass, then spun her around.

"I give you permission to continue." Her crimson mouth opened into a taunting smile.

"I don't need permission to do anything. I need answers. And I'm just in the mood to wrap my hands around your throat to get them."

"Threatening to kill Nellis *and* me, David? All in one night?" She laughed. "Isn't that out of your moral character these days?"

"Does your job entail sleeping with Munro?"

"Among other things, Mr. Munro is a powerful man in this part of England. I believe you've done worse in my place."

"You haven't seen my worse, Pamela."

"Mum." Pamela's servant Agatha stood on the stairway, wringing her hands in her white apron. "Would you be needin' something to eat before ye retire to your chambers?"

Pamela slanted him a glance. "Would you care to join me?"

"What are you doing, Pamela?"

"I'm a whore." She flailed her gloved hand and stumbled

slightly before tilting her chin. "Hasn't my husband told you that, yet?"

David looked at Agatha. "Make her something to eat."

"You are not my protector. Nor is Ian, though he likes to think of himself as one. And because I like you"—she set her gloved hand on the door latch—"I'll warn you to get out of this town house now."

David caught her arm. "Tell me about the gold locket."

A momentary flash of fear in her eyes vanished as quickly as it came. "I have no idea what you are talking about."

"Pamela." His fingers tightened on her arm. "If you are involved with Colonel Faraday you are in way over your head."

"Why? Because you failed?"

"If you know where he is—"

"I don't." She yanked away and leaned against the door. "Besides, I grew up in a family of eight big strapping brothers in the slums on East Holborn. I've been managing men my entire life. If you want to be afraid, be afraid for yourself." She swung open the door. "Now I wish for you to leave."

David hesitated, and then walked out into the night. He mounted Old Boy, looked one last time at the town house, and reined the horse around. The fury that he had known since leaving Kinley had not lessened.

An hour later, wrapped in an oilskin slicker, David slowed Old Boy as he rode into the churchyard, surprised to see lantern lights blinking in the church. Dawn was still an hour away. Blakely came out to greet him, excitement lighting his eyes.

Hunkered in an oilskin coat, he told David the tunnel had been found. "Mister Rockwell discovered it. Took himself in and came right out again. Said a man would be a fool to go inside. We're waiting for daylight." Blakely cleared his throat. "You'll also be interested to know you'll not be havin' trouble with missing posts and stolen telegrams any longer," Blakely said with no small amount of pride. "There's not a man workin' that office what fears Nellis Munro more than he fears me after today." His tooth flashed in the dim light.

David peered down at him from the saddle. A gust of wind drove the chill against him. "Tell me you didn't maim or kill anyone."

"I didn't lay a finger on a one of them."

Knowing it was better never to delve too deeply into Blakely's approach to his business affairs, David rubbed the heel of his hand against his temple and ruthlessly blocked out the distraction weighing foremost in his thoughts.

Blakely shifted. "Is there anything more that you be needin'?"

"Send Rockwell to me. I'll be at the house."

"I've not seen him since he came out of the tunnel."

He gave Blakely his attention before looking at the church. "Where is my wife?"

"The old man, he took ill. She and the nipper stayed the night at the cottage. We've two men with her. Why don't ye take yourself off to bed and go home?"

Home.

The notion was no longer a stranger to his thoughts as he stood in the middle of Meg's chambers a half hour later and found no relief for the heaviness in his chest. He had not removed his coat, and the collar still hugged his neck as his masculine presence, so out of place among the lavender and lace, filled the room. How profoundly she had captured him, he thought, touching her pillow, for he felt, not caged by her dreams and her heart, but freed to live.

He pulled open the drawer beneath her night table and removed the locket he knew she kept there. A pale hint of growing daylight favored the scrolled lilies. He found a chair a faced the fireplace. Closing his eyes, he leaned his head back and let the silence fill him.

The fact that Kinley knew about David's attempt to seek a pardon for Meg led to one conclusion. He was getting information either from Nellis or from someone in contact with Nellis. No doubt, Nellis had not only paid the telegraph operator for the contents of all missives David sent out the past few weeks, but had somehow gotten hold of the post he'd sent Ravenspur.

Except, David knew from the man he'd set to watch Nellis's movements, even before Meg's visit to the man, that there had been no meeting with Kinley.

Pamela remained the thread connecting every incident.

Victoria placed a steaming bowl of broth in front of Sir Henry and bit back a smile when he groaned. "Not again, Victoria." He accepted her aid as she fluffed his pillows behind him. "Is it your intent to starve me?" he asked.

"Count your fortune that I don't give you a needle full of morphine." She patted his bristly cheek and hoped she worried him a little bit. "It would serve you right if I was the vindictive sort who had a long memory with which to contend."

Sir Henry refused to pick up his spoon, so she stirred his soup for him. Esma had hurried her down from the manor house last night, fearing Sir Henry had grown ill. But after spending last evening and the entire morning with him in the cottage, Victoria had concluded something else entirely.

"Chadwick has not given me any answer concerning the will," he said.

"You should not have poured it all on him so thick, Sir Henry. A man can drown in that kind of responsibility."

He eyed her shrewdly. "But you believe he is learning to tread the water."

"I believe he might want to learn." Victoria sat on the mattress and balanced the tray so that it would not slide off Sir Henry's lap. "Promise me you'll say no more on the topic."

"Hmmpf. I will do no such thing."

She assumed not. Once Sir Henry set his mind on a goal, he was apt to see it accomplished. If his orneriness served to keep him alive longer, then she would aid as much as possible in his purpose. She did not tell him that David had left yesterday and had yet to return from his meeting with his brother-in-law.

The last few days had given her more than the last twenty-eight years of her life. Whatever it was she suspected of keeping David away, she had found something of his strength to hold to her heart. "I would have you move to the manor house, Sir Henry."

"Pah, I would only be underfoot." He dawdled over a piece of bread. "Now off with ye. If you have a need to starve me, I'll dine alone."

Victoria gave him the spoon so he could feed himself. "Unfortunately"—she stood and fluffed her skirts—"you are not all of a piece, Sir Henry. Esma said that you ate a strawberry tart last night and suffered for it. Do you think I would have ridden through the rain if you were merely lonely for company?" Knowing that was exactly what she'd done, she turned toward the window. The curtains were closed to the light outside. She ran her hand across the moorings and opened them.

A shaggy horse pulling a heavily laden dray appeared at

the top of the drive. She watched it lumber into the yard as she moored the second tier of draperies. The sun made a feisty appearance over the treetops, illuminating the driver. A floppy hat covered his head. It was market day in town. Someone was delivering a load of coal that she'd ordered last week. Nathanial appeared from the stable to help Mr. Shelby unload the dray, and she turned away.

"I will come again tomorrow," she said, tucking the blankets over Sir Henry's feet. "I can either feed you more broth or you can decide you are well enough and we'll play a hand of cards. But if you wish to speak to Lord Chadwick, then you will come to the manor house and do so. I am not your bridge."

He grumbled obstinately, and she kissed his cheek. After closing the bedroom door, Victoria walked to the kitchen. Esma stood over a washboard in the sink, her long sleeves drawn up to her elbows and a mist of perspiration on her upper lip. Victoria grabbed a pad and lifted the pot of coffee from the stove.

"I want him to move to the manor house, so I can be closer to him, Esma." She poured the steaming brew into a cup.

"He'll not be a burden, mum." Esma worked one of Sir Henry's shirts over the washboard and dunked it in a bucket of water.

Victoria set the pot back on the low fire. Laughter in the yard pulled her to the window. Leaning against the countertop, she lifted aside the curtain.

Bethany and Nathanial were talking to the dray driver. Carrying a basket of eggs, Bethany wore a cloak but no hood covering her head. Sunlight captured the gold from her hair, and her smile was bright for the older man performing some sleight-of-hand for Nathanial. Victoria shifted her scrutiny to the driver as he presented her son with a piece of candy that had magically appeared from behind Nathanial's ear.

"Who is the dray driver?" she asked Esma.

Esma peered through the window above the sink. "He and Mr. Gibson deliver goods from town. Always brings sweets for the boy."

That was odd for a man who didn't look as if he had two shillings to his name. After Nathanial and Bethany returned to the stables, Victoria remembered that she was going to take him coffee. She walked to the mudroom and drew her cloak off the wall. She pulled it over her shoulders and returned to the kitchen to retrieve the coffee. Shielding the brew with the palm of her hand, she negotiated her way across the yard. Mr. Shelby and the man Mr. Rockwell had sent to watch over them were unloading buckets of coal.

The driver squatted behind the back wheel of the dray, and Victoria saw that he was scraping clumps of mud from the spokes with a large knife. She couldn't see his face. He'd wrapped heavy wool around his palms, but his scabbed fingers were still exposed to the elements. Yet there was no hint of vulnerability to those hands.

"I thought perhaps you might want something warm in your stomach," she said.

At first, she didn't think he heard her. Then his head tilted and he was looking at her feet. Slowly he rose. His shoulders hunched, she saw that the knife remained in his hand. He turned his head, and she was suddenly looking into his eyes.

"Hello, daughter."

Her heart slammed against her ribs. She would have dropped the cup if he had not found it in her grip and gently detached it from her palms. Her father had aged twenty years from the time she had last seen him. His once-dashing features were gaunt behind a beard now feathered with gray, though his hazel eyes remained sharp. No one questioned his presence, which meant he'd been coming and going for some time. Who knew him after all, except she and David? Yet her father was also a chameleon, and somehow she knew this version of him was another masquerade.

"Smile, Maggie." He nosed the steam rising from the cup. "We are being observed. If you give me away, Donally's son won't grow up. I am not working alone."

The words were a promise. If something happened to him, someone somewhere would carry through on the promise. Today. Tomorrow.

Her father still held the knife in his hand; though his sleeve shielded the blade, it would take little effort to strike at the flesh of a person. "If you so much as harm a hair on my son's head, I swear I will kill you with my own hands."

"Now, that's the spirit." Her father drank from the cup, eyeing her over the rim. His knuckles bore evidence of a recent fight. "Nice boy, my grandson, despite his bastard of a father. You know why I am here, Maggie."

At once, her son emerged from the stable where he had gone to find eggs with Bethany. "Mother?" He ran toward her.

Her breath caught, and she felt an overwhelming sensation of drowning. She could have screamed, but it had not occurred to her to do so. Anymore than it had occurred to her father that she would do just that and risk the lives of her family.

"Please . . . don't hurt him."

"Mother." Breathless from his obvious foraging in the stables, he stopped in front of her. Straw stuck out of his hair.

His eyes sparkled as he held two eggs out to her. "Bethany said if I wrap these in blankets, they'll hatch chicks."

Victoria stepped between her father and her son. "I think Bethany was just teasing."

"She said she's done it a hundred times and that I should keep the eggs in my room near the stove."

"She's jesting, Nathan." She set her palms on his arms and gave him a little push. "Now, go inside and have Esma make you lunch with those eggs."

His expression growing mutinous, he looked past her to her father. Out of the corner of her eye, she could see him as he crooked an elbow against the wagon.

"But why?" he asked. "I don't want to eat—"

"Just do as I say, Nathanial!" Her son was too young to hide his hurt, and she wanted to touch his cheek. "Now!"

He took his precious eggs and walked toward the cottage. When she finally faced her father, she knew a ferocity born of her past, the need to protect her family and the knowledge that she would fight.

"He's just a little boy, Father."

"How very quaint." Handing her the cup, he smiled. His teeth were still nearly perfect. "If I wanted to harm Nathanial, I could have long ago."

Hearing her son's name spoken with such familiarity accomplished what nothing else had. A strange sort of calm settled over her. It kept her chin high. She watched as he hitched the gate on the dray and turned. She should have been afraid, as they faced each other. Father and daughter. He had molded her so perfectly into his shadow.

Perhaps he did not realize just how perfectly.

He blew into his hands to ward off the chill, his gaze catching hers and perhaps the thoughts behind her eyes, as even the silence framed her memories of him. A visceral mixture of love and hate that had forever defined her image of herself.

His slow smile told her that he recognized her weakness. "Watching you these last months, I have decided you can have your little family, Maggie, unhindered by the burden you've carried for me all these years. No one need ever know the machinations of your devious little heart. I will forgive you your betrayal of me. I'll leave the country, and you'll never see me again." He walked to the front of the dray, and climbed onto the bench. He retrieved the reins. "I want the locket, Maggie. My time is up here and now I must go."

"It was you that night in the church after the storm."

He did not deny it.

The dray lumbered in a turn as her father brought the horses around. She could do nothing to stop him from leaving, for catching him did not erase the danger to her son, or his purpose for finding her. She walked beside the slow-moving wagon.

"Did you shoot me?"

"Assuredly I did not," he said as casually as if they were discussing the weather.

Then there *was* someone else.

David's man walked outside the stable and, thumbing his hat back on his head watched them. She lowered her voice. "Is Nellis working with you?"

"Nellis is a preening maggot who overplayed my patience and put his nose where it does not belong." Pulling the floppy hat over his forehead, he smiled down at her. "Donally has settled that particular problem for me."

Her hand went to her chest. "What do you mean?"

His eyes were laughing as if he were privy to some great

joke, as if the last laugh belonged solely to him. "He has great affection for you, daughter. He always has. Alas, he is walking the line of treason to save you."

She came to a stop. Dizzy and disoriented. She stood on the drive, her mind a total blank as she struggled to think. Pressing her hand against her waist, she only knew if she took a single step from where she stood, her knees would fold.

She waited until the dray disappeared before turning to look at the trees and surrounding rooftops. Nothing moved. There was no flash of field glasses staring down at her. No hint of any sharpshooter ready to drill her through the heart.

She called to the man standing outside the stable. "Where is Mr. Rockwell?"

"I don't know, mum," he replied as she approached.

"Take Bethany and go inside the cottage. If you leave my son alone, so help me, you will regret my wrath to your dying day. Do you understand?"

She darted past him into the stable. She didn't want her father to get too far a start, but it took precious minutes arguing with Mr. Shelby the entire time he saddled the horse.

The mud from the recent rain made following the heavy wagon tracks simple. Fifteen minutes later, she rode into the busy churchyard. With no thought as to what she should do, she searched for the dray and saw the man at the reins set the brake.

Victoria stared in disbelief as Mr. Gibson climbed out of the seat. She nudged the horse forward. "My lady." His expression showed surprise as she rode up beside him.

"What happened to the man driving this wagon?"

"I met him a ways back. He said that you asked him to return to town for more supplies. He took my horse and went the way of the old drover's trail."

Victoria twisted in the saddle and glared at the woods. The neglected trail went down the bluff to the river bridge. She had taken the same path when David found her in the cemetery. Her burst of vim died inside her almost at once. She would not find her father unless he wanted her to find him.

Turning her attention back to the churchyard, she sought out Mr. Rockwell. More than that, she wanted David—if only to know that he was safe. The sight that met her eyes stopped her. "Mr. Rockwell found the tunnel, mum," Mr. Gibson said.

Men filled the churchyard, thirty or forty strong, standing in a line passing down buckets filled with dirt. "They have come to help, my lady."

They were the same men and their sons who had walked away from their farms afraid of reprisal, now back with more numbers than before.

"But how did David get them here?" She said the words without realizing that she had spoken them aloud.

"I don't know. But they came, mum. They came for Lord Chadwick."

Chapter 21

Victoria arrived upstairs from the servants' entrance. Gripping the edge of her skirt, she hurried down the corridor to her chambers and slammed the door behind her. With a flick of her wrist, she snicked the key in the lock, spun on her heel, and walked through her private sitting room to her bedroom.

With little regard for her cloak, she threw it on the bed. It wasn't until she'd dropped on her knees in front of the night table that she felt her muscles drain of strength. She wanted to close her eyes and disappear. Tears grabbed at her throat. But she would not allow herself to cry.

After a moment, she rallied herself and pulled open the drawers in her night table. When she could not find the locket, she dumped the contents on her bed.

The locket wasn't there.

Victoria returned to her sitting room and emptied the contents of another drawer. In desperation, she made her way through cabinets and articles of clothing. When she could find nothing else to tear apart, Victoria stepped back, saw the destruction, and gasped at what she had done. Her hair had loosened from its pins. Long dark strands fell over her shoulders. She shoved it off her face with hands that trembled, prepared to move the furniture and carpets. She stopped in her tracks.

David was standing in the doorway between her sitting room and bedroom. There was something restrained in his eyes as he met her horrified look, as if he had been watching her for some time. She did not know how he had gotten into her chambers.

Yet she felt relief. He was here and he was whole, and he filled her vision. She ran to him. He wrapped his arms around her and held her.

"You're shaking, Meg."

It didn't matter that his clothes were damp or that his face scratched the tender under-curve of her cheek. She held him to her with all her strength. "He's here, David. He has been living beneath our very noses. He left by way of the old drover's trail."

His head angled back. "Who, Meg? Your father?"

"He's been making deliveries to the cottage for Mr. Gibson. He stood close enough to Nathanial to touch him. He knows that he is our son. He knows everything. He knows—"

"Shh." He brought her against him. "Where is Nathanial now?"

"He's at the cottage. I sent Blakely to be with him," she said, trying to regain her equilibrium. She felt as she had when she was a little girl, before her mother had gone away. When a scrape or a bump was perfectly tolerable until her mother had appeared and the tears she'd been able to hold back rushed to the surface.

"He wants the locket, David." She pushed herself to arm's length, aware that his hands held her shoulders. "I must have dropped it behind the furniture, though I don't know where. I have to give him the locket. He said he would go away forever."

"Why does he want the locket?" He looked at her hard. "How does he even know you still have it?"

Shaking her head, she heard herself falter. "I tried to take her image out of the locket. I should have thrown it away years ago, but I couldn't. I hid it away. When I made up my mind to fight him, I thought if I didn't have the locket . . . he would never have the treasure. But you brought it back to me."

"He gave you something that he knew you would never throw away. Something so important that he would want it back after a decade. Why? What is the locket to him?"

"A long time ago, he told me it was the key to my mother's heart. That if I wore it long enough, it would lead me to her."

"He is a bastard, Meg. You know that, don't you?"

She nodded slowly. "He is the only one who ever knew where the treasure was. I told you the truth when I said I didn't know." Was David ashamed of her? she wondered.

She had no more secrets. David knew them all as intimately as he knew her body and her heart. If he turned her over to the authorities this time, there would be nothing left of her to salvage.

"After the treasury theft in India, the Circle began crumbling," she explained. "Father seemed bent on doing things that drew attention to us. Everything was a game for him. He allowed you into the Circle. He must have known what would happen. And I did exactly what he wanted me to do. He always knew I would be the one to betray him to the authorities all those years ago."

He framed her face within his palms and forced her to look at him. "But you didn't know that, Meg."

"Don't you see? He could not have planned the last ten years better. For who in the Circle of Nine remains to claim the treasure, but the one who created the scheme?"

He started to say something else, but she forestalled him. "There is someone else working with him, David. Someone other than Nellis is involved."

"I know."

She pushed away from him. "He promised Nathanial would not be hurt. He'll go away forever—"

"Meg . . ."

"We can finally be free. Do you understand?" She walked to the window and flung open the curtains. The glass framed a dome of sky. "I want to wake up and feel the sunlight on my soul and know that I am free of him. I have lived in fear for nine years that my father would find my son, but now if I give him the locket, our son can be free. My father will go away." She dropped to her knees and began rifling through the drawer contents she'd dumped on the floor. "This can be over."

David stood at the edge of the carpet, his heart torn in half, unable to move farther into the room, yet helpless not to go to her. He stepped over the scattered papers, buttons, pens, and knelt beside her. "You're not alone anymore, Meg."

She sat back on her calves, her violet skirt spread around her, achingly beautiful. "Will you help me find the locket?"

A strand of her hair had fallen over her shoulder, and he brushed it off her face. A faint frown marred his mouth as he considered what she had yet to say. David angled his palm around her chin. "He gave you his word that he would not harm Nathanial. But he did not give you his word that he would not harm you. I won't help you find the necklace."

Meg pressed her lips together. Her fingers folded into her skirts. She struggled to her feet. "I don't need you to help me," she said, sidestepping him. "I will search alone if I have to tear this place apart."

David watched her walk to the door that separated this room from her bedroom. She stepped over the threshold and pulled shut the door. The sound of a key clicking in the lock followed.

David looked at the door behind him that led into the hallway. She had locked that door earlier. The key was not in the lock. He drew in his breath and, bracing his wrist across his thigh, swore before he rose to his feet. Did she even know she'd locked him in her sitting room?

He sat on the chair next to the window and removed the locket from his waistcoat pocket. He turned it over in his hands, studying the intricate lily flower design.

Something crashed to the floor in the other room. "Damn, damn, damn," he heard the muffled feminine expletive.

Returning the locket to his pocket, he walked to the connecting door. "Meg?"

"Go away, David." He could hear the scrape of furniture. "If you aren't going to help me do this, I'll do it alone."

"You're not doing anything alone."

There was a long pause. After a moment, he pressed an ear to the panel. He could feel her doing the same on the other side and knew she could feel him, too. "Just open the damn door, will you? I'll injure myself if you make me break down this door."

After a moment, he heard the lock click and the door flung open. Meg looked past him to the other door before she deigned to give him her attention. When she did, he saw that her eyes were wet. Leaning a palm against the frame, he spoke without touching her. "You know I love you," he said.

"I love you, too," she answered.

"You should not have had to face your father alone today." This was his fault for allowing himself to get unfocused. For forgetting why he was here.

"I wasn't frightened for myself, David."

He touched her face. "That is what frightens me."

Tears clung to the rims of her lashes, and he took her into his arms. "Why?" Her voice was a whisper, but David heard the quiet mutiny framed by that one word.

"Because you *should* be afraid. Because I love you and I would not lose you again."

"He knows where my mother is buried." Her voice was muffled against his shoulder. She curled her fingers in the cloth of his shirt. "He has always known."

David brushed the hair from her cheek. "Kinley's people went through Faraday's holdings before his trial looking for any shipments made during his tenure in India. Do you remember anything about your mother?"

She shook her head. "I know that she and my father were married in Brighton. My mother always talked about a chapel on the sea someplace." Dabbing at her eyes, she studied him. "She loved the sea."

"Anything else?"

Her smile wobbled a bit. "Are you interrogating me?"

"Do you trust me to know how to help you?" He spoke against her hair.

He felt the slight stiffening of her spine beneath his palm and felt her hand against his pocket. "Is this an issue of trust between a husband and his wife?" she asked. "I recall that you asked me that same question before, David."

That afternoon like a thousand days since, he regretted. He had destroyed her trust, and, carrying his son, she had walked out of his life. "I know what I said, Meg."

Taking his face between her palms, she pressed her lips against his and, after she kissed him, looked deeply into his eyes. "Then do *you* trust me?" she asked.

"I trust you."

"Will you give me back my locket?" Her voice sharpened slightly. "The one you must have forgotten you put in your pocket?"

Leaning one palm against the doorjamb at her back, he stopped her from reaching for his pocket. "Not in a thousand years, love."

"You want this to end as much as I do. If my father is ready to flee, then whoever is working with him will flee as well. We have to catch them all."

"I won't let you be bait."

"Give me the necklace." She nailed him with the tip of her finger. "This is my fight more than yours, Donally. I have to finish this for us."

His eyes narrowed, and he was a second too late in intercepting her hand. She grasped the pocket in his waistcoat, wrapped the loose fabric in her hand, and pulled the cloth. He enfolded his palm around her wrist, and they stood rooted to the floor like two battling warriors.

"Let go, Meg."

"I will not."

He didn't want to hurt her, but neither would he relent.

She swore at him, but he was stronger and pulled her hand

from his pocket, securing both her wrists. He pinned them to the wall at her back. And knew a slow sweet hunger inside. Her eyes glittered with their own searing fire. "I am part of this fight, David. I will finish it with or without your permission."

She was right, of course. Everything she'd said was correct, but he could not allow her sacrifice. If she stayed and helped him do this, he would have to turn her over in the end. He could not. Nor could he allow her father to get his hands on her.

"You're thinking like my husband, David." The quiet intensity of her voice drew his focus back to her face. "You cannot."

He could.

And he did.

"You are my wife."

His mouth covering hers, he could think of her as nothing else. She did not twist away, and he kissed her deeply. The shocking hunger of his passion swept through his veins. It didn't matter that he'd made himself vulnerable and in doing so found her vulnerable, too. Her mouth opened over his, and he thrust his tongue inside. He fit her there as he did everywhere else, and she kissed him back with dizzying need. When he broke away, it was to carry her to bed.

"I think you are a witch," he said against her lips, falling with her to the mattress, without minding that either of them had yet to divest themselves of clothes. "A sylph, nymph, my Lorelei, Meg."

She unbuttoned his waistcoat and shirt, her hands needy and eager as he opened her bodice with an urgency that matched hers. He knew every inch of her limned beneath the thin cloth of her shift. She kissed him. "Then I am glad of it,

David." Moving across his body to straddle his thighs, she slid the locket from his waistcoat pocket.

He snaked his hand upward and caught her wrist, entwining his fingers with hers, the locket pressing between their palms, as his other hand pulled her to his mouth and took the initiative from her. "No, Meg," he rasped against her lips.

Then he drank her protests and finally her surrender in a possession that was total. The soft inflection of her breath humming in his blood, he bore her beneath him, in a rustle of fabric, holding to their kiss. His knee insinuated itself between her thighs and found the slit in her drawers. He loomed above her, unyielding muscle to her softness. She saw the banked fire in his eyes, felt it in the tension of his arms, and let the currents rise between them. His shirt spilling around her, he pushed himself into her. She drew in a breath of air, her body contracting around him in an intimate embrace.

Deep within his throat, he groaned. He withdrew, then rocked again. "I love you." His voice a groan, he pulled back to look down at her, beautiful among the pillows, until his breath came in short rasps. Her half-closed eyes on his, she whimpered and slid her hands through his hair in a ragged cry, a sound that changed into pleasure against his mouth. Then neither one of them was thinking about the locket or anything outside this room. His mouth sheered across her temple to slant against her lips. Her limbs twined around his hips. Reality ceased to matter.

If only it could never matter again. He could not love her passionately enough. She wanted his kiss. So deeply that she grabbed his head and held him to her as he rocked against her again and again, his mouth on hers. Together they came hard in a shuddering climax, and he pushed inside her, drawing on her orgasm as long as he could.

When it was over, he sank against her, his chest heaving, and she was clinging to him. He'd ruined her pretty dress, he realized. The skirt was crushed beneath him, and he promised her he would buy her another gown. "Ten gowns," he said, after she laughed, but there was somberness in her tone. And he was smart enough just to let her cry. "I would take you away from here," he said, pulling her against him.

She did not ask why he had yet to tell her about his visit last night with Kinley and Ravenspur. "You didn't come to the cottage last night."

"I came here."

"And sought out the locket. Why?"

His hand smoothed the tangled hair from her face. "Kinley asked about it."

"They found the tunnel," she said, her mouth pressed against his shoulder.

"I know."

"What are we going to do, David?"

"I'm going to get you, my son, and everyone else out of here."

Suddenly rising on one elbow, he looked toward her sitting room, leaving her staring at him. Then she heard what had drawn his attention. A horse was approaching at an urgent pace. David was already out of bed, pulling up his trousers.

He walked into the sitting room to the window, and Victoria remained in bed, unwilling yet to move. "Bloody hell." David was already shoving his shirttails into his trousers when he returned. "It's Ravenspur," he said.

Less than fifteen minutes later, Victoria had washed and changed her clothes. David had told her to stay in the bedroom until he came to her. But she was finished letting other people protect her. She had meant it when she told David this was her fight. After combing her hair, she'd pinned it in a chignon, and flung a red knit shawl over her shoulders. Clutching it tightly, she followed the sound of voices as she descended the stairs.

David had taken Lord Ravenspur into the bookroom and closed the door. Rather than eavesdrop, she entered. Both men stopped talking and turned.

David stood near the window, a hand on his hip, his eyes stark as they found her. The second man beside him, she assumed, was his brother-in-law, and she paused. His gray eyes were even now assessing her.

He had the eyes of a hawk. Of a man who did not ask but simply took. A man who had just delivered some very bad news, she thought as David walked toward her.

"What happened?" she asked when he pulled her to his side.

"Nellis Munro was murdered sometime last night," His Grace said when David would not, or could not reply. "It seems your husband was the last person to see him alive. A warrant has been issued for his arrest."

Chapter 22

❦❦

"**D**id you or did you not go to the town house last night?" Kinley threw David a scornful glance, his eyes amplified behind his spectacles.

"Obviously you know that I did," David said.

"Witnesses claimed you threatened to kill Mr. Munro. You ordered him out of the town house," snapped Kinley. "Did you see him later?"

"Witness. I saw Agatha. And I *was* angry. But not for reasons you think. Does anyone want to tell me where Pamela is?"

"Her room was not all of a piece. As of now, you are also a suspect in her disappearance as well."

"This is bloody rich and you know it."

Rain pebbled against the window behind him. Already Moira had lit the lamps in the room against the approaching night. Ravenspur faced him from across the room. "I have to ask this," Ravenspur said, having patiently listened to Kinley interrogating him for the last two hours. "Did you go to Mrs. Rockwell's bedroom last night?"

"Ian and Pamela are married?" Meg quietly asked.

"Yes," David said to her, sitting with her hands clasped on the chair in front of him, then looked at Ravenspur. "No, I did not go to her bedroom. Yes, I have been in her bedroom before and she has been to mine. I had a room in the town house." He raised his eyes at the ceiling at the banality of the next statement. "No, nothing ever happened."

"Pamela's servants say otherwise." Kinley had the good grace to look embarrassed. "Someone of your description has been seen there frequently—"

"Do you think it's possible that man could be Faraday?" David sat with his arms folded, leaning against the desk, half listening to Kinley and Ravenspur only because respect bid him to do so.

He was looking at Meg. Her eyes on his, she had said little since Kinley's arrival, and he'd listened helplessly as she endured insinuations that he was Pamela's lover, and that he had snapped Nellis's neck last night in a fit of jealousy, which was laughable if the whole thing had not been so bloody tragic.

But whatever Pamela was, he *had* been at her town house in the middle of the night. He *had* ordered Nellis to leave. Someone else had been in the town house waiting for her when he was there. Pamela had practically thrown him out the door, he realized. "Have you considered that had Nellis gone with Pamela to her room last night as planned, he would have been killed there?" David asked. "Someone clearly wanted him dead."

"We need to find her husband," Ravenspur said.

"Ian hasn't been seen since yesterday," David replied. "He left after going into the tunnel. Something must have happened. I need to go down there and find out what it was he saw."

"No, you don't, David." Meg rose and shook out her skirts as she looked at Ravenspur. "My husband came home angry last night. He wouldn't tell me what happened. I should have pressed for more answers."

David shifted his gaze in disbelief but she looked away from him. Red flags brightened her cheeks. "He wanted me to go away with him," she continued.

"What are you doing, Meg?"

"Telling the truth for once," she said in an uneven voice. "Look in his pocket. He has my locket. We were going together to find the treasure."

"Bloody hell." Kinley set down the drink. "Is that true?"

Meg saw the furious expression flicker across his face and folded her arms. He could see hurt and fear in her eyes and knew what she was doing, damn her. "It's all true," she said. "I feared he might even try to kidnap me away from this place."

The corners of David's mouth tilted. "Did you now?"

"Check his pocket," she said. "I'm telling the truth."

David denied nothing. But telling anyone that Colonel Faraday had made contact with her that morning would confirm Kinley's allegations that she was working with her father. "You're playing a dangerous game, Meg," he quietly warned.

"I play no games, David. You've always known me for what I am." Tilting her chin, she gave Ravenspur her full attention. "My father contacted me this morning. David wanted to protect me. I think he believes he can still save me. He has an unrealistic picture of the situation. Do you not think so?"

Ravenspur looked at her closely and said, "I know what he's asked for on your behalf."

"Then you understand that if it isn't granted, I won't allow him to sacrifice his future and that of my son. I won't."

David came to his feet. "Don't even think about removing me, Ravenspur."

"Do it," Meg demanded. "I don't trust him. He . . . he—"

"Is in love with you?" David asked, pulling her around and looking into her eyes, willing her not to turn away. "I didn't kill Nellis, Meg."

Tears welling, she shook her head. "This is my fault," she told Lord Ravenspur, her eyes pleading. "My father will kill him. I don't want David here."

"That's unfortunate, Meg. I'm not leaving. And you still aren't getting the locket."

"Let go of me!" Her eyes flashed. "You are the most infuriating man I have ever known. I won't forgive you your stubbornness this time."

Whirling in a flurry of lavender silk, she nearly made it to the door before David intercepted her departure. "You're not leaving, love."

She tried to twist away from him. "Let me go." When she spoke again, her voice was broken. "Please," she whispered.

David turned with her in his arms, his chest heavy. Ravenspur and Kinley were watching him, and he wrapped Meg to him as if that would shield her vulnerability from them. He didn't want her so exposed and sought to protect her. "You said Nellis had struggled and had blood on him?" he asked Ravenspur. "I'm wearing the same clothes I was wearing when I left here yesterday. Would you not agree, Meg?"

She wrenched her chin away. He merely pulled her along

the length of his body. "Would you not think if I fought Mr. Munro they would be bloody or torn? Where are my wounds?" He held up his hands and turned them over. "No sign of trauma here. I am guilty of nothing but a moment's rashness for going to the town house in the first place." He looked into Meg's eyes. "No one is taking me away from you. I did not kill Nellis."

"A man came here six months ago asking questions about the lady doc." Sheriff Stillings stood outside the doorway. His wet cloak opened to reveal a heavy truncheon hanging from his belt. "Asking if she had lived in Calcutta before coming here. When we did not hear from him again, I assumed he had not found what he was looking for and left." He looked at Meg. "Except I knew you were from Calcutta. Munro got it in his head to do his own investigating." Stillings assessed David next. "He had his neck broke, like my men did when we found them on the old drover's trail after the storm. Who knows how to do that? Kill so efficiently, my lord?" His brown eyes did not waver, and his smile turned unpleasant. "I've only seen one person fight with that kind of skill."

Meg took a swift step in front of him, but David held her back, his fingers wrapping around her arm tightly enough to warn her that she was finished fighting his battles for him.

"Whatever your nature, you've brass for bollocks, lordship," Stillings said. "Maybe even ballsy enough to walk into a room full of cutthroats with the promise of riches and walk out alive."

David's mouth stretched into an unsmiling grin. "If a man were to do something so foolish, the last thing I'd expect is to see him back in your town."

"I have a dozen men outside and a warrant for your arrest," Stillings said mildly. "There are not any of us around here that will be missing the magistrate, but if whoever killed him killed my men. I want to find him."

Stillings looked past David to Meg. "You once came to me for help."

"I did." Her voice was a whisper.

He stepped into the room, his boots muddy. He carried a rifle in his hand. "You are looking for the tunnels, my lord. I came up from the river. This is what I found beneath the church."

David took the Enfield. He held it, stock high to the light, and traced the faint indentation of a single letter once burned in the stock. David handed Ravenspur the rife as he looked over at Stillings. "Will you show me where you found this?"

"The letter R?" Ravenspur asked.

"Rockwell?" Kinley took the rifle and turned it over in his hand. "This rifle belonged to Ian Rockwell's father."

David pulled Meg to a more private distance. He cupped her chin so she could not avoid his gaze. "You've done your job here. Now let me do mine." He looked past her at Ravenspur. "I intend to clean out the caves. Blakely should be here soon with my son and ward. I need you to get my family somewhere safe until this is over. Telegraph Halisham or New Haven. Have them hold the train tomorrow if need be. We can be there by early in the morning if we leave tonight."

"You can hold the train?" Meg asked.

"No, but Ravenspur can." He wedged her hair behind her ear. "Pack only what you and Nathanial will need. I'll be back as soon as I can." To Kinley, he said, "You can arrest me later."

"You can arrest me now," Victoria said after David and Stillings rode out of the yard.

Outside, she heard the jangle of a carriage and harnesses

and knew Blakely was returning from the cottage. She planted herself in the doorway. Ravenspur could not leave the bookroom without walking over her.

"My lady." He folded his coat over his arm and waited for her to move out of the doorway. "With all due respect—"

"There isn't any pardon for me, is there?" she asked him.

When no answer was forthcoming, she lifted her chin and ignored the burn behind her eyes. "I wasn't lying when I told you David wants to take me from here. I won't let him do something noble and treasonous to prevent the inevitable."

"What do you suggest that we do?" Lord Ravenspur asked.

"I'll go with Kinley. As far away from my family as possible." She pulled her shawl tighter. "My father has gone to ground. You won't catch him unless you lure him into the open. After all, he thinks I have something he wants. If I'm not here and there is no one to play with, he will come after me. When he does, I don't want to be anywhere near my family. David won't catch him unless I am the bait."

Nathanial burst through the front door. Water dripped from his hat. He saw her standing in the hallway and ran to her. "Do we have to go away, Mother? Do we?"

She looked over her son's head at Bethany. Removing a soaked pelisse, she raised her head. She wore a periwinkle blue traveling garment. Her eyes, so like the sky in summer, wavered only slightly as she joined them.

"Is Sir Henry not with you?" Victoria asked.

"He could not abide the carriage. The Shelbys will remain with him." Bethany placed an arm across Nathanial's shoulders. "I told him I would help him pack his trunk. We're about to embark on an adventure. Aren't we, Nathan? He will be fine, Victoria."

And never at that moment had she loved Bethany more.

"This is Lord Chadwick's brother-in-law." To her son, she said, "Your uncle, His Grace, the Duke of Ravenspur. He is arranging a place for you to stay."

Both Nathanial and Bethany raised their eyes to look at the tall imposing figure standing in the doorway. Bethany dipped into a curtsy. "Your Grace."

"You are his ward," Lord Ravenspur said, then shifted his eyes and knelt on one knee in front of Nathanial. "And you are my nephew. My name is Michael," he said. "Uncle Michael. That is what your cousins call me."

"Can I bring Zeus?"

Lord Ravenspur looked up at her. "A cat," Victoria explained.

He laughed. "You and your Aunt Brea are cut from the same cloth. She loves cats. We have five. But don't you think Zeus would prefer to catch mice here and not be caged for the next few days?"

Victoria agreed. "He will remain and keep Sir Henry company."

Lord Ravenspur came to his feet and bowed over Bethany's hand. "It was nice meeting you as well, Miss Munro."

After Nathanial and Bethany went upstairs, Victoria raised a brow. "Five cats?"

"And they all sleep with us."

She smiled then. Even if it wasn't true, it was an outrageous statement, and, though she sensed in him a will of ducal iron, not easily bent, the clear gray eyes betrayed a hint of charm, maybe even softness if she looked hard enough. She no longer wondered what kind of man he was within the arms of his own family. Or whether her own family would be safe with him.

"My lady—"

"Victoria," she said. "My name is Victoria, Your Grace. Few know me by any other. Since we are related, I would prefer you call me Victoria."

"I haven't gotten used to calling Donally, Chadwick."

"I love him, Your Grace," Victoria said before Lord Ravenspur could turn away, and she would never be able to say to him again what she wanted to say now. "I need his family to know that and not judge me. I want them to accept our son."

"Victoria." Lord Ravenspur shrugged into his coat as she walked him to the front door. "David would never forgive me if I did what you asked me to do." He pulled on his gloves. "I trust you'll go upstairs and pack instead? If I'm to get to the telegraph office, I need to leave."

"But I can't—"

"You're going to London, Lady Chadwick."

She remained on the threshold as he jogged down the steps into the rain and out of the enclosed yard. A man stood beside his horse picketed near the fence. Lord Ravenspur spoke to him, then mounted. She was surprised he had not arrived by carriage. As he rode out, she looked through the darkness toward the church. An eerie luminosity colored the sky. A hundred lantern lights had caught the moisture in the air and set the night aglow.

David was out there. Stillings's loyalty worried her, but Tommy, being intelligent when it came to his survival would surely acknowledge where the future bread and butter of this town lay. As for Nellis?

She should have felt something. Instead, she felt . . . helpless.

Victoria shut the door. She didn't want to face Kinley. But the least she could do was see the man comfortable before

David returned. She walked back to the bookroom.

At first, she didn't see Kinley beside the window. His gloved hands clasped behind his back, he stared out across the darkened valley.

A distant flash of lightning silhouetted the orchard below the bluff. "Like a soliloquy in a Greek tragedy," he said before she could speak. "How very quaint."

Victoria looked from the window to Kinley standing in the shadows. He turned and regarded her over the pair of gold spectacles on his nose.

How very quaint.

Her father had used that very phrase that morning.

And at once, as his eyes touched hers, the air froze between them, like ice and death, and what her thoughts had initially refused to acknowledge, now warned her to run.

They both moved at the same time.

Footsteps hard and fast behind her spurred her toward the door, but she was not fast enough. The door slammed shut in front of her face. A hand on her shoulder jerked her around as fingers wrapped about her throat and pinned her to the door. "Was it my word choice that gave it away, Maggie?" he asked.

Chapter 23

❧◦◦◦❧

"**G**et away from me!" Victoria pressed her palms against his padded shoulders, and he balled up his fist. The one that wasn't wrapped around her neck and cutting off her air.

"Don't make me strike you, girl. I've never hit you, but so help me, I will."

"Strike me?" Fighting the constricting vise around her lungs, she focused on separating her heart's frantic hammering from her need to breathe. "You murdered Mother."

He laughed. "Your mother died birthing another man's child. You pitied and loved her when she left you. Did I leave you, Maggie? Never."

Her vision swam in currents. "How could you pull it off?"

"How could I impersonate Kinley?" He spat out stuffing that puffed his cheeks. "That bastard shadowed me for nine bloody years. So clever, a man of rules and agency decorum. I knew his every nuance, his every thought and expression. I

340

knew his family. The names of his children. He would visit me. We'd play cards and talk over brandy. He would ply me so cleverly with questions and I would tell him about the treasure. You see, he was the one who had my earring all these years. Then he made the mistake of telling me he believed you were alive. My clever, clever girl. That was what I thought. You are your father's daughter after all."

She cried out and covered her ears. "Stop it!"

"Donally is all that remains," he said. "My only loose end. Now he has my bloody locket. I would have left Nathanial alone. Didn't I tell you I would?"

Victoria's eyes widened.

Nathanial.

He and Bethany were upstairs unaware.

"My partner will have already found your son."

She went slack. She was winning the battle against the fog in her head. But she had to think. One hand went to her pocket. She found the key that remained there. Sensing her fading strength, her father loosened his hold on her neck.

"There now, isn't that better?"

She suddenly had the advantage. She knew he was dangerous, but he had no idea that she was as well.

She burst into sobs and leaned against the door, underscoring her helplessness, yet careful not to overplay the part. He loved his drama, but he would not believe she had changed *that* much. His hold loosened just enough.

She rose with force, throwing out her arms to break his lock on her. He stumbled back and hit the corner of a table. Victoria flung open the door, slammed it shut, and locked it just as he pounded his fists against the other side.

"You won't leave without your son!" He kicked the door.

She turned and ran down the hallway, dousing each wall

sconce along the way. But she had forgotten the servants' entrance. A panel door slammed open in the foyer. Drawing in her breath, she dipped into the dining room. The curtains were drawn. Her breath coming in gasps, she stopped and tried to listen for any pursuit.

Nothing.

The room was dark and cold. She slipped behind the folding doors that led downstairs to the kitchen, and leaned against the wall to catch her breath. She remained there for several minutes listening, making sure her father had not found his way into the corridor. The house had few enough servants as it was, but she passed no one as she made her way downstairs, through the kitchen corridor and to the servants' stairway that led to the second floor.

Victoria extinguished each lamp and wall sconce as she edged up the back stairs. Her palms pressed against the wall, she rounded the corner and slid into another servants' panel. She wanted to get to Nathanial's room, but instinct told her that her father would be prepared for her to make that move. Holding her hands against the wall, she felt her way along the corridor to the studio. As she edged back the panel and looked into the room, a flash of lightning revealed the studio empty.

"Maaaaggie?"

Her father's lilting voice sounded from somewhere down the hallway. A door slammed. "I don't like it when you hide from me."

She didn't know who else might be in the house. She could hear her father's muffled voice speaking in low tones. She dashed across the room and retrieved David's sword from high on the wall. Had she been a shorter woman, she would not have been able to reach it.

She ran across the studio floor, pressed her back against

the wall, and peered around the corner. All the lights in the house had been extinguished, she realized, as she looked out into complete darkness. Holding tight to the sword, Victoria left the studio.

The hunted had now become the hunter. She knew her father wanted David more than he wanted to kill her at this moment, and that gave her a slight advantage, as he would be looking out the windows for his approach from the church. She wasn't yet willing to give away her location. She had to know who else was in the house.

God don't let him hurt Nathanial and Bethany.

Slipping into the servants' corridor, she exited in the other wing. She made it to her chambers and went at once in search of a second weapon that she could use more to her advantage. Night pressed against the windows, but she dared light no lamp.

Her physician's bag still sat next to her bed, and, dropping to her knees, she fumbled with the latch and withdrew a syringe. Better yet, she sucked morphine into the narrow vial connecting to the needle and filled it. More than enough dosage to knock out a grown man her father's size. Maybe even kill him. Holding the plunger like a knife, she rose, careful not to trip on anything scattered over the floor and inadvertently stab herself.

She grabbed the sword and made her way out the door. Halfway down the corridor, Victoria slid across the hallway, pressed her back against the wall, and tried desperately to swallow the rising panic. Darkness stood between her room and her son's. The weather hampered her ability to hear anything beyond the trace of her ragged breathing.

She reached her hand out to open her son's door. Turned the glass knob and let the door swing wide.

Nothing.

"Nathanial?" she called, then said his name louder. "Nathan?"

She stepped into the room. He wasn't there. She ran through his dressing room to the classroom. Her son wasn't there, either. A broken sob escaped her lungs. "Nathanial?"

Thunder crawled across the sky and she glared at the ceiling. The rain outside didn't nearly equal the ferocity of the growing storm swirling inside her chest as she backed a step. The rage was red as something erupted in her chest.

She was beyond caring about her own life. If her father harmed one hair on Nathanial's head, she would hunt him down, the face of her nightmares, the stealer of her soul. She would skewer him. Her voice catching on a sob, she spun on her heel and slammed into a body.

The scream tore from her throat and she swung the sword, even knowing she was too close to maim. But the left hand that caught her wrist did not prevent her from using the syringe, and she stabbed it into his shoulder before she realized that the man standing in front of her was not her father.

"Oh, God!" she cried, as she heard David swear.

"Meg . . ." He yanked the syringe from his shoulder, but she'd already flown into his arms and he stumbled backward into the corridor, catching his hands around her waist.

"You're here. You're all right. Oh God, ohgodohgod . . . I gave you all of it," she whispered as she flung away the syringe.

She heard footsteps down the corridor. David turned as a bullet splintered the doorjamb and, with a scream, she pulled him back into the room and slammed the door. She fumbled for the key in her pocket and locked the door. Then she stripped David's shirt from his shoulder. His clothes were soaked and caked in mud.

"*Bloody, bloody* hell." He bent and placed his hands against his knees. He fell back against the wall.

Blood oozed from the wound on his arm. "You're hit. Oh, Lord, David. He shot you."

"Tell me you didn't just inject me with poison."

"Morphine." She cupped his face desperately and kissed him. "I'm so sorry. I'm so sorry. You're going to go out, David. I don't know what to do for you."

With a start, she realized someone was moving in the next room. A door slammed. If her father found David now, he'd kill him, if she hadn't already done that with the morphine. "It's Kinley," she said, her voice frantic, as she tried to pull David to his feet. "He's my father. The real Kinley is dead."

His hand cupped her cheek. "Ian found me. Pamela . . . is working . . . with Kinley. Are you hurt?"

"Nathanial . . ." she sobbed her son's name.

"Nathanial and Bethany are safe. Downstairs. They are with Stillings. The tunnel," he whispered. "The tunnel from the church leads to your cellar. Your father has been visiting here for months . . . before we moved in here. Doyle was afraid of this damn house." He was sliding down the wall. "I should have known . . . Kinley."

"You've not seen either Kinley or my father in years. Not even Lord Ravenspur knew." She struggled with his weight. "I have to get you out of here."

"My men should be here." His voice slurred. "Find them."

She fell to her knees in front of him. "I'm not leaving you," she said over the tears. "Now, hush. No more noise."

"Tell me you love me."

"I love you."

"You'll run away with me. We'll get married all over again."

"And live happily ever after." She stemmed the bleeding on his arm. "I know the ending."

It was a fairy-tale ending. One that would never be theirs.

Then he closed his eyes.

In a panic, she checked his pulse and found it still beating a moment before she heard the hammer of a revolver cock. "How very quaint." The voice came to her from the darkness, and her father's presence displaced the shadows.

Her heart nearly leaped from her chest, so strong was the panic. Her father held the gun pointed at David's head.

"Does he have the locket?"

"Take it, Faraday." David's raspy voice came from behind her. The locket landed with a metallic *clink* on the floor. "Go find your gold. Just leave my family alone."

The sword lay at her knees. Victoria grabbed the locket as she stood and raised the weapon. "I won't let you kill him, Father."

Outside the room, she could hear shouts. People were in the house.

"Come with me, Maggie."

"Don't . . . , Meg. Don't . . . bloody leave here."

Her father took a step around her, but she moved in his path. "Can he offer you your freedom?" he said, his spectacles catching what little light was found in the room. "No one understands you better than I do. Don't you miss the excitement? After all these years, everything we worked for is within our grasp. We'll be free."

But she wasn't free.

She would never be free.

Wiping the tears from her face, she did not look from her father's eyes as David slumped to the floor unconscious. Nor did she give him her back as she dropped to one knee and checked David's pulse. He would never understand why she was running again.

Would he forgive her?

Perhaps it was a matter of her own honor this time. She had to see this finished.

"I won't let you kill him."

"Ask like you were my daughter, Maggie."

"Please . . . don't kill him, Father."

He removed his thumb from the hammer and drew the gun back. "As you wish. Now, give me the locket, or give me your hand and we'll be on our way."

Chapter 24

$\sim\!\!\!\!\gg\!\!\infty\!\!\sim$

Victoria stumbled as her father pulled her beneath a tree. Her breath came in gasps and she sucked in air when he removed the gag in her mouth. A flash of lightning revealed that the road leading into the valley lay empty before her.

"You don't have to tie my hands, Father."

Victoria flinched as he yanked on the piece of cloth binding her wrists. "I'm doing it for my own peace of mind, Maggie." He adjusted her cloak and pulled the hood over her hair to protect her from the driving rain. "You have not proven that I can trust you."

"Then why take me at all?"

She heard an uproar in the darkness behind her. Shouts grew louder. Even if it hadn't been raining, the night was dark. She could not see anything as they moved through the yard. And then they were running, stumbling down the hill through the mud and the rain.

Pamela was waiting at the bottom of the ravine. She held two horses. Both were pulling at the reins. Victoria recognized Old Boy.

"What is she doing here?" Pamela demanded.

Colonel Faraday took Old Boy's reins. "She's going with us."

"Not with me, Faraday. We only have two mounts."

"Then she'll ride with me."

Pamela pulled out a revolver. Wearing a heavy oilskin slicker, she was barely visible. "She's *not* coming with us!"

"Dammit, what the bloody hell are you doing, Pamela?" Rain plastered her father's white wig to his head, and he tore it off. "We don't have time for this."

"Drop the gun, Pamela." Ian stood behind her, his arm raised to fire. He shouted above the rain. "I swear I *will* shoot."

Pamela didn't move. Ian looked past her to Victoria. "I'm sorry I didn't get here sooner."

"Oh, please," Pamela scoffed. The gun remained pointed at Victoria's chest. "Could you be more of a bore if you tried? I'll kill her if you don't put down the gun."

"My wife sold out." Ian's revolver wavered. She could see he wore a bandage around his head. "I found the rifle last night in the tunnel. It belonged to my father. She was the one who shot you. Did you bloody think I wouldn't come after you, Pamela?" Ian yelled over the wind. "Where will you go?"

The dark eye of the revolver in Pamela's hand remained steady on Victoria, but when she spoke, she spoke to her father. "I haven't done your bidding for these years for you to double cross me now, Faraday." Pamela cocked the hammer. "She betrayed you. She is not going anywhere with us."

Victoria moved, her father moved faster, shoving her out

of the way as the gun fired. She landed on her knees. At the same time, Old Boy reared, flailing his hooves, and she twisted away from the thrashing forefeet. Then her father loomed over her, tall and forbidding as he blocked the horse from trampling her. Somehow, even sheltering her with his body, he held to the reins. He finally mounted, missing the stirrup the first time. "Get on!" he shouted, holding out his hand to her.

Victoria shot her gaze to her father's, seeing what the brief staccato lightning flash revealed against his chest. A dark, growing stain spread.

"Don't go, my lady." Ian had wrestled the gun from Pamela's hand and sat astraddle her thrashing body. "It's over. You don't have to do this."

"Maggie," her father's voice came to her. "You'll never be free if you stay. I know where the treasure is."

"Bastard!" Pamela screamed at Ian. "Kill him."

In the distance, Victoria could see lantern light moving down the hill. She looked at Ian. His gun lay a few feet from Pamela. It was all he could do to control his wife. "When David awakens, tell him . . . I'm sorry."

Pamela started laughing. "Who is the real traitor now?"

Victoria took her father's arm and he helped her mount behind him. Her father spurred the horse forward, and she caught hold of him for dear life. His body blocked the wind and rain, and she lowered her head against his back.

Victoria came to consciousness slowly. The ground was cold beneath her back, the blankets damp. She lay beside a fire in a dilapidated barn. Nothing about her surroundings was familiar and, as her sluggish senses grappled with her memory, she struggled to sit and found her hands still bound.

Every part of her body ached. Too exhausted to care about her physical state or the precarious state of her future, she turned her head and found her father sitting on a log, his elbows braced tiredly on his knees, watching her.

"You've been asleep for hours." He poured coffee into a battered tin cup. "Are you hungry?"

Squatting in front of her, he set down the coffee tin with hands that contained a curious suggestion of unsteadiness. With the makeup scrubbed off his face, her father looked younger than his forty-nine years. His hair was the same color as hers, a dark brown with a feathering of gray at the temples and tied back in a queue. The spectacles were real, and he wore them now. The flames from the cooking fire reflected from the lenses. "It isn't my wish to hurt you," he said, pressing a red-stained kerchief to his mouth. "I've missed you and would prefer your conversation to my own, which on a good day is not so pleasant to my ears. If I untie your hands, do you give me your parole that you won't escape?"

Her fingers rethreaded themselves and she looked out into the darkness beyond the barn. Thick groves of naked-limbed trees cloistered close to the abandoned farm they had found for the night. They'd played this game for two days, traveling the cold, wet country roads. She had no plan to escape him, but neither would she surrender an ounce of cooperation. He seemed to recognize this and accepted the gauntlet thrown as the price for her company. For she would allow him nothing more.

"Where do you go when you are with me, Maggie?" Her father held her chin and forced her to look at him. "You used to talk to me. I remember how much you loved talking. I remember the little girl you were."

Noting his ashen pallor, she knew he was dying.

"Why did you take that bullet for me?"

"What makes you think I did anything for you? You had the locket."

She didn't have the locket now, and he still had not hurt her. "You are a liar, Father."

His eyes narrowed and she saw something dangerous glint in them, before his expression vanished as quickly as it came. "Maybe I should reconsider gagging you, after all." He struggled to his feet, and she saw that he wore another change of clothes from the ones he'd worn yesterday. Obviously, he had prepared well his escape across country. He just hadn't prepared for the bullet Pamela put somewhere in his chest.

"I have no change of clothes for you." He slapped food onto a tin plate. "I was expecting Pamela. Not you. I do not believe her dress will fit."

"You sound sorry that she didn't make it. Doesn't that leave more treasure for you?"

"Pamela was Kinley's close protégée these last few months. I will miss her company."

The thought revolted her.

"Why did you kill Nellis?" she whispered.

"He figured out who you were and was planning to blackmail Donally for his silence, without understanding who I really was. Donally was already piecing together everything too fast. Alas, Nellis ended the game sooner than I wanted." Her father set a tin pan smelling of burned beans beside her. "Donally was the only one who ever understood me completely, always my most worthy adversary. I thank you for single-handedly defeating him for me, both times."

Dropping her gaze, she looked at the fire and watched the flames blur behind tears. She had given him a huge amount of morphine. She did not dare entertain the horrible thought she might have killed him.

"Hold out your hands, Maggie." Shaking her head past the tears, she did as her father asked, and he cut her bonds. "Would you believe I never wanted to see you hurt?"

"No."

He laughed shortly, but his laughter spasmed into a cough. She saw pink-tinged spittle on his lip. The infamous, larger than life Colonel Geoffrey Faraday was not immortal after all, yet all she could feel was a strange loss she could not explain. "Perhaps you should consider making your peace with God, Father."

His mouth crooked in a parody of a smile. "God and I never cared to know one another. He was your mother's hypocrisy. Not mine," he said, struggling to sit upright.

"Will you let me look at the wound?" she asked quietly.

"When we get to Brighton, I have a cottage waiting. Not far from where your mother is buried. The chapel is a beautiful place by the sea. She loved the sea," he said, studying the place on his finger his gold band had once been. "Even you would approve."

After so many years of wondering and waiting, she would finally know where her mother rested. Something she never thought possible.

"You want to see her, don't you?" he asked.

She nodded, for more than anything, she wanted closure to her past. She desperately needed closure with her mother. Knowing where she had been buried all these years would give her that.

"Why would you do that, Father? Bury her someplace she would have loved?"

He never answered, and she knew as she followed him to Brighton over the next few days that she would never learn the reasons.

Maybe he had enshrined her mother's memory in death because he could not hold on to her in life, anymore than he could hold on to her. But from the moment her father had stepped in front of Pamela's gun, that one unselfish act had forever imprinted itself on her.

It was the reason she stayed with her father in the following days, feeding him and taking care of Old Boy.

He brought her to a cottage as he'd promised, the only promise he'd ever kept, and, too weak to stand, he had needed her help to walk inside. The cottage was set back in a forest of trees, something out of Grimm's fairy tales, covered in a century of thorny vines.

David did not appear in the days that followed her arrival in Brighton. At night as she'd slept on the settee beneath the window, she would sometimes hear a distant foghorn. Here where there were only her private thoughts and a sky filled with stars until she'd begun to believe that David was not looking for her because he believed that was what she wanted, until she almost believed it herself.

By the end of the second week, her father had become so ill, Victoria knew he would not survive another night, but he continued to do so. She fed him his meals, bathed his face, and kept him alive longer than he deserved.

Until her father's voice drew her from her sleep near dawn ten days after their arrival at the cottage. He was muttering incoherently. His fever was high. She gave him water. Wet his lips with cool water.

And quietly, she watched him die.

*   *   *

Victoria wrapped him in blankets. Forcing herself to stand, she washed her teeth, face, and hands, scrubbing beneath her chipped nails until her flesh was raw. She removed her gown and washed her arms and neck. She washed everything before sinking to the floor. For a long time afterward, holding the locket in her hand, she sat with her back against the tub, the single lamp beside her throwing shadows on the water-stained walls, then, drawing her knees to her chest, she buried her face against her skirt and wept.

She didn't know why she wept. But she was no longer that frightened, angry nineteen-year-old fleeing from her life. All that was strong in Meg had now become Victoria. Sir Henry and David had given her back the very things she'd once allowed her father to take from her. Her honor, her dignity, and her heart. The revelation did not take away her fear, but it did give her courage.

When she again lifted her head, the sun was coming up and the room filled with light. She walked to the window.

She had been at the cottage almost two weeks and never once stood at this window as the sun topped the trees. Now, as she breathlessly watched, the morning light caught the golden spires of a distant church tower.

The trek to the church took her across an open field visible to an entire town. Moisture in the grass soaked her shoes, but she didn't care about the dampness against her feet or the icy December cold beneath her rag of a dress as she clasped her cloak to her. She flung open the huge wooden doors and stepped inside the quiet sanctuary.

Morning sunlight captured the stained-glass windows, spilling color over the pews. Walking forward into the gauzy light, she looked upward at the painted wooden and elaborately carved ceiling, a giant eight-sided lantern tower. Victoria had never dreamed that heaven truly existed. But in here, as she stared in awe, she could believe it surrounded her. The Italianate Roman church was heavily decorated with marble and statuary. Only the stone was cold beneath her slippers, and she looked down at her feet. The stained glass cast colored images over the floor, and when the sun was just right in the sky, the images became floral pictures. Like those on her locket.

Victoria held out the locket, realizing that the image engraved on the front was a special flower. A white lily.

She took a step backward and examined the colored definitions marking the stone floor and walls. She walked back and forth across the length of the church, looking at the stained glass and all the names on every stone, looking for her mother.

A laugh finally escaped her. One filled with irony. She was at the wrong church. After all she had been through, she was at the wrong church.

Victoria didn't know how long she sat with her hands folded in her lap. A shadow fell over her, and a young vicar spoke. "You look a little lost, miss."

She *was* a little lost and wanted to go home. "Is there a Margaret Victoria Faraday buried here?"

"No, miss," he said and handed her a slim wedge of paper. "But there is a Lady Margaret Victoria Sullivan buried in the chapel by the sea," he told her. "If you go outside, you will see the dome on the next rise."

Victoria stared at the paper in her hands, giving no hint that she wavered between feverish exhaustion and disbelief.

But her hands trembled as she opened the folded paper and read her mother's name. "I don't understand. Who gave this to you?"

"That young man sitting behind you. He told me to give you that slip."

Victoria came to her feet and turned.

David was sitting in the last row of pews. His arm in a white sling, he came to his feet, and her heart leaped with an aching love. His dark hair fell over his brow and white collar. He did not walk toward her, but in standing surrendered that choice to her.

She stopped in front of him. She did not touch him for fear she would crumble if she did.

"Is Nathanial safe?"

"Are you all right?" he asked.

They had both spoken at the same time.

And a sob formed in her throat. "I think so. Yes," she whispered, perhaps not so well physically, but her strength and purpose had never been clearer. "I am very all right."

He held out his hand as if she had not gone missing for three weeks, as if it was the most natural thing in the world that he should do. She looked at that hand, aware of the constancy of its strength, and let him take her fingers, his height bringing her chin higher.

Then he pulled her to him within the protective circle of his arm, and pressed his mouth against her temple. He'd not shaved. His shirt was unbuttoned at the collar. He was not so well put together as she'd originally thought.

She set her fingers against the loose wave of his hair that touched his collar, and, closing her eyes, she felt everything dark inside her simply disappear in the peace that filled her.

She was crying but they were not tears of sadness. "How did you know where to find me?" she rasped against the dark stubble of his chin.

"I've been staying at the inn that overlooks this cathedral. I saw you walking from the direction of the field."

"My father is dead."

"You cannot know how I wish I had been there for you." He turned his face against her cheek, then he cupped the back of her head and kissed her, finally searing her with his need and hers. Their lips met again and again, openmouthed and hungry. "I missed you." He turned his face against her cheek and she choked on the intensity of his emotion as he moved his lips back to her mouth. "I couldn't get to you sooner. I thought I had lost you."

And like the whisper of her name, the words echoed with tenderness of her own feelings. She had lost weight and her clothes were in disrepair, but she was better than all right, and she held him to her, her heart brimming. But before she could speak, movement drew her attention to the back of the cathedral where she saw the young vicar leave, his echoing footsteps fading in the empty silence surrounding her. A glance around David's injured shoulder told her that they were alone. The morning was too beautiful to be so void of life.

It occurred to her then that she had not seen anyone else since she had entered the cathedral. Her hand closing around the precious paper the vicar had given her, she met the searing blue of David's eyes. She would not allow him to hold himself responsible for what had to be done, and with a sudden vulnerability and weakness she could not fight, she was glad everything was over. "Am I under arrest now?" she asked.

His smile hinting at so much more than love touched her with sudden splendor. "Come," he whispered against her temple, withholding nothing from the force of his words. "I have something to show you."

Chapter 25

⟨⟩⟨⟩

The carriage stopped near an isolated cemetery. Victoria looked out the window at the white caps on the sea. David had found her mother for her. The locket pressed in her palm, she looked out across the cemetery. Her eyes touched the small Romanesque chapel on the knoll overlooking the sea, then the marble mausoleum next to the dormant gardens, a smaller version of the cathedral she'd just left. A pair of Doric columns supported a domed roof. She turned her head to find David watching her.

After years of hiding, this moment felt surreal. Her gaze dropped to the gold band on David's hand, then on hers. "If you can't do this, we'll leave now." He took both her hands in his and brought them to his lips. "I'll take you back to the inn. You can bathe and sleep. We'll do this tomorrow or never if that is what you want."

She was a little afraid, but she was no longer frightened. At least she wasn't as much about what tomorrow held as she was about the next ten minutes. Ten little minutes that had her quaking in her shoes.

"Wait." Pulling his hand to her cheek, she held his gaze. "I need you to promise that no matter what happens . . . that come tomorrow . . ." A brief gust of wind buffeted the carriage, and she tightened her hands around David's. "I don't want you and Nathanial involved in this case anymore. Please tell me that you will protect him and yourself. Promise me that you will tell Sir Henry . . . that I love him. Bethany . . . she is tenderhearted and needs to know that she is important. People will not be kind to any of them."

"What about you?" His eyes softened on her face. "What do you ask for yourself?"

"That my son will have a future untarnished by me."

"Remember you promised to trust me? That includes with our son's future."

David reached around her and opened the door. A groom set the step and stood aside as he stepped down and waited until she was ready to descend from the carriage. The wind played with her cloak as he took her elbow and led her to the steps between the columns. "I didn't know your mother's middle name was Victoria."

"She was named for her mother. I didn't know her maiden name was Sullivan."

Victoria looked up at the circular stained-glass window above the weathered door depicting a white lily. She stopped.

The inscription above the lily had been carved in Latin.

It was the same inscription in her locket.

"*There are no miracles to the man who does not believe in them,*" David said, standing behind her. "A proverb. It is a ceremonial to life."

"You can read all of this?"

He opened the door and stood aside for her to enter. "Something of my old ecclesiastic training," he said.

Victoria entered and, for a moment, blinked trying to adjust her eyes to the shadows. Candles fluttered in wall sconces and she looked around the empty room before realizing David had not followed. A question formed but he touched a finger to her lips.

"This, you have to do alone," he said.

Victoria stood silent as he shut the door, leaving her in semidarkness. The room smelled of earth and dead flowers. The window slats opened to the sea, and, as she stepped beneath the archway into a veritable Garden of Eden, she stopped.

Breathless, she lifted her gaze. A stained-glass skylight domed the ceiling in a heavenly tableau. An angel cloaked in flowing white lilies spread her arms.

Victoria turned and touched her hand on the names and dates of those buried within the granite wall. She found her mother's name engraved on the floor nearest to the garden, and she sank to her knees. For a long time, she leaned with her palms pressed to the name.

And as the sun shifted across the morning sky, she held her hands to the stone marker inscribed with her mother's name. The bright light spilling through the stained glass revealed two slight indentations on the stones next to her mother's. Wiping away the tears, Victoria withdrew the locket and held it to the oval dimple. She slid her fingers along the heavy square granite, working her nails around a wedge of stone, and realized it could be removed. The blood left her face. Then she stood, backed away from the stone and sat on the bench, opening her palm that held the locket.

"It's a key," a voice said from the shadows behind her.

With a gasp, she bounded to her feet. Lord Ravenspur sat on a stone bench against the back wall, the top half of his body shadowed. "Once the locket is inserted, you twist the lid. Your father built this mausoleum with the stipulation that no one but his wife ever be buried in the floor." He rose to his feet as if unfurling to face a sudden gust of wind.

He wore no hat, and he held his gloves in his hand. He'd folded his coat beside him.

"But if someone already knows where the treasure is, one doesn't need the locket—"

"One does if one doesn't want to use dynamite to blow up this mausoleum." He did not approach her. Instead, he walked to the window and looked out across the sea. "There is a recompense for the one who finds that treasure. Even a small percentage would make a person wealthy."

"But I didn't find it. David did."

"David is giving you his percentage. I promised him that should you choose to leave, I would not stop you. Or he wouldn't tell me what he'd found."

She closed her eyes briefly. "He is a stubborn man who walks the line of sedition as if it were a two-foot high tightrope. Give it back to him."

Ravenspur narrowed his eyes on her, but they had lost some of their sterling brittleness. His hands behind his back, he rocked on his heels, then returned his attention to the window. "He was laid up for three days. I thought he would kill himself trying to get to you. I don't know how he knew that you would be in Brighton. But he wouldn't leave. A week ago, he located your parent's marriage record. Your mother's name was Sullivan. She and your father were married in the Chapel by the Sea." Lord Ravenspur nodded to the stone plate on the floor. "We can open it."

Victoria looked at the locket in her hand, and then held it out to him. "I don't want any part of that treasure. And I'm finished running. Open it after I leave here, please. Then give my locket to my son."

Ravenspur's mouth pulled at one corner as he approached and took the piece of jewelry from her. "He told me you'd say that."

"Then this was some test?"

"No, I did have to swear I'd let you walk out of here if you chose." He pulled a fistful of paper from his jacket. "He will do what it takes to see you free. Are you worthy, Victoria?"

"My name is Margaret Faraday, Your Grace. I think we both know that."

"Except I have witnesses that claim Margaret Faraday died, December 18, 1863, off the coast of Bombay."

"What?"

"It's true, Lady Munro. You see, not even Lord Ware can wave a magic wand and erase the first eighteen years of Meg Faraday's life. Even if she received a new tribunal and was acquitted of all charges, once the recovery of this treasure becomes public, she could never lead a normal life. Her connection to Colonel Faraday would forever make her a prisoner of her own reputation and mark those she loves most. It is a stain not so easily erased."

Victoria comprehended his words only too well.

"And, as it is, witnesses have died—"

"Do you think *I* killed them?"

"Pamela Rockwell is responsible for that. We believe she married Ian Rockwell three years ago to get closer to his father. She gained access to Major Rockwell's papers on the case, worked her way to Kinley and through him to your father. She was our mole, and committed high treason for her share in gold. Unfortunately, we don't know how much damage she and your father did to the department."

"Where is she?" Victoria whispered.

"As we speak, her husband is taking her to an asylum in the south of Wales. In lieu of a public trial and her execution, she will spend the rest of her life confined in a stone cell. Do not feel sorry for her," he said when she looked away. "She tried to kill her husband and would have hurt your son had Rockwell and David not come in time."

"It was Pamela's bullet that killed my father. That he should save my life, in the end, at the cost of his own must be the ultimate Greek tragedy for him." She folded her arms. "His body is in a cottage not far from here."

"David's men followed your tracks to the cottage."

She tightened her arms over her torso. "What happens now?"

"You are all that remains of the original Circle of Nine," he said, pulling her gaze back to his face. "But since Meg Faraday aided our agents in Calcutta and helped break a major case there as well as here, the government is willing to see that her past is buried here in this vault and that her name is cleared posthumously. There will be no reopening of the case. No public tribunal to endure. After today, the files on Colonel Faraday's daughter will be destroyed. As Victoria Munro, she'll be given a chance at a new start in life. I can offer her that much to protect her identity and that of her family."

She pressed a fist to her mouth. Even now, she could not comprehend the words. "But Meg Faraday is David's wife. We have a son. Does David understand how this could affect Nathanial?"

"I believe this was his idea, as well as Sir Henry's."

"What?" she rasped.

"David has secured a special license. He will marry you before your return to Rose Briar. Life may never be a hundred percent perfect, but it can be damn close. When you walk outside this chapel, you will be free, Victoria."

Free!

Her heart raced until she thought she could not take another breath. Would anyone possibly understand that one word represented all the riches in the world to her? "You have no idea how many years I've waited to hear that word."

Lord Ravenspur laid his jacket over his arm and held out his hand. "Let me be the first to welcome you to my wife's family, Lady Chadwick."

She flung her arms around him. "Thank you, Your Grace. Thank you." Even if it wasn't a proper show of restraint, she couldn't help herself.

"Your son and Bethany have been staying with my wife for the past few weeks at my estate in Aldbury. The entire family is with them by now. You can thank David's brother Christopher for the new puppy Nathanial is about to bring home. Chris enjoys sharing. He is generous like that. Just ask Ryan or Johnny or Colin."

She laughed through a watery smile. "They sound perfectly wonderful."

"They are," Lord Ravenspur said with heartfelt sentiment that she had not seen in him.

Dashing the tears away, she looked down at her feet. Victoria bent and touched her mother's name, then looked up at the stained-glass angel peering down on her. If anything good had come from the first eighteen years of her life, he was standing outside this marble sanctuary waiting for her.

She saw David sitting at the top of the broad white steps of the chapel overlooking the sea. He looked up as she appeared in the garden and stopped, the wind buffeting her hair and cloak.

Only when he rose did she hike up her skirts and run toward him. He bounded down the stairs, and she flew into his arms laughing, his arm wrapping around her, and, when he kissed her, it was as if it was for the very first time. It was a long kiss, warmed with passion and love, and remarkable tenderness. There was only his mouth on hers, his hand in her hair, her body pressing against the length of his, his warmth and hers. She took it all into her heart and returned it tenfold, until she grew dizzy in his arms and he at last lifted his head and looked into her face.

"I'm sorry I couldn't tell you," he said against her hair. "How this played out had to be your choice."

"We have a son, David." Years of protecting him continued to make her cautious. "How will this affect him?"

"We still have a son, and Sir Henry has a grandson. I've no entailed estate, and my title cannot be inherited. When Nathanial is older, we can tell him more about the circumstances of our decision today. He will never know uncertainty about his legitimacy."

"You are sure. No doubts? This will not be easy."

"Would a lifetime be enough time for us to make everything work?" he asked, pulling her into the circle of his arms and holding her tightly. "Whatever we have to face, we'll do so together this time."

Voices behind her lifted his head, and David looked over her shoulder. Three men stood in front of the mausoleum carrying pickaxes and shovels. Victoria did not move from his arms, but she'd seen what caught his attention and turned her face against his shoulder. David regarded her profile, his mood frayed by her silence. "Do you want to wait and see what they find?"

"I already know what they will find," she replied, and he immediately regretted that he had asked. She had been through hell these past weeks. He would not ask her to go there again.

"There will be a bath and a hot meal waiting for you at the inn," he said. "We will talk more after you have rested."

"I would like that."

Together they walked to the carriage. "What else would you like?"

"I'm all right," she said, leaning against his shoulder. "Truly."

"I know."

But he still did not let her go.

Chapter 26

⌒⌒◯◯⌒⌒

Victoria came awake with a gasp to uncertain darkness. Cocooned in the down mattress of tester bed, she tried to remember where she was, breathing again when she saw David asleep in a chair near the hearth. She had not seen him at first in the darkness. His arm in a sling, he no longer looked disheveled and exhausted, far less vulnerable than he had earlier that day.

A voice startled a gasp out of her. "I don't think he's slept in two weeks."

"Sir Henry?" She twisted against the pillows. He sat next to the bed gnawing on a corncob pipe. His features were pale, his eyes infinitely weary, but she felt only gentleness in their touch. "He hasn't left that chair since he returned to find you asleep."

She sat up. Her hair still damp from her bath fell over her shoulders. "I had no idea you were—"

He waved her words away. "What am I going to do all by

myself at Rose Briar? Play tiddlywinks with Stillings? I came down with Chadwick on the train. Esma and William are also here. She'll be in the kitchen downstairs overseeing the preparation of your meal. She's been as firm with Chadwick's health, making sure he was eating properly. Surprised the young man hasn't had her bound and gagged and put on the first train out of here."

Emotions shimmered in her eyes. "You've all been taking care of him."

"Or him of us," Sir Henry said. "I see he got you something proper to wear."

Glancing down at her lavender and lace wrapper, she knew that Sir Henry must have been the one to see her things packed. "Do I have you to thank for my clothes?"

"Esma packed a valise. We had to move quickly or that young whippersnapper would have left us. I only hope the cottage is still standing when we get back."

"Is Sheriff Stillings causing trouble again?"

"Worse," Sir Henry snorted. "He and Chadwick's man Blakely have become friends. He practically lives at Rose Briar now. Though he did spend two days looking for your trail. Got to respect a man for that, even if there's nothing else about him to like," he said, wiping a red kerchief across his nose.

He talked on and on about the train ride, the miserable late December weather, and what the cold and rain did to his joints. His head bowed over his folded hands, he leaned forward against his knees and talked about missing Nathanial and Bethany, and how nothing was the same without them. Startled by the sudden wetness in her eyes, she slid off the bed, dropped to her knees on the floor beside Sir Henry's chair, and took his aged hands between hers.

"I love you, Sir Henry." She cradled his palm against her cheek. "If I've not ever said that before, I'm saying it now. Thank you for everything you have given me and for taking nothing less than my very best. Nathanial and Bethany are fortunate to have you for their grandfather."

He let her hold his hand a moment longer, then cleared his throat. "He is a fine boy. A fine boy, indeed. He already plays a respectable hand of gin. Knows his way around an ear tube and can take a pulse. Bethany could show him a thing or two about the herbal though."

"I believe if you ask her, she will."

"Now, up with you." He patted her shoulder. "Do you want to wake Chadwick with all this nonsense?" Sir Henry nodded to the other side of the bed where David slept. Only he was no longer asleep but was watching them.

The light of the fire behind him cast his face in the shadows, but as he leaned forward, she could see one corner of his mouth tilt. "Too late," David said, looking between Sir Henry and Victoria.

He'd shaved and changed his clothes, but for all his respectability, the look in his eyes sent her heart racing, and she found it nearly impossible to answer. Impossible when hot shivers raced up her spine, when she was still afraid that she might be dreaming.

Sir Henry took his cane and stood. "I'll leave the two of you alone."

But at the door, he turned and surveyed them both. "You *are* married? Correct?"

"Our state of affairs is somewhat ambiguous at the moment." David looked across the bed at Victoria. "But in a few days Victoria will no longer be a Munro."

"I was not for certain that you would choose to keep the name, Victoria." His sudden pause sounded loud, but his proud face had filled with emotion as he shifted his attention to David. "If I have not thanked you yet—"

"You have, Sir Henry." David nodded in deference. "More than you know."

"I've yet to misjudge a person's character. It is nice to know my family is in capable hands, Chadwick."

Sir Henry left the room, the sound of his cane thumping across the sitting room as he limped toward the door. David moved into the bedroom doorway and, leaning a hand against the doorjamb, watched the outer door shut. Victoria joined him. After a moment, she regarded David's profile, and he felt an enormous surge of love.

"Have you decided to formally accept the terms of the will then?"

He turned into the room, leaning his back against the door as it clicked shut, and suddenly he wanted to laugh with the relief of a hard-fought day, as if he had just come from battle unscathed and very much alive. His wife was free, and he'd never felt more confident of his future. "I think you know I have."

"Where did you go today while I was in my bath?"

"Ravenspur asked to see me." David slipped the locket out of his pocket. "He said that you wanted Nathanial to have this."

She almost didn't take the locket. Neither of them spoke a word about the treasure, but the topic was there between them. He knew only time could truly eradicate the past. But nine years had been a good start.

"Then everything is finally over?" she asked.

"Or it is just beginning." David reached behind him and

carefully eased the sling from his arm. Ignoring the pain, he tossed the fabric to the floor.

Her eyes widened in alarm. "Should you be doing that?"

He slipped his arm around her waist and, with only the slightest encouragement on his part, she moved into his arms. "Probably not." She had used his soap. His lips brushed her forehead and the fine hairs at her temple, then his hand tilted her chin and he pressed the advantage. "Have I ever told you that I like the way you smell?"

"David?" She pulled back. "We really *were* legally married in Calcutta, correct?"

"You are questioning the legitimacy of our civil ceremony?"

"If you were supposed to be working on a covert job, why did you use your real name?"

"As luck would have it, my brother served in India before I got there," he said in the manner of someone confessing for the first time. "The governor general recognized the family resemblance my first hour at the consulate. Denying it would only have raised questions. None of that mattered anyway."

"Why didn't you leave and let someone else take the job?"

"Because I saw you." And smiling that familiar smile she loved so much, he framed her face with his hands. "I only know that I love you, Victoria or Meg, I will love and honor both of you through sickness and in health until death. You are the mother of my son. The mistress of my new home, and everything that I hold dear. I don't ever want to wake up and find you gone from my life again."

Clutching his lapels, she regarded him with shining eyes and laughed. "We will love and honor you back. In fact, we are all going to grow very old together."

With a reverent touch, he slid his fingers into the warm

sable of her hair and tilted her face. They'd been lovers for weeks, but this was different. He was about to be exactly where he wanted to be. Where he thought he would never be again when he'd awakened that stormy morning at Rose Briar to find her gone from his life—in her arms.

Yet, in a way, Meg had vanished, for he no longer saw the woman he'd married in Calcutta all those years ago. The girl he'd fallen in love with and lost had matured into a woman he would love forever. When he'd seen her in the church that morning, he'd seen only Victoria.

A devilish twinkle appearing in his eyes, he backed her to the bed. "Where do you want to honeymoon?"

He smiled like a saint but promised sin, leaving her breathlessly aware that she was ready for her honeymoon now. And closing the distance, his mouth sinking onto hers, David sealed the private vows they had just spoken, melding her past to his future, and knew he had found his piece of heaven in his arms.

They were married just after the New Year at St. Mary's in London. With her hands clasped to his, his body warmed by her gentle strength, they faced each other and spoke the promise in their eyes. Sir Henry, Nathanial, and Bethany stood around them. His family was also there. His brothers and sisters and their children were present to share this moment in his life. He felt blessed and, as he met the conviction in Victoria's gaze, he felt alive.

More than alive. He felt peace as he spoke his wedding vows for a second time in his life. For he had found purpose. Or it had found him. He was not sure of anything except its steadfastness in his life and his promise that he would never forsake his family.

Eight months after they were married, he and Victoria

christened their second child in the church at Rose Briar, a
little girl who looked the image of her mother, more fragile
than a sunbeam, and David had held her in his palms, caught
by the tiny miracle of life that never ceased to amaze him. Sir
Henry passed away shortly after that day, but not before he
held his newest granddaughter in his arms.

The funeral took place in September, a year after David's
arrival, where long rows of meadow hay lay drying in the
fields, ready for gathering. The weather had grown cooler and
autumn set in on the banks of the Cuckmere River where the
measure of a man's dreams could be found in the fruits of his
labor, a child's sparkling laughter, and a wife who loved him.

"There you are," Victoria said, finding David in the cemetery one day after she was leaving the cottage to return to
Rose Briar. She saw patients there these days, and most days
the tenants kept her busy. She carried their baby. Nathanial
and Bethany were with her.

David was looking down at the tilled earth beneath his
feet. Someone had set flowers on Sir Henry's grave. "Don't
you think it strange that you and I came here and both found
the same thing?" he asked as she held out her hand to him.

Victoria glanced up at the church and the beautiful
stained-glass windows and smiled. David pulled her against
him, then told her that he loved her, outdoors beneath a bright
bold sky amid the modest zephyr and surrounded by angels.

It only seemed fitting, he thought as he took his tiny
daughter from her arms, for fate had returned to him a second
chance and the promise of a shiny gold future he never
thought possible. The treasure he'd been searching for his entire life. David laid his arm across Victoria's shoulder, and together with Bethany and Nathanial flanking them, they
walked home.

Coming in May from Avon Romance

Duke of Scandal by Adele Ashworth

An Avon Romantic Treasure

Lady Olivia is a wife in name only, returning to London determined to confront her dastardly husband. But the man who stands before her is her husband's twin, the Duke of Durham, and now Olivia must make a scandalous choice.

Vamps and the City by Kerrelyn Sparks

An Avon Contemporary Romance

Can the undead really find love on Reality TV? Producer Darcy Newhart thinks so. But this sexy lady vampire is distracted by a hot, handsome contestant named Austin . . . who just happens to be mortal, and a slayer! What next?

What to Wear to a Seduction by Sari Robins

An Avon Romance

Lady Edwina is putting on clothes . . . only to take them off again! But she's determined to seduce notorious rogue Prescott Devane, the one man who can help her find a blackmailer . . . and also steal her heart.

Winds of the Storm by Beverly Jenkins

An Avon Romance

Archer owes his life to Zahra Lafayette. Now, in the days after the Civil War, he needs the help of this beautiful former spy again. Posing as an infamous madam, Zahra is willing to help in his cause, but she's unwilling to grant him her love.